June Drummond had her first book published in 1959, and has been published worldwide ever since. She lives in South Africa.

LOOSE CANNON

A peace accord is due to be signed in Jerusalem in two weeks' time, but it is threatened when a Boeing airliner, leased by charity organization Dove International, catches fire and crashes in the Mediterranean, killing one hundred and fifty-five people. Political and commercial powers, fearing that charges of sabotage will enable extremists to wreck the frail truce, frustrate investigations and blame the crash on pilot or mechanical failure. It is left to individuals — the pilot's brother and ex-girlfriend, a forensic psychiatrist, a Roman policeman, an FBI investigator and a Mossad agent — to challenge authority and track down the criminals endangering world peace.

Books by June Drummond
Published by The House of Ulverscroft:

THE IMPOSTOR

JUNE DRUMMOND

LOOSE
CANNON

Complete and Unabridged

ULVERSCROFT
Leicester

First published in Great Britain in 2003 by
Robert Hale Limited
London

First Large Print Edition
published 2004
by arrangement with
Robert Hale Limited
London

The moral right of the author has been asserted

British Library CIP Data

Drummond, June
    Loose cannon.—Large print ed.—
    Ulverscroft large print series: adventure & suspense
    1. Crimes against peace—Fiction
    2. Terrorism—Fiction 3. Suspense fiction
    4. Large type books
    I. Title
    823.9′14 [F]

    ISBN 1–84395–346–3

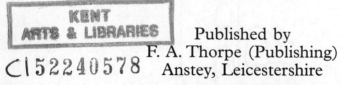

Published by
F. A. Thorpe (Publishing)
Anstey, Leicestershire

Set by Words & Graphics Ltd.
Anstey, Leicestershire
Printed and bound in Great Britain by
T. J. International Ltd., Padstow, Cornwall

This book is printed on acid-free paper

When Powers and Principalities fail, individuals of diverse faith, colour and race may lean on the lever of good conscience to alter the course of history

Prologue

The Board of Inquiry appointed to investigate the Omega Airlines disaster in which one hundred and fifty-five people died, is charged with the duty of determining the cause of the accident.

Experts will examine and report on every aspect of Paloma's last flight — the condition of the aircraft, the fitness and skill of the crew, the nature of the cargo on board, the weather, all these things will be studied in great detail.

Perhaps most of the truth will be established, but not the whole truth, for in a tragedy of such magnitude, it's not possible to assess the part played by human failings. Ignorance and malice, sloth and greed, the amounts may be small in themselves, but weighed together they may tip the scale from life to death.

1

London — Thursday

In the last week of June three people met in an office overlooking the Thames. The youngest of the trio, Oliver Hudnut, was well named. His prematurely wizened features would have looked at home in a dish of walnuts. He was a civil servant inasmuch as the British Government paid his salary, but his true allegiance was to the machines in the seventy-foot-deep, specially insulated, bomb-proof basement of the building. There, with his hand-picked staff, he sifted and collated the information flowing from the media networks of the world, and fed the resultant pabulum to people like Sir Clive Radnor, now seated across the table from him.

Sir Clive was barely computer-literate, his expertise lay in other directions. He loathed Hudnut and snubbed him at every opportunity. He dabbed a bored finger at the printouts presented for his inspection.

'Nothing of value there,' he said. 'Straws in the wind.'

Hudnut's eyes became opaque. 'They show

that Iraq is still shopping for pilotless planes and smart missiles, which would allow them to wage bacterial warfare on neighbouring states. They have put in a bid for the Macaque — '

'Which was turned down — '

'On financial grounds, not in principle. They'll come back to the bargaining table.'

'Hudnut, I'm not here to discuss wild theories, what I want is facts. Your department wastes time and money on material we will never use; eighty per cent of what you produce is trash.'

Hudnut giggled, a sign in him of acute annoyance. 'Oh, ninety-nine per cent, I'd say. The remaining one per cent is of course crucially important to our national security.'

'This lot doesn't qualify.' Radnor thrust the printouts aside. 'Have you anything else to offer?'

'I think the information on Joel Moshal merits attention.'

'Why? The man's decided to duck out of a small-time conference staged by some idiot do-gooders. Hardly earth-shaking news.'

'It's out of character. Moshal has a reputation for keeping his commitments — particularly to small-time do-gooders.'

'Huh. And what, I ask, does Tel Aviv claim is the cause of this grievous falling-off?'

'Circumstances beyond their control.'

'What an admission: one imagined they controlled God.'

'It seems not.' Hudnut's tone was bland, but Radnor eyed him suspiciously. The little squirt was capable of withholding information. These days, people lived by new rules. There was no loyalty, no sense of public duty, which was why the world was in such a stinking mess.

'How did you learn about Moshal?' he demanded.

'Routine monitoring.'

'That doesn't answer my question, damn it.'

Hudnut shrugged. 'He was due to fly to London on Monday to attend Dove International's summer conference. He cancelled his flight early this morning, and we were informed.'

'By whom?'

'The airline volunteered the information.'

'Why? What made them think the cancellation is significant?'

'Moshal's a significant man.'

'Who decided not to waste his valuable time on a bunch of cranks.'

'Dove doesn't fit that description. It has important patrons. Moshal's one of them, he wouldn't pull out from choice.'

'Meaning he was pressured?'

'Probably.'

'By Mossad?'

'I have no idea. Not by lightweights, certainly.'

Radnor's ire rose. 'This is perfectly absurd. I don't know why you waste your time and mine on an outfit like Dove. International affairs are complex enough without the meddling of these latter-day saints with their half-baked relief schemes.'

'They only go where they're invited, and they sometimes achieve remarkable success.' Where you fail, Hudnut's tone implied, and Radnor leaned forward aggressively.

'You listen to me — '

'No!' The third person in the room, an enormously fat woman who, sat crouched in her chair like a toad wondering which fly to swallow, spoke sharply and both men turned to look at her. Rylda Warne linked her small plump hands on the table.

'In a sense you are both right. Moshal is a financial genius, vital to Israel and influential throughout the world. He is, as Oliver says, significant.

'Our priority, however, is the Jerusalem Accord, which we hope and trust will be signed in two weeks' time. We've achieved a truce which has the token support of all the

6

Middle East states, and of major powers elsewhere. I say token support because there are groups of fanatics, of both the right and the left, who are set on breaking the truce, and who don't give a damn if that brings about World War Three.

'The last round of talks at Camp David went well. All the parties made concessions, but selling those to their followers is something else again. Meanwhile there are religious extremists converging on Jerusalem, and certain business and oil cartels are more concerned with their profits than with a peace settlement.

'Anything that threatens to wreck the truce, and so prevent the signing of the Accord, is significant. Oliver, if before this afternoon you stumble on anything which you consider remotely relevant to what I've said, you are to inform me at once. Clive, we need to talk.'

She heaved herself to her feet and waddled from the room, Radnor trailing in her wake.

Hudnut gathered up the despised print-outs. He knew that 'this afternoon' meant COBRA, when top-level government, security and intelligence personnel would meet. It was a body that liked to deal in certainties.

Certainty, in Hudnut's experience, was a rare bird. He dealt in scraps of knowledge which, cobbled together, could cast a shadow

7

of things to come. He acted on hunches because they were often all he had. He had a hunch about Moshal, and he was buggered if he was going to kowtow to Sir Fatarse Radnor.

He remained at the table for several minutes, brooding over Moshal's change of plan. It was uncharacteristic and therefore interesting. Mossad was being cagey about it, also interesting. He would have to seek enlightenment from other sources.

Straws in the wind, Radnor said, but Hudnut was in the business of clutching at straws. Straws showed which way the currents flowed. Without straws, you couldn't make bricks of certainty.

He took the lift down to his basement kingdom and there set underlings to enquire into the activities of Joel Moshal, and the do-gooding of Dove International. He directed his own attention to the man who provided Dove with financial muscle, mega-tycoon Daniel Roswall.

★ ★ ★

At a convalescent home near Ashford in Kent, Dr Kevin Marsh was ready to sign James Brock's discharge papers.

'The ribs are fine,' he said, 'and the knee's

mending nicely, but I'd like you to keep up the physiotherapy for a while.'

James Brock frowned. As long as he concentrated, the doctor stayed in focus and his words made sense, but if he allowed his mind to stray, the drumming swelled behind his temples, and the room began to expand and contract like a tickle-toby. He turned his head carefully and stared at his reflection in the dark glass wall of the examination cubicle. Not 'the' ribs, he thought, and not 'the' knee. *My* ribs and *my* knee, my face with the scar from eyebrow to hairline, my body back from the edge of death.

He said loudly: 'I know who I am. I'm not crazy.'

The doctor looked startled. 'Of course you're not. You've made an excellent recovery. You had a nasty head wound there.'

James knew all about that. He remembered purple pain and yellow bile, a quagmire of nausea in which he struggled to reach Clare, screamed for help and received no answer.

'Any headache now?' the doctor asked.

'No. Feel a bit muzzy.'

'Vertigo. A couple of days on the new pills will fix that.'

'Yes. Thank you.' James found to his horror that tears were welling in his eyes and he smudged them away with his hand. 'I'm fine. Really, I'm fine.'

The doctor leaned forward, his expression kind.

'Mr Brock, in your circumstances, some depression is natural. You were badly injured in the accident, you lost your wife, it will take time for you to recover from the trauma.' He consulted the file in front of him. 'I see you name your brother David Brock as next of kin. Perhaps you could stay with him for a spell? Find your sea legs?'

'No.' James gripped the arms of his chair and made himself speak quietly. 'I'm not crippled, I don't need a minder.'

Dr Marsh raised a calming hand. 'I'm not suggesting anything of the sort, but company's no bad thing, is it?'

'I'm going back to work. I'll have plenty of company.'

'When you're fit, of course . . . '

'On Monday. I'm going back on Monday.'

The doctor studied him and sighed. 'Well, don't overdo it. Keep up the therapy, stick to your medication, get plenty of sleep. Come and see me in two week's time, and if you need to talk, give me a call. Don't feel you have to soldier on alone.'

He walked James to the door and left him

with a friendly clap on the shoulder. Back at his desk he made notes in the file.

Post traumatic stress syndrome. Withdrawn, refuses to acknowledge the gravity of his injuries, unwilling to face the fact of his wife's suicide.

He sat back in his chair, his face puckered. Brock was lucky to be alive. Twenty-seven stitches in his forehead and scalp, three cracked ribs, a fractured patella, bruising and lacerations all down the right side of his body. The wounds had healed well, but the man's mental state was less satisfactory. He'd spent two weeks in hospital and another two convalescing here. For ten days after the crash he'd suffered appalling nightmares and panic attacks. He'd retreated into numb silence, refusing to see any visitors, even his brother. Today the mere suggestion that he might stay with his family had drawn an angry reaction.

Anger was the third phase of the stress syndrome. The fourth was recovery and the long return to normality.

Severe head injury could result in personality change, loss of confidence, moodiness, even violent outbreaks. One had to protect society against psychotic behaviour. One had to protect the patient himself.

Marsh shook his head. Brock wasn't

psychotic or neurotic. He was stubborn as a bloody mule and didn't always listen to advice, but one couldn't force healing on a patient, one could only help him to heal himself.

★   ★   ★

In the foyer, James settled his account, and collected the keys of the Camry his secretary Edith Morrow had hired for him. His own BMW was a write-off, smashed on the rocks at the bottom of Bansford Quarry, and Candida had taken Clare's Rover, claiming it was hers now.

Time to leave. Scary thought.

Folk out there considered him a success. Popular attorney, happily married man. He'd maintained that last web of pretence for ten long years, mending and patching like a demented spider. Clare had beaten him in the end, there was nothing more to be said or done.

Well. Back to the real world, Brock.

He drove with caution at first, then with confidence, and by eleven o'clock was crossing the Weald. The air was warm, the sky tightening towards thunder. Reaching Bansford, he skirted the market square and took the river road past St Swithin's and

Brock's Wood, to Badger's Sett on the crest of the hill.

He drove into the garage, carried his bag into the hall and up the stairs, to the bedroom that overlooked rolling downs and the quarry where Clare died.

His cleaner Mrs Commins had done a good job. All Clare's things had been shifted to the walk-in cupboard next to the bathroom ... clothes, make-up, jewellery, photos. But removing Clare's effects wouldn't eradicate her. She was everywhere present. He could hear her now. *You could make more if we moved to London. We never do anything exciting. Why can't we go somewhere warm this winter? You're such a stick-in-the-mud!*

They'd quarrelled and he'd ended up yelling, 'Why in God's name did you marry me?'

She'd given him a lopsided smile. 'I suppose because you loved me. It was a new experience. I was never very loveable.'

Trying to mend things, he'd said, 'We've had some good times, haven't we, Clare? Some happy times?'

She'd shrugged, her turquoise eyes indifferent. 'I suppose.'

That denial hurt more than her outright hostility, because it was a lie. They'd had plenty of good times; good holidays, good laughs, good sex.

Now she was dead. Trying to recall her face, he could only see it skewed by murderous rage.

He would sell the house for what he could get. He would move away from Clare beautiful, Clare beloved, all her days and nights, including those final minutes when he'd stood on the brink of the quarry and watched her gun the BMW towards him. He'd put his body between her and death, but she'd neither braked nor swerved. Her white luminous face stared past him into eternity.

Dr Quinell, who lived on the far side of the quarry, had heard the crash. He'd driven round and rushed James to hospital. The doctors thought he'd die, but he'd lived — after a fashion.

He made his way downstairs to the television room. Best room in the house, Dave always said. In summer the french doors stood wide to let in the scent of roses, in winter apple, or cedar-logs burned in the grate.

Dave's belongings were scattered about, his rackets in a corner, his fax machine on top of the bookcase, his instant camera lying on the coffee-table. One of his photo-albums lay

14

next to the camera. James flicked over the pages. Dave and James riding ponies on the beach. Dave winning the hundred yards at prep school. Dave in captain's uniform when he was still with BEA. Dave at James's wedding reception, proposing the health of the bride and groom.

James slammed the book shut. Straightening, he caught sight of his reflection in the mirror above the mantelshelf. He looked crazy, the scar pulsing across his forehead. He pressed his fingers against it. He had to stay cool.

A whirring sound made him turn his head. The fax machine was spilling a waxy sheet into the catch-tray. Mrs Commins must have switched the fax on.

The message was addressed to Captain David Brock, c/o Badger's Sett, Bansford, Kent, UK. It made no sense to James.

Dave, re your query, the mark's not known to anyone here. I'll have it checked by the Assoc and ask around. Let you know soonest. Regards. BORU.

The page carried no heading and no return address, only today's date.

James's first impulse was to drop the sheet into the waste-basket, but he thought better of it. He laid it on top of the machine, lifted that into its box and secured the lid. He stacked Dave's rackets and camera and Raybans on top of the box and carried it all to the garage. There he packed it into a carton, sealed that with masking tape, and wrote Dave's Rome address across the top. He loaded the carton in the boot of the car.

He felt light and empty then, as if a devil had left him.

Back in the hall he found a box of groceries and vegetables, and a pile of junk mail. Edith must have dropped it off. He stirred the envelopes with a finger.

I used to know the people who lived here, he thought. James and Clare Brock. But that was a long time ago. Four weeks ago.

★ ★ ★

In his basement fortress, Oliver Hudnut brooded on the meteoric rise of Daniel Roswall, billionaire. He pushed aside the reams of data concerning the manifold business achievements. He wanted the personal stuff, of which there was very little. A mighty private person, Roswall.

★ ★ ★

At age ten, owned a bicycle and had a grocery delivery-round. By age 23, had a Cambridge degree in chemistry, and had founded Roswall Chemicals, now dominant in the industry.

Everything Roswall touched, turned to platinum, thought Hudnut.

Plenty of women, no commitments ... until at 33, while skiing in Aspen, he met Sophia Lang, daughter of a US senator. Fell in love, married the girl, and according to True Love Stories 'shared three halcyon years' with her.

One son, Stephen; doctors advised against further pregnancies. When the boy was two, Sophia took him to visit her father in Washington. On the return trip she suffered a burst aneurysm and bled to death before the plane reached Heathrow.

Roswall's life then centred on his son. Took him along on his travels, bought the estate Mallowfield in Kent and made it his headquarters, 'for the boy's sake'. (Family Journal).

In 1974 married Helen Blundell, heiress to Blundell's Dental Aids, mother of two. The Toothpaste Fairy didn't match up to the Snow Queen and the marriage failed. (Helen kept the Roswall name, which opened many doors.)

Stephen Roswall didn't follow in his dad's footsteps. Qualified as a doctor, went to Gabon, Africa, to study tropical diseases, contracted a virulent strain of malaria and died in a Johannesburg hospital with Daniel at his bedside.

Roswall fell apart. Retreated to Mallowfield and drank himself into a stupor. Word went out he was on the skids. Roswall stocks plummeted.

Enter Hugo Spinner, the company's Maidstone manager, who told Roswall to get his act together and do something positive, like set up a memorial for his son.

Roswall told him to fuck off, but a week later recalled him and announced he would launch a project in memory of Stephen. It would supply disaster areas with fertilizers, pesticides, and chemicals needed for disease prevention, also the trained staff to see the goods were properly used. Spinner would convene and develop the project. Its title would be 'Dove International.'

Officialdom protested that Roswall would have to proceed through the correct channels. Roswall replied that the correct channels handed most relief material straight to crooks and profiteers. He intended to change that.

Roswall pulled strings, Dove got clearance, and against expectations, it flew. Hugo

Spinner moved to London as general manager, and ten years later Dove was aiding famine and flood victims in Asia and Africa, and war refugees in the Balkans and Middle East.

(Sharp operators, Roswall and Spinner. In Dove, Roswall had a massive outlet for his chemicals, and enough free publicity to make a tycoon drool. Spinner had a plum job for life.)

Dove's Central Council, consisting of reps from over forty countries, was due to meet at Mallowfield next week. Moshal was to have been among the delegates. He'd reneged. Why?

Hudnut scowled at the papers on his desk. There were no answers in this load of pulp fiction. He'd have to dig deeper. One thing was sure. Roswall and Spinner would defend their brainchild like pit bulls. He felt almost sorry for Radnor and Warne.

Hudnut would have been astonished to know that what prompted Roswall to create Dove was not greed, but a postcard from his step-grand-child, Lucy. It was hand-made, of white paper clipped into the shape of a dove.

Dear Grandpa, it read, Mom only just told me Stephen died, I am so sorry. Mom said not to write because you not my real grandpa and we not blud kin, but you wrote to me when Dad dumped us and other times as well, and I like to have your letters. This one is cut like a dove because doves mean hope. It was 'sposed to have a leef in its beek but the sissors slip and cut it off. With all my love. Lucy Ann Roswall.

2

Daniel Roswall stepped from a side door of Mallowfield and strolled towards the helipad two hundred yards away. An armed guard already stood there, gazing skyward.

The estate lay in peaceful country, between the headwaters of the Medway and Rother rivers, but it was protected by every security device known to man. Roswall's huge fortune made him a target for criminals, political fanatics, and common cranks.

The helicopter was a twinkle in the sun's eye. It sparked south-eastward, veered, hovered and settled neatly on the tarmac. A man in city clothes jumped down from the perspex bubble and ducked to where Roswall waited.

'What the hell does Moshal think he's doing?' Hugo Spinner was pallid, his reddish hair dark with sweat. Roswall dropped an arm round his shoulders.

'Relax, Hugo, it's not the end of the world.'

'It could be the end of Dove. It wrecks months of work, our whole Israeli project. Moshal was to lead the debate. His resolution is the guts of the conference.'

'Gerda can speak to it. She's Israeli.'

'Expatriate.'

'That doesn't preclude her from putting the case. She knows the arguments on both sides.' Spinner swung his briefcase like a cat lashing its tail. 'She's no Moshal.'

Roswall didn't argue. Hugo didn't get on with Gerda Marcus; few people did, she tended to ride roughshod over people's feelings. He said mildly, 'She and Kyle will be here about four. Harry and Dieter are coming over later, from Paris.'

Once in the house, Hugo hurried away up the stairs. Watching him go, Roswall sighed. Hugo was a workaholic. He'd been a fine athlete once, eagle skier, scratch golfer. Now he took no holidays and no exercise. He lived alone, parents dead, no siblings. His taste in women ran to busty redheads from behind the bar.

Once the conference was over, he must be made to take leave, relax and live a little.

* * *

In his suite upstairs, Spinner changed into casual clothes. He kept outfits at each of his several addresses — a fat-cat trick, he thought, as he thrust his feet into soft loafers, a far cry from the alley cat days when he

22

washed his only shirt in the sink every night.

That was the difference between him and the rest. Except for Dan, they'd all been born mega-rich; if Dove went down the tubes they'd cut their losses and move on.

Sod Joel Moshal, why had he pulled out? What did he know, what did the Israelis know?

Moshal was the goose that laid their golden eggs. They'd trash anyone and anything that threatened him.

Moshal was also vital to Dove. He was a conduit to substantial funding, especially in the USA. He could bridge frontiers that were closed to lesser mortals. His withdrawal could damage Dove, mess up its plans.

My plans, said Spinner savagely.

He had to start damage control, warn key people to watch their words. Starting with the executive, tonight.

★   ★   ★

The company of six was gathered on the terrace in front of the house. Below them, lawns rolled to the sunset lake where midges danced. A barman served drinks from a mobile trolley, then moved out of earshot.

'Did Moshal jump, or was he pushed?' Roswall wondered. 'Gerda, what's your view?'

'I think it's probably a security move. Israel's lost two top-liners recently, Abrams to a car bomb and Zachary to a sniper. Moshal's too precious to risk.'

Hugo said sharply, 'That's guesswork. Can you confirm it?'

Gerda gave him her saurian smile. 'I'll exert my charms in the cause.'

She was forty-one years old, squat of build, with dusty fair hair that curled close to her skull, and a small bulbous nose. Her appearance was redeemed by eyes as large and golden as an eagle's, and an air of sparkling intelligence.

By contrast, the man next to her seemed colourless. He sat quietly. His hair lay sleek across his head, his pale skin showed no furrow of thought or emotion, his eyes were blank behind gold-rimmed spectacles. Roswall addressed him with deference.

'Dieter, can you shed any light?'

'Not on Moshal, no.' Dieter Engel blinked rapidly. A financier based in Zurich, he had access to an information network that surpassed that of many police forces. Occasionally — very occasionally — he let fall a crumb of knowledge. 'There have been enquiries,' he admitted. 'The FBI has asked questions about certain accounts.'

Roswall nodded, unsurprised. It was hardly

news that the FBI hoped to break the silence of the Zurich bankers. Tax-evaders and racketeers, not least the Mafia, salted away billions in Swiss secret accounts.

Hugo said impatiently. 'Why do you raise this? Is someone in Dove involved?'

Engel shrugged delicately. 'My informant knows that Dove is one of my interests. He hinted at the FBI's concern. He didn't mention names.'

'Hints, rumours Moshal wouldn't ditch us for so little.'

Engel eyed Hugo in mild surprise. 'Moshal's priority now has to be a peace settlement between Israel and Palestine. If he suspected that Dove had a hand in something that might upset the current truce, he would of course distance himself and his government from us.'

Hugo's face flamed. 'As you would, no doubt!'

Engel's only answer was a slight tilt of the head.

Roswall frowned. 'Hugo's right, we need facts, not rumours. I'll see what I can learn from the Americans.' He turned to the young man on his right. 'Kyle, we need your skills. See what you can discover, will you?'

'Be glad to.' Kyle Parnell's face shone with pure pleasure, and Hugo glared at him.

The fool thinks it's a game, he thought. Break some codes, tap into other people's systems. Hooked on adrenalin, always looking for a new rush.

There were photos in Dan's study of Kyle on Annapurna, of Kyle a white speck on a black wall of surf; last week he'd appeared on a magazine cover, doing the Arctic explorer bit. Silver fox parka, blue eyes circled with black, you couldn't tell him apart from the bloody huskies.

Roswall turned to a plump man who was sitting a little apart from the group.

'You'll check on flight security, Harry?'

'Sure, sure.' The fat man was all smiles. He used *bonhomie* the way Engel used silence, to conceal his intentions. Harry Solomon — or was it Hari Sulamein, no one was sure — had interests in oil and shipping, and owned Omega Airlines, which leased an aircraft to Dove.

'I already upped the insurance,' he said. 'I'll play it safe, don't worry.' In days to come they were to remember his words.

'Good,' Roswall said. 'Dinner's at eight. After that we'll work on the conference agenda.'

As they strolled back to the house, Hugo spoke to Gerda.

'Talk to Kyle,' he said. 'Tell him not to hack

into any FBI computers. He's daft enough to try.'

'Leave Kyle to me,' Gerda said shortly. Hugo ignored the danger signals.

'And keep me up to speed on Moshal, hear? There are people out to smash us.'

'I'll keep in touch,' Gerda said. Hugo was paranoid about Dove. One had to weather his nerve storms.

Roswall walked between Kyle and Dieter, aware of the tensions they generated. Banker and playboy, getter and spender, they were often at loggerheads. He said gently:

'We have a delicate situation, you know. We have to find out what's going on, but we must tread warily.'

It was a command. Dieter was to tell what he knew, withholding nothing. Kyle was to ferret out the truth, without attracting unwelcome attention.

★   ★   ★

James Brock woke early on Friday morning. He dressed in jeans and shirt, went to the kitchen and made coffee and toast. As he was finishing his breakfast he heard a car draw up to the gate. Peering through the window he saw that Candida Woodley was coming up the path. He opened the front door and she thrust past him into the living-room, swung round to face him.

'I've come from the rectory,' she said. 'Mr Wallis says you refuse to hold a service for my sister.'

James shook his head. 'Clare was agnostic. She told me more than once, she didn't want a church service.'

'She was a Christian! She was baptized, married in church!'

He nodded tiredly. 'I know. I was there.'

'You're disgusting!'

He shrugged. 'Why don't you hold a service at Staplehurst?' Clare's parents lived there, and Candida and her husband were a few miles further on, at Chart Sutton.

'Don't worry, we intend to.' Candida stepped closer to James. 'We at least mourn her. You wanted her to die. Did you know she phoned me that last morning? She said I must take her car, she wasn't going to need it any more. She meant to leave you. You couldn't face that, could you? Couldn't face looking a fool to your precious friends!'

James ran a hand over his eyes 'Clare made up her mind to leave life, Candida. Not just me.'

'You could have saved her. You could have pulled her out of the car.'

'No. The door was locked. She wouldn't open it.'

Candida made a wild gesture. 'You let her die! You let her drive over the edge. You're a coward, a weakling, a useless failure.'

James made no answer. His silence seemed to madden Candida, and she struck out at him, lurching unsteadily. He caught the blow on his upraised arm and pushed her away.

'Go, please,' he said.

She made for the door. Reaching it she stood for a moment, her face curiously blank, as if she was suffering some sort of fugue. Her lips moved sluggishly.

'Clare never loved you. She told me. She said you were her cross in life. Her very words. It was David she loved. He had her before you did. They used to sleep together when he came on leave. That last time, too. The truth is, you're nothing without your precious brother. Not a husband, not a man, nothing at all.'

She turned and walked from the room. James heard the clatter of her heels as she crossed the hall. The front door slammed.

He stood without moving until the sound of her motor car faded down the lane. Then he collected his bunch of keys from the hall table, walked through the side door to the garage, and set out to drive to Heathrow.

3

On arriving in Rome late on Saturday afternoon, Hugo Spinner went straight to the Dove warehouse, which adjoined Rome airport. The freight-manager, Andrew Fermoy, was in his office, a glass eyrie suspended above the warehouse floor.

In his youth Fermoy had been a quarter-master in the British Army. He was stocky, crinkle-haired, with pale-brown eyes under the calloused eyebrows of a boxer. He greeted Hugo without enthusiasm.

'Back early, aren'tcha? Thought you was slummin' with the top brass.'

'I was. We have an emergency. Joel Moshal's pulled out of the conference and Gerda Marcus thinks there may have been a terrorist threat. We have to step up security, especially on Monday's flight. Omega one-nine-seven.'

'*Paloma*'s clean. She's not carrying illegal substances, no hazardous materials, we've done random samplings. We've checked the cargo against the waybills and there's no discrepancies. We're not breakin' any IATA rules. Airport security will run its own tests

30

before take-off. That satisfy you?'

'I'm not criticizing, Andy. Just doing my job. Have you heard from Mr Solomon?'

Fermoy scowled. 'Yeah, fat fart's been bashin' my ear since yesterday, have we done this, have we done that. I sent him copies of the manifests. Passenger list's not my worry.'

'I gave him a copy of that, before I left England.' Hugo fixed Fermoy with a cold stare. 'You guarantee there's no suspect cargo? Nothing unusual?'

Fermoy shrugged. 'There was a carton came from Rome office this arvy. Addressed to Captain Brock.'

'Who sent it?'

'His brother. Took it to Heathrow. Old Summers checked it and sent it over with our courier.'

'Did you check the contents?'

'With me own lily-whites.' Fermoy pointed at the open box standing on a trestle near the windows.

'What's in it?'

'Fax machine, two rackets, camera, pair of Raybans. Captain Brock wants it all sent back to Mallowfield. We'll load it in the conference container. There's room.'

Hugo went over to the carton. He lifted out the fax machine and examined it, plugged it in and switched it on to see if it was working.

He hefted the rackets to test their weight. He dipped a hand into the carton and retrieved a sheet of paper, scanned it and slid it into his pocket.

'Fax message,' he said. 'I'll see Captain Brock gets it.'

He strolled across to the windows and stared down at the warehouse floor, with its rows of numbered crates, pallets and containers. The bay for *Paloma*'s freight was over to the right of the road that led to the main cargo-doors.

Without turning his head, he said; 'Dieter Engel reports that the FBI's been sucking up to the Zurich bankers, fishing expedition. You heard anything about that?'

Fermoy said softly: 'If you're askin' have I been saltin' away bread with the gnomes, the answer's no.'

Hugo turned to face him. 'There are those who might have. I don't want the law on Dove's back, Fermoy. Anyone who tries fancy footwork answers to me. Is that clear?'

'Sure.' Fermoy's pale eyes were expression-less. 'I'll pass the word, but I don't reckon any of my lads are runnin' scams.'

'If you hear anything, let me know. Use my mobile phone. Monday I'll be at the airport first thing, to meet the Balkan delegates. We'll have to go over their stuff

32

carefully. We'll check the manifests together.'

Hugo took his departure, his steps brisk on the metal treads of the stairway. Fermoy watched his progress on the photoscanner, saw him disappear among the canyons of freight. Spinner always used the door marked STAFF ONLY. A real Nosy Parker, that one, but sharp. Better warn the lads; now wasn't the time to let things fall off the truck.

He closed and sealed the carton, affixing his clearance label to it. That done, he carried the box down to the *Paloma* bay and stacked it with the rest of the goods to be loaded into the Dove container for Mallowfield.

★　★　★

Moshal's defection caused deepening anxiety at Dove and Omega. On Saturday evening Gerda Marcus called Hugo at his Rome apartment.

'I spoke to a friend at the Israeli embassy,' she said. 'Moshal's to join the Washington talks on the Accord; he leaves Tel Aviv in three days' time. Till then he's wrapped in cotton wool.'

'Mallowfield's secure.'

'No. We're talking state troopers with Uzis.'

'Has there been a terrorist threat?'

'They say not, but I smell brimstone.'

33

Gerda paused. 'Dan wants me to join you in Rome. Lend you a hand.'

'I don't need a bloody hand!'

'It's what Dan wants, Hugo.'

Hugo said sullenly: 'So when do you arrive?'

'Tomorrow morning, by Alitalia. I'm booked at the Orsini. I'll be in touch.'

★ ★ ★

At Mallowfield, Gerda tried a fresh number, let it ring.

'Where is Adri,' she muttered. 'That number's supposed to be fail-safe.'

Kyle Parnell said: 'Try again later.'

She waited ten minutes, then dialled again. Shook her head.

'Could be a fault on the line,' Kyle said.

She nodded, but in her mind's eye she saw Adri's office, the phone on his desk ringing, ringing, and the people in the room listening, waiting for the ringing to stop.

★ ★ ★

Hugo called Iain Kincraig, the maintenance chief for Omega Airlines at Rome.

'Iain, I'm sorry to trouble you, I've just heard from Gerda Marcus. It seems the

34

Israelis have wind of a terrorist attack. Andy Fermoy is double-checking all *Paloma*'s cargo. I need to be sure you're exercising the same vigilance with the aircraft.'

Kincraig answered with icy politeness.

'*Paloma*'s in prime shape, Mr Spinner. She's passed her Phase A and terminal inspections; my teams have run special checks on her mechanical, electrical, fuel and computer systems. Her engines are just fine. I told Mr Solomon he's no need to concairn himself about her.'

'Good. Good. I don't doubt your efficiency, you know. Merely a word to the wise, you understand.'

'Aye, weel, that word's a'ready been spoken, by those who've the right to speak it, so I'll bid you goodnight, sir.'

The line went dead.

★ ★ ★

At a table outside his favourite trattoria, Andrew Fermoy opened his second bottle of Chianti. He brooded about Monday's flight. He hated working with Combi aircraft. Passengers and cargo on the same deck, it wasn't safe. After the *Helderberg* caught fire and crashed off Mauritius, the board of inquiry wanted all Combis banned, but the

US Federal Aviation Association just issued new directives 'to minimize the risk of cargo fires'.

A mess of new rules about how cargo must be stored, packed, consigned. Passing the buck to the handlers, that's what it was. If anything went wrong with *Paloma*, he'd have to carry the effing can.

He finished the bottle, paid his shot, and left, slouching bearlike through the pavement crowds, shouldering aside anyone who stood in his path.

Hugo's last call was to Vitagas, the firm that supplied Omega and Dove with oxygen- and halon-gas-cylinders.

Alonso Vespucci, the son of the owner, took the order.

'I want delivery tomorrow,' Hugo told him. 'I want to see the stuff loaded — with Kincraig present, of course. That clear?'

'Certainly, Mr Spinner. I'll see to it myself.'

As Alonso hung up, his father looked at him questioningly. 'What was that about?'

Alonso waggled his fingers in the air.

'Spinner wants new oxygen- and halon-cylinders delivered to the airport tomorrow. For *Paloma*.'

'Why? The stock he has is recent.'

'He's in one of his states. Some terrorist scare.'

'Well, it's their money. You'll come in early tomorrow, eh?'

'No, I'll make it up tonight. Don't you wait, Papa. It won't take me long.'

Alonso went off to the storage area where rows of gas-cylinders stood on their specially made racks. One of the men on night duty came forward to help him lift the larger canisters on to a trolley.

★ ★ ★

Hugo walked out on to the balcony of his apartment. Below him the lights shone vivid green on flowering chestnuts and a twist of the Tiber.

He'd covered everything — security at the airport, *Paloma*'s airworthiness, the cargo checks.

There remained the fax in Brock's carton. Brock could be the weak point in his defences. The record rated him one of the best pilots in the business, but he'd left BA to join tinpot outfits in Colombia and Greece. Did they offer more profitable sidelines, perhaps?

Brock was a big spender, lived high on the hog, gambled.

37

Hugo chewed on a hangnail. Tomorrow he'd chase Brock, corner him, find out exactly what he was up to.

★ ★ ★

David Brock stood at the window of the master bedroom of the Villa d'Ascani.

In a few minutes the sun would rise. The sky glowed blood-red, the village two miles distant flamed on its round Tuscan hilltop. Far to the south, mist marked the course of the Ombrone River. It would be a hot day.

He decided to go for a swim, wrapped a towel round his hips and moved quietly through the bedroom. Pia was still asleep, sprawled on her back with the sheets twisted across her legs. She breathed heavily, and her skin shone with oily sweat.

Five years ago it had been a pleasure to watch her sleeping. She'd been like a peony, richly coloured and opulent. Now the contours of her face were blurred, her breasts were flaccid, and her hair, that had been soft and silky as maize tassels, had faded to dull ash. She was forty-five, but she looked a lot older.

She'd had a tough life. When they met she was married to Nicolo d'Ascani, who was dying of multiple sclerosis in a clinic in

Lausanne. Pia had in tow a freeloader who spent her money, cheated on her, and insulted her in front of the paid help. One night at a party he slapped Pia's face. David punched him out, and drove Pia back to Tuscany. A few weeks later he moved into the Villa and Pia's bed.

Her household and the village people accepted him as a fixture. Even Father Stefano, the local priest, seemed to consider him a trespass that might be forgiven. Roman society sneered, saying Pia d'Ascani had a new chauffeur. David didn't care. His job took him away a lot, but when he was in Italy, he came to Pia.

For a few years the arrangement held. Then Nicolo died in his Swiss clinic. Pia told David she loved him and wanted to marry him. If marriage wasn't to his liking, they'd go on as they were.

For ever, till death did them part.

David tried to break with her. He transferred to Omega's African sector, cut all links with Pia, and spent his leave periods in England with James and Clare. Then in 1997 Omega signed the agreement to lease planes to Dove International, and appointed David chief pilot for its operations. Just before Christmas of that year he arrived in Rome to sign his contract.

When he set foot on the concourse of Rome Airport he found Father Stefano waiting for him. The old man announced he'd come to drive David to the Villa.

'No way, Padre,' David said, 'I'm leaving for England tomorrow, to spend Christmas with my brother.'

A thin hand fastened on his wrist. 'You don't understand, my son. Pia is very ill. She had typhoid fever. We thought she would die. She is still very weak, she won't eat, she has sometimes,' Stefano sought for a word, waving thin fingers, 'illusions, in the head. She needs you.'

They faced each other on the concourse, resentment face to face with compassion. Compassion won.

'If I come, I won't stay,' David warned.

Father Stefano nodded and smiled. 'God will reward you,' he said.

They drove through fields thinly powdered with snow, the frozen furrows gleaming like bone against the dark flesh of the plough-lands. Pia was in the living-room of the Villa, curled on a sofa before the fire. She half-raised herself, staring at David. Her lips framed his name and tears welled in her eyes. He leaned down and took her hands. They were cold and frail as twigs. He kissed her forehead.

'I've come for Christmas,' he said.
That was two and a half years ago.

* * *

They'd come to terms. Pia accepted the limits he set. He would stay at the Villa on his Rome stopovers, sleep with her sometimes, write to her if he was away for a long spell. She didn't expect more.

He had an easy lifestyle, no clouds on his horizon — not until March of this year when he decided to spend a fortnight's leave at Badger's Sett with James and Clare. The holiday was jinxed from the start by Clare's behaviour.

Her moods had always been chancy, but this time she was downright erratic, swinging from feverish gaiety to bleak silence. He wondered if she could be on drugs and thought of speaking to James, but what would he say? *Hey, by the way, I think your wife's a user?*

At the start of the second week, James announced that he must go to London for a couple of days. 'The contract means a lot to the firm,' he said, 'I'll be back by four on Wednesday.'

On Tuesday night, Clare and David were invited to dine with the Woodleys. They returned home at midnight. Clare suggested a nightcap, but David declined and went up to bed.

He fell asleep quickly, to wake an hour later with a coldness on his skin. The duvet had been flung back and Clare was lying beside him, mother-naked. She pressed herself against him, wound her legs about him and tried to fumble his crotch. Her flesh was cold, it was like being in the coils of a snake. He tried to break her grip but she clung fast, muttering that he needn't worry, they had the house to themselves, it was quite safe.

He thrust her away and rolled out of bed, snapping on the bedside lamp. In the pool of light her face glistened, her eyes were black as stones. He pulled on his bathrobe and tried to calm her, telling her she'd had a bad dream and must go back to her own room. For answer she clawed at his face, screaming obscenities. He wrapped the duvet round her and carried her along the passage. At the door of her room, she wrenched free of him, ran inside and slammed the door in his face. From the far side she yelled at him:

'Get out of my house. Get out now!'

He went back to his room and sat on the edge of the bed. He felt sick and confused. His first thought was that he should do as Clare told him, but he couldn't leave her alone. She was ill, she needed help. He'd have to stay at least until morning, when the cleaner arrived. He dressed, packed his belongings and spent the rest of the night on the living-room sofa.

When Mrs Commins came, he told her he'd had an urgent summons from Omega and must return to duty at once. 'Mrs Brock isn't well,' he said. 'Some kind of feverish attack, I think.'

The old woman gave him a shrewd look. 'Aye, she's given to 'em,' she said. 'Lives on 'er nerves, she does . . . and other people's.'

David put through a call to James and told him he had to report on emergency standby. He told him Clare wasn't well, and that Mrs Commins would stay with her.

James said he'd come home early, David mustn't worry. His voice sounded tired.

Later, David understood that what drove Clare was neither drugs nor lust, but anger. She was in a blind rage against James, against herself, against life. She was set on a course of self-destruction, and by failing to recognize that, he'd given her time to kill herself, and almost to kill his brother.

★   ★   ★

David climbed out of the pool, picked up his towel, and walked slowly back to the house.

He had to stop worrying about James and Clare and the past. He had to focus on the present.

He still hadn't heard from Boru. It was weeks since he'd sent that first fax. He'd sent others, but there'd been no replies. All he had was a fuzzy photo, and a vague feeling it was linked with Colombia. That wasn't enough to take to Harry Solomon, and it was no use talking to Spinner, the silly prat would throw hysterics and very likely land them all in a major libel suit.

There was nothing to do but wait, and hope that Boru would come up with something conclusive.

Pia met him at the front door and handed him his mobile phone. Spinner's voice shrilled at him.

'Brock, why the hell aren't you at the apartment, I've been trying to reach you for hours!'

'What's your problem?'

'That carton that came for you yesterday . . . there was a fax message in it.'

'Who from?' David said sharply.

'Someone called Boru. Who is he, Brock? He talks about an association. What association, what's going on?'

'The Pilots' Association in Washington. Omega's looking for recruits.'

Spinner's voice climbed higher. 'I don't believe you. Something's going on. I demand to know — '

'It's Omega's business, Spinner, not yours.'

'Don't you tell me my business! We have an emergency, we're facing terrorist threats, it's my duty to protect *Paloma* and everyone on tomorrow's flight. I won't tolerate your behaviour, I shall take this to the highest level — '

'For God's sake, cool it! There is no terrorist threat, if there was Omega would have been warned of it. If you keep screeching 'terrorist' you'll start a panic that will paralyse every airport in Europe. Get a grip on yourself, man.'

Hugo sucked in a shuddering breath. 'Yes, I'm sorry. There've been disturbing rumours.' He hesitated, then went on: 'Tell me, do you think any member of Omega or Dove could be acting as an agent for a criminal organization?'

'How the hell should I know?'

'Pilots hear things.'

'Not this pilot.'

'Let me be plainer. Do you know of anyone who pays money into a Swiss numbered account?'

45

'No, I don't.'

'Have you such an account, yourself?'

'No! What are you saying, Spinner?'

'Nothing, nothing. But if you do hear of anyone who's salting money away in Zurich, I rely on you to tell me at once. Goodbye, Brock.'

David went upstairs to dress. Spinner was probably overwound, but his questions about Swiss accounts could be significant. Boru would have to be told. He'd send a fax tonight.

He toyed with the idea of phoning James and telling him about Boru, but decided against it. James was in no state to be burdened with new problems.

This trip, he'd go to Badger's Sett for a couple of days, talk to James, maybe bring him back to Italy for a holiday in the sun.

4

Arriving at the airport on Monday, Kincraig went directly to the zone where *Paloma* was taking on cargo. Andy Fermoy was watching the loading of containers to the main deck cargo-hold. He had stationed himself near the loading-door at the rear of the aircraft, and was racing about, swearing at the handlers. Kincraig knew Fermoy to be a hard worker, but disliked and mistrusted him. Fermoy was what the army had made him, a grafter. Too canny to breach airline regulations, he worked points with the firms supplying Omega, saw that contracts went the right way, and that the beneficiaries looked after him.

As Kincraig approached, Fermoy turned to face him. For a moment they looked like fighters squaring up, Fermoy restless and aggressive, Kincraig tall, watchful, solid.

Fermoy said: 'You're here early. Aunty been after you, has he?'

Aunty was the name the ground crews gave to Spinner. Kincraig ignored the gibe.

'Spinner does his job,' he said.

'Long as he doesn't try to do mine. He'll be here to see us load the cylinders from

Vitagas. Got his knickers in a knot over nothing, as usual.'

'I wouldn't say it's nothing.

Kincraig left the loading zone and walked out on to the tarmac apron. He felt uneasy. He couldn't shrug off Spinner's fussing, the way Fermoy did. He'd seen the aftermath of air disasters — the dismembered bodies scattered across scorched earth, or dangling from trees, the fields gouged and stinking of fuel, fire and death.

Whenever he heard of an air crash, he sweated. Rumours affected him like warnings from the oracle. He always did his best, but he never quite shook off the fear that one day his best wouldn't be good enough.

Spinner arrived and the gas cylinders were loaded. Fermoy made a final inspection of the hold, checking the stacks and the fire-resistant linings. The main cargo-door was closed and the linchpins that secured it were examined and seen to be firmly engaged. Later in the day *Paloma* would be fuelled and moved to the final boarding zone, where the crew and passengers would embark.

The main concourse of the terminal was already seething with activity: pilgrims, business groups and holidaymakers laying siege to the information desk. Gerda Marcus, dressed in tracksuit and trainers, was

48

shepherding her Dove delegates to their departure zone. The Turkish delegate, hugely fat and totally hairless, was distraught.

'I have pay first class,' he wailed, 'I have pay for effeeciency and comforting and what is result? I lost all my suitcase. All.'

'Your baggage isn't lost, Dr Isnik,' Gerda said. 'It's at Athens and they'll send it direct to London.'

'Who will send? Same idiots who make the first rubbish? My things will go to Timbuktu. I wish to make complain in writing.'

Gerda soothed, and Isnik subsided. Gerda turned to the man on his left.

'Dr Kesh, I have a favour to ask of you. Joel Moshal can't make the conference and we need to rearrange the programme. Can you speak at two o'clock tomorrow, instead of three-thirty?'

'Sure.' Kesh nodded amiably. He was forty-two, but his mop of fair curls and unlined face made him look younger. His accent marked him as coming from the southern USA.

Dr Isnik, diverted from his troubles, squinted at his companion.

'So Doctor, what is your topic this time?'

'Communicable diseases of cattle and sheep.'

'Aha, very current, very urgent matters.

Bovine tubercle. Foot an' mout', mad cow, anthrax. Also shigellosis. After the earthquakes, many in my country die of such disease. I have myself much to say about infected meat.'

Kesh nodded, smiling slightly. Isnik had much to say on every subject. Sometimes what he said was useful.

At the main ticket-office a clerk was having trouble with a teenager.

'I'm sorry, *signorina*,' he said, 'your card is no use, it is invalid.'

'What do you mean, invalid? Your machine must be wrong. Try it again.'

'The card has been stopped. Someone has cancelled it. You cannot use it.' The clerk studied the girl on the other side of the glass. About fourteen, he judged. Designer jeans, Nike trainers, pricey shades. Not hard up, but hyped-up and scared. Could be a runaway.

He said kindly: 'Why don't you go home, my dear, talk to the mamma and papà, they'll sort things out. There's plenty of other flights.'

'I don't want other flights, I want *Paloma*, today, now! My grandpa owns Dove, he charters effing *Paloma*; if he was here I wouldn't have to pay at all!'

Her voice was soaring towards hysteria. The people in the queue were listening, it

50

could build into a big scene. The clerk summoned the airport PRO, Fiamma, explained the situation to her in rapid Italian.

Fiamma glanced at the girl's passport.

'You have been in Italy only two months? You are on holiday?'

'Yes. I stayed with my mother, but she's gone to Salzburg.' The girl was close to tears.

Fiamma nodded at the clerk and said quietly: 'Put out a call for Mr Spinner. He's Dove's manager. I'll take Miss Roswall to his office.' She put an arm round the girl's shoulders. 'Come, Lucy, let's go.'

Hugo arrived at the office white-faced. He stared at Lucy and threw up his arms.

'Girl, what in hell are you doing here? Why aren't you with your mother in Salzburg?'

'Salzburg sucks,' Lucy said. 'The river stinks and there's no action. I'm going home to England.'

'Wait now. Does your mother know about this?'

'I phoned her hotel. She hasn't called me back, she's cancelled my card. How'm I supposed to live without money? I want to go home, on *Paloma*.' Lucy's voice broke, and Hugo came to a decision. He called Dan Roswall.

'Dan, it's Hugo. I have Lucy with me, at the airport. Erica's in Salzburg with new talent, she's stopped Lucy's cards. The kid's very upset, she tried to book a flight on *Paloma*. Yes, I told her, but she's in a state.. Yes, right . . . '

Hugo held out the receiver and Lucy snatched it. 'Grandpa? Please can't I come home on *Paloma*?'

'That's not possible, darling, she's due to take off in a hour and that doesn't give me time to settle Erica's hash.'

'She won't let me go, Grandpa I'm her meal ticket, she said so. This new man's the pits, he's always after me, I told Erica but she just says I'm making it up, I can't stand any more . . . please . . . '

'Lucy, darling, listen to me. You are coming home, very soon, and for good. You will never have to worry about Erica again, I promise. Hugo will lend you some money, and drive you home to the apartment, and I'll call you again when I've fixed things. Soon. OK?'

'Cool! Thanks, Grandpa.' Lucy heaved a great sigh. 'How are you all, over there? How's Bojangles?'

'We're fine, and Bojangles is in full control. He brought me a fine fat rat, yesterday, put it on my pillow.'

Lucy giggled. 'That shows my cat likes you.'

'Yeah. He sends you his love. Put Hugo on,

now, honey, and don't worry. I'll see you very soon.'

Hugo took the receiver. 'Yes, Dan?'

'Lucy's to stay in Rome,' Roswall said. 'See she has all she needs. How's the flight shaping? Any more security scares?'

'No, nothing.'

'Good. Thanks for your help, Hugo. I'll call you later.'

Hugo cut the connection and spoke hurriedly to Lucy. 'I have to see the delegates board. Just sit tight, understand?'

When he reached the departure bay, the delegates were already moving through the gate. Gerda came to meet him.

'What kept you?'

'Lucy Roswall. She's split from Erica. She tried to book herself on *Paloma*.'

Gerda said sharply: 'She's not booked, is she?'

'No, I'm to take her to the apartment, till Dan's sorted things out.'

He made his way back to the main concourse and entered a public phone cubicle. The number he dialled rang for some time before a voice said: 'Kyle speaking.'

'Hugo. Do you know of any individual or organization that goes by the name of Boru: B-O-R-U?'

'Nope.'

'It might be an airline pilot, someone registered with the IAP in Washington or elsewhere.'

'You're talking needles in haystacks, man.'

'Chase it, will you Kyle? It could be a tie-up with what we discussed at the last meeting. Dieter's report, remember?'

'I'll do what I can.'

The line went dead. Hugo hurried back to the office to cope with Lucy's problems.

5

Paloma was ready for departure.

Her flight plans had been checked and registered by air traffic control. She was linked to the intricate web that stretched across Europe, beneficiary of the resources of major airports: the batteries of telephones, radios and computers, the maps, charts and weather machines, the ground and long-range radar, the VOR, DME and NDB systems, the thousands of technicians, supervisors and managers who made the immense plan function.

David Brock and his co-pilot Sandy Rossi had boarded early and were already on the flight deck. Dropping into his seat, Rossi said in a voice a little too casual:

'You feeling lucky?'

'Sure,' David said. He had no expectation of trouble. Iain Kincraig was one of the best maintenance chiefs in the business, and he was happy with the aircraft. Fermoy swore the cargo was clean, no explosive or hazardous materials in the holds. The passengers and their baggage had passed an extra-vigilant inspection.

Spinner's jitters and his own unease had to be put aside. Boru hadn't come up with anything. It was time to quit dithering and get on with the job, fly the bloody plane.

He started the routine cockpit drill, scanning the instruments on the console, a multitude of dials and switches that in flight would become an extension of his brain. He paid special attention to the communication systems. The flight deck was fitted with 'hot-mic' equipment, microphones that ensured that not only the flight crew's speech, but all the cockpit sounds in range were picked up and stored by the cockpit voice recorder on the tape in the Black box.

He checked the area mikes that allowed the pilot to talk to the flight engineer's station. This was next to the fibreglass barrier that separated the passenger cabin from the cargo hold. A service galley formed part of the barrier, and two flight attendants were busy there, sliding trays of plastic cups and soft-drink cans on to a trolley.

David asked the flight engineer, Len Oakley, who was on fire duty for the flight.

'Ted Doubleday,' Len said, 'and Wally Prout's the back-up. Ted's checking the hold, now.'

According to regulations, once the main cargo door was closed and secured, a crew member trained in fire-fighting must inspect the hold, to see that the pallets and containers were correctly stowed, with enough space round them to allow access to any part of the cargo. He would also make sure that the extinguishers, cargo-nets and flame-resistant compartment linings were securely in place.

Doubleday came on the intercom to report everything was in order, and David switched to the controller in the airport tower. He received and acknowledged the controller's flight instructions, and noted the weather conditions prevailing along *Paloma*'s route to London. Violent thunderstorms were flailing the southern coast of France, and the controller cited the altitude that would best avoid them.

The passengers came on board and were shepherded to their seats. Hand luggage was packed into the overhead shelves, pleasantries were exchanged. An air hostess came forward to tell David that Dr Isnik wished to visit the cockpit during the journey. David sighed, but nodded.

'OK, he can come. I'll tell you when.'

The checks were complete: aircraft doors closed, flaps set, controls operating freely, instruments correctly set. David signalled the control tower that *Paloma* was ready for take-off and awaiting final clearance.

Clearance was given, the controller citing the altitude and course *Paloma* must maintain after take-off. David spoke his brief welcome to the passengers, the chief cabin steward recited his routine safety instructions, piped music flowed. The engines purred, roared, and the aircraft moved slowly from the holding area to the taxi lane.

Reaching the appointed runway, *Paloma* turned into the wind, gathered speed along the tarmac, soared and climbed steeply. Beneath her belly, Rome dwindled, the land became turquoise-blue sea, shimmering yet milky, furrowed by the widening wake of a small tramp steamer.

★   ★   ★

By 16.16 hours, *Paloma* had reached an altitude of 26,000 feet above the Mediterranean. Visibility was patchy. To the north, curdled clouds rolled before the wind, but the coast of Corsica was clear, and the route ahead sunlit.

The passengers relaxed in their seats, chatted or dozed. On the flight deck a steward handed a mug to Rossi, who grimaced as he took it.

'Two months from now,' he said, 'I'll be in the US of A, where they know how to make coffee.'

David nodded. Rossi was leaving to join Pan Am, a good career if you could stand the monotony.

Len Oakley moved into the engineer's jump seat behind David and began to describe a smallholding he was planning to buy.

'Near Luton,' he said. 'The soil's in good nick, but the cottage needs a lot done to it. Em and I can tiddle it up when I retire, I don't fancy sitting on my bum all day, and Em's brother and sister are close to Luton; it'll be nice to have family around.'

His chatter was interrupted by the sharp ringing of an alarm-bell, and the flashing of a red light on the pilot's overhead module. At the same time the intercom from the fire-fighter's station crackled, and Ted Doubleday's voice said urgently,

'Skip, we have a smoke alarm. Detector number four in the main-deck cargo hold.'

'Yes, we have it here, too.' David reached to silence the alarm bell, his mind fighting the paralysis of shock. 'Is the passenger cabin clear?' he said.

'Clear, yes. No smoke. Yet.'

Ted was issuing a reminder that in a

Combi aircraft like *Paloma*, air was distributed to the cargo compartment through the passenger-cabin system. Some of that air flowed through both cabin and hold, to exit via the outflow valve in the belly of the aircraft, but some was returned by circulating fans to the passenger area. That stream could carry traces of smoke, and if the passengers smelled smoke, they'd panic.

Rossi said harshly: 'It can't be a fucking fire, everything's flame-proof.'

David cut him short. 'Could be a fault in the detector, or the electricals. Len, fetch up the checklist, main-deck cargo-fire stroke smoke.' Len moved quickly from the jump seat to his work desk, and David switched back to Doubleday.

'Ted, you and Wally get kitted up fast and make a hold inspection.'

Oakley had the plastic-coated checklist in his hand and began reading aloud. 'All flight-deck crew on one hundred per cent oxygen. Cockpit door closed. Right. Non-flying pilot establish all crew communications OK.' Rossi nodded and set about calling the various crew stations to put them on alert.

David was making a rapid check of *Paloma*'s systems, looking for defects. All seemed normal, but now a second smoke warning sounded, and he swore under his breath.

Oakley kept up his incantation. 'Bleed air switches open, duct isolation valve switches open, pack valve switches open. Recirculating fan switch off.'

The closure of the fans would halt the flow of smoke-contaminated air to the passenger cabin, and the reduction of airflow would cut the supply of fire-feeding oxygen to the cargo hold.

David called Doubleday. 'Ted? You and Wally ready to go in?'

'Going in now.' Ted's voice was muffled by his mask.

'Check the hold, make sure the smoke barrier is secured once you're through it, report conditions ASAP.'

'Roger.'

Just over two minutes had passed since the first alarm-bell sounded. Oakley said: 'The passengers, Skip? When will you announce . . . ?'

'Soon as I know what we have back there.' David sent Len a warning glance. In theory, the barrier between the passenger and cargo compartments should prevent smoke or fire from leaking forward, but they both knew that theories were fallible. An aircraft fire could burn with demonic speed, building in minutes to the point where combustible gases would ignite at ceiling level, and flames flash from end to end of the hold at temperatures close to 2000 degrees Fahrenheit. That kind of heat destroyed the pressure differential between hold and cabin, so that smoke-laden air was forced back into the passenger area.

David said: 'Sandy, check the situation in the cabin, bring me a report. Len, brief the crew. Tell Liz to be ready to move the passengers as far forward as possible, and help them on to oxygen if necessary.'

That was a big if. Humans lived on oxygen. So did fire. You couldn't feed one without the other.

As Rossi and Oakley moved away, David called Rome airport on VHF radio.

'Roma. Roma. This is Omega one-niner-seven, do you read me?'

Static crackled, then Rome control tower answered.

'Omega one-niner-seven, this is Roma, go ahead.'

'We have a problem. A smoke warning from the main-deck cargo-hold. We are proceeding on emergency checklist for main-deck cargo smoke, we are assessing the position in the hold, I will report to you as soon as possible. Over.'

'Roger, Omega, we will await your report.'

In the control tower, the controller had already summoned chief supervisor Benno Capriati. Capriati hurried across the floor, taking charge, issuing the instructions that placed the airport's complex systems on emergency alert.

★   ★   ★

Ted Doubleday and Wally Prout, sci-fi figures in protective overalls, gloves, oxygen masks and carrying cylinders, moved through the partition that divided the rear galley from the cargo hold, securing the safety door behind them. They encountered a thick pall of smoke that veiled the twin rows of containers, and rolled sluggishly against the ceiling. Heat puffed and sucked at their bodies like a snuffling animal.

'Christ, it's a bugger,' Ted said. He snatched up the intercom phone and called the flight deck.

'Skip, we have heavy smoke in the hold, visibility's fuck-all. Looks like there's a fire in one of the rear portside containers. We'll try to locate and extinguish.'

'Roger.' David looked up as Rossi gripped his shoulder.

'There's no smoke in the cabin, but they

know something's wrong. You better talk to them.'

'OK. Are the cabin signs operative?'

'Yes.' Rossi turned back to the entrance to the flight deck and David reached for his mike.

'Ladies and gentlemen, this is your captain. I'm afraid we have a problem and I'm asking for your close attention and co-operation. The trouble is in the cargo area and we are dealing with it there. There is no cause for alarm but we may have to alter our flight plan. Please realize that this is a routine safety procedure. Remain calm, and do exactly as the crew-members tell you. I will keep you fully informed. Thank you.'

He knew what it would be like, back there, voices yelling, people trying to jump out of their seats. He heard the uproar begin, and Rossi shouting to quell it. Most people behaved well in a crisis, but you could count on a few going hysterical. Liz and the cabin crew would have to cope, that was their job. His was to look after the aircraft and bring it safe home.

It was 16.25 hours. He called Rome again and was answered this time by Chief Capriati. David heard the basso-profundo voice with relief, and launched into his report.

'Chief, our fire-fighter reports heavy smoke in the main-deck cargo-hold. The probable source is one of the portside containers at the rear of the stack. The fire-fighter and his assistant are in the hold and will try to locate and extinguish the fire.'

'Roger, Omega.' As he spoke, Capriati was watching the radar screen that showed the aircraft's course. 'Is the smoke confined to the hold? Do you have smoke in the passenger cabin or on the flight deck?'

'Negative. As of now, the smoke is confined to the hold.'

Len appeared at David's side and David signed to him to wait. He said: 'Roma. Request clearance for an immediate descent to flight level one four zero.'

'Roger, Omega, you are cleared for an immediate descent to flight level one four zero.'

Capriati watched the screen display *Paloma*'s steady loss of height. His skin felt clammy. Brock had said there was no smoke in the passenger cabin or flight deck, yet he'd decided to take the aircraft down to 14,000 feet. That was the required procedure when there was heavy smoke penetration to the forward areas. Was Brock expecting the situation on *Paloma* to worsen? He was a highly experienced pilot with a cool head. He wouldn't make such a move without good reason.

No smoke without fire.

Capriati thought of the rumours that had plagued the airport for days: tales of terrorist threats, sabotage. Brock must be taking them seriously.

So what was the right course? Stick with the known facts, or go with the captain's gut-feeling?

Capriati cleared his throat. 'Omega one-niner-seven, do you wish to declare a full emergency?'

There was a brief pause, then the answer came flatly.

'Affirmative.'

'Roger, Omega. I declare a full emergency. Request your exact position and flight details.'

Rossi relayed the information, which Capriati acknowledged. All over the airport the emergency programmes sprang into effect. Ranks of computers, telephones, radios, spun a network of links with other airfields, ships at sea, fire and police departments, search-and-rescue operators. The airlines were scanned and a path cleared for *Paloma*.

David said: 'Roma, what is my nearest suitable airport?'

Capriati was ready for the question. 'Roma,' he said. 'Marseilles has a ground-crew strike, also gale-force winds. Advise you return to Rome.'

David acknowledged the message and directed Rossi to set the course for Rome. *Paloma* began to describe a half-circle across the sky.

★　★　★

In the cargo hold, Ted and Wally had unfastened the gate in the net that enclosed the double row of cargo stacks. Ted lifted a three-metre-long hose from its retaining clips and attached it to the nozzle of a sixteen-pound halon-gas extinguisher. Wally picked up a smaller cylinder, and Ted signed to him to spray the outer flank of the portside containers.

He himself moved into the narrow aisle between the two rows, and directed a stream of chemical extinguishant at the boxes to left and right of him. The containers at the front of the hold were relatively small, made of high-density polyethylene with aluminium doors — not as flame-resistant as fibreglass, but good enough to pass the regulation tests. As he swung the heavy canister in a smooth arc, the air about him cleared slightly,

67

confirming his belief that the source of the smoke lay further aft.

He paced steadily through the murk, remembering his training: don't run, breathe easily, keep calm. Questions raced in his brain. How did this thing start, the containers were supposed to be fireproof, so it had to be the contents that were burning. He noted that the smoke was whitish, not black, not oily. He remembered that when some plastics burned, they produced lethal gas. People died of suffocation, not burns.

He made himself think about the canister he carried. The small ones only lasted twelve seconds, even this sixteen-pounder was nearly dry; he could tell by the weight. He had to nail the source of the smoke. It was further aft. He quickened his pace. He could see Wally, level with him on the outer side of the stack. They'd reached the third set of containers. From here on it was all the new type, all metal, each one with its own extinguisher attached to its side, you shoved a patent nozzle through a seal on the side of the box, pressed the tit, and released a stream of gunge to douse the contents.

The smoke was coming from the last container in the port stack, the one with Dove's stuff for the conference. It was rising fast, sooty as well as white, twirling up towards the ceiling. Gas? Gas could start a flash fire that would wreck the tail controls, total fuck-up.

He emptied the last of his halon over the container, and turned to reach for a fresh supply. It was then that Wally went crazy. He went stumbling back to the safety barrier, plunged through it and passed the galley, to burst into the passenger cabin beyond, trailing smoke and fumes like a demon from hell. Lurching in pursuit, Ted saw Len Oakley spring to grapple Wally to a halt, and slam the cabin door.

6

Pandemonium erupted.

Wally had torn off his helmet and was blubbering, arms flailing wildly. One of the cabin attendants, a burly Scot, seized him in a bear hug and, at Len's nod, bundled him away to the stairs that led up to the crew's rest area.

Len raised his voice to maximum pitch.

'Ladies and gentlemen, stay in your seats, there is no call for panic. Sit down, stay calm. *Stay in your seats.*'

A woman in the back row started to scream hysterically and Liz Corbett leaned over to soothe her. Len continued along the aisle, repeating the same phrases.

'Stay in your seats. There is no cause for panic. The smoke is confined to one container, it's under control. Stay calm.'

Half-way along the aisle a thin man snatched at Len's sleeve.

'Why are we losing height? We should remain at altitude to starve any fire of oxygen. I'm a scientist, I know we must maintain height.'

Len shook himself free. 'Captain Brock

knows what he's about, sir. Please sit down at once.'

The thin man started to argue and the woman next to him struck him a back-handed blow in the chest.

'Sit down, you fool! Do as you're told!'

Len moved on, past clutching hands and a clamour of voices. Co-pilot Rossi met him at the front of the cabin.

'Skip wants you, Len. I'm to move the passengers forward.' He lifted a hand-mike and began to talk into it. The babble of sound diminished and Len hurried forward to the flight deck.

David signed to him to take the co-pilot's seat.

'What happened?'

'Wally freaked, bolted to the cabin, brought some smoke through with him. Rossi's talking to the passengers, going to move them forward.'

'Are they under control?'

'Pretty good.'

'How much smoke is there? Are you sure it came through with Wally, and not through the ventilators?'

'I'm sure. It's not heavy. We can clear it by opening vents.'

David stared at the instrument panel. He shook his head. 'Get me the checklist for

71

smoke evacuation.'

'I don't think that's necessary, sir. We can clear it — '

'Get the list!' David was almost shouting, and Len moved fast to do his bidding.

★ ★ ★

Alone in the cargo hold, Ted Doubleday contemplated the last container. Smoke still billowed from its base. Fermoy had sworn it couldn't happen, no dangerous cargo aboard. Sod Fermoy.

He called the flight deck.

'I've located the source of the smoke, Skip. It's from the aft portside container. Dove's stuff.'

'How bad is it?'

'There's a lot of smoke, visibility's still poor, but I can fix it.'

'Do you need back-up?'

'Nah.' Ted sounded relaxed. 'On'y get in my way. This shouldn't take long.'

'Report as soon as you've got it under.'

'Roger.'

David reported to Capriati in Rome.

'We've located the source of the smoke. It's in the rear portside container, main-deck cargo-hold. Our fireman is dealing with it but there's been a small amount of smoke leakage to the passenger cabin. We're moving them forward.' David's voice was partially swallowed by a burst of sound, voices shouting. Then the interference disappeared, and Capriati intervened.

'Omega, what is your present altitude?'

'Altitude is one-four-zero. We are operating the checklist for smoke evacuation.'

'Roger, Omega.' Capriati gave the course *Paloma* must follow to Rome, and David acknowledged the instructions. Turning back to the intercom he called Doubleday.

'Ted, what's the situation?'

'Smoke's still coming. I'm going to use the extinguisher attached to the container.'

As he spoke, Ted was lifting the patent hose from the clips that secured it to the side of the box. His fingers felt for the spot where the sharp nozzle of the hose would pierce the seal.

'Going in now,' he said.

Liz Corbett appeared in the doorway of the flight deck.

'We've moved them forward as far as we can. They're very stressed. Is there anything we can tell them?'

'Yes. Ask Sandy to talk to them, explain that we have things under control, we're heading back to Rome.'

The door closed after Liz and David

studied the checklist. He handed it to Len Oakley.

'Set it up,' he said.

As Len moved towards his workstation, a series of clicks sounded from the instrument console.

David swore. 'Circuit breakers,' he said. Several of the switches that protected the aircraft's wiring systems had dropped down, and as the two men watched, more clicked into position.

'Ted?' David was already calling the cargo hold. 'Ted, do you read me? We have circuit breakers down. What is the temperature . . . ?'

His voice was drowned by a thunderous rush of sound, a whoosh and thump like the lighting of a mammoth gas oven. In the control tower at Rome airport, Capriati spoke urgently.

'Omega one-niner-seven, do you read me?'

The roar of noise intensified. Capriati called again.

'Omega one-niner-seven, this is Roma, please respond.'

At Capriati's elbow, a junior engineer said anxiously, 'What is it, are they opening the entry doors?'

Capriati shook his head. He was deadly afraid that what they had heard was not a rush of air, but the roar of a flash fire

74

breaking its bonds.

The time was then 16.32.25

Rome called *Paloma* repeatedly, but there was no answer.

Just silence, silence, silence.

★   ★   ★

At 16.42 hours, the captain and mate of the luxury motor cruiser *Amethyst, en route* to take on passengers at Genoa, saw an aircraft crash into the sea off the coast of Corsica. The captain took accurate bearings and signalled the harbour authorities at Ostia.

'She went straight down,' he said, 'like a gannet after a fish. Struck the water at a very steep angle, broke up on impact. The nose section sank at once, the tail section cartwheeled, then went under.'

Ostia passed the news to Rome air traffic control. *Amethyst* changed course and headed at full speed for the site of the crash.

★   ★   ★

At 16.50 hours, Rome ATC issued a DETRESFA, the formal declaration of disaster, to the Civil Aviation Authority of Italy, and also to that of England as the state where *Paloma* was registered.

Within minutes the search-and-rescue centres of both countries swung into action. Italy deployed reconnaissance aircraft and rescue helicopters. Britain sent a rescue plane and diverted a minesweeper from its Mediterranean manoeuvres.

The official search was joined in short order by a polyglot fleet of coastal launches, cargo-and fishing-boats, and private yachts.

First to reach the accident site was a coastal-patrol aircraft of the French Air Force. Its pilot reported seeing wreckage on the surface of the sea: sections of fuselage, baggage and human remains. He dropped a locator beacon to mark the area.

Amethyst arrived soon after, and scoured the site in a vain search for survivors. The debris was widely scattered, and already drifting westward, driven by wind and current.

A lifeboat was lowered to retrieve bodies. An hour later it returned, and four tarpaulins were hoisted to the *Amethyst*'s deck. The young seaman in charge of them was green-faced and trembling.

'There's just pieces,' he told the mate. 'Two on 'em's about 'uman, but the rest, it's just bits. Gawd, I never seen nothin' like it. They wasn't wearin' life-jackets. Din't 'ave time, I 'spose. We brung all wot we could find, but

I dunno wot's the good of it. It's not like you can tell 'oo they was.'

The captain said: 'They'll do post mortems, check DNA and dental records. It may help them to decide how it happened.'

The young man rubbed sweat off his face. 'Where'll we put 'em, sir.'

'In the refrigeration room. I've had it cleared. It's the best we can do.'

The tarpaulins were hauled away and the boat made further sweeps, retrieving a few items of luggage and small pieces of wreckage. Examining those, the captain pulled down his mouth.

'Signs of smoke and fire damage,' he said, and the mate nodded.

'Yuh. I didn't see fire outside the fuselage, though. She didn't torch, far as I could tell.'

'Hard to know, at that distance, and looking into the sun.' The captain raised his binoculars to study a trawler that was forging towards them from the south. It was a welcome sight. *Amethyst* wasn't equipped to retrieve or stow big pieces of wreckage, and her owner was a money-grubber who'd winge about the cost of delay, never mind the remains in the fridge.

He exchanged signals with the captain of the trawler, and thankfully handed over operations to him. His own radio was receiving a stream of questions and instructions. The answers he gave were short. In a few hours he'd be in Genoa. He'd make his report to the authorities there, and leave them to deal with what he'd dredged from the sea.

★　★　★

At Britain's Department of Civil Aviation, clerks were compiling a full list of *Paloma*'s passengers and crew, and settling to the task of locating their next of kin. The director issued a statement designed to prevent public panic, but *Paloma* was already world news. By nightfall, not only Omega Airlines, but government offices and foreign embassies were dealing with a flood of anxious enquiries.

Press and television teams were deployed to cover the disaster. Evening papers carried a picture of a Lockheed 382 circling above the oily surface of a darkening sea. The BBC set up a special desk to feed information to an avid audience.

In the home counties, transport aircraft, medical teams and hospitals were on standby for possible survivors, although as the night wore on, it became clear that there would be none.

Experts gathered, consulted, planned.

Boeing's head office in Seattle, as well as its British and Italian counterparts, were already collating facts and figures about *Paloma*, checking her certificate of airworthiness, the number of operational circuits she had completed, the records of her maintenance and inspections.

Also in frenetic action were the firms that had played a part in building *Paloma*, her superstructure, engines, electrical and computer systems. Officials of the Federal Aviation Association and the National Transportation Safety Board of the USA were summoned to emergency meetings, and representatives of the Pilots' Association to which David Brock belonged conferred across the globe.

The brokers and companies that had insured *Paloma*, her crew and her passengers, were busy with preliminary assessments, and all those concerned with *Paloma*'s cargo began an intensive scrutiny of their manifests.

The police forces of Europe, the intelligence and counter-intelligence services of many nations watched for any sign that their interests were threatened by the disaster.

In their boltholes around the world, terrorists and political fanatics absorbed the news of the crash, but none of them dared to claim responsibility for it, because the Jerusalem Accord was in the balance, and anyone who destroyed that fragile truce could expect swift and relentless retribution.

7

Ashford, Kent

James Brock spent Monday morning in Ashford, trying to pick up the threads of his working life. At noon, Reg Purviss knocked on the door of his office.

'Lunch,' he said. 'I'm off to the Fife and Drum. Come on.' As James hesitated, Reg said; 'I want to discuss Clare's estate. I'm executor, remember?'

They ate at a table in the garden behind the pub. Reg dealt briskly with the terms of Clare's will.

'Straightforward,' he said. 'Ten thousand and the car to Candida, three gifts to charity of five thousand each, and the rest to you, over two hundred thousand.'

'I don't want Clare's money.'

Reg took his time answering. Salt of the earth, old James, honest as the day, loyal friend and good at his job, but Clare's death had changed him. Didn't seem in full control, somehow. One must tread carefully. He smiled across the table.

'It's your money, mate, you can give it to

charity if you choose, though I hope you won't.' He paused, uncertain whether to broach the other matter on his mind. He said slowly:

'I had a visit from Candida last week. She's round the twist, that one.'

'Why, what did she say?'

'Er . . . that you planned to divorce Clare, that . . . ah . . . Clare and your brother were . . . involved.'

'Sleeping together,' James said.

'Yes.'

'Rubbish.'

'That's what I told Candida.' Reg rubbed an eyebrow. 'She's a nasty piece of work. You want to watch out for her.'

'Always have.'

They finished their lunch and went their separate ways. Back in his office, Reg brooded over their conversation. Candida Woodley was a bitch. No one would listen to her spiteful jabber, but James didn't help things. Refusing to hold a service for Clare, and now this nonsense about not taking her money. People would talk. James must be warned to watch what he said and did.

★ ★ ★

James visited three motor-sales rooms, looking for a replacement for his car. He settled on a BMW, delivery in two weeks' time. The papers signed, he left for Bansford and reached home at 6.45 to find Police Sergeant Galgut on his doorstep. Galgut sometimes dropped in at Badger's Sett for a pint and a chat, but this evening he silenced James's welcome with a sombre shake of the head.

'Been trying to get hold of you since six,' he said. 'Rang the rector, too, but he's over to Tunbridge with the choir. It's bad news, James. I'm sorry.'

'What?' The word came out a croak and Galgut put a hand on James's shoulder.

'It's your brother, lad. There's been a terrible accident, his plane crashed in the Med. They're looking for survivors, but they've not found anyone. They say, not much hope, see?' As James neither spoke nor moved, Galgut gripped his arm. 'Come in the house, now. Sit for a while.'

In the kitchen, Galgut brewed mugs of sweet tea, talking as he worked.

'It was Civil Aviation phoned us. I couldn't get much out of 'em; all the man said, the plane came down in the sea between Corsica and Italy. It was on the six o'clock news that there'd been a fire in the cargo hold. First off they thought they had it under control, like, but it must of got away from them. The plane hit the sea and broke up. There was a ship saw it happen. I tried to see if I could get any sense out of Heathrow or the airline, but they couldn't tell me any more. I left your number with all of 'em; they promised to call if there's any news.'

James nodded. He made himself take deep breaths, and when the whirling of his thoughts settled, he said: 'Do you have Civil Aviation's number?'

'Yeah.' Galgut handed over a slip of paper. 'You'll go straight through to a special desk.' He eyed James with concern. 'Do you have anyone can come and sit with you tonight?'

'I don't need anyone. I'm OK, I'll be fine.'

'I'll be getting along then. I'm on duty. You need anything, call the station.'

'Thanks, Ed. Thanks for coming.'

When Galgut left, a veil of silence closed over the house. James called Civil Aviation, and a brisk voice repeated an approved message:

Wreckage identified as belonging to Omega Airlines 197 had been located. An intensive search for survivors was under way. So far none had been found. Mr Brock would be kept informed.

James cut short the platitudes.

'Where will they take survivors?'

There was a brief hesitation. 'To Heathrow if they are well enough to travel. Those with serious injuries would be taken to the nearest hospital . . . Rome.'

James licked his dry lips. He wanted to ask about the dead, but his voice was lost in the void of his being. He replaced the receiver, groped for a handkerchief and wiped his hands and face. He was shivering.

He switched on the TV set and saw David's face, larger than life, smiling at someone off-camera. The picture was replaced by a still of an aircraft, then by a long-shot of an airport concourse, crowds pressed round an information desk. The announcer was saying that a room had been set aside, relatives could wait there.

He switched off the set, went upstairs and changed into jeans, windcheater and trainers. He checked that he had money in his wallet, and that the house was locked.

By 7.15 he was driving north to Heathrow.

Mallowfield

Hugo Spinner called Daniel Roswall, almost incoherent, teeth chattering against the rim of the receiver.

'Dan? You've heard? *Paloma*. She's a total loss, Dan, no . . . no survivors. Mother of God — '

Dan cut him short. 'Lucy? Is Lucy all right?'

'Yes, she's fine. I called the apartment. She's very upset, but she's OK.' Hugo sucked in gulps of air. 'I did everything I could, Dan, I swear. There was nothing . . . I don't know how it happened . . . '

'You did your best, Hugo, this wasn't your fault. Where are you speaking from?'

'Rome. The airport. It's bloody chaos. Nobody knows any thing . . . they can't . . . they don't tell me . . . '

'Is Gerda with you?'

'She's here, somewhere. We were booked to leave for UK tomorrow, but now . . . '

'Call her to the phone, I want to talk to her.'

After a moment, Gerda's voice came on the line, husky with strain.

'Hullo, Dan.'

'Gerda, my dear. This is a horrible thing, horrible. Thank God you and Hugo weren't aboard.'

'Yes. Dan, does Harry know?'

'Yes. He's liaising with Civil Aviation. What's it like, your side?'

'We're being hammered. Press, TV. I don't

know how long we can duck and dive. Once they hear about Moshal . . . '

'Refer them to me. And Gerda . . . keep an eye on Hugo.'

'Yes. Right. Can I speak to Kyle, please?'

'Sure.' Dan handed the receiver to Kyle Parnell, who was standing close to the desk.

Kyle said softly: 'You OK, Gee?'

'Yes. No. I will be. Can you come to Rome?'

Kyle closed his eyes, opened them. 'Dan wants me to stay here until we know the official line.'

'Which officials are we talking about?'

'Good question. *Paloma* came down in the sea, outside of territorial waters. Dan's lawyers say the enquiry could be in Britain, as it's the state of registration. It'll be a long process. There's not much we can do, except wait.'

'Not I! I'm going to get Moshal by the neck and choke some answers out of him. He should have spoken up, if he knew something. He might have prevented this horror.'

'Can you reach him, if he doesn't want to be reached?'

'Maybe. I know a few people.'

'Take care, Gee.'

'Don't worry. See you soon.'

Kyle hung up with a grimace. 'She's going

after Moshal. She could run into trouble with his minders.'

Dan considered the younger man. He was puzzled by Kyle's devotion to Gerda. A prince kissing a frog. Aloud he said, 'Sometimes the most dangerous course is to do nothing. Paralysed by the headlights.' He was silent for a moment, then sighed. 'Everyone will be looking for scapegoats, you know. We have a lot at stake.'

Dieter Engel, who'd been standing at a window, came to sit facing him.

'We have to talk about that,' he said. 'We have to discuss the money.'

'Money?' Dan stared blankly.

'Certainly. There will be a lot of questions, very soon, about the insurance, about compensation to the relatives of the victims. Some of them will be ready to wait. Others will ask: 'How much do we get?' and they'll want answers right away. They'll engage lawyers. We must brief ours.'

Dan nodded wearily. 'Very well. Speak to Philbrick.'

'I already have. We're covered by a consortium of listed brokers. We insured the passengers, all the Dove affiliates. Omega covered the crew, and the aircraft. Payouts are of course subject to due process of law. If there is proof of negligence, or criminal intervention, that will cause delays, and possibly alter the awards.'

'Delays of how long?'

'Months. Years. There'll be a board of inquiry. That in itself is a long process.' Dieter steepled his fingers. 'We might be well advised to offer early settlement of claims, on an individual basis.'

'How does that benefit us?'

'If the inquiry shows that there was a threat — even a suspicion — of terrorist action, that we knew of it before the flight, people might bring cases against Omega or Dove or both. An offer of early settlement could pre-empt that. Most people go for the bird in hand, and once a claimant accepts payment, he can't come back for more.'

'There was never a suspicion of terrorism,' Dan said.

'The lawyers might disagree with you. Lawsuits could cost us millions.'

'The crash cost a hundred and fifty-five lives,' Dan said roughly. 'I can't put a price on them.' Dieter started to protest, and Dan waved him to silence. 'Sort it out with Philbrick, and keep Harry's people informed.'

Kyle touched his shoulder.

'It's on TV,' he said.

The screen in the corner of the room showed a stretch of indigo sea, incongruously barred by the path of a rising moon. As they watched, a helicopter swung across the foreground, its belly-light illuminating a number of small boats that bobbed round a floating marker. To the right of the picture loomed a vessel broad and squat as a tug, with a tentlike structure sticking up aft of the bridge. Luminous letters glinted the length of her side: SEASCANNER.

Dan exclaimed under his breath, and turned up the sound.

' . . . search for the survivors of the one hundred and fifty-five people on the Omega airliner *Paloma* continues. A minesweeper of the Royal Navy is making all speed to the scene of the accident, and a Red Cross helicopter is ready to render help. The search will be augmented at first light by support vessels and aircraft from neighbouring territories.

'Her Majesty the Queen has expressed her deep distress at the disaster, and representatives of the Government and the Directorate of Civil Aviation are already on their way to Rome.

'Relatives and friends of *Paloma*'s passengers and crew are gathering at Heathrow to await news of possible survivors.'

The camera panned across what appeared to be a VIP lounge, touching people huddled in groups, an elderly woman hobbling beside a uniformed attendant, a young girl who wept in a corner, body rocking, face red and swollen.

'The bloody thing makes voyeurs of us all,' Dan said.

Kyle said: 'I'll set up a data base.' He left the room, and after a moment, Dieter Engel followed him. Dan turned back to the television screen. It displayed the weather chart for Europe. Tomorrow the west coast of Italy would have cloud, and rain.

That would hamper the search-and-rescue operation.

He reached for the massive atlas on his desk and leafed through it. The stretch of sea where *Paloma* had crashed was coloured medium blue, which meant that what was left of her was now lying under 500 feet of water.

Dan sat for some time with his head in his hands. At last he reached for the telephone and dialled the number of the Department of Civil Aviation.

8

At Rome airport, Gerda Marcus confronted
Hugo Spinner in Dove's office.

'You have to make a statement,' she said.
'You have to speak for Dove. You can't hide in
here all night.'

'I'm not hiding.' Hugo's eyes were black
holes in the mask of his face. 'I can't speak
until I have Dan's say-so.'

'You do have it. He appointed you to handle
the situation here, that includes the media.
They're waiting outside that door. If you
don't give them facts, they'll print fiction.'

'I can't tell them anything they don't
already know. *Paloma* is a total loss, there are
no survivors.'

'We don't know that, yet.'

'Oh, for God's sake, Gerda, they won't find
anyone alive, you know that! I can't mention
the names of the crew and passengers until
the next of kin have been informed.'

'So tell that to the press. Refer them to
Harry Solomon. Just say something before
they suck stories out of their thumbs.'

Hugo's mouth twisted. 'They'll do that
anyway.'

Gerda moved to stand over him. 'They'll ask about the pilot. By now they know his name, so tell them about his fine record, tell them he's brought refugees out of Colombia, done mercy flights to Rwanda and Angola and the Balkans.'

Hugo squinted up at her. 'Why don't you tell them; you knew Brock much better than I did. Tell them how he was in bed.'

'David was my friend, you bastard, and now he's dead.' Gerda turned away, snatched up her bag. 'I don't have time for this, I have to meet someone.'

'Who?'

'Someone who knows Moshal.'

Hugo pointed a warning finger. 'You mind what you say, Gerda. We don't know what we're up against here.' She made no answer, sliding into her jacket. Hugo scrambled to his feet. 'All right,' he said. 'All right, leave it to me. I'll cope.'

He stepped out of the door and was at once engulfed by reporters. Gerda watched until they were in full cry, then slipped past them and made her way to the carpark.

Heathrow

'I'm James Brock.' James showed his passport photograph to the clerk at Heathrow's information desk. He had to brace himself against the mass of people who surged and fought around him. 'My brother David Brock is the pilot of the Omega plane that crashed.'

The clerk nodded and opened a hatch in the counter, hauled James through it and slammed it shut.

'Relatives are gathering in the first class lounge, Mr Brock. If you'll follow this lady?' He beckoned a girl in BA uniform.

As she led James away from the crowd, he said, 'Is there any news of survivors?'

The girl shook her head. 'Not yet. They'll be able to tell you more upstairs, they have a direct link with Rome.'

They rode an escalator up to the mezzanine floor. Below them on the concourse, flashbulbs exploded and the girl said something under her breath. She drew him along an upper corridor, past a uniformed guard, and into a lounge already full of people. A man in a dark suit came forward and held out his hand.

'Mr Brock? They told me you'd arrived. My name is Darby. I understand you're brother to Captain David Brock?'

94

'Yes. Have you any news?'

'They've located the site of the accident, and a search-and-rescue programme is operating. It will continue, to a limited degree, throughout the night. There are ships and aircraft involved, and also the smaller boats of Sea Rescue. We're in constant communication with the people on the spot, and we'll do our best to keep you informed, but at the moment all we can do is wait. If you'll take a seat, someone will attend to you.'

He turned away as another group of people came through the door. James edged across to a chair on the far side of the room, sat down and leaned against the wall. Someone proffered a tray laden with mugs of tea, but he waved it away.

His throat ached and there was a droning in his ears. He turned his head and saw that the people next to him were praying. A priest in a cassock, and an elderly couple, they sat with hands linked and heads bent. Their agony was palpable, but watching them James felt nothing, nothing for them or for himself or for David. It was as if a life-support switch had been thrown, leaving him dead. He closed his eyes.

'Mr Brock?' The voice came from far off. He looked up to find a woman stooping over him. 'Mr James Brock?'

He nodded, and she crouched on her haunches beside his chair.

'I'm Natalie Lomax,' she said. 'I heard you tell Mr Darby that you're David Brock's brother. I knew him, a while back, in the States.' James tried to rise but she pressed him back. 'No, don't get up. I'll have to move on in a moment. I'm helping out, checking names and addresses and phone numbers. If you'll give me the details . . . '

James gave them and she wrote them in the file she carried. He wondered how many times he'd have to supply the information. The woman was staring at him. Her eyes were huge, blue-green, and her hair was dark gold, her skin pale and clear. She made him think of surf on a white beach. Her voice was more Irish than American.

'Are you an air-hostess?' he asked, and she smiled.

'Was, until I married. That was years ago, about the time Dave left for Europe.' She was watching him the way the nurses had done, in the hospital. Kind, but making assessments, looking for certain signs. He turned his head away, and she got to her feet.

'Dave's a great pilot,' she said. 'The best. I hope he's OK.' She touched light fingers to James's shoulder and moved away. The man called Darby came to meet her. James had the feeling they were discussing him.

A man tugged at his sleeve; paunchy, with heavy jowls and small, suffering eyes.

'That woman. Did she tell you anything?'

'No. She's just taking names and addresses.'

'Didn't say anything about the accident?'

'No.'

'Close as clams, all of 'em.' The man leaned towards James. He smelled of whisky and violet sachets. 'It's the money, see?'

'What money?' James shifted to avoid the loaded breath.

'Compensation. We'll have to be compensated, no doubt of that. That blonde you were chattin' up, she's from one of the big insurance companies, that's why she's so pally. I reckon they should come clean with us, tell us the form. I mean, there's families have lost breadwinners, how're they going to manage, without they get compensation? My wife's brother was on the plane, his wife hasn't a penny to her name, and three young kids to raise. We can't keep them all, not in a house our size.'

James said stiffly, 'I'm sure she'll be looked after.'

'Yeah, well, people can't live on promises, can they? I mean, we should be told, they should set our minds at rest, that's what I say.

You can't bring back the dead, but the living should not have to suffer. I'm going to have a word with that young lady. See we get our rights.'

He set off in pursuit of Natalie Lomax. She'd vanished in the crowd. James wished she'd stayed. He wanted to talk to her about David.

David was dead.

The knowledge stabbed through the protective layers of shock, white-hot pain, and James groaned aloud. The clergyman next to him stopped praying, and the woman next to him put out a hand.

'Are you all right, dear?'

James focused on a face soft and crumpled like a fading flower. He said: 'Yes. Thank you.'

'You have someone on the plane?' There was compassion in her gaze, not curiosity.

'My brother,' James said. 'He's the pilot.'

'Then he knows my son. Leonard Oakley. Len's the flight engineer on *Paloma*. He's flown with Captain Brock, many's the time. Perhaps you've met Len?'

She's using the present tense, James thought. She's keeping her son alive in the present tense.

'I'm afraid we never met,' he said.

She nodded, hiding disappointment. Her

husband leaned across her, extending a blue-veined hand.

'I'm Bill Oakley. This is my wife Rose and our friend Pastor Lampert. He came to keep us company while we wait.'

There were tears in the old man's eyes and his lips trembled. James dredged for words and found a memory.

'David spoke about your son, said he was great at his job. A first-class engineer.'

The tears spilled over. The old man nodded again and again.

'Yes. Great. Len's great. First-class. Yes.'

★　★　★

Natalie Lomax walked briskly along the gallery that overlooked the main floor of the terminal. Some way along it, she turned through a door marked STAFF ONLY.

The room she entered was small, containing a table, four chairs, and a telephone. Natalie glanced about her.

'Camping out?' she said.

The massive black man behind the table went on talking into the telephone, waved her to a chair. The other occupant of the room glowered at her.

'They said we could wait here. We don't have status yet.'

He looked like a man who cared about status. His face was predatory, a high-domed forehead, beaked nose, and prominent eyes the colour of iced tea. He wore a linen suit, a fine cotton shirt, and hand-stitched loafers.

Natalie grinned at him. 'Hi, Sim. When did you get in?'

'Twenty minutes ago.' Simeon Todd pursed his lips as if he resented her question, jerked his chin at the file she carried.

'So what have you got?'

'Sweet FA.' Natalie dropped into a chair and kicked off her shoes. 'Except I met James Brock who's brother to Captain David Brock.'

'The pilot.' Todd's pale eyelashes flickered. 'What did he tell you?'

'Nothing. I introduced myself and told him I knew David a way back. It didn't seem to mean anything to him.'

'Perhaps they weren't close.'

'Or perhaps he's still in shock.' Natalie touched fingers to her forehead. 'He has a recent head wound. I'll get more out of him, later.'

The black man, who hailed from Boston and whose name was Eugene Lafayette, slammed down the receiver of the phone and growled: 'They won't give us shit.'

'Go higher,' Todd said.

100

'That was higher. That was as high as it gets, 'less you have a hot line to God.'

'It's surely too early,' Natalie said. 'They won't allow us odds and sods to play till they've fixed the ground rules.' She was watching Lafayette closely. 'What about the NCIC? Did they find anything?'

Lafayette rubbed a palm over his mouth. '*Nada*.'

Natalie looked disappointed, but said nothing.

'What about the aircraft?' Todd asked. 'She a total loss?'

'They think so.' Natalie laced her fingers together. 'She burned before she crashed.'

'They know what made her burn?'

Lafayette shrugged. 'That's the question the Brits are asking. They'll set up a board of inquiry.'

'Are they entitled?'

'Sure they are. *Paloma* crashed outside of territorial waters, Britain's the state of registration, they get to conduct the inquiry. They like to clean up their own messes.'

'What's Rome feel about it?'

'Happy to pass the buck. They're not exactly off the hook; they'll have to work closely with London.'

'Who'll head the investigation?'

'Probably Geoffrey Waldron. I'm told he's a

good man, authority on aircraft accidents and knows how to reconcile all the conflicting interests. I expect Barry Coburn will handle the technical side. Also a good man.'

'What are the odds on terrorism?'

Lafayette shook his head. 'No organization has claimed responsibility — yet. Right now it's anyone's guess what downed *Paloma*. Accident, negligence, pilot error, sabotage, we don't know. What we do know is, all the big boys will be trying to shift the blame on to someone else. We keep an open mind. Pursue options.'

Todd sniffed. 'How long before we get an invite to the party?'

'Hours. Days. Sooner or later they'll have to include us. Thing is, what do we do when we get there? There's a lot of people will try to tell us, pull us this way and that. We're involved in a lot of ways. First, as the state of manufacture. We built the fucking plane. Once the board of inquiry gets going, it'll suck in Boeing, Federal Aviation, the Safety Board, Airline Pilots, all of them with ideas about what Uncle Sam owes them. Then there's the individual experts, medical, scientific, you name it. We'll be invited, don't you worry.'

'And until we are, we just sit on our asses?'

'No way.' Natalie stood up and thrust her

feet into her shoes. 'I'll be checking insurance claims.' She looked pointedly at Lafayette. 'You'll let me know if you hear anything I can use?'

Before he could answer, Todd cut in: 'You don't have any authority, you know.'

She looked at him coolly. 'I don't need your permission to do my job, Sim. I don't work for Uncle Sam, I'm employed by Seabright and Boyce who insured the crew of *Paloma*. I can go where you can't, for the moment at least, so better be nice to me.'

'I demand to know your intentions.'

She laughed. 'Sorry, I can't make an honest man of you.' She picked up her file and smiled at Lafayette. ''Bye, Gene. It was nice to see you again.'

''Bye, girl. Keep in touch, hear?'

'I will.' Natalie sketched a wave and left the room. As the door closed after her, Todd swivelled to face the big man.

'Are you crazy? That woman's a maverick. You've no control over what she says or does.'

'None, except friendship.' Lafayette met Todd's furious glare. 'Let me remind you, she came to us, she volunteered information that may be crucial, she did us a big favour.'

'Crap, Gene. She's using you, trading on the fact you knew her husband. She wants something from us. What was that about the NCIC?'

'She needs help in tracing a missing person, and I'd say she's entitled. Lomax was the best investigative agent I ever had, and he died in the line of duty. I owe his widow.' As Todd opened his mouth, Lafayette held up a hand. 'No, boy, I talk, you listen. We don't have to pay her, we can't be held responsible if she gets in trouble. And as she says, she can go where we can't. She can be useful.'

Todd chewed his lip. 'I'd like to know just what there was between her and David Brock.'

Lafayette's smile was benign. 'Then make that your first assignment. Find out, and make it fast, we don't have a lot of time.'

'It's not my job to — '

'Your job is to do what I say. Right now, we have a few disconnected facts. Tax-evaders who bring money through Rome and stash it in Zurich. An organization called Dove that sends missions to Arab states. A plane chartered by Dove that's crashed in the sea.'

'I don't see the connection.'

'There may not be one. On the other hand, there could be a connection with the Jerusalem Accord, which is due to be signed in less than two weeks. Like I said, we don't have much time, so get to work.'

9

On her way into Rome Gerda stopped at a petrol station and used the payphone. She spoke briefly, first in Italian and then in English. The call concluded, she drove to the hotel where Dan had booked a room for her. She signed in, dumped her suitcase, and walked two blocks to a small restaurant next door to an amusement arcade. Settled at a table, she ordered ravioli, green salad and Chianti.

The owner brought the dishes himself and lingered to chat. His topic was *Paloma*: what a terrible disaster, one could think of nothing else, God help the poor souls who most surely perished out there. A bad thing for Rome at the height of the tourist season; who would wish to fly to Italy after such a tragedy?

'It wasn't an Italian plane,' Gerda said.

'No matter, Italy will be blamed. People will blame us, they won't come to Rome, they'll go elsewhere.' The man moved away, shaking his head.

Gerda ate slowly, filling time. Her bill paid, she walked to the far side of the square, where dusty lime-trees shadowed a drinking-fountain and a stone bench. Adri Romm had said ten o'clock. Twenty minutes to go.

Adri was the only child of prosperous Genoese parents. When he was three they emigrated to Israel and settled in Haifa. Adri had a privileged childhood, did well at school and university. It was expected he'd make a career in medicine or the law. Instead he turned to politics, not the overt hustings, but the covert intrigues and manipulations of the Middle East.

Gerda met him when she was twenty, in New York. He was attached to the Israeli Embassy. She suspected that his work went far beyond the bounds of diplomacy.

They became lovers, on her side a blundering passion, on his a tolerant, half-amused expertise. She knew from the start that it wouldn't last. He didn't need her as she needed him. He probably needed no one. He left her without pretence or apology, moving on to something he considered important. It took her two years to recover, and in that time of misery she reached a decision. Adri owed her, and one day, if need be, she would call in the debt.

Now was the time.

She saw him on the far side of the square. He stood with hands in pockets, appraising the area. Adri was never off guard. He started towards her. He had the smooth, prowling walk of a leopard. She'd read somewhere that a leopard hunted alone, and killed face to face with its victim, jaws crushing head and throat while hind feet raked out the intestines. He reached her, smiled and bent to drop a kiss on her forehead.

'Gerda, it's good to see you. I was afraid you were in that aircraft. Shall we sit here, or walk?'

'Walk,' she said. She rose and paced beside him along the crowded sidewalk. 'I didn't expect to find you in Rome, Adri. I thought you were in Tel Aviv.'

He turned his head to look at her. She met his eyes calmly, letting him see she wasn't here for old time's sake, but on the terms he preferred, to make a trade.

'I'm here on business,' he said.

'Moshal business?'

He smiled faintly. 'In a sense, yes.'

'Are you his minder?'

He made a movement as if applying an invisible broom. 'Crossing-sweeper; I see he doesn't step in any shit.'

'I hear he's received threats.'

'All the time. The story of his life.'

'Was that why he cancelled his flight on *Paloma*?'

They had reached the north-eastern corner of the square and Adri signed to her to turn down a lane that ran past a row of small shops, to debouch on a major thoroughfare. He answered her question with one of his own.

'Have you any idea what caused the crash?'

She shook her head. 'According to Rome ATC, the captain reported a fire that started in a container in the main-deck cargo-hold.'

Adri's eyes narrowed and he said sharply, 'Which container?'

'I don't know. I do know that the whole cargo was checked very carefully before it was loaded.'

'Who did the checking?'

'Omega's warehouse supervisor and his team; and airport security did spot tests, comparing the manifests with the cargo. They didn't find any unlisted items.'

'And who checks the checkers?' mused Adri. He stood still, watching the traffic that poured along the road ahead. He said: '*Paloma* went down in five hundred feet of water, they know the exact position. They'll get the Black boxes fast.' He shifted his gaze to Gerda. 'What about the captain? What's his record?'

'Excellent.' Gerda was sure that Adri already knew the details of David Brock's CV.

He was fishing for personal stuff, the dirt. She decided it was her turn to direct the conversation.

'Tell me about Moshal,' she said. 'Why did he cancel?'

Adri tilted his head to stare at the pallid city sky. He said: 'Moshal's field is money. He watches the things money does, the way it moves around the world, he translates the flow of money into political forecast, he interprets for those of us who don't speak the language.

'A few weeks ago, he sent in a report that in his view, money from certain Arab states was being laundered by a cartel in Rome and transferred to secret accounts in Zurich. From there it will be disbursed to buy materials that can't be bought on the open market. We keep a sharp eye on such transactions. We need to know what hostile countries are buying — and who's selling to them. We asked Moshal to follow the money trail and keep us informed.'

'Did he identify this cartel?'

Adri shook his head. If he knew, he wasn't going to tell. Gerda thought rapidly. A lot of states were hostile to Israel. Iraq, for example, was always in the market for war materials: mechanical, chemical or biological. If Moshal had sicked Mossad on to the Iraqis, he'd put himself at risk. But her mind baulked at what Adri was implying.

'I can't believe that *Paloma* was sabotaged because Moshal was booked on the flight. A planeful of people murdered to eliminate one man?'

Adri's glance was pitying. 'It wouldn't be the first time, Gerda. Planes have been sabotaged so someone can claim the insurance on a single passenger, they've been brought down out of petty spite, or to issue a warning to a political enemy. An assassin doesn't care who dies, as long as he gets what he wants, makes his point.'

'But Moshal wasn't on that flight,' Gerda said. 'He cancelled days ago. Whoever wanted him dead must have been watching him, must have known he wouldn't be on board.' She swung to face Adri. 'And if Moshal wasn't the target, then who was? A different target could mean a different assassin. Just who are we talking about here?' As Adri made no answer, she seized his arm and shook it. 'Tell me the truth! Innocent people are dead, I could be dead. Tell me what you know.'

He stared at her, his eyes sombre. 'Maybe you should look closer to home,' he said.

'Home? What do you mean, what are you saying? Adri?'

But he freed himself from her grasp and

stepped away from her. 'I have to go, Gerda. I've a lot of work to do.'

She knew it was no use trying to detain him. She said desperately: 'Will you be staying in Rome? Where can I reach you?'

'I'll be in touch.' He raised one hand in a gentle gesture. 'Take care of yourself, Gerda. Remember that curiosity killed the cat.'

He walked off and was quickly lost in the throng of people on the sidewalk.

Gerda started back to the hotel, walking slowly, trying to make sense of what Adri had said. Middle East principals were sending money through Rome to Swiss accounts. Money to be used to buy materials that posed a threat to Israel. Moshal had warned Israel of the situation. Mossad had pulled Moshal off the flight. *Paloma* had crashed, even though Moshal wasn't on board. Different target? Different assassin?

Adri could be lying. He was trained to lie, a professional deceiver.

Look closer to home, he'd said, and meant it. No lie.

So what was home?

Not Dove. Dove was a job, a bunch of boffins who were in no way suited to cloak-and-dagger stuff; as well ask hippos to dance on a tightrope.

Paloma's crew was a better bet. Gypsies

with a lifestyle that laid them open to shady deals. Some of them were big spenders. Dave Brock lived it up, he had a mistress who was one of Rome's beautiful people; in those circles there'd be plenty of ways to launder money.

Except Dave was an honest man, salt of the earth.

Home is where the heart is.

Gerda stopped dead in her tracks.

Her heart was with individuals, not groups; with Adri, once; with others after, and now with Kyle. Kyle was home. He couldn't be involved in a scam, he had no need of money, or power. But excitement? A new rush? Might he go for crime, just for kicks? Get caught in the undertow and swept out past saving?

Music hammered her ears. She was close to the amusement arcade, and its black glass pillars reflected her tenfold, frog face twisted in horror. A line of youths swung out into the street, arms linked, and she stepped back to let them pass. She groped for a handkerchief and wiped sweat from her face, made herself take deep breaths, hurried on to the hotel.

In her room she sloshed brandy into a glass and drank it, grimacing. She turned on the television. A newscast showed a small boat rising and falling through a shaft of light. A piece of wreckage banged against its prow, an escape slide with the Omega colours on its side. A sailor was lifting something pink and sodden from the water. He slid it into a plastic bag; a human foot with painted toenails.

Gerda doused the picture and pressed her hands to her mouth, trying to think.

Adri had agreed to meet her, to make a trade. The stuff he'd given her about Moshal must be valid. He'd also issued a warning. The *Paloma* disaster involved her, and that could mean danger for herself and for the people she loved. Take care, Adri said, don't ask questions. He'd issued a warning, and in return he wanted information. He would let her know what, and when. He would stay in touch.

She thought, we are like the honey-guide and the honey-badger. The bird leads the badger to the hidden, impregnable comb, and waits nearby. The badger breaks out the comb and the two share the spoils.

'Deal,' she said aloud.

She tried to call Hugo at his apartment, but there was no answer. She called the airport and was told Signor Spinner was at the emergency centre at Ostia, where they were bringing in debris from the wreck. She rang Mallowfield and spoke to Kyle, who demanded to know where the hell she'd been.

'I went to meet Adri Romm,' she said.

'What for?' Kyle's voice sharpened from anxiety to anger. 'What's he after?'

She thought, not me, don't worry, but she said quietly: 'I can't talk about it on the phone. Tell Dan we have to meet, all of us.'

Kyle growled under his breath, and Gerda said, 'Please. It's important.'

'All right, I'll tell him. Where's Romm now?'

'I don't know. He promised to keep in touch.'

'Well, bugger him. You keep away from him, hear? He won't care what he gets you into. He's a creep.'

'He's only doing his job.'

'So let him do it, he doesn't need your help. By tomorrow, every agency on planet Earth will be in on the action, including Mossad, CIA and FBI. Leave the work to the cruds who are paid to do it. Just stay in your own back yard.'

'I don't think we'll any of us be able to do that. Kyle, are you setting up a database?'

'Yeah, I am. Why?'

'I want the records of all the personnel — Dove's and Omega's — who were on board *Paloma*. Hugo has copies, but I can't get hold of him at the moment, and it's urgent.'

114

'OK. I'll fax everything to you at the Rome office.'

'No. Send it by courier, for my eyes only.'

'OK. Will do.'

Gerda knew he'd send a flood of material. Kyle had his electronic sources, some legitimate, some not, and welcomed a chance to use them.

10

London

The operations room set up by the Directorate of Civil Aviation was large and well equipped. Behind the glass wall at its west end, banks of telephones were already in service, the operators mouthing silently. There were more telephones on the near side of the glass, and when one of them shrilled, a clerk signalled to a thick-set, shock-haired man seated at the central table.

'Geoffrey? For you, the red line.'

Geoffrey Waldron, the assistant director of the organization, hurried to take the receiver. The red line was reserved for Donald Porteous, head of the search-and-rescue unit that had been flown to the site of the *Paloma* crash.

Waldron listened without comment to what Porteous had to say, and at the end said: 'Yes, I agree. I have a meeting here, now. I'll put it to them and let you know as soon as I can. Yes. Right. 'Bye, Don.'

He cut the connection and stood for a while contemplating the three men who sat at

116

the table, listening to the tape that Rome's air traffic control had rushed to him.

Rupert Sandiman from the Department of Transport's Accident Investigation Branch, was flat Lancashire with a voice like a buzz-saw and the manners of a baboon, but his experience of disasters was unrivalled, and he could magic workers and supplies from thin air.

Barry Coburn was a hard-packed Australian who smoked his black cheroot as if he'd rather chew it. He'd arrived from Seattle an hour ago, and would lead the technical investigations, mechanical, electrical and aeronautic.

The third man was an unknown quantity: in a sense an experiment. John Thorneycroft's CV described him as a forensic psychologist. His career had been varied, to say the least. At eighteen, he'd joined the army, and later transferred to the SAS. After four years he was invalided out of the corps, back surgery having made him unequal to its demanding lifestyle.

He studied medicine at Edinburgh and qualified with distinction. His interest in forensics led him to work with the police on several important cases, and he was now an official consultant to London's CID. He was building a reputation as a profiler, a discipline whose followers advised honest flatfoots what kind of perps might have committed the crimes under investigation.

Thorneycroft, thought Waldron, looked a tough customer, hard and fit despite the surgical history, with deepset dark eyes and a flat, uncompromising mouth. Now he met Waldron's gaze and smiled. The smile made him look even tougher. Waldron decided to tread carefully in Dr Thorneycroft's vicinity.

The ATC tape ended and Waldron switched off the recorder. Sandiman looked up and said: 'How many, Geoff?' He meant, how many dead. When an aircraft came down from that height, the sea was like concrete. No flesh survived the impact.

'One-fifty-five,' Waldron said. 'Nine crew, one-forty-six passengers. The ministry has all the names.'

'Who've we got from there?'

'Blore.' Waldron saw Sandiman's grimace, and said, 'He'll be useful if we strike political log-jams. Superintendent Parrish will handle the police investigations. He's a good man.' He turned to Barry Coburn. 'What did you make of the tape?'

Coburn shrugged. 'The pilot didn't send a Mayday signal. He sounded calm, perhaps he didn't expect to crash. Another thing, there was no smoke in the passenger cabin, but he took the plane down to one four zero, preparing for smoke clearance.'

'He may have thought there was likely to be smoke penetration. That's possible with Combis, isn't it?'

'Yeah. The cabin and the cargo hold share a common ventilation system. Who reported the accident?'

'A Captain Hennessy, of the pleasure yacht *Amethyst*. He was first to reach the accident site, retrieved two bodies, some body parts and light wreckage. Some of the wreckage was fire-damaged. Two of our forensic surgeons are in Rome, to make preliminary examinations of the human remains. The detailed autopsies will be done in England.' Waldron hesitated. 'Apparently one of the bodies retrieved was so badly burned they couldn't even determine the sex.'

There was a brief silence, then Waldron said, 'Blore's arranging a memorial service, and his team will handle the insurance matters. I'm setting up the Board of Inquiry, I hope Judge Osbert Finney will head it. Don Porteous is in charge of salvage. He's raised a point we must discuss.'

Waldron settled in the chair at the head of the table. 'As you know, our priority is the search for survivors and the recovery of human remains, but there's also an urgent need for us to retrieve the wreckage and the cargo, because that may help us to decide what caused *Paloma* to crash — whether there was sabotage, and if there was, who was responsible. There is great concern, not only in our own government circles, but around the world, that the aircraft may have been the target of political extremists aiming to destroy the Jerusalem Accord.

'*Paloma* came down in five hundred feet of seawater. The floating wreckage may be easy to recover. The stuff at depth presents greater difficulties.

'We must locate the key items as fast as possible — especially the cockpit voice recorder, the digital flight data recorder, the quick access recorder if there was one, the engines, engine-cowl and so on. Also the fuselage and structures close to the area where the fire started.

'Normally, we'd use one of the major salvage companies — they're already after the job — but that would involve us in delays; contracts to be signed, heavy tackle to be moved to the site, the whole tender process. For reasons of international peace, we can't afford delay. Porteous has suggested a short cut.' Waldron's gaze fixed on Sandiman. 'One of the vessels already at the crash site is a marine exploration ship named *Seascanner*.

You may have heard of her?'

Sandiman's eyes narrowed. 'The treasure-seeker that's been working round Crete?'

'Crete, and the Tyrrhenian Sea. She was making for Ostia when she picked up the DETRESFA about *Paloma*. She's a highly specialized search craft. She was designed and built for a multimillionaire named Hamish Trotter, owner of the Clydeside shipyards of that name. Since retiring, he's spent his time — and a deal of money — raising artefacts from the seabed.

'*Seascanner* is state of the art. She has sonar scan, photomapping equipment, and a remote-controlled vehicle capable of loading wreckage on a cradle lift, and bringing it to the surface. Trotter has offered us the use of the ship for as long as we want, and at a figure that's way below that quoted by the regular operators.'

'Why?' demanded Sandiman. 'What's in it for him?'

Waldron shook his head. 'It seems he's a friend of Daniel Roswall who's the kingpin of Dove International, the organization that chartered *Paloma* on a more or less permanent basis. When Trotter picked up the distress signals on *Paloma*, he got in touch with Roswall and offered to help, any way he could. Roswall informed us, and we asked

Porteous to give us his opinion.'

'Which was?'

'He thinks we must use *Seascanner*.'

'I don't like working with amateurs.'

'Trotter's not an amateur. He's built ships, he's done salvage work for several big airlines, and for the US Navy. He's an expert.'

Barry Coburn grunted. 'Expert or not, you'll need to clear him with the major interests — airline owners, manufacturers, insurers. They're tetchy about salvage.'

Waldron looked at him. 'As I said, the pressure's coming from top levels, government levels. They're demanding quick answers, I believe they'll opt for *Seascanner*. The rest will fall in line.' Waldron leaned back in his chair. 'But let me make one thing clear. *Paloma* is Britain's tragedy, and therefore our responsibility. We are in charge of the investigation, the inquiry, and whatever follows. We call the shots.'

Sandiman spread his hands. 'Reet, then. We go with Trotter and his treasure-boat.'

The meeting ended, Coburn and Sandiman left, but John Thorneycroft lingered.

'I've a couple of questions,' he said. 'This Daniel Roswall, has he been in touch with you since the accident?'

'Yes, twice,' Waldron answered. 'He phoned a quarter of an hour after the crash, wanted news, wanted to know if there were survivors. He sounded very distressed. I told him what I could. A couple of hours later, he phoned again, to put me in the picture about Dove. It's his brainchild. Once a year they hold a conference at Mallowfield, his estate in Kent. A lot of the delegates were aboard *Paloma*. One of them was supposed to be Joel Moshal. You've heard of him?'

Thorneycroft nodded. 'Israel's financial genius. Four days ago he cancelled his flight, pleading urgent talks in Washington.'

'Right. Roswall told me that his manager in Rome, Hugo Spinner, is convinced Moshal pulled out because of terrorist threats. Roswall checked with Home Affairs, who asked around. Sir Clive Radnor's response was that no one had informed our security divisions of any such threats. On the strength of that assurance, *Paloma*'s flight went ahead, as scheduled.'

Thorneycroft blinked slowly. 'Let me guess. Radnor is now busy closing the stable door, and the powers that be are demanding instant answers to the question of what caused the crash.'

'That's it.'

'Hence their willingness to use *Sea-scanner*.'

'Yes. Make no mistake, in some ways she's

a godsend.' Waldron hesitated, wondering how far he should confide in a relative stranger. Thorneycroft grinned.

'But you're troubled by the friendship between Trotter and Roswall. You're afraid Roswall might persuade Trotter to manipulate evidence?'

'It's crossed my mind.'

'Why would Roswall want to conceal the truth? I don't see him blowing up his own enterprise. Dove isn't just his brainchild, it's his memorial to his son. I doubt he'd do anything to harm it.' Thorneycroft tugged at his lip. 'You could put someone aboard *Seascanner*, a man from one of our special units, underwater expert, knows his way round ships. Someone to keep an eye on things, when Porteous isn't around.'

'Good idea. I'll suggest it to Porteous.' Waldron fixed Thorneycroft with a speculative eye. 'Tell me, how do you fit in with the police team? What's your status?'

'I'm not a member of the Force, I'm a consultant. I've worked with Superintendent Parrish before. He's a smart cop, hardworking. Doesn't go much for fancy footwork, meaning people like me, but we'll scratch each other's backs.'

'And how will you divide the labour?'

'Parrish and his team will look after the

heavy sweat. They'll interview the relatives, friends and workmates of the victims, talk to the airline employees, the people who serviced *Paloma*, the baggage-and-cargo handlers. They'll listen to god-a-many boffins rabbiting on about avionics and cargo fires and explosive charges. They'll look for the facts you need.'

'And you? What's your job?'

'I cover some of the same ground, but in a different way. I talk to the people who do the post-mortems, I check the medical records of key players in Dove and Omega, I study reports from Coburn and Porteous, and from the experts who run tests on the wreckage. I try to build a picture of what happened to *Paloma*, and why. I build a profile of the sort of people who played a part in what happened.'

'It sounds time-consuming.'

'Normally, it is. In this case, we don't have the luxury of time.' As Waldron made no reply, Thorneycroft said: 'You mentioned Radnor. Who else is with him?'

'Mrs Rylda Warne, and Mr Oliver Hudnut.'

Thorneycroft blew out breath. 'A clever bitch, a secretive nerd, and a fussy old fart. God help us.'

'You've met them before?'

Thorneycroft fingered his back. 'In a

previous existence.'

'Our best agents are already deployed, keeping the Accord on track.'

'Chasing terrorists.' Thorneycroft grimaced. 'This may not have been a terror attack. *Paloma* wasn't hijacked, the ATC tape proves that.'

'It wasn't a terrorist hijacking, but it may have been terrorist sabotage. Even that's not proven. Eye-witnesses say the aircraft didn't explode, didn't torch. No terrorist organization has claimed responsibility . . . yet. Her cargo manifests were thoroughly checked, the airport did spot checks on the freight, no dangerous substances were found. Spinner and the Omega warehouse chief watched the stuff loaded. Those factors combined tend to rule out sabotage.'

'And the aircraft itself?'

'Entirely airworthy.' Waldron's mouth had a bitter twist. 'They always say that, but the catastrophes keep happening, the victims keep dying, we keep having to pick up the pieces.'

Thorneycroft lifted the canvas bag that served him as a briefcase.

'I can be here at eight tomorrow, if you need me.'

'I do. The reports are pouring in.'

'Right, then. See you at eight a.m.'

After Thorneycroft left, Waldron summoned his chief assistant, and together they
briefed a second shift of clerks and telephone
operators, drew up lists of teams, and
discussed potential team-leaders. Waldron
took the more important of the calls that were
flooding the incoming lines.

At half-past four, he went to the quarters
set aside for him at the Centre. He showered
and lay down on the bed. He managed to
snatch two hours of sleep before he was
wakened to take a call from a presidential
aide in Washington.

★   ★   ★

Thorneycroft walked the few blocks to his
apartment off Victoria Street. Walking at night
in the city helped to clear his thoughts.
Boiling traffic, crowded pavements, and a
sour-smelling sky acted as a balm rather than
an irritation.

He was glad that he'd had a chance to talk
to Waldron, a useful man, he thought, one
you couldn't push around, but ready to
consult and to listen, a pragmatist like
Parrish. Those two would accumulate a
mountain of facts.

Thorneycroft wriggled his shoulders. Facts
could recreate the skeleton of events that

made up the *Paloma* disaster, and if they proved mechanical failure or pilot error, that might be enough. On the other hand, if there was the suspicion of sabotage, of mass murder, the bare bones of fact must be fleshed out with imagination. It would be his job to probe old case histories, look for hidden thoughts and emotions, think himself into the mind of a criminal, and produce a profile of that criminal that could guide the investigators towards an arrest and conviction.

Guesswork, some said, and in a sense it was, but in dealing with abnormal people, serial killers, hijackers, political fanatics, reason and logic weren't enough. You had to track them through the dark abnormal paths of the mind.

His apartment, closed for nearly twenty-four hours, was hot and stuffy. He turned on the air-conditioner, collected cold beer from the fridge, and settled in the armchair facing the television. Looking for news, he found a documentary on Jerusalem. Old hat, and the commentary was junk, so he cut the sound and watched the pictures.

White-clad Muslims, shouting with raised fists, moved in a stream along a narrow street. Christians sang carols by candlelight. Jews gathered at the Wailing Wall.

The faithful were converging on Jerusalem now, all of them rooted in faith, all of them determined to claim their slice of the holy city. Most came to seek peace. Some came to stir up hatred and violence. The politicians debated. The tanks, planes and warships moved into position. The world waited for time to run out.

Accord, or cataclysm.

Multitudes, multitudes in the valley of decision.

★ ★ ★

Clive Radnor was fond of saying that the best form of defence was attack. He was also fond of finding scapegoats, and tonight his choice fell on Israeli Intelligence.

'Mossad failed to communicate,' he complained. 'If they anticipated terrorist action of any sort, they should have informed us at once. They never at any time intimated that Moshal was under terrorist threat.'

Seated at the far side of the desk, Rylda Warne fixed Radnor with a basilisk stare.

'Hudnut did warn that Mossad was nervous about Moshal's safety.'

Radnor primmed his mouth. 'Rumours, mere rumours. Hudnut said that Moshal had cancelled his flight to the UK, and that that was cause for concern. On my instructions, he approached Mossad, and was assured that there had been no threats against Moshal. Moshal, they said, had been summoned to top-level talks about the Accord, in Washington, and naturally that invitation took precedence over Dove's little tea party.' Radnor smoothed an eyebrow with a delicate finger. 'Dove's manager in Rome, a Mr Hugo Spinner, made waves at our embassy in Rome.'

'Perhaps he'd also heard these ... rumours?'

'No, no. He's a hysterical creature; he was upset by Moshal's defection, and jumped to false conclusions. We were able to confirm, through diplomatic channels, that Moshal's decision was based purely on Israel's political interests.'

Oliver Hudnut shifted in his chair, and Mrs Warne's cold stare swivelled towards him.

'Oliver?'

The young man blinked thick lids. 'I'd like to know why Moshal was invited to the talks. He's not a politician.'

'You think he was invited for his financial expertise?'

Hudnut placed his hands on the edge of the table, slid them apart and together again. 'I think,' he said, 'that Israel believes that if the Accord fails, she will come under immediate attack by Iraq. A year ago, Iraq was negotiating to buy Macaque pilotless planes. The deal was blocked by international action. Latest information suggests that Iraq is now back in the market — the very black, very expensive market. The question arises, how will payment be made, where is the cash coming from, who is assisting the transactions? Perhaps Moshal crossed the money trail and informed the Israeli authorities. If so, he's put himself at risk, which makes Mossad nervous on his account.'

'Ifs and ands,' said Radnor pettishly. The fat woman ignored him.

'How does all this tie in to the *Paloma* crash?' she demanded.

Hudnut sighed. 'I don't know. I do know that if the Iraqis have those Macaques, they can take out any major city in the Eastern Mediterranean — which is scary for the Israelis, and for the rest of us.'

11

'Mrs Lomax.'

Natalie Lomax turned. James Brock was standing behind her. He looked terrible, deathly white and shivering. She reached out to steady him, but he thrust her hand aside.

'I'm all right.' His voice sounded thick. 'I'm leaving. There's no point in waiting here. David's dead. They all are.'

'We can't be sure,' she began, and stopped at the look in his eyes. He was right. It was wrong to raise false hopes.

'Will you go home?' she asked. 'Is there someone there for you?'

'I'm all right,' he repeated. 'You have my name and number, if I'm needed.' He managed a travesty of a smile. 'Thank you for your help.'

He shouldered his way through the crowd and out of the door.

Natalie glanced round the room. None of those near at hand appeared to have heard what he'd said. Some of them huddled in corners, some stared at the giant TV screen on the wall, some sat in groups, praying together. A few pressed close to the airport officials, seeking the latest news. Those were the worst, the ones who hoped against all reason that there would be survivors.

★   ★   ★

Back at Badger's Sett, James found messages, some on the answering-machine, some written in Mrs Commins's looping hand. The old girl must have come over specially. A note from Elizabeth Wallis urged him to stay with them at the rectory. It was too late to phone and thank her now.

He stretched out on the sofa in front of the television. He was aware of newscasts, that showed the wreckage of *Paloma* as a scum in pale spotlights. People gave interviews. The assistant director of Civil Aviation, Geoffrey Waldron, said the search for survivors was continuing. His eyes made no promises.

None of it made sense. James's mind was full of David alive. Once, waking from a half-sleep, he thought he heard Dave's voice in the hall, and hurried out, but there was no one.

In the early hours of the morning, he switched off the TV and slept.

★   ★   ★

In their bedroom at the rectory, Elizabeth and Charles Wallis stood at the window and looked across the village to Badger's Sett.

'He's home,' Elizabeth said. 'The lights are on. He shouldn't be alone.'

Her husband put an arm round her. 'We'll speak to him tomorrow.'

Elizabeth turned back to the room. 'I called Candida Woodley as soon as I heard about the accident. She was out, her husband said, playing in a bridge drive. He said he'd ask her to return the call.'

'I expect she called James direct.'

'She won't do that. She hates him.'

'My dear, in these terrible circumstances — '

'She won't, Charles. She hates him. James is well rid of the creature.'

But that was wishful thinking on Elizabeth Wallis's part.

Mediterranean — Tuesday

Hamish Trotter leaned on the rail of *Seascanner,* and watched the sun rise on a slice of Hell. Under a blood-red sky the water slid black and sluggish, glistening with oil and dotted with pieces of wreckage, some of it human. The stench of oil clogged the air.

134

Overhead, spotter planes of the Italian Air Force directed the small craft that trawled for detritus and hoisted it to the deck of an anchored minesweeper.

Trotter loved ships, had made his immense fortune building them, and on retirement had realized a lifelong dream by creating *Seascanner*.

She resembled her maker; brute strength concealing a surprising range of skills. Her hull was broad and squat, her forward deck bristled with ungainly machines. Aft of her bridge loomed a structure like something from a child's meccano set, massive metal pillars and girders supporting a flat asymmetric roof. Aft of that again, the rear deck lay ready to receive whatever was dredged from the sea. Four clawlike cranes were ranged along her sides.

One of the spotter planes flew low overhead, and Trotter's mouth twisted in a sardonic smile. No doubt they were watching him and his ship, and carrying tales to the local competition. Plenty of operators would be snapping for a piece of this action. That didn't bother him, turned him on in fact.

He wanted this job. If he got it, there'd be battles to fight. Opponents would be quick to point out the smallest error of procedure. He'd have to be bloody careful, record every move on tape, keep a full computer log, see that the evidence was flawless, and above all, keep his temper.

He squinted down at the water, considering his priorities. The Black boxes first. He knew where to go for those, his sonar cable was picking up the pinger signals loud and clear. Once the boxes were recovered and sent off to whoever was going to vet the tapes, there'd have to be a survey of the seabed. All the heavy wreckage would be down there; he'd have to map the whole area, send the ROV down to take photos so that Don Porteous could decide which items to lift first.

The ROV would lift as much as it could. Once on deck, every piece must be hosed down and treated with lubricant to prevent salt-water erosion, labelled, photographed again, recorded in the log, carted off by air or sea to Ostia or London or wherever. Then it would be up to the experts to identify and piece together the fragments of *Paloma*.

Trotter thought about the human remains. There'd be some trapped in the sunken wreckage, very likely. He'd have to ask Porteous about handling those.

He wondered if Don planned to use drivers. They were useful on or near the surface, but at depths like these, the ROV worked better and faster — and it didn't get the bends.

The throb of an engine broke across his thoughts. A naval launch approached on the starboard bow, slowed and nudged the ship's side. A deck-hand flung down a ladder and a small man in jeans and windcheater climbed up it, followed by a young man in dark-blue overalls. The launch pulled away and Trotter moved to greet the newcomers.

'Don. Welcome aboard.'

Porteous shook hands and indicated his companion. 'Jack Lawrie,' he said. 'He'll be working with me during the investigations.'

Trotter nodded, bright-eyed. 'So is it settled, do I get the job?'

Porteous tapped his own chest with a gnarled finger. 'The buck stops here. Why don't you show us what's on offer?'

'I'll give you the luxury tour,' Trotter said.

They moved through the vessel, Trotter pointing out features, Porteous stopping to ask questions or examine a piece of equipment. Lawrie followed a pace behind, silent until they reached the video-control room. There his face lit up.

'Man, you've got the lot,' he said.

Trotter nodded. 'Aye, we have.'

Porteous moved along the row of screens that lined the far end of the cabin. They were dark at the moment, but he wasn't deceived. Trotter would have a cable over the side, had probably already located the pinger signals from *Paloma*'s grave.

The sonar worked on echoes. A line was lowered, it trailed a device that emitted sound waves. The signals bounced off the seabed or objects lying there, and were transmitted back through the cable's optical fibres to this control room, where they appeared on the screen in the form of shadows.

It took a skilled operator to interpret the meaning of those shadows. Trotter had the skill, but he also had a major defect. He was a devil for bending the rules. That could be disastrous in this investigation; it could lead to dissension, and even to international incidents. The usual course, the safe course, would be to wait for a salvage ship to be sent from England.

On the other hand, there was no time to waste. London was screaming for fast answers, even Geoff Waldron, who never rushed things, had said: 'All possible speed'. Trotter, for all his faults, was here and now and he owned the best small recovery vessel in the business.

Porteous turned to face his host.

'Show us the ROV,' he said.

Trotter led the way to the deck where the

Remote Operated Vehicle stood, square and compact, crowned with a dome. He traced the letters painted on its side. 'Tethys,' he said, 'wife to Oceanus. She's based on my '96 model, but with improvements. She's better able to deal with sand on the seabed, doesn't kick up such a dust with her thrusters, so you can see what you're doing. She's better in rough weather, too. She has full video and photo capabilities.'

He pointed to two big drums mounted close to the rail. 'Those carry the remote operation cables. Each cable contains eight strands of optical fibre — Eastport's special — they connect the ROV's video camera with the screens in the control room. You can guide your underwater operation from the comfort of your chair. That allows us to inspect wreckage, decide what we'll retrieve, and how. We can also use the video digitizer to freeze a frame and print it for closer inspection or enlargement. You'll be needing that to assess damage to big structures, airframe, engines, and so on.

Trotter turned to face Porteous. 'While the ROV's in action we have two men on duty in the control room, twenty-four hours a day. Directing Tethys — driving her as you might say — is tricky, especially during lifts. Four of us, myself included, are trained for the job, and we'll not be handing over to anyone. You and Lawrie are welcome to watch and learn, but you'll not touch unless I say so.'

Porteous nodded. 'The ROV's your baby. General strategy's mine.'

Lawrie ventured a question. 'Sir, last time I worked on this, like, we'd grief with acoustic interference. We'd to switch off the ROV every time we needed to make a fix.'

'You won't find that here,' Trotter said. '*Tethys* has inertial navigation.' Now fully into his stride, he leaned forward to touch the machine's pincers, thick and shining. 'The lifters will handle medium-sized objects, place them in the cradle, and bring them up here, but anything really big needs to be done by conventional salvage.' He turned to Porteous. 'Was there an explosion aboard *Paloma*?'

'Can't say yet. They don't think so. There was certainly a fire. The wreckage shows soot and fire damage, and they've fished out a head and torso with soot in the throat.'

'So the smoke reached the passenger section?'

'We don't know that the victim was a passenger. Could have been the fire-fighter. The ATC tape suggests that the chief fireman was in the cargo hold at the end. The torso could be his. The pathologists will run DNA tests and dental records to try to establish the identity of victims, but that will take time, and we've a need for speed. Speed and accuracy.' Porteous was staring at Trotter with intensity. 'Whatever we recover from that devil's broth out there becomes part of a chain of evidence that may tell us if *Paloma* was brought down by accident or intent. That in turn will determine issues of insurance payouts, criminal charges, future aircraft design. What we do here can have international repercussions. There has to be absolute integrity. Our reports must be totally accurate, and totally confidential.'

'They will be,' Trotter said, but Porteous continued to hold his gaze.

'Tell me, Hamish, why do you want this job? You don't need the money.'

Trotter smiled. 'Anything I make goes back into funding *Seascanner*. She's an expensive lady. I want the job because I'm an old friend of Daniel Roswall. We go back a long way.'

'So I'm told.' Porteous tilted his head. 'And how far would you go to oblige an old friend, may I ask?'

Trotter looked away to where a motor-launch circled the oil-slick. The well of the boat was piled with black body-bags. Overhead the sun battled against clouds that

141

thinned and scattered before a toothed wind.

He said: 'That out there — it's an abomination. If it was an accident, we have to know the cause, so it can't happen again. If it was sabotage, we have to find who's responsible, and put them away. If I get the job, I'll do the best I can. I'll not tamper with evidence, I'll not perjure myself, I'll see the work gets done, to the end.'

Porteous slid his hand inside his windcheater and brought out a bundle of papers.

'I'll need some signatures,' he said.

Rome — The Dove Warehouse

'They'll hold us responsible for all those deaths, the plane, the cargo . . . ' Hugo Spinner swept an arm across Fermoy's desk, knocking a pile of waybills to the ground.

Fermoy retrieved the papers and glared at Hugo.

'For God's sake, cool it! It won't help to throw hysterics!'

Spinner collapsed backward in his chair.

'Capriati says the ATC tape shows the fire started in the rear portside container, the Dove container.' He banged both fists on the desk. 'I want to know everything that was in it, you hear? I want a full breakdown.'

'What d'you think I've been doin' all this time?' Fermoy's puggy features were dark with rage. 'I've gone through them waybills with a fine-tooth comb, an' I'm tellin' you, there weren't any dangerous materials in our container, nothin' that could've started a fire.'

Iain Kincraig, who was sitting at the side of the room, rose and came to stand beside Fermoy.

'There are plenty of things can start a fire, Andy. Friction, chemical interaction . . . '

Fermoy drew a hissing breath. 'Before *Paloma* loaded, I was instructed by Mister Spinner here to take special care with the cargo checks.' He jabbed a finger at Hugo. 'You gave the order, an' you saw it carried out. *Paloma* wasn't carryin' lighter-fluid, or nitric acid, or peroxide, or phosphorus, or any other effin' no-no in her cargo-hold.'

'I want printouts,' Hugo said. 'Printouts of the contents of every container in the main-deck cargo-hold.'

'It's not that ruddy simple!' Fermoy tapped the papers in front of him. 'These here are master waybills. Your office booked all the stuff for the Dove conference on one waybill, but that don't mean it was all packed in the one container.'

'Then give me the breakdown of the master

143

waybills.' Hugo swung round to confront Kincraig. 'And from you I want a full report on the maintenance of the aircraft, all the records, details of past repairs, past problems . . . '

Kincraig said quietly, 'I'll see to it, but they'll run their own checks, you know, and make their own reports.'

' 'They'? Who's 'they'?'

'The Board of Inquiry, the Boeing Airline Company, the manufacturers, the electrical fitters, old Uncle Tom Cobley and all. They're as scared as you are of being blamed for what happened.'

'And you, I suppose, are not scared?'

'Oh aye, I'm scared, but I don't think Omega's to blame. *Paloma* was in good shape, well maintained, correctly loaded. I don't think the trouble lay in her legitimate cargo.'

'Meaning there was undeclared cargo?'

'That's ma gut feeling, yes.' Kincraig's deepset eyes were sombre. 'I think there was sabotage.'

Hugo shook his head helplessly. 'But how? How could anyone get past our checks, not to mention airport security, and the electronic scanners? They have TNA here, you know. That would have picked up any explosive material, even Semtex.'

'Maybe it wasn't explosive they used, just a routine incendiary device. I'm no' an expert in the matter, but you can be sure there'll be those who are.' Kincraig glanced at the wall clock. 'I'm away to the terminal. There's a lad from head office wants to talk to me.' He saw that Hugo wasn't listening, and leaned towards him.

'Mr Spinner? Are ye coming, or not?'

Hugo looked at him blankly. 'The carton,' he said.

'What carton?'

'The one that was sent on by Omega's Rome office. Fermoy and I checked it, right here. It was sent to Captain Brock by his brother in England.'

'Is that so? What was in it?'

'A fax machine, two rackets, a camera, a pair of Raybans. Gemelli contacted Captain Brock and asked him what he wanted done with the stuff; Brock said send it to Mallowfield, he'd collect it there.' Hugo wiped his hands on the lapels of his jacket. 'I'll swear there was no incendiary device in that carton, Fermoy will bear me out.'

Fermoy was scowling, searching his memory. 'Unless there was something inside the fax machine or the camera . . . or the racket-frames.' He riffled through the pile of manifests and selected one. 'This is it. It's all listed, confirmed by Heathrow, contents kosher.' Fermoy lifted his head to stare at Kincraig. 'What sane man would want to bring down the aircraft his brother was flying?'

12

Bansford

James woke at sunrise.

His body was stiff and his mouth sour. He went upstairs, and used the bedside phone to call Heathrow. There was no news of survivors, he was told. An intensive search was being conducted; he would be informed as soon as news came through.

He bathed, shaved, dressed, went down to the kitchen and made coffee and toast. At six, he phoned the rectory. Charles Wallis answered and repeated his offer of hospitality. James thanked him, but declined the invitation.

'People know where to find me, here,' he said. 'In case I'm wanted.'

Soon after that, the telephone started to ring. Friends, colleagues, the press called. After a while he switched on the answering-machine.

He wandered round the house and garden. Today wasn't one of Mrs Commins's days.

Calls came through on his mobile, but the screen showed they weren't from the airport, and he didn't take them.

At eight o'clock he backed the car out of the garage and headed north, circling London, to Slough. Dave's flat was on the outskirts.

He couldn't have said why he wanted to go there. Since his accident he'd been prey to sudden impulses. Dr Marsh said it was a recovery mechanism, part of his brain was drawing on past experience, prompting his actions, sparing him the need to make conscious decisions.

He parked his car close to the service stairs at the back of the building. A man on the property next door was cutting grass, the sweet, sharp smell filled the air.

James climbed the stairs and let himself into the flat. The curtains in the living-area were closed, and he drew them back. Light slanted on to dusty surfaces. Dave hadn't used the place much, only when he was on standby.

A thought floated into James's mind.

Boru. Dave sent a fax to Boru. Boru was important, maybe crucial. He'd have to tell someone about the fax.

He needed to know who Boru was. If he could find an address book. He crossed to the desk. It wasn't locked. There was very little in it, some stationery in the pigeonholes, a bundle of receipted accounts, an Omega pamphlet. No unopened mail, no business or legal documents.

No letters. Dave was never a good correspondent. When he wanted to communicate, he used the telephone, an occasional fax or e-mail. There'd be no paper-trail to follow.

Dave wasn't here. Badger's Sett was the nearest he'd had to a home in England, and out of England he'd made Italy his base. Tuscany, with the Countess Pia d'Ascani.

I never met her, James thought, I don't know what she looks like, she doesn't know me.

But he was going to meet her. He was vaguely surprised at the firmness of that intention. He said aloud, as if Pia d'Ascani was here in the room with him: 'I have to find the reason. I have to know why he died.'

The silence didn't argue.

'I don't know what to look for,' he said. 'Who, or what, is Boru?'

He remembered the albums.

Dave was an avid photographer. He always carried a camera and he used it constantly. He kept the photos in albums that went all the way back to his schooldays.

James searched the flat. Cupboards in the living-room and bedroom, linen-closet.

No albums.

Kitchen cupboards, broom-cupboard. Nothing. At last, in the space under the boiler, he found a couple of empty suitcases and a folded aluminium ladder.

Of course! The flat was on the top floor, and there was a ceiling hatch in the bathroom. He carried the ladder to the hatch and climbed up to the attic.

The albums were packed in boxes, each box labelled by year. There were far too many to carry away.

He selected the ones that covered the past seven years, lugged them down to the kitchen and packed them into one of the suitcases. He returned the ladder to its place, locked the flat and carried the suitcase to his car.

The neighbour had finished mowing his lawn and was tossing cuttings into a garden incinerator.

Man is as grass which today flourishes and tomorrow is cast into the fire.

James pressed his hands to his eyes. Fire had consumed Clare's body, fire had killed Dave. The numbness that had gripped him all these weeks suddenly evaporated, to be replaced by a pain so acute that he cried out and leaned both hands on the bonnet of his car.

'You OK?' The grass-cutter was at his

fence, craning to peer at James. James straightened up.

'I'm fine. Just a cramp in my back. I carried a load of books.'

'Ah. You want to be careful with backs. Slip a disc and you're in real trouble.' The man leaned on the fence, ready to chat, but James slung the case into the back of the car and drove off.

Rome Airport

When Hugo left the warehouse, the sky was like a new bruise, purple, crimson and yellow. Inland over the mountains, thunder muttered.

He drove round to the airport parking lot, and hurried into the terminal. On the way to the control tower he caught up with Gerda Marcus. He greeted her pettishly.

'Where've you been, I've been looking all over for you?'

She shrugged. 'I've been here most of the night. Dodging the press, preparing statements, talking to reps from airlines and insurance companies and God knows who else. And to Dan. He called ten minutes ago. He's meeting with our executives this morning. Harry's spoken to the civil aviation

151

authorities. Are you coming to listen to the ATC tape?'

'Yes.' His face twitched, and he put up a hand to massage the back of his neck. 'What's the latest from the accident site?'

'They haven't found anyone alive.'

They reached the room set aside for the viewing of the tape. A number of people had already settled in the seats facing the screen. As Gerda sat down, a young man next to her smiled at her.

'Hi. I'm Fergus Carnegie. I hold kind of a watching brief for the FAA, just till their man gets here from the States. And you are?'

'Gerda Marcus. I'm with Dove International.'

'That so? A bad day for you, then.' He shook his head, pulled down his mouth. He had ingenuous blue eyes and tombstone teeth, a frank manner. Gerda was not deceived. This was no puppy-dog.

Capriati, who had been standing to one side, talking to Boeing's Rome agent, now moved to the front of the audience.

'Ladies and gentlemen,' he said, 'I have called you here to listen to the air traffic control tape that records the last communication with the aircraft which has crashed yesterday — Omega 197, known to many as *Paloma*. You have all special interest in this

152

disaster, will be part of the enquiries that must come. Please to understand, what you will hear is privileged information. You must not reveal it to others, or make it public in any way. I will run the tape to the end, then you ask questions. That is satisfactory? Very good, then we proceed. The first voice you hear is of Captain David Brock, pilot of Omega. He makes the routine checks before take-off.'

Capriati switched on the recording. Gerda clasped her hands tightly. To her right Hugo fidgeted and sighed, to her left Carnegie scribbled notes. Gerda flew with *Paloma*.

The voices on the tape were clear. Phrases stayed in her mind. A problem, a smoke warning from the main-deck cargo-hold. Heavy smoke in the hold, none in the passenger cabin. The fire-fighter and his assistant in there, looking for the source of the smoke.

There was a break in the recording, but no one in the audience spoke. Gerda closed her eyes. She wanted to pray, but it was too late for that. David spoke again, asking for clearance to descend to flight level 140. Capriati answered, declared a full emergency, requested Omega's position and flight details.

David asked for his nearest suitable airport.

Rome, Capriati told him, Marseilles was not an option.

There followed a break of four minutes, Capriati trying to make contact with *Paloma*, but receiving no reply. At last David spoke again, his tone higher and louder than before. They had found the source of the smoke, it was in a rear portside container. They were at flight level 14,000 feet, trying to deal with the fire, working towards smoke evacuation.

There was more background noise now. Static. Voices shouting across each other. Something about circuit breakers. Then a thumping, rushing sound, and the tape soared into a high, wavering whine. Nothing more from *Paloma*, and from Capriati only a constantly repeated appeal: *Omega one-niner-seven do you read? Please respond. Please respond.*

* * *

In the viewing-room, Capriati stooped to switch off the recorder.

'Questions,' he said.

For a time no one spoke, then Carnegie raised a hand.

'Of course we will have to hear what skilled analysts make of the tape, but certain things spring to mind.'

Capriati nodded, waiting.

Carnegie consulted his notes. 'At the first alarm, when Captain Brock reports a smoke problem, he sounds calm and . . . in control. A few minutes later, he reports heavy smoke in the hold. He sounds much more strained. It seems that in that short period his sense of danger has dramatically increased. He doesn't say why, he doesn't give any facts to explain why, but he requests clearance to make an immediate descent to flight level one four zero — fourteen thousand feet. That is surely significant?'

As Capriati remained silent, Carnegie continued, 'Level one four zero is the level at which an aircraft can be depressurized to allow smoke to escape . . . if there is smoke in the passenger cabin.' He swivelled in his seat to survey the audience. 'You see the problem? In his first call, Captain Brock says there is no smoke in the passenger cabin, but a couple of minutes later he asks to descend to level one four zero. He was planning to evacuate smoke before there was any smoke to evacuate.'

Capriati tilted his head. 'What is your point, Mr Carnegie?'

'My point is that Captain Brock's request could indicate an element of confusion . . . under strain, he made an error of judgement. Perhaps he was affected by some flow of fumes from the hold.'

Capriati interrupted him. 'No. When he receive the smoke warning, Captain Brock must call for the check list for smoke infiltration. All on the flight deck must at once put on oxygen mask. He could not breathe fumes.'

'Then maybe it was simply pilot error. Under stress he made a wrong decision.'

'One moment.' A man at the back of the room rose to his feet. He wore the uniform of a senior pilot of British Airways. 'My name is Gascoigne,' he said. 'I'm here to represent the Pilots' Association of Great Britain. I'd like to say that Mr Carnegie has no right to accuse Captain Brock of error. Brock was an experienced pilot with a fine record. He obviously felt that *Paloma* was in a critical situation. There was a fire in the cargo hold. It could spread rapidly. He decided to be ready to evacuate smoke. It was a wise precaution.'

'Or an unfounded guess. There was no smoke in the forward part of the aircraft.'

Gascoigne's jaw jutted. 'Are you a pilot?'

'I'm an engineer, I have knowledge of avionics.'

'Let me tell you something. Fire is a pilot's worst nightmare. You have no idea what

156

Brock had to cope with in those circumstances. He had to monitor all the systems, keep the aircraft steady, control the crew, calm the passengers. A Boeing isn't a bloody armchair, you don't just sit on your arse — '

'Brock panicked, he demanded a full emergency — '

'And he was right, wasn't he? *Paloma* burned. Our job is to find out why, not try and shift the blame on to the pilot!'

'You have an axe to grind, I want the truth . . . '

Capriati held up both hands to halt the argument.

'*Signori*, please. We have not yet all the facts. Soon we will have the other tapes. CVR and DFDR.' He looked at Carnegie. 'I can say now, Captain Brock did not panic. He was very calm, to the end.'

He turned to take a question about airport security. The discussion became technical and Gerda picked up her handbag. Before she could move from her seat, Carnegie bent towards her.

'Brock said the smoke came from the rear portside container. I understand that that belonged to your organization, Dove International?'

She nodded, and he flashed the tombstone

teeth. 'I'd be interested to talk to you about that, some time.'

Someone in the row behind hushed him, and he settled back in his chair.

Gerda got to her feet and headed for the door. After a brief hesitation, Hugo followed her.

13

In the Dove office, the receptionist and an assistant were dealing with a steady stream of telephone calls. Hugo beckoned Gerda through to the inner office and slammed the door.

'That prat Carnegie,' he said, 'why was he on about our container? Does he think we'd sabotage our own plane, murder our own people?'

'The fire started in our container. Something in it burned. We have to have a full list of the contents.'

'I've already told Fermoy to give me the breakdown.' Hugo flung himself down in a chair, fumbled for a handkerchief and mopped his face. Aware that Gerda was staring fixedly at him, he said defensively: 'What?'

Gerda sat down facing him. 'You tell me, Hugo.'

He thrust out his lips. 'Something I remembered. There was a carton. It was sent to David Brock by his brother in England. Brock wanted it sent back to England, so it was loaded in the Dove container.'

'What was in it?'

'Nothing out of the way. Rackets, a camera, a fax machine. Fermoy and I checked it.' As Gerda started to speak, Hugo waved an impatient hand. 'All right, I suppose there could have been incendiary material in something.'

'Have you told the authorities about this?'

'No. I only remembered the damn thing an hour ago.'

'Then tell them, right away. Tell Capriati or the airport manager or security. For God's sake, Hugo, if you say nothing, they'll think we have something to hide.'

'They'll say it's not their job, they're not in charge of the investigation.'

'Then tell whoever is in charge.' Gerda reached for a file and flicked over pages. She twisted it round for Hugo to see. 'Rupert Sandiman of Air Accident Investigations, Geoffrey Waldron of Civil Aviation, speak to one of them, I'm going to call Dan.'

Hugo looked morose. 'They won't talk to the likes of me.'

But Sandiman took the call himself, and questioned Hugo at length about the carton, its provenance, and its handling at Heathrow, the Omega office and the airport warehouse. He wanted to know who had checked the box, what was in it and how it was packed and loaded aboard *Paloma*. At the end, he thanked Hugo for the information, and hung up.

Hugo slammed down the receiver.

'Waste of bloody time,' he said. 'All he's interested in is rules and regulations.'

There he was wrong. Sandiman was already relaying what he'd learned to Geoff Waldron, Barry Coburn, Mrs Rylda Warne, and Dr John Thorneycroft. Waldron in his turn put through a call to old acquaintance Benno Capriati.

'Benno? Geoff Waldron. How are you?'

'As well as you can expect. You receive the tape?'

'I did, thank you. We're working on copies here and in Washington, to get maximum definition. You did a good job, Benno.'

'Not good enough. *Paloma* went down.'

Waldron cleared his throat. 'Er . . . your session this morning . . . I've had some fast reactions to the tape. One from Ed Gascoigne. He claims someone named Carnegie tried to blame the accident on pilot error.'

'*Sí*, he says Brock started procedure for smoke evacuation, before there was smoke in the cockpit. He says Brock was confused.'

'I'd say he was far-sighted.'

'I also. Brock was not confused. He was to

the end in control — of himself, of the aircraft.'

'Umh. Well. One more thing, I don't know if you're aware, there was a carton of goods in the Dove container that was sent from London by Brock's brother . . . '

'I heard, ten minutes ago.'

'Who told you?'

'A Mr Hugo Spinner, from Dove.'

'Has he told anyone else?'

'That I cannot say, but Rome is the home of the press scavengers, my friend. By tomorrow the story will be all over the world.'

★   ★   ★

At Mallowfield, Daniel Roswall spoke to Kyle Parnell about the carton.

'It looks bad for us,' he said. 'Goods sent at the last minute, not on the regular manifests, packed in the Dove container, where they say the fire started.'

'So what do we do?'

'We report it at once to the Directorate of Civil Aviation, I'll see to that. You get me everything you can about this James Brock, and the carton. Use our London agency, tell them we want the facts fast.'

'You aiming to say J. Brock murdered his own brother and took out a planeful of

162

innocent people? You want to make him the prime suspect?'

Dan raised cold eyes to Kyle's face.

'No, but if he becomes the prime suspect, I want to be sure that Dove isn't accused of complicity or negligence. My job is to protect this enterprise, and I'll do whatever it takes.' He drew the telephone towards him and began to punch digits. Kyle shrugged and went off to do his bidding.

★   ★   ★

Capriati was right about the press scavengers.

An hour after *Paloma* plunged into the sea, they were swarming at Leonardo da Vinci airport, cornering distraught members of the public and harassing officials, lavish alike with bribes and threats.

One of them, sharper or luckier than the rest, made the Omega office in Rome his target, and carried chief clerk Gemelli off to the nearest bar. Gemelli was both stupid and greedy. (It was only next day that he realized he'd sold his gossip far too cheaply). He told everything he knew about the carton, how it had been sent to David Brock by his brother, and given onward passage to England in the Dove container.

The story was sold at a handsome profit to a news syndicate, and on Tuesday it appeared in numerous newspapers. Follow-ups established that the fire had started in the Dove container, and by evening the yellow press was giving banner headlines to what they termed the killer container.

* * *

James Brock read the early editions, and phoned his partner Reg Purviss.

'Have you read today's *Clarion*?' he demanded.

'Yes. It's garbage.'

'It's more than that. It infers my carton set that plane alight. It's bloody nonsense, Reg, there was nothing flammable in the box, it was cleared at Heathrow. That story is actionable.'

'I don't think so, James. There is no suggestion it was your stuff that started the fire.'

'But the juxtaposition . . . the inference is clear . . . '

'There must have been a helluva lot of goods in the Dove container, besides yours. I agree the story is tasteless, but it's not libellous — not as it stands.'

'I'm going to blast that dirty little rag off

the face of the earth.'

'Tomorrow we'll take advice. If there's cause for action, we'll have the *Clarion*'s balls. Until then, stay cool. Is there any news of David?'

'No. Nothing.'

'If you'd like company, I can come over.'

'No. No thanks. I may have to . . . go out.'

'Call me tomorrow, James, will you do that?'

'Yes. Sure. Thanks Reg. 'Bye.'

After a few minutes' thought, James put through a call to the office of Geoffrey Waldron. He was told Mr Waldron was in conference but would return the call as soon as he could. Surprisingly he did, listened closely to what James had to say about the carton, assured him that close attention was being given to every item on *Paloma*'s cargo manifests, and advised him to leave the press 'to the proper authorities.'

'There are elements of the media,' Waldron said, 'that exploit tragedy, they thrive on controversy. Have a go at them and you'll boost their circulation, they'll do all they can to keep the pot boiling. Ignore them and they'll look for other targets. They'll find plenty, believe me.'

James hung up in a mutinous mood. All

165

very well for Reg and Waldron to urge caution. They weren't being accused of mass murder.

His anger was somewhat eased by the messages that started to come through to his answering machine. Some were from old friends, others from people he'd never met. All of them expressed sympathy, and outrage at the press stories.

He went to the kitchen, heated a frozen meal, added a tankard of beer, and carried the tray back to the television room. He turned on the set, but left the sound low.

Waldron was right, he knew. The yellow press would exploit every lead, and they'd have powerful backing. The big airway corporations, the insurance companies, the firms who built *Paloma*, would be on the look-out for scapegoats to carry the burden of all those deaths. They'd blame him, and Dave as the pilot, and anyone else they could think of, because their reputations and their profits were at risk.

Raging against the heavies was farting against thunder.

So what could he do? What did he have?

He had his knowledge of Dave, his skills and character. Dave could fly an aircraft better than most. He would never be slipshod at his job. He was loyal to his mates and to

166

his employers, to Omega and probably to Dove.

What else?

There was the fax Dave sent, asking someone called Boru about a photograph.

If the fax had a bearing on the *Paloma* disaster, he had to find out how.

The first step had to be Dave's photograph albums.

He piled them on the coffee table and chose the earliest of them, which went back seven years. He ignored the landscapes, concentrating on the pictures of people. Some of these had no captions, in other cases the caption was there but the photo itself was missing; lost, perhaps, or given away to someone.

A few of the people were known to him, but not many. After a while, feeling stiff and somewhat discouraged, he took a break, to check the messages on the answering machine. One of them caught his attention and he called the number indicated.

A no-nonsense voice answered and James said, 'Captain Gascoigne? This is James Brock.'

'Oh. Good. I called to offer my support. I represent the Pilots' Association, here in the UK. I did my initial training the same time as Dave. If anyone tries to suggest *Paloma* crashed through pilot error, refer them to me. Dave's the best in the business.'

'Thank you.'

'I hope you have good news of him.' Gascoigne hesitated. 'I'd like to talk to you, some time.'

'I'd welcome that.'

'There'll be a memorial service soon, for . . . those lost. I'll be at it, perhaps we can meet then?'

'Good idea.'

'I'll be in touch.' Gascoigne rang off.

James wondered if there was a picture of Gascoigne in the albums. He found one, near the end of the first volume. It showed David and Gascoigne standing together in the mouth of a hangar. They were both pointing at the camera and laughing. Gascoigne was tall and heavy-set, with deep-set eyes and wiry hair cropped close to his skull.

James extracted the photo and slid it into his wallet. He worked on until eleven. He was about to go upstairs to bed when his mobile phone beeped. A woman spoke, her voice sibilant with venom.

'I suppose it was you who sicked your tame priest on to me.'

'Candida?'

'The old fool gave Tom a lecture, a lot of sentimental crap. Said I should call you, so

I'm calling. I'm glad of a chance to speak my mind. You did it, didn't you? You packed something in that box. You meant David to die and I know why. Don't think I'll let you get away with it. All those people dead! You're a murderer, a filthy murderer and I'm going to tell the world about you, I'm going to see you get what you deserve!' The receiver crashed down.

James went to bed, but sleep was slow in coming, and when it did, Candida Woodley's voice buzzed like a blowfly through his dreams.

London

On Wednesday morning, John Thorneycroft, heading out of his flat to his car, found Rod Gamage of the Special Branch leaning against its bonnet. He straightened up at Thorneycroft's approach.

'Morning, sir. Could I have a word?' Seeing Thorneycroft hesitate, he grinned. 'The Chief knows I'm here.'

The backscratching begins, Thorneycroft thought.

'Make it fast,' he said. 'I'm running late.'

'I received a call, eight o'clock this morning, from DCI Bob Evans, Maidstone

Central. It concerned a carton of goods sent to Rome from Heathrow by a Mr James Brock. He's the brother of Captain David Brock, who's — '

'The pilot of the plane that crashed on Monday. I know about the carton. Go on.'

'Evans had a visit, sir, crack of day he says, from a Mrs Candida Woodley of Chart Sutton. She'd read this, story in yesterday's *Clarion* . . . '

'Yes, yes. So?'

'Seems Mrs Woodley is sister-in-law to James Brock. She swears he loaded the carton with incendiaries and sent it to his brother with the intention of setting fire to *Paloma*.'

'She sounds like a right nutter.'

'My first thought too, sir, but Evans is a mate of mine, Maidstone was my manor before I transferred, and I asked him would he do a quick check on Brock and the Woodley woman. Evans came back to me twenty minutes ago, said Brock lost his wife, who was Mrs Woodley's twin sister, a couple of months back. She topped herself. Drove off the edge of a quarry and ran her husband down on the way. Damn near finished him. Split his head open, broke his leg and some ribs. He was in hospital quite a few weeks.

'While he was there, he acted pretty queer, wouldn't have any visitors, not even his own brother. It caused talk. You know how talk spreads, in these country places.' Gamage saw Thorneycroft glance at his watch, and quickened the pace of his narrative. 'Point is, Mrs Woodley told Evans that the reason for Mrs Brock's suicide was, she'd been having it off with Captain Brock, quite a long affair, and her husband caught them at it and threw the brother out. So the wife topped herself and tried to take hubby with her.

'According to Mrs Woodley, as a result of it all — the finding out, plus the head injury, plus losing his wife — Brock went off his rocker and decided to do for his brother by sending the carton to start a fire, never mind all the other poor sods who'd go too. It's a crazy story, but the Chief thought you'd want to know.'

Thorneycroft. nodded. 'I'm grateful. Will you be following it up?'

'Yes. Me and Fay Cowper'll be going down to interview the both of them.'

'Does Mr Waldron know?'

'Not yet, sir. The Chief said it was your department.'

Thorneycroft smiled. 'Set a nutter to catch a nutter? All right. I'll tell Mr Waldron. You keep me up to speed.'

Watching him gun the Rover through the flood of traffic, Gamage decided that being kept up to speed was something Dr Thorneycroft had no need of.

The Mediterranean

Early on that same Wednesday, Don Porteous left Hamish Trotter to bring *Seascanner* into position for the start of the retrieval of debris from *Paloma*, and had himself ferried across to a sleek freighter anchored at the edge of the disaster site. *Celtic Rose* was a modern refrigerator ship which had been dragooned into handling the human remains taken from the sea. A team had worked through the night, and a second shift was still at work, packing body parts into heavy plastic sacks and taking them through to a refrigerator room. The freighter's broad rear deck had been cleared of containers, and a military helicopter squatted there, its crew standing by.

Porteous spoke to the freighter's first mate. 'How many bodies so far?'

The mate grimaced. 'More or less whole bodies? Seven or eight. There's substantial parts of thirty or forty more, but which belongs with what, that's someone else's job. And there's stuff you can hardly tell what it is, just that it's been bled white.' He brushed a hand over his mouth. 'None of 'em were wearing life-jackets, so please God it was quick at the end. The parts'll keep coming for a while. They sink, y'see, then rise again when gas forms. And there'll be some trapped in the wreckage under water.'

Porteous glanced at the helicopter. 'It would be a great help if you could send the first load away to London as soon as possible. They're already started on the post-mortems at West Middlesex mortuary.'

'Rather them than me. Must've been a bomb on board, wouldn't you say, to smash the poor buggers up like that?'

'Not necessarily. Could have been impact injuries. If there was an explosion it'll show in the wreckage of the plane, and there'll be opaque fragments lodged in the bodies, that'll show up in the X-rays.'

The mate made a savage gesture. 'Well, if it was sabotage and you find the lot that did it, hand 'em over to me and the lads.' He walked away to discuss Porteous's request with the pilot of the helicopter.

★　★　★

Back in the control room of *Seascanner*, Porteous found Trotter and two of his technicians poring over piles of charts and scale drawings. Trotter signed to Porteous to join them.

'I want to get the ROV to work as soon as may be,' he said. 'We need to make accurate maps of the wreckage down there, photograph it and decide which items we must lift first. You have a list of priorities, I take it?'

'I have, and we'll be getting instructions from the DCA, drawn up in collaboration with Omega and Boeing and the rest. They'll fax us diagrams of the key parts. Meanwhile . . . ' he placed a sheet of paper before Trotter, 'here's what I think:

'Number one target is the Black boxes: cockpit voice recorder, digital flight data recorder, and quick access recorder.' He jerked a thumb at a machine at his elbow which was emitting a steady pinging sound. 'You picked that one up pretty fast, I see.'

Trotter smiled blandly. 'Luck. Just put the scanner over in the right place. So we know the approximate position of at least one of the tapes, but we still have to pinpoint it and see if we can lift it. I take it the boxes were in the usual place?'

Porteous nodded. He spread out a scale drawing of an aircraft skeleton.

'The CVR and DFDR were here, right at the rear, close to the stabilizer area.'

'And right behind the rear portside

container, where the fire started.'

'That's right.' Porteous met Trotter's troubled gaze. 'The Black boxes can withstand enormous heat and heavy impact, you know.'

'Let's hope so. What else are we after?'

'First, the main-deck cargo-area — stabilizers and crown skin, rear pressure bulkhead, rear superstructure, the walls of the cargo hold, anything that will help us to determine the course and nature of the fire. But the whole of the aircraft is important. We need the engines, the flight deck, the passenger area, the ventilation and electrical systems, and of course the cargo, especially from the rear of the stacks.'

'I doubt there'll be much left of Dove's container. We'd a message from Rome an hour ago, there was a carton loaded in it that might have held an incendiary device.'

'The container was a new design. Highly fire-resistant.'

Trotter pulled down his mouth. 'What sort fire, laddie? I'd a flash fire once in a storeroom at the shipyard. It was out of control in seconds. The assessors said it probably reached two thousand degrees Fahrenheit. The place was gutted, there was a stack of graphite sheets that melted. Graphite melts at huge temperatures.'

'Well, we'll have to do the best we can.' Porteous was turning the pages of a bulky manual, marking some of the pages with a star. 'How fast can you get the ROV in action?'

'Fast, starting now.' Trotter moved to study the marked diagrams. 'The deck team's ready. Lawrie can work with them. You and I will watch the video with Bob and Ty, here. We'll need to take stills of key parts.'

Porteous persisted. 'How fast is fast?'

'Couple of hours,' Trotter replied. 'With luck we'll be getting good pictures by noon.'

14

'Take the next left,' Sergeant Cowper said, and Gamage obediently swung the car from the fast to the slow lane, cutting neatly into the gap ahead of a refuse truck. The truck driver opened his mouth to yell, but closed it again on meeting the sergeant's stony glare. She'd been christened Fay, a cruel misnomer when one considered her heavy thighs and bulldog jowls.

'What d'you make of the report?' Gamage asked, and Fay pursed her mouth.

'No family feeling, I'd say. James Brock didn't want any of 'em visiting when he was in hospital. His wife's family was at the inquest, sour as lemons. They wanted a memorial service for Mrs B. but hubby said no. Now Mrs Woodley's saying he's committed arson and mass murder, just to get back at his brother.'

'She claims the brother was screwing the wife.'

Fay sniffed. 'Yeah. Take the right-hand fork a mile on.'

'You don't believe her?'

'Won't know till we've talked to her, will

we? I do wonder, how could James be sure his brother would put the carton aboard *Paloma*? More likely to stash it in the Omega office, or wherever he hung out in Rome. No one could tell if that fire would happen anywhere near Captain Brock, and even if it did, it mightn't do any harm. It was a potential killer if it was put aboard the aircraft. It could've been a damp squib off of it. Bansford's five miles from the fork.'

'It's a point,' Gamage agreed. Cowper's features were blunt but her mind was sharp and her instincts were to be trusted.

Bansford basked in pale sunlight, the cattle in the fields turned to face a south wind. Gamage eased through a square with market stalls, negotiated a hump-backed bridge, passed shops, a church, and a small wood, to the gate marked BADGER'S SETT.

The front door was opened to them by a small, gnomish woman in a flowered overall. She indicated a door to their left.

'Mr Brock's in the telly-room, doin' 'is photos,' she said. 'Will yer 'ave tea er coffee?'

'Bring both, Mrs Commins.' The man who had appeared in the doorway was above average height, lean, with dark hair that only partly hid the scar on his forehead. His eyes were dark blue, his expression both reserved and diffident. He shook hands, and waved them into a pleasant room that faced south. A heavy scent of roses flowed through the french doors.

Gamage made the routine remarks: need to collect as much information as possible about *Paloma*'s last flight, crew, cargo, anything you can tell us will be appreciated. James listened politely and poured tea. He answered questions about the carton, its contents, its dispatch to Rome. Fay made notes.

Gamage said: 'Your brother stayed here sometimes, did he sir?'

'Sometimes, when he was in England. He has a flat near Slough, but it's dreary; he preferred to stay with us.'

'So he'd have been back some time to collect the things he left? The things in the carton?'

'They were things he used a lot. His rackets, his camera, his fax machine. I thought he'd want them with him.'

'But he had them loaded on the plane, to come straight back to England.'

'So I'm told. Perhaps he was going to be based here for a while. A change of schedule. That happened sometimes.'

'You were on friendly terms with your brother, were you?'

'Yes, I liked having him here.'

Gamage cleared his throat. 'I understand

you lost your wife very recently, sir?'

'Yes.' The single word was a door closing.

Gamage said stolidly: 'I'm sorry, Mr Brock. We have to ask these questions.'

The blue eyes regarded him without expression.

'Why?'

'I beg pardon?'

'Why do you have to ask these questions? Why are you here?'

Brock's tone was reasonable, and Gamage hesitated. Be tactful, his orders were, meaning don't give the subject cause to claim harassment, don't show your hand, go by the book. But he had the feeling James Brock had read the book, maybe written it. Shove him around and he'd close up like a clam.

Gamage plunged off the high board.

'I have to tell you, we received a report from a Mrs Candida Woodley, early this morning. She claims — '

'I know what she claims,' James said. His voice remained calm, but suddenly the scar on his forehead burned red like a new brand. 'My sister-in-law claims that my brother David seduced my wife, that they slept together here in this house. It's a figment of her sick imagination. There was no seduction. No affair.'

'You're sure of that, sir?'

180

'I am. I know my brother.'

'Why would Mrs Woodley make such an allegation?'

James Brock leaned back and closed his eyes. After a moment he opened them again and said, 'Candida is mentally unstable. She suffers from violent mood-swings. She's capable of saying anything.' He paused, frowning. 'She's twin sister to my wife Clare. They had a disastrous upbringing. Their mother was a selfish neurotic who spent a lot of her life in expensive clinics. Clare and Candida had no proper family life. Their father didn't care for them enough to make the effort. He was a gambler, he brought call-girls to their home whenever his wife was taking one of her cures.

'I met Candida before I met Clare and took her out a few times, but then I met Clare and fell in love with her and married her. I think Candida resented that. I suppose your next question is, was my marriage happy?'

Gamage spread his hands and James gave him an ironic smile.

'The answer is, sometimes it was, sometimes it wasn't. This past year, Clare was very unhappy. She suffered from depression. She wanted to leave Bansford and move to London. We talked about moving. I considered job offers but . . . it's not easy to break away from one's firm, friends, clients. I didn't try hard enough. Before I could arrange anything suitable, Clare killed herself.'

'I understand you were injured in the accident?'

Again came the smile, sadder than tears.

'It wasn't an accident, Inspector. Clare drove over the edge of the quarry at the foot of our property. I tried to stop her. She tried to take me with her.'

'Where was your brother at that time?'

'In Hong Kong. He came home at once.'

'You were in hospital?'

'Yes.'

'You refused to see him. Why was that?'

'I . . . couldn't. I couldn't deal with anything or anyone. I just wanted to be left alone. Looking back, I suppose I was a bit off my head.'

Fay Cowper spoke for the first time. 'You say your marriage had its ups and downs, Mr Brock. Did anything happen between you and your wife . . . a quarrel or such . . . that could have made her want to kill herself?'

'No, absolutely not. I had to be away on business for a couple of days. When I left, Clare was in good spirits. Dave was staying with us, the two of them went to dine with the Wallises — our rector and his wife — while I was away. At the inquest Mr Wallis said she was cheerful, not depressed. When I came home, Dave had left. Omega had recalled him, some emergency, he said in his note. I packed up the things he'd left behind and sent them to Rome. There was nothing in the carton that could have started a fire. I don't know why all this happened. I just don't know.' James leaned his head on his hands.

'Lots of things can start a fire,' Gamage said. 'Battery fluid, chemicals reacting, a fault in the wiring.' As James made no answer, he sighed. 'Well, sir, if you think of anything that can help us find out what caused the plane to crash, let us know.'

James raised his head. His expression was blank and fixed, as if an idea had come to him, but he said nothing, and Gamage got to his feet. As he stepped past the coffee table he glanced at the photo albums lying on it.

'Your photos, sir?' he said.

James nodded. He shepherded his visitors to the door and walked with them to the front gate. He was still standing there when their car reached the end of the lane and turned towards Bansford village.

They headed north to the wooded area of Chart Sutton. Candida Woodley's home was at its western tip; lush country, old money, a garden patrolled by a pair of brindle bull-terriers, a breed Gamage disliked.

Candida appeared on the parking circle, called the dogs to heel and led the way to a conservatory at the side of the house. They settled in garden chairs. The air was humid and the chair-cushions felt clammy. Candida offered no refreshment.

'I haven't time to waste, Inspector Gamage,' she said. 'I have a luncheon date. Frankly I can't see why your visit is necessary. I made my suspicions perfectly clear to your man in Maidstone.'

The woman wasn't bad-looking, Gamage thought; a straight nose, high cheekbones, the eyes large and luminous. The mouth spoiled her, too thin and flat, with a tightness that matched the pettish tone of voice. She wore a plain linen dress that must have cost plenty, real suede shoes, a spiky gold necklace, a flat gold watch with a black face. All set to lunch with the right people.

Gamage reminded himself that it was unprofessional to dislike anyone on sight. Same as it was unprofessional to like James Brock. He said quietly:

'I'm afraid we can't act on suspicions alone, Mrs Woodley.'

She eyed him coldly. 'You can hardly expect me to provide proof. That surely is your job.'

'You told Inspector Evans that you suspect

your sister was having an affair with Captain David Brock.'

'I know she was. She told me so, the day she died.'

'Did she tell you face to face, ma'am?'

'No. She telephoned.' Candida drew up her shoulders, tightening her muscles defensively. 'She was very distressed, crying all the time. She said David was her lover, and James had found them in bed together. Dave left the house. Clare asked James for a divorce, but he wouldn't even discuss it. He was obsessed with Clare, bitterly jealous of her. He never considered her happiness. He was utterly selfish.'

'What did you do on receiving the call?' Gamage asked.

Candida stared at him.

'To help your sister,' he prompted, and she shrugged. She reached for a gold case on the table, took out a cigarette, and snapped a lighter. Her hands were trembling violently.

'I tried to calm Clare,' she said. 'I told her I'd drive over and see her next day. I couldn't get away immediately, I had an important appointment with my lawyer. Clare didn't wait to see me. She killed herself that evening.' Candida stared at the cigarette in her hand, thrust it into the soil-filled pot beside her. She lifted her head to glare at

185

Gamage. 'James was responsible for Clare's death, David's death, all those others on *Paloma*.'

'Why do you say that, Mrs Woodley?'

'It's obvious. He sent that carton. There was something in it to start the fire and make the plane crash.'

Questioned further, Candida stuck to her accusation, though she could give no solid information, either about her sister's relations with David Brock, or the carton James had sent to Rome. Pressed for facts, she said snappily that she had none.

'I'm not a keyhole-snooper. I leave that to the police, but I can see what's in front of my nose. James was crazy about Clare, he'd never have let her go. After she died, he was off his head. He wanted revenge on David, for taking her away from him. If you people know your job, you'll find proof and put him in gaol where he belongs. He's a bloody murderer.'

She got to her feet. 'I'm afraid I don't have any more time. No doubt you'll be in touch with me later. Good day, Inspector, Sergeant . . . Er.'

She walked through a door into the house, leaving them to find their own way out. The bull-terriers were not in evidence. Turning the car on to the London road, Gamage said: 'Well, what do you make of all that? You were

186

right about family feeling. No love lost between those two, I'd say.'

'Candida hates James,' Fay said.

'And vice versa?'

'I don't think he's much of a hater, but if his brother was banging his wife, that could've turned him nasty. Also there's the crack on his skull. That's a big scar he has.'

'Difficult to prove there was adultery. Hubby off at work, no servants around except the daily, and her on duty mornings only.' Gamage chewed his lip. 'No talk of bonking at the inquest, either. I doubt we'll prove anything. Brock struck me as a good witness. Truthful, I'd wager.'

Fay frowned. They both knew a great deal about liars and the body language that gave them away. She said: 'I think he told the truth most of the time.'

'Oh?'

'Right at the end. I think he remembered something. He clammed up. He could be withholding information. Know what I mean?'

Gamage did know. Those small hesitations could give the suspect time to think, time to frame a lie. He said: 'Brock said the photo albums were his, but the top one had D.B. on the cover. Could stand for David Brock. I daresay it doesn't mean much.'

'The *carabinieri* will be checking out the

carton,' Fay said, 'and the salvage people may find something.'

'Leave it to the men on the spot?' Gamage made a wry face. 'The frogmen on the spot. How about Mrs Woodley?'

'I think she told it the way she sees it, but . . . '

'It could be nothing but spite and malice. I wouldn't like to be on the wrong side of her. She's a right bitch.'

★   ★   ★

Parrish relayed Gamage's report to Thorneycroft. Two points came under discussion.

The first was the carton. Both agreed that James Brock could not have foreseen that it would be returned to England aboard *Paloma*, and that the contents of the box had been cleared by Omega's chief cargo-handler, Andrew Fermoy, and Dove's manager Hugo Spinner.

'Rome police will cover that investigation,' Parrish said.

'Who's in charge?'

'Vincent di Maggio. He's capable.'

The second point of interest was the impression created by Candida Woodley and James Brock.

'Gamage says Woodley told the truth as she

saw it,' Parrish said, 'but he said she's a bad witness. She hates Brock and it skews her judgement.'

'And Brock? What did they make of him?'

Parrish rubbed his nose. 'He had a stack of photo albums on the table. He said they were his, but the top one had the initials D.B. on it. We've had a report that a man visited David Brock's flat in Slough, yesterday. A neighbour spotted him leaving with a suitcase. The neighbour gave a description that fits James Brock. The car he was driving was a hire-car. It was rented by Brock when he left hospital. The suitcase could have had the albums in it. I'd like to know what he wants with them.'

'Photos of his brother?'

'Gamage didn't see Brock as the sentimental sort. Cowper thinks he's hiding something.'

'Who isn't?' Thorneycroft said. He was wondering who had insured the Omega crew. Payouts to crash victims, these days, could be upwards of $1,000,000, which might be a powerful incentive to murder.

★　★　★

Aboard *Seascanner*, Donald Porteous, with Hamish Trotter and two of his technicians, were watching a video. The screen showed

189

lumpish objects against a murky background pierced by a finger of light. The ROV was on the seabed, sending its pictures through the optical fibres of its cable. As they watched the image on the screen was veiled by a swirl of what looked like dust, and Porteous swore under his breath.

'She's hit a patch of sand,' Trotter said. 'It'll settle.' The tension in the cabin was acute. They were so close to the Black box that the pinger was sounding at maximum pitch. Trotter looked at his watch. 'We've plenty of time.'

He spoke into the intercom that linked them to the ROV controller on the deck. Nick had his own video and directed the handling of the ROV from deck level, but Trotter was the expert on marine salvage.

'Give it a few minutes,' he said, 'then move ahead slowly.'

They waited. The sand sank. The shadowy shape on the screen grew clearer in the probing beam of light. It was cone-shaped, ribbed, and it trailed a length of heavy cable.

Porteous said excitedly: 'That's the crown-skin of the main cargo deck. Can you get us closer, Hamish?'

Trotter gave orders. The ROV edged forward. Light focused on the cone, then swung across the surrounding dark. Trotter stared at the screen, his lips moving silently. He said: 'Nick. Make a slow turn, a degree to port.' The picture changed a little, stopped at a tangle of fine wires.

'Electricals,' Porteous said. The picture changed again. More spaghetti wires. The ROV seemed to climb a slope, then suddenly bucketed backwards.

Trotter muttered, 'For Chrissake hold her steady!'

Nick's voice answered calmly. 'There's a sea building, sir. The cable's reacting. I've got her now.'

Porteous jerked to his feet, waving an urgent hand. 'Wait, wait. Left of the screen, d'you see it?'

Trotter leaned to peer. 'What? Yes, by God. Nick, you have it, back a wee bit. Yes. Right. There, bingo! Black box.' The sound of the pinger filled the cabin. Trotter said: 'Lift away, laddie, it's all yours.'

They watched as the ROV was manoeuvred gently into position. The picture showed the box, partly buried in silt. The ROV's steel pincers stretched towards it, paused, closed. The beam of light now shone full on the box. Trotter snapped his fingers at the technician next to him.

'Get it on the digitizer, fax the picture to London.'

The ROV's jaws were clamped on the box now; moving it delicately, lovingly, towards the cradle that would bring it to the surface.

Porteous wiped sweat from his face. 'How long before it's up on deck?'

'An hour or so,' Trotter said. 'We have to move slow and steady. We'll shift the box from the cradle to the transport container under water, so we don't get air-bubbles building on the tape — they could deposit seawater chemicals. When we get the box on deck we'll replace the sea water in the container with deionized water. We have to keep the temperature between four and twelve degrees centigrade, until the box is safe in the lab.'

Young Lawrie was exuberant about the find. 'You said the CVR and the DFDR were lodged next to each other, sir. Now we've found one, it won't be long before we get the other.'

Trotter, who knew how widely debris could be scattered by a fall through deep water, said quietly, 'Let's hope that that's the way of it.'

★   ★   ★

The rescued box proved to be the direct flight data recorder. Porteous went up on deck to watch it lifted from the sea, cleaned and resettled in its container. Care was taken to allow no air to enter the box, and the metal tools used in the operation were demagnetized.

The container was placed aboard a naval helicopter and flown to a specially equipped laboratory in London, where the unit was once more submerged in deionized water, and the precious tape removed and dried in a vacuum chamber by regular nitrogen purging.

Only after the completion of these rituals was the tape ready to be handed over to the experts to be examined, copied, and analysed.

In the event, Lawrie was right about the second box. The cockpit voice recorder was located and lifted from the sea late on Wednesday afternoon, and subjected to the same meticulous treatment as the DFDR.

On Thursday morning, Geoffrey Waldron released the news of the double recovery to the media, which was complimentary.

'Exemplary speed,' was the comment of *The Times*.

The analysis of the tapes was of necessity a much slower process, involving the experts in discussion, and sometimes in acrimonious dispute, with a great many interested parties.

Aboard *Seascanner*, work went on to map and retrieve the wreckage of *Paloma*. Day by day the debris was pin-pointed, photographed and marked on the charts. Important pieces were lifted, hosed down, treated with preservatives and flown to the high-security Debris Centre in England. There they were placed on a full-scale floor diagram of the *Paloma*. The bare bones reunited, but never to fly again.

The four great engines were retrieved by a salvage ship, along with larger segments of frame and superstructure. Smaller pieces, mangled seats with the unused life-jackets still attached, galley bulkheads, doors, electrical conduits, fire-extinguishers, luggage and cargo, were left to *Seascanner* to raise.

One section of bodywork bore the lettering and bright logo of Omega Airlines.

No trace was found of the Dove container where the fire had started, nothing of the carton said to have been sent by James Brock to his brother David.

A squash racket was retrieved, its graphite handle almost entirely consumed by the flames, but there was nothing to prove that it had belonged to Captain Brock.

15

Mallowfield

'I thank God Lucy wasn't on that plane. That fool of a mother, letting her jaunt about the world alone ... well, that won't happen again, Lucy stays with me from now on.'

Dan Roswall had had little sleep since the disaster, and his face was haggard. Hugo Spinner, seated on the opposite side of the table, nodded sympathetically, but Dieter Engel cut short the older man's flow of words.

'Where's Gerda?' he demanded.

'Telephoning.' Dan drew a long breath, forcing himself to consider the matters on hand. 'She won't be long. Did you speak to Philbrick about the insurance?'

'Yes.' Dieter tapped the pile of papers in front of him. 'I have the details.' His gaze switched to the two men at the foot of the table. Harry Solomon had drawn his chair close to Kyle Parnell's and was talking volubly, his plump hands making agitated gestures. He had shed his jacket and his shirt was transparent with sweat.

'We'll have to keep an eye on Harry,' Dieter said. 'He's all to pieces.'

Dan said fiercely: 'For God's sake, Dieter, he's chairman of Omega, he feels responsible for all those deaths, never mind the huge financial loss.'

Dieter pursed his lips. 'Then I hope he keeps his feelings to himself. Admitting responsibility can be very expensive.'

At that moment Gerda entered the conference room. She came over to embrace Dan and sat down next to him. 'I am so sorry, my dear,' she said. 'This terrible thing.'

He patted her hand. 'Terrible for all of us. Did you book your flight?'

'Yes.' She caught Hugo's eye. 'We're on the last flight.'

Dan tapped the table to draw the attention of Solomon and Kyle.

'We'll begin, please. I appreciate your presence. I know that's difficult right now, but we have to share our thoughts and make decisions together.

'Since Monday's unspeakable tragedy, we've been thinking of the people we know, praying for their survival . . . for a miracle. An hour ago, I spoke to the head of the search-and-rescue operation. No one has been found alive, and I'm afraid what they aim to do now is retrieve the dead, not rescue the living.

'We have to face the fact that our friends and colleagues are gone. It's a time of loss. Of mourning, but we have to do more than mourn, we have to concern ourselves with the dependants of those who died, and we have to play our part in determining what caused the accident, so that such a thing can never happen again.

'My good friend Hamish Trotter is engaged in salvaging the wreckage of *Paloma*. I've spoken to him ship-to-shore, and he told me they hope to retrieve the Black boxes today. Thereafter they'll continue to lift the debris and return it to the UK. The experts will examine it for signs of explosion, engine failure, metal fatigue and the rest. Pathologists will examine the . . . the human remains.

'In short, there'll be exhaustive efforts made to find the source, the course, and the extent of the fire that destroyed the aircraft. The police and security forces will be doing all they can to establish whether or not there has been criminal action of any sort.

'Understand, all of you, that over the coming weeks and months there will be a sustained, trenchant, highly skilled investigation of everything and everyone connected with *Paloma*. As executives of Dove, we will be asked searching questions. Those questions must be answered fully and honestly. There can be no withholding of information. We have to give the authorities our full co-operation, however uncomfortable that may be. There is no other way to safeguard Dove's reputation as an agent for good.'

Dan glanced round the table. No one spoke and he leaned back in his chair. 'Good, then. Our first task must be to consider the compensation due to relatives of the victims. Dieter will report.'

Engel nodded and opened the file in front of him.

'The insurance of the Dove employees is handled by a consortium of brokers, all listed on the LSE. I have consulted with them and with our lawyer Mr Philbrick. I asked them about making immediate payouts. They advised against it, because at this stage it is difficult to decide on the amount to be paid.

'A basic payment might be one million American dollars, but the earning capacity of the victim could be a factor. If it is found that there was structural defect in *Paloma*, or pilot error, the manufacturers or the airline could face large additional claims. There would be much legal argument. Our own liability could be affected.

'You understand, only one payment is

made per person, so it is important to make the correct evaluation before one makes payment.'

'And while you debate that,' Kyle said, 'the dependants starve.'

Engel said coldly: 'In the event of financial hardship one could arrange an immediate settlement, but I must warn you not to allow sentiment to cloud judgement. Claimants can drive hard bargains. Some even study the market to file their claims in the country that offers the biggest payment.'

Dan intervened. 'So Philbrick's advice is, 'wait and see'?'

'Yes, at least until the Board of Inquiry makes its final report. That could take months, even years.'

Dieter frowned, pressing a finger to his upper lip. Watching him, Dan reflected that Dieter might be unmoved by the violent deaths of the victims, but he was as sensitive as a sea anemone to the smallest ripple in the oceans of finance.

Sure enough, Dieter said: 'Delay could be very costly. If we make payments now, people cannot make further claims, but if we wait for the Board to report, and it lays blame on us, we might face ruinous demands.'

Dan stared. 'What blame could possibly attach to us?'

Dieter did not answer at once. He gazed at a point above Dan's head.

'If, for example, the report found that we knowingly chartered an aircraft that was unsafe — '

'Unsafe? What you mean, unsafe?' Harry Solomon was stuttering with rage, his face purple. '*Paloma* was safe, we have a certificate of airworthiness, we have records of maintenance, everything in order. What you mean, unsafe?'

Dieter raised plump hands. 'In 1987 an SAA Combi plane suffered a fire in the main-deck cargo-hold. The aircraft crashed. One hundred and fifty-nine people were killed. The inquiry that followed found that Combi-type planes should be prohibited — '

'But federal authorities of the USA said Combi planes must be modified, obey new rules. We modify *Paloma*, we obey the rules. Better training for our crews, new smoke detectors, flame-resistant linings to holds, modern containers for goods. Everything has been done. God will judge me, Omega has made *Paloma* safe.'

'Which God?' Dieter leaned towards Solomon. 'Allah? Jehovah? Christ? I'd say Allah. You're a Muslim. Who knows what a Muslim might do, these days?'

'I am man of peace!' Harry was struggling

200

to rise, hand stabbing at Dieter, and Roswall banged a fist on the table.

'Quiet. Both of you. Sit down, and hear me. Your private views are not at issue here. The issue of *Paloma*'s safety will be decided by experts, which we are not, and I accept Harry's assurance that all the rules have been complied with. To return to the question of insurance. Harry?'

'We have full cover.' Solomon was breathing heavily and his lips were bluish. 'For the crew and for *Paloma*.'

'When was your last policy update?'

'Last month; and after the attacks on the USA, we increased all our cover.'

'Was there a blanket policy for the crew?'

'No. Every member could state preference, who would benefit and how. A straight payment, a trust . . .'

'So you know who benefits,' Kyle Parnell said.

'It will be on record, of course.'

'Can you get us that information, Harry?'

'It is confidential.'

'Nothing is confidential any more. The brother of the pilot, James Brock, sent a carton of goods to Captain Brock. It was packed in the Dove container.'

'So?'

'I'd like to know if James Brock inherits

under the terms of David Brock's insurance policy.'

Solomon shook his head. He said with quiet dignity: 'It is confidential. If I am asked by proper persons, I will answer.'

There was a short silence. Gerda Marcus raised her hand.

'I have a question for Dieter.' Dieter turned to face her, and she said: 'When we met here last week, you told us that the United States FBI was 'sniffing around' — I think that was the phrase — for information about tax evasion, and the use of Swiss secret accounts. We asked you to try to find out if that could involve any member of Dove. Have you done so?'

Dieter bridled. 'One does not run about asking questions. Discretion is essential in these matters. I have . . . put out feelers.'

Gerda eyed Dieter's well-manicured hands. 'With what result?'

'So far, none.'

'In other words, you don't know if anyone connected with Dove uses a secret Swiss bank account?'

He smiled. 'The point of a secret account, my dear, is that the identity of the client is not bandied about.'

Gerda looked ready to pursue the argument, but Dan lifted a warning hand. 'You were asked to enquire about Moshal, Gerda.'

'I did. The night of the accident, I spoke to Adri Romm. He's an Israeli diplomat and probably a Mossad agent. He told me that a few weeks ago Moshal sent in a report that he believed certain Arab states were sending money to Rome, it was being laundered there and transferred to secret accounts in Zurich. It would be used to buy materials that can't be bought on the open market. Adri said Moshal was asked to watch the money trail, and keep Israel informed.'

Dieter said angrily: 'You Jews are paranoid about Arabs. Always accusing Iraq. The Iraqi power was broken by Desert Storm, their war factories were demolished — '

'And rebuilt,' said Gerda furiously. 'Underground where they can't be detected. They're manufacturing weapons of mass destruction, biological and chemical weapons, Israel is the target of extremists and madmen — '

'And what's more,' cut in Hugo Spinner, 'if Moshal did as he was asked, and spied for Israel, he's made dangerous enemies, people who might well have decided to sabotage *Paloma*.'

Gerda said impatiently: 'Moshal wasn't on *Paloma*, he cancelled his flight days before, and anyway, Adri doesn't think Moshal was the target. He said we should look closer to home.'

Hugo gave an angry laugh. 'That's absurd! Closer to home means Dove or Omega. Our people don't work with warmongers.'

'There's another way of looking at it,' Roswall said. 'If one of our people crossed the same trail as Moshal did — the secret accounts, the money-laundering — that person could have become the target. *Paloma* may have been sabotaged to eliminate him.'

Kyle was watching Dieter. 'Do you know anything about funds being channelled from the Middle East, through Rome, to Swiss accounts?'

'I know it is stupid to put faith in rumours fed to us by a Mossad agent!'

Gerda said sharply: 'Adri had nothing to gain by talking to me.'

'Then why did he trouble to meet you?'

'He's an old friend.'

'You're naïve, my dear. Mossad has no friends.'

She held his gaze. 'Answer Kyle's question. Do you know anything about funds going from the Middle East, through Rome, to Swiss accounts?'

Dieter sighed heavily. 'Every country in the Middle East conducts such deals. Money comes to us from every country in the world.

Most of it is from individuals, or cartels, not from governments. I know nothing of the . . . undertaking Mr Romm hints at, but I will make enquiries.' He bowed towards Kyle. 'Discreet enquiries.'

Dan nodded. 'Very good. Hugo, what's happening in Rome?'

'Too many bloody cooks,' said Hugo sourly. 'Roman, British, embassy people, press, all stirring the pot, and the police underfoot all the time. Fermoy and Kincraig have been questioned, so have Gerda and I. The Board of Inquiry has asked for copies of our manifests and other documents, and I have that in hand.'

'You're keeping in touch with Benno Capriati?'

'Yes. He's the best of the Iti bunch. He invited us to hear the ATC tape. He gave me a copy.' Hugo laid the cassette on the table.

'We'll listen to it later,' Dan said. He waited, his eyes fixed on Hugo. After a moment, Hugo drew a paper from his pocket.

'Last night, I remembered this,' he said. 'It's a copy of a fax message that was in the carton James Brock sent to his brother.'

Dan took the paper and spread it open. He read aloud: 'Dave, re your query, the mark's not known to anyone here. I'll have it checked by the Assoc and ask around. Let you know

205

soonest. Regards. BORU.'

'Who's Boru?' Kyle said.

'I don't know,' Hugo answered, 'but I think we should find out.'

Dan passed the sheet of paper to Kyle. 'What do you make of it?'

Kyle studied it. 'David Brock wanted someone identified. He probably attached a photograph. The recipient — Boru — didn't recognize the person, but handed the photo to an association, probably someone who was familiar with Brock's world, people in aviation, air transport, perhaps a pilots' association? I can look into that.'

'Do so,' Dan said, then added: 'Be careful about it. We don't want the search to go on the Internet, not until we're sure of our own position. Harry, can you talk to David Brock's associates, see if anyone knows who this Boru may be?'

'Who, or what,' Gerda said. 'Boru could be a group, a company, a society.'

Kyle said, 'Brian Boru. The Irish king who drove off the Danes, about eight hundred years ago. Maybe Dave Brock was in touch with the IRA.' He encountered a frowning glance from Dan, and held up both hands. 'Sorry.'

Dan said: 'Hugo, did you report the fax to anyone in authority? The police, the DCA?'

Hugo reddened. 'I told Capriati. No one else. Frankly, I forgot all about it, I've had other things on my mind.' He glanced round the circle of faces. 'All right, I kept my trap shut because I didn't want Dove to carry the can.'

'What do you mean,' Dieter said. 'What can?'

Hugo made a hissing sound of irritation. 'The fax is suspicious, wouldn't you say? I questioned Brock about it and he was extremely cagey, he refused to tell me who — or what — Boru is. Brock was a maverick. We have to consider the possibility that he had information that he didn't choose to share with any of us. He may even have been involved in some illegal practice. Smuggling, money-laundering, something of that nature. I would be interested to know his financial position. If this investigation were to show that he had an income in excess of his legitimate earnings . . . ' Hugo looked sideways at Dieter, 'money in a Swiss bank, perhaps . . . then Dove would be in a very unpleasant situation. We could all find ourselves smeared by association.'

Gerda said angrily: 'You are a disgusting little man! Dave Brock was incapable of doing what you suggest!'

Hugo rounded on her. 'Disgusting, is it, to

put Dove first, to try to protect Dove? I've spent the best years of my life building up a great team, one that's effective, noble, above reproach. Dove is my only concern.'

Dan said quietly: 'It's everyone's concern, Hugo.'

'Then you should all put your mouths where your money is,' Hugo retorted. 'You should check out David Brock's finances: how much he had, and just how he obtained it.'

★ ★ ★

At five o'clock the meeting broke up and its members dispersed, Harry Solomon to be driven back to London, Dieter to continue on by ferry and road to Zurich, Hugo and Gerda to catch the last flight to Rome.

Dan Roswall and Kyle Parnell remained in the conference centre, working through piles of messages and queries that had come in during the day. After a while, Dan pushed the papers to one side.

'Can you produce a list of all the countries Dove has worked in over the past five years?' he asked. 'I need dates, names of team members, places visited, as much detail as you can find.'

'No problem,' Kyle said. 'It's all in the

memory. Why do you want it?'

'I want to give it to the investigators, so that they can check Dove's activities against known terrorist attacks for that period.'

As Kyle stared, Dan smiled. 'They'll be working on it, you know. We can save them time, and ourselves tiresome interviews. Better for us to come clean than to force them to drag the facts out of us.'

'Right,' Kyle said slowly. 'You don't believe what Hugo suggested, do you? You know how he works himself up. He gets hysterical.'

'Adri Romm doesn't,' Dan said. 'Get me that list.'

Bansford

Reg Purviss called at Badger's Sett at noon on Wednesday. It had been announced on earlier newscasts that the searchers at the site of the *Paloma* crash had found no survivors, and there was now little hope of finding any.

A red-eyed Mrs Commins met Reg at the front door.

'Such a terrible thing,' she said. 'Our Mr David and all them other poor souls. You can't 'ardly believe it, can yer?'

'No. How's James, Mrs C?'

'Bearin' up, but it's an 'ard time. 'Ardly

spoken, just sits with the telly and the books of photos. Taken the phone off the 'ook, well yer can see why, Nosy Parkers that don't even know 'im, ringin' up an' askin' questions. Newspapers even come right 'ere to the door; well, I sent 'em packin', I told 'em don't come yere where yer not wanted. Puttin' all that in about Mr James, as if 'e'd burn up 'is own brother, it's anythink for a story these days an' never mind 'oo gets 'urt. Dunno what the world's comin' to.'

As she spoke she led Reg to the dining-room where James was busy clipping items from a pile of newspapers. He looked tired and drawn, but the deathly languour of the past few weeks had gone — as if, Reg thought, the shock of David's death had shaken him from a trance.

Reg sat down facing James.

'Everyone sends messages. They all want to attend the service here. I don't suppose you've made plans?'

'Not yet. The civil aviation people phoned this morning to say there's to be an official memorial service for all the — all of them — on Sunday afternoon. Charles Wallis suggested we do a private service on Sunday morning.' James's fingers strayed to the scar on his forehead. 'That might be a good arrangement.'

'Joanna and I will be glad to help, so will Edith.' Reg pushed the newspapers to one side. 'We need to talk, James.'

As James looked at him enquiringly, Reg cleared his throat.

'Normally, I'd have waited a bit, but in view of — of all the circumstances I think we must discuss the matter now. In case there are — er — any questions.'

'What about?'

'David's will. You know I handled his affairs, I drafted the will. It's a very simple one. Some money to charities, and a few bequests to friends, but the bulk of his estate comes to you. It's a very substantial sum, James; in fact it's over a million and a half pounds, and that doesn't include the insurance on his life, which will also be very substantial.'

James was shaking his head dazedly, 'I'm not interested in the money.'

'You have to be. Tell me, did you realize what was the size of Dave's bank balance?'

'No. We both had money from our grandparents, but Dave was a big spender, he was generous to charity and to his pals.'

'He had plenty to spend,' Reg said, 'much more than he could have earned as a pilot for *Paloma*. He had investments that date back to pre-Omega days, to the time he was working for Sirius. Do you know anything about that?'

'No. David didn't talk about money, to me.'

'You don't know how he made all that cash?' James was silent for a space, then he said, 'I think it was danger money.'

'What do you mean?'

'When he was with Sirius he may have flown cargoes that were . . . a bit unorthodox.'

'You mean illegal? Drugs? Arms?'

'God, no! Dave loathed the drug trade, he'd never have touched it, and the same goes for arms-dealing.'

'So what were these unorthodox cargoes?'

'I know he transported Green Peace campaigners, and sometimes he ferried cargoes that the big companies thought were too risky: chemicals, and so on. There were a couple of jobs with animals that needed special handling, and I think sometimes Sirius accepted passengers that other lines refused.'

'Like illegal immigrants?'

'No. But people who were out of favour with the US government, or their own.' James met his friend's eyes. 'Dave was paid well because he had the skill and the nerve and the moral commitment to go into dangerous territory on difficult assignments.'

'I see.' Reg hesitated, frowning. 'You realize that all this has implications for you, James. You're Dave's heir and there's a lot of money involved. If the gutter press finds out about that — '

'They'll conclude I had a motive to kill Dave. They'll suggest I sent a carton full of incendiaries to bring *Paloma* down, in order to inherit Dave's estate.'

'Exactly. They won't say so straight out, but they may drop hints, poison people's minds.'

'So what do you want me to do?'

'Tell the truth to people who have a legal right to question you; otherwise keep your trap shut. Tell the press nothing. If they harass you, refer them to me. You don't need to worry too much. The public aren't all that gullible. Reasonable folk don't like the way you're being smeared, but I do think you should leave the enquiries to the police. Don't try to take the law into your own hands. It's a dangerous pastime.'

James nodded a little abstractedly.

'Thanks, Reg. Thanks for coming, I appreciate it.'

Reg waved a dismissive hand. 'And take some leave, why don't you?'

'I may do that. I may go to Italy. Dave had friends there.'

'Umh. Well, remember what I said. Watch your step.'

★ ★ ★

When Reg had left, James put through a call to Pia d'Ascani. He'd spoken to her a few times in the past, but had never met her. Her major-domo answered the phone and it was a minute or two before the contessa came on line. She sounded very tired.

'James? How kind of you to call. I have been wanting so much to talk with you.'

'And I with you. I waited because . . . I hoped there might be news . . . but now . . . '

'Yes.' She drew in her breath. 'We have to accept he's gone. He leaves . . . such an emptiness.'

'Contessa, in a day or two I hope to visit Rome. I'd like very much to meet you.'

'Please, yes. Please come. Come soon.'

'There's to be a memorial service here on Sunday. Do you think you might come to that?'

'No.' Her voice was emphatic. 'That would not be wise. The newspapers would make scandal. But come to Italy, James. Stay with us at the villa. You will be most welcome.'

'Thank you. I'll call again as soon as I'm

214

free to travel. I look forward to meeting you. Goodbye, Contessa.'

★ ★ ★

Back at the office in Ashford, Reg Purviss spoke to Gordon Abercrombie.

'I have a nasty feeling that James is planning some sort of crusade,' he said.

'Oh come! He's not the sort.'

'He's exactly the sort. Stubborn as a mule when his principles are challenged — and he was devoted to his brother. I think he means to go to Italy.'

'No harm in that, surely? Lovely country, perfect place for a holiday.'

'And the current target of the sensation-mongers,' said Reg grimly. 'Think of it, Edward. A pilot who made a stack of money with a questionable airline, who kept a rich, titled mistress, who died violently, perhaps as the victim of terrorists, perhaps murdered by his brother who stands to inherit his fortune. It's jam for the press blowflies. They'll make a meal of James, and of this firm. What's more, if David Brock was in a shady deal, he'll have had associates who won't like James nosing around. He could run himself into real danger.'

'I see what you mean. So, what do we do?'

215

'There's not much we can do. I've warned him to leave things to the police . . . not to talk to the press. But I know James. I don't think he'll take a blind bit of notice, of me or anyone else.'

16

'Nerves at the top?' suggested Geoffrey Waldron.

On arrival at the airfield where the wreckage of *Paloma* was being assembled, he and Thorneycroft had found themselves facing elaborate security checks. Now, searched, questioned and issued with plastic tags, they were being driven across the landing-ground in Barry Coburn's Jeep.

Coburn said shortly: 'Blore's going ballistic.'

'Doesn't he always?'

Coburn gave a sardonic smile. 'He's worse this time. Rylda's been at him, so has Radnor. They must be getting pressure from on high.'

'Tell me about it,' muttered Waldron. Every hawk in government was on the hunt. Foreign governments were yelling for information, the Home Office was demanding absolute silence, the FBI wanted an invitation to the party, and the media came uninvited. It was like trying to pick daisies in the path of a buffalo stampede.

In the back seat of the Jeep, Thorneycroft stared out of the window. The airfield normally handled freight, and at the far end a team of men in blue overalls were unloading goods from a refrigerator plane. At the opposite end a hangar had been set aside to house the *Paloma* debris. It had been provided with its own landing-strips and a parking zone.

The two great ports of the hangar stood open. Coburn parked beside the nearer of the two, and led his visitors inside. A girl at a desk checked their tags and logged their names. The three men moved past a barrier on to the main floor of the hangar.

Here there were several distinct areas of activity. To the left, near the second entry port, teams were sorting through piles of wreckage, stacking it by category. Thorneycroft saw large sections of *Paloma*'s fuselage. He recognized part of a wing. It looked clean, not burnt. There was an escape slide, almost intact; broken and twisted seats, one of them with its headrest driven down into its framework. Some of the seats were blackened by soot or oil.

In another area lay smaller fragments, pieces of machinery, tangles of wire as fine as spaghetti. A third sector contained cargo, blistered, warped, melted beyond recognition. Items of luggage stood in the fourth sector.

Waldron and Coburn studied the debris,

talking together, brisk and matter-of-fact. Thorneycroft moved away from them. He'd seen plenty of death and destruction in his time, but he couldn't share their professional detachment. To him, these mounds of wreckage represented human carnage. Looking at it he was trapped in the burning aircraft as it plunged towards the sea, smoke filled his throat and lungs, all around him people screamed and choked.

He wiped sweat from his face and walked to the far end of the hangar. Here, on the cement floor, had been painted the outlines of a Combi aircraft — cigar-shaped body, backward-sloping wings — and on this outline the pieces of *Paloma* were being placed. To one side, a number of men and women appeared to be studying certain items and marking them with cabbalistic signs. A clerk listed the results and fed them into a computer.

Some of the debris, apparently not yet identified, was carried away to a separate part of the floor.

They were rebuilding *Paloma*. Fascinated, Thorneycroft stood watching. Presently Coburn joined him.

'We're getting shipments fast,' he said. 'We'll be able to do a good reconstruction. Each item of the model is being numbered, and the heat and smoke damage to it recorded.'

Thorneycroft pointed. 'Those blackened bits at the back — that's the tail section, right? The cargo hold?'

'Umh. The source of the fire. My boys will start work there.'

'Your boys?'

'Assessors. Engineers and technicians. Avionics specialists, they're the scientists who study the development of electronic and electrical devices for aircraft. A lot of fires start because of failure in those systems. You remember the Swissair one eleven crash? That was put down to electrical faults. Then there are specialists on propulsion systems, the engines, the actual structure. That fat man over there is our Boeing adviser. And we'll have to study the maintenance records, the effects of weather at the time of the crash, and of course the aircraft's personnel.'

'It sounds like a long process.'

'Normally it is. Normally we like at least six months to make intensive tests, consult all the fundis, but the way the top brass are carrying on, we don't have months, or even weeks.'

'Can you give fast answers?'

'Not with the right degree of accuracy.' Coburn's face was morose. 'I told them, you want guesses, go to someone else. I've got my good name to protect.'

'Why are they in such a hurry?'

Coburn didn't answer at once. At length he said:

'Could be politics. Could be they're scared of a repetition. That can happen if there's a basic defect in a class of aircraft. Remember the Comet? That was metal fatigue. There was more than one crash.'

Thorneycroft looked at the metal and fibre scattered over the area. He shivered.

'So if you take your time over the tests, this could happen again?'

'Yeah, it could.'

'So what will you do?'

'Give some fast answers but make it plain they need a lot more work. Make some informed guesses, strictly not for publication.' Coburn swept a hand in an arc that covered the whole area of the hangar. 'I can make some good guesses now, from the evidence we already have. Witnesses saw *Paloma* go down and hit the sea. She didn't torch and she didn't break up before she hit the water. We've got a lot of pieces of the superstructure, some close to the main deck cargo area, and they don't have the shockwave patterns you get when there's an explosion in flight. Rome airport has sent us a copy of the ATC tape, and there's no sign on that of an explosion.'

'Will you examine the tapes?'

'Sure, but the definitive answers come from experts — here and in the USA. They'll enhance them, nurse every last sound out of them. It's not just the voices that count, it's all the sounds picked up by the mikes. Even the silences can help you to read the story of what happened.'

Coburn stooped to pick up an object from a pile of blackened articles. It was the remains of a squash racket, the frame half-eaten away.

'Graphite,' he said. 'Graphite melts at many times the temperature of boiling water.'

Thorneycroft said: 'There were rackets in the carton sent to David Brock.'

Coburn shook his head. 'Those were probably totalled. I doubt we'll retrieve them. The team on *Seascanner* have been combing the seabed for the Dove container and found no sign of it. I reckon it was completely consumed by the fire.'

Thorneycroft stared at the racket. 'Heat like that . . . God, what a way to die.'

'There'd have been a lot of smoke and lethal gases, they may have lost consciousness quickly.'

Thorneycroft brooded. 'How often is fire the cause of an aircraft disaster?'

'Not often. The first I can recall was an Air

Canada DC Nine. There were forty-six dead. The fire started in the rear john, an electric fault in the flush-motor. In 1973 there was a Varig Airlines Boeing 707, a hundred and twenty-four dead. November of the same year it was a Pan Am Boeing 707, three crew dead. 1979 a Pakistan Airlines Boeing came down in Saudi Arabia, killed a hundred and fifty-six. 1980 a crash at Ryadh, a Lockheed 1011 with three hundred and one dead. 1983 an Air Canada McDonnell Douglas DC Nine, killed twenty-three. 1987 a South African Airways Combi caught fire and came down in the sea off Mauritius, a hundred and fifty-nine dead. And now, *Paloma.*'

Coburn was staring into space, and Thorneycroft tried to recall him.

'Barry? Do you think this fire was sabotage?'

'Maybe. Saboteurs study the ways to bring down an aircraft. Fire is one way, not the most efficient. But there's a chance someone set the fire in *Paloma*'s hold and caused her to crash.' Coburn's mouth twisted. 'That, my friend, is a guess, strictly not for publication.'

Waldron rejoined them, and Coburn led them on a tour of the hangar. On the way out they passed a long line of board frames, on which photographs of the wreckage had been mounted. There was also a video room where the controllers of the debris centre could view the footage taken by *Seascanner*'s underwater ROV.

In the parking lot an army truck was waiting to convey them back to their own cars. As they were crossing the airfield Thorneycroft said:

'I'm going to the morgue. I want to hear about the first autopsies. You want to come?'

Waldron nodded. He hated this part of the job, but he felt he must show solidarity with an important member of the investigatory team.

'I'll follow you there,' he said.

★ ★ ★

The morgue where the victims of the *Paloma* crash had been brought for post-mortem was close to the debris centre, a modern block in a municipal complex. Waldron knew that there were several surgeons engaged in the autopsies. The man in charge was a Dr Hirsch: younger than Waldron expected, plump, bespectacled, and pursey-mouthed, with thinning red hair. He greeted the visitors in the entrance hall, offered a cold pink hand and a colder blue stare, and addressed Thorneycroft.

'There's a batch ready for dissection now.

You want to watch?'

'Please,' said Thorneycroft.

Hirsch jerked a thumb at a uniformed attendant standing in a doorway.

'Morris will get you kitted up. When you're ready, come to the carvery.'

He walked off. Waldron muttered: 'Charming little tick.'

'He's competent.'

'I suppose you're used to this sort of thing.'

'Inured.'

The attendant provided them with sterile suits, masks, theatre boots and rubber gloves. They were ushered into a lift that bore them down to the basement, and were admitted through a metal door to the autopsy chamber. The air stank of formaldehyde, disinfectant, and death.

Hirsch was already stationed next to the central dissection table. Brilliant overhead lighting gave his figure a surreal sharpness. He was dictating into a microphone suspended near his head. Behind him a nurse presided over an array of instruments, bags and metal containers. Behind her again, a male attendant appeared to be busy with some sort of machine.

Hirsch signed to the newcomers to stand out of the way, near the wall. They had a good view of the operating area. Waldron forced himself to look at the object on the steel table. It looked like a Sunday roast. His stomach heaved and he clamped a hand over his mouth.

Hirsch took the scalpel the nurse held out to him and made his first incision. His hands moved with firm delicacy. He kept up a steady discourse with the microphone and the nurse. Waldron gathered that he was working on a throat and section of chest. From time to time Hirsch lifted out pieces of tissue which the nurse sealed in specimen bags, and labelled.

Occasionally Hirsch addressed a remark to Thorneycroft.

'Soot in the trachea,' he said, and later, bending to peer at the scorched chest, he smiled. 'Tattoo,' he said. 'That should help.'

Thorneycroft answered: 'We need all the help we can get.'

Waldron sighed. His office was being besieged by people wanting to claim their dead. It was hard to explain to them that there were few bodies complete enough to allow quick identification. What had been recovered was an obscene jigsaw. It would take the best efforts of the orthodontists and the DNA experts to put names to the pieces.

Thorneycroft said: 'If we can find which

seat he was in, we can determine how far the fire spread.'

Waldron shook his head. 'He may have been an attendant, or one of the firemen.'

After two hours Hirsch declared a lunch break. He led them back to the ablutions room and thence to the staff canteen. Over coffee and sandwiches he waxed voluble.

'What you saw today was upper torsos and throats. They're our priority. In a case of fire, the first thing we look at is the lower respiratory passages. The soot we're finding in some of the windpipes shows the victims inhaled smoke before they died. We'll examine any closed thoracic cavities, where there's been no exposure to outside air or seawater before death. That'll tell us important things about the period leading up to the crash, and the nature of the crash itself.'

Waldron closed his eyes, gulping lukewarm coffee.

Thorneycroft said: 'The chief technical investigator at the debris centre says they haven't found evidence of an explosion.'

'I'd support that,' Hirsch said. 'The X-rays don't show foreign bodies lodged in the flesh, which is what we expect when there's an explosion. The injuries we have here suggest massive impact, that caused multiple fractures, dismemberment, evisceration. Nobody

227

survived that crash, I can tell you.'

'We have to know how they were affected before impact,' Thorneycroft said.

Hirsch nodded. 'We're running blood-tests to determine if there was carbon monoxide or dioxide intoxication.'

Waldron opened his eyes. 'If there was, does that mean the victims were unconscious before . . . ?'

'Yes. The first results of the blood-tests show a high level of carboxy-haemoglobin saturation — over sixty per cent in fact. We used gas chromatography, which gives very reliable results.'

'What does that mean?'

'It means that towards the end a lot of smoke penetrated to the passenger cabin . . . at least, the rear portion of it.'

'And the flight deck?' Waldron asked. 'If the pilots were affected?'

'I can't say anything about how far the smoke travelled. I can say that a fire generates smoke and lethal gases. Synthetic materials like seat-cushions can be deadly. The victims could have lost consciousness quite quickly.' Hirsch's cold eyes flickered. 'Not quickly enough. There'd have been a period when they choked and fought to breathe.'

'They'd have switched off the oxygen at 14,000 feet,' Waldron said, 'to starve the fire.

But this is all guesswork. The cockpit voice-recorder may help us fix the spread of the fire.'

Hirsch looked at his watch. 'And now, if you gentlemen will excuse me, I have a lot of reports to write.' He rose to his feet.

'You'll be called to give evidence at the inquiry,' Waldron said.

'I don't doubt it.'

Thorneycroft shook the pathologist's hand. 'I'll keep in touch.'

'You do that,' Hirsch said, and hurried away.

★ ★ ★

Returning to their cars, Waldron and Thorneycroft found little to say. Waldron was in a hurry to reach the open air and rid his lungs of the morgue smell. Thorneycroft walked more slowly, head bent and hands behind his back.

Oddly enough, he was not at that moment thinking about the fragmented bodies in the morgue, but about David and James Brock. One of them had piloted *Paloma* on her last flight. The other had dispatched a carton of possibly lethal goods to form part of her cargo. It was time to learn more about the brothers Brock. Thorneycroft made a mental note to phone his sometime friend and antagonist Eugene Lafayette as soon as he reached his office.

★ ★ ★

The late edition of the *Clarion* continued to feature the *Paloma* disaster on its front page.

It is not yet known, what sent *Paloma* crashing to its doom in the Corsican waters with the loss of so many lives.

Experts are considering two possible causes, namely engine defect and pilot error. It is known from the tape recording made by Rome's Air Traffic Control that at 16.21.04 the pilot, Captain David Brock, called Rome to announce there was a smoke warning from the aircraft's main deck cargo hold.

Four minutes later he called again to say there was heavy smoke in the hold but it was confined to that area and had not penetrated to the passenger cabin or the cockpit.

Despite this, Captain Brock requested permission to take *Paloma* down to 14,000 feet, the procedure laid down when an aircraft is to clear smoke from the forward section. It is significant that at this flight level, there is enough natural oxygen in the air to fuel a fire.

Expert Mr Karl Heiniger, who has headed many investigations into air disasters, has said that it is better to keep a burning plane at great altitude, in order to starve the fire and so help to extinguish it. Whether such action might have helped to save *Paloma* must be decided by stringent and skilled enquiry into all the circumstances surrounding her tragic end.'

Sir Clive Radnor, having read the story, handed his copy of the *Clarion* to Rylda Warne.

'Did you arrange this?' he demanded.

She glanced at the passage, brows raised. 'I did not,' she said.

Rylda distrusted the press, and avoided pressmen like the plague; but there were times when a word dropped into a receptive ear could produce very satisfactory results.

17

Thorneycroft and Eugene Lafayette met for dinner at a quiet restaurant in Mount Street. Their meeting carried no official blessing. Lafayette had no status in the *Paloma* inquiry nor indeed in Britain. However, when heads of departments needed quick solutions to crucial problems, they turned a blind eye on protocol.

Thorneycroft had booked a table in the bow window that had once been the preserve of Regency rakes. The Paragon's bill of fare was best of English, its wine list best of Europe. Thorneycroft waited until the second bottle of burgundy had been broached before he asked the question that irked him.

'Gene, why are our elders and betters so uptight about *Paloma*?'

'They think . . . they're scared . . . the investigation might upset the Jerusalem Accord.'

'How? What's the connection?'

'Your guess is as good as mine.'

'So what is your guess?'

Lafayette hesitated, studying the wine in his glass. His answer might be off the record

232

but it was by no means sacrosanct. Thorneycroft would use it if he had to. On the other hand, silence, right now, wasn't worth a cent.

'My guess is WMDs,' he said.

Thorneycroft nodded. That was his own gut-feeling, nothing to do with reason or the established facts. These days, it was weapons of mass destruction that made the boss-boys twitch. They were in a muck sweat about who had the nuclear bomb, who was stockpiling the material for chemical and biological warfare, and who was crazy enough to use it. So far there was nothing to link *Paloma* with WMDs, but the possibility was there.

'Is that what brings you to these parts?' he asked. He knew the official explanation for Lafayette's presence in Europe, having been given it by a toffee-nosed prat on the American desk, who, claimed Gene and his team were after US citizens, who were dodging tax and hiding fortunes in foreign accounts.

Could be true, as far as it went, but Gene's interests didn't stop at tax evasion. Certain Swiss and German banks were holding huge sums for faceless clients, some of whom were fronts for criminal organizations such as the Russian Mafia. That crowd, driven from their home sewers by Yeltsin's purges, had deployed to countries that were less vigilant. They sent their profits to European banks, and used them to finance crime in the developed world, notably the USA.

If dirty money was being moved around the world, there had to be points where it was laundered, and couriers, and safe methods of transport. Like *Paloma*?

Lafayette broke into Thorneycroft's train of thought.

'The carton that was sent to the pilot,' he said. 'Has it been retrieved?'

'No. They think it's a total write-off.'

Lafayette speared rare beef and chewed abstractedly. 'You reckon James Brock planned the fire?'

'No. The contents were checked before the carton left the UK, and again at Rome airport. No dangerous materials were found.'

'Who did the checking at Rome?'

'Omega's warehouse foreman, and Dove's manager.'

'Both insiders. Has James Brock been questioned?'

'Yes. By people I trust.'

'And?'

'They believe he's clean.'

'What about the press stories?'

'Muck-raking.' Thorneycroft saw by Lafayette's jutting lip that that wasn't good enough. He elaborated. 'James Brock's sister-in-law, Mrs Candida Woodley, showed up at our Maidstone station with the story that her late sister Clare had been unhappy in her marriage to James, and was sleeping with David Brock. She claimed that James found them in bed together, and went off his rocker. She says he wanted both of them dead, didn't try to prevent the wife's suicide, and sent his brother a boxful of incendiaries.'

'But you don't buy it?'

'The facts don't support it. Planting fire-starters in the carton couldn't guarantee David's death. Secondly, Clare and sister Candida share a history of mental instability. Clare probably made up the story of seduction to put the knife into her husband. Thirdly, James did try to stop her driving off a cliff. His prints were on the car door and on the bonnet, his footprints show he stood in front of the car and was deliberately forced backwards, and run down. She drove clear over him. He was lucky to survive.'

'He suffered severe head injuries, I'm told.'

'Yes.'

'Which might have caused brain damage? Personality changes?'

'The doctors say not in Brock's case. He's made a good recovery, he's rational, he's been cleared to return to his legal practice. He's co-operating with us. He's doing all he can to find out what caused *Paloma* to crash.'

'Does he inherit?'

'Yes, a considerable sum. He's David's chief heir, but I have to tell you, he doesn't need the money. He's already a rich man. He and David were left a bundle by their grandparents.'

'Even the rich want to be richer.'

Thorneycroft saw the gap and took it.

'David Brock did, it seems. He made a lot of money in America and the West Indies, flying for Sirius Freight. You know anything about that?'

Lafayette grinned. 'Yeah, I do. Sirius isn't a US line. It operates mostly in South America. A few years back, the owners were pally with what Washington considered was the wrong side, in Colombia and Guiana. Brock was their chief pilot, around then.'

'Did they carry cocaine or arms?'

'If they did, they never got caught. They got up some noses, just the same. Flew medical supplies, ferried people who didn't favour the regular airlines.'

'How about dangerous substances? Flammables?'

'Maybe. To make big bucks you have to take big risks.'

Thorneycroft thought that over. World

opinion was divided on who were the right people to back. One man's freedom fighter was another man's terrorist.

'Is there any chance David Brock was carrying on the bad work in Europe?' he said.

Lafayette rolled heavy shoulders, and Thorneycroft tried another tack. 'Do you know who were David's associates when he worked for Sirius?'

'No. Those tinpot lines have a changing population.'

'How about women?'

'Plenty of those. A passing trade, y'know? He laid 'em and left 'em.'

'Do you have names?'

Now Lafayette looked distinctly cagey. He shook his head. 'Tell me about the fax in the carton,' he said.

It was on the tip of Thorneycroft's tongue to ask how he knew about that, but he refrained.

'It was an answer to a request from David Brock, who it seems wanted the subject of a photo identified. The fax was signed BORU. You know anyone of that name?'

'No. Brock must've met up with some smoky characters.'

'Can you ask around, about BORU?'

'Sure.' Lafayette seemed to lapse into some private dream. Thorneycroft asked him if he wanted dessert and received a blank look. He beckoned the wine steward and ordered brandy. When it was set before them, he said:

'What's Mossad's interest in all this?'

Lafayette looked surprised. 'Same as always. The well-being of Israel and bugger the rest.' He picked up the brandy balloon and stared into it as if consulting the oracle. He said slowly: 'Maybe they pulled Moshal off that plane because they smelled something nasty — like dirty money, going where it shouldn't, to buy what it shouldn't?'

Bingo, thought Thorneycroft. 'I've wondered,' he mused, 'if they knew *Paloma* was going to crash?'

Lafayette's head jerked up. 'Hell, no! They're a hard-nosed set of bastards, but I don't see them letting a planeload of innocent folks roast alive.' He leaned forward, eyes bright and challenging. 'What's the official position on Dove?'

'I believe Radnor's people are running checks on all the Dove personnel. I'm not in his confidence.'

'And what's your own opinion of Dove?' As Thorneycroft hesitated, Lafayette persisted. 'I hear no members of the Dove executive were aboard *Paloma* when she crashed. You think they knew what was going to happen?'

Thorneycroft sipped his brandy. Caution

advised him to ignore awkward questions, but was this a time for caution? He said:

'There was one occurrence that could be significant. Roswall's grand-daughter turned up unexpectedly at Rome airport, wanting to travel on *Paloma*. Luckily her mother had blocked her credit card. There was a scene at the ticket-office, Hugo Spinner, the Dove manager, phoned Roswall, who vetoed the girl's flight and arranged for her to come home overland.'

'Could be Roswall and Spinner had foreknowledge of the crash.'

'Could. But why would any member of the Dove hierarchy want to bring down the plane that was the mainstay of their operation? Leave alone it was carrying all their skilled workers.'

'If we knew why, we'd know who.' Lafayette set his brandy-glass aside. 'Roswall has the reputation of being ruthless. In New York they call him the Rottweiler.'

'He's experienced a Damascene conversion,' Thorneycroft said. 'His son Stephen renounced the family fleshpots and went off to Africa to uplift the poor. He died there, of malaria. Roswall created Dove as a memorial to Stephen. It's by way of being a holy cow. He'd never do anything to harm it.'

Lafayette sniffed. 'Everyone has his price. Roswall's in the business of manufacturing chemicals. Chemicals are used to make poison gas, explosives, and other weapons of mass destruction. There are ready markets for banned substances in the Middle and Far East.'

'I don't believe Roswall sabotaged *Paloma*.'

'How about Spinner? He let that carton through.'

'Only after he'd searched it in the presence of an experienced cargo operator. He also alerted people to the fact Moshal had cancelled his flight. He was the one who told Benno Capriati about the carton. He spoke to David Brock about the fax that was in the carton. It wasn't his fault that Brock didn't tell him what it meant.'

Lafayette rubbed his nose. 'What kinda man is Spinner?'

'By repute he's hugely efficient, dedicated to his job. Bit of an old woman. Doesn't make friends easily; he didn't get on with David Brock. Chalk and cheese, it seems. But that's water under the bridge.'

'Who else is on the Dove executive?'

'Harry Solomon, who owns Omega Airlines. He was admitted to the London Clinic this evening. Heart problems, and I imagine a severely stressed wallet. He'll face massive

240

losses. Passenger confidence will take a helluva knock.'

'What is Solomon? British? Jewish?'

'He has a Turkish and a British passport. His wife and family live in Italy.'

'Is he Muslim?'

'Christian, he claims.'

'Who handles the Dove finances?'

'Roswall controls it. A banker named Dieter Engel, of Zurich, is the chief custodian of Dove's off-shore assets.' Thorneycroft caught a flicker of surprise in Lafayette's eyes and said, 'You know Engel?'

'We've met.' Lafayette leaned an elbow on the table. 'Who else are we talking about?'

'Kyle Parnell, the youngest member of the pack.'

Lafayette looked startled. 'Kyle Parnell of Parnell Electronics? Man, he has to be one of the richest men in the world. Rich as Roswall, maybe richer.'

'They're all rich.'

'So what are they doing in a small-time operation like Dove?'

'I'd say that Solomon, Engel and Spinner are in it for the money. Working with Roswall opens a lot of doors. Parnell is probably in because of Gerda Marcus, the last member of the group. They're lovers.'

Lafayette shook his head, laughing. 'Hey,

man, wonders never cease. He's the golden boy. She's ten years older than him and she looks like a frog.'

'Or a primitive fertility goddess. She has a certain reputation.'

'That I know. Gerda worked at the UN for a spell. We met now and then, in the way of business. She's one smart lady, speaks five languages better'n I speak English, has a nose for politics. She's a redhot Zionist, none too fond of Americans, but I guess she makes an exception in Parnell's case.' Lafayette's grin faded suddenly. 'I'll be damned!'

'What?'

'I just recalled. Gerda was involved with a guy at the Israeli Embassy in New York. Name of Adri Romm. Romm was — is — a Mossad agent. Lately he's been based in Tel Aviv, but I happen to know he was in Rome at the time of the *Paloma* crash.'

'You know why?'

'No.' Lafayette brooded for a moment, then said, 'There has to be a link. Romm, the Brock brothers, Dove's fat cats, the carton, and the fax from Boru. They tie it together. There's a link.'

Off the top of his head, Thorneycroft said: 'The Jerusalem Accord.'

'Sure, sure, in the long run everything's linked to that, if we don't make the Accord,

242

we fry in World War Three, but that's not what I mean. There's something more . . . immediate.'

'Maybe you should follow the money trail.' Thorneycroft met the big man's eyes. 'Money coming to Rome, laundered there, sent to Zurich so someone can draw on it to buy the raw materials for weapons of mass destruction. Moshal crossed the trail. Maybe you did, too.'

Lafayette's jaw muscles twitched. He stared at Thorneycroft through narrowed lids, answered at last at a tangent.

'The money flows through Rome and all the major cities. We don't get word of it. The crooks don't talk for obvious reasons, and the honest citizens . . . if they think something's going on, they don't come to us because they don't trust us. They don't trust the law any more. They just keep quiet. Folks die as a result.'

Thorneycroft leaned back in his chair. He knew they'd left the realm of hard fact and entered his realm of guesses and gut-feelings.

'You say you've met Dieter Engel,' he said. 'Can you make him talk?'

'Not unless you tell me how.'

'Maybe I can.' Thorneycroft traced lines on the tablecloth, a six-pointed star. He rubbed out the lines.

'Engel was born in 1938,' he said. 'to Jewish parents in Munich. When he was six weeks old, they sent him to friends in Switzerland, who raised him safe, well-educated, and very, very rich. His parents died in Buchenwald, and the friends adopted him.'

'So Engel's a Jew.'

'By birth only. At age twelve he opted to join the Catholic faith of his adopters. He's more Catholic than the Pope. He refuses to admit he's Jewish, won't support Israeli causes, won't even contribute to Jewish charities. He will do whatever it takes to preserve his nice, plush, Gentile identity. If you were to talk to him . . . tell him you're on the track of money coming from Middle East extremists to a Zurich bank . . . he might become quite chatty.'

'Yeah,' said Lafayette softly. 'Yeah, so he might.'

18

Rome

Captain Vincent di Maggio of the Rome police had arrived at the airport within half an hour of the declaration of the *Paloma* disaster. He had worked with Benno Capriati on other airfield inquiries, and was allowed to snatch a brief interview with him. He came straight to the point.

'Any leads?' he said. Sometimes one got lucky, a crackpot had been seen hanging round the departure bays, or some political arsehole had claimed responsibility.

But Capriati shook his head. 'Nothing. It came out of nowhere.' He broke off to yell an order to a scurrying computer clerk, then turned back to face di Maggio. 'You'll have access to our premises, tapes, records, but you'll get the rest secondhand. Britain's in charge of the investigation.'

'Not in Italy,' di Maggio said. 'We'll start with the people who work here. You got the list?'

Capriati handed him a file that contained the names not only of the staff on the airport, but also of key personnel at the offices and warehouses on the neighbouring industrial complex. Omega Airlines and Dove International were among those. Di Maggio flicked over pages to reach the list headed 'Suppliers'. It included all the concerns that placed materials aboard aircraft, everything from high-octane fuel to soap and potato crisps.

Di Maggio sighed. He was envisaging the piles of paper that would engulf his desk: depositions, false claims, expert opinions, accounts, a mass of chaff to be sifted for a few grains of fact. The investigation could drag on for months, maybe years, and like as not, at the end there'd be no firm answers.

'Better get started,' he said.

'A moment.' Capriati eyed him, chin on chest.

'What?'

Capriati jabbed a forefinger skyward. 'The big boys are screaming for quick results,' he said.

'Like always.'

'Now especially,' Capriati said, 'because of the Jerusalem crisis.'

'What's that got to do with an airline disaster?'

'Find out, and they'll promote you.'

Capriati hurried back to the control tower, and di Maggio began his wearisome round of interviews. He took Capriati's tip about pressure from the government — politicians in his view were a bunch of crooks who got their smeary hands into everything — but he found nothing to convince him that the destruction of *Paloma* was politically motivated. He decided that Capriati had picked up false vibes — easy enough, in the panic of the first hours, with every major interest in Italy sweating to shift the blame somewhere else. In a day or so, they'd fix their sights on pilot error or mechanical failure. Until then, it would remain open season.

He began by questioning the security personnel on the airport, and from there moved on to general staff. He spoke to key people at Omega Airlines and Dove International. He appointed teams to investigate the scores of firms that had supplied *Paloma*, and to question the dozens of men and women who had dealt with her maintenance and loading. Nowhere in this mass of information did he find clues to why the aircraft crashed.

At one a.m. on the Wednesday after the accident, di Maggio was preparing to go home for a shower, food and some much-needed sleep, when his belt-pager bleeped. The caller was Willi Huber, the man he'd deputed to visit the Vitagas company which supplied Omega Airlines with fire-depressants and oxygen-cylinders. Huber looked and moved like an Emmentaler bull, but there was nothing slow about his thought processes, and he was good with people. He told di Maggio that Signor Emilio Vespucci, who owned the Vitagas company, had called him to report his son was missing.

'He says his son believes he caused the *Paloma* crash, sir, he says the young man's in a suicidal state.'

Di Maggio groaned. 'Hell, Willi, papa's boy is probably sitting in some bar, getting ready to wallow in publicity. Every time there's a major disaster, some perv claims he did it.'

'I don't think that's the way of it, sir. I think you should talk to the old man.'

'Where is he?'

'At the warehouse. It's not far from the airport.'

'All right. I'll come.'

A police car conveyed di Maggio to the Vitagas yard. Lights blazed along the perimeter fence and the central block was fully lit. A uniformed guard checked him through the main gates and admitted him into the building through a door marked STAFF. Huber came to meet him, accompanied by an elderly man in a dark-blue track

248

suit. Di Maggio identified himself and the old man nodded.

'I am Emilio Vespucci.' He looked like death, di Maggio thought, the yellow skin drawn tight across the bones of his face, his scalp showing through thinning hair. One hand was pressed to his chest, the other clutched a mobile phone. His lips moved, but no words came. Di Maggio wondered if he was senile.

'You sent for me, Signor Vespucci? In connection with your son?'

Vespucci turned away, beckoning them to follow him. They crossed the concrete floor, passing storage racks where cylinders of various sizes were stored roof-high. Two guards stood duty at a security door, one watching a row of video screens, the other drinking coffee. Vespucci continued through the gate to a reception area, where there were chairs and a low table.

'Please.' Vespucci gestured and the police-men sat down, one on each side of him. Huber drew out his notebook. Di Maggio offered civilities but Vespucci wasn't listening. He reached inside the jacket of his track suit and hauled out a sheaf of papers which he thrust towards di Maggio.

'It's all there,' he said. 'Everything we delivered to Omega for that flight. We delivered on Sunday. It's all there.'

Di Maggio leafed through some ten pages of printed forms, listing halon- and oxygen-cylinders. Each item was numbered, and separate columns noted the holding capacity of each, with its appointed place on the aircraft.

Vespucci sat back, spreading his hands. 'All in order, you see? Your man here knows. If you wish to check our records you can do so at any time. You will find all is as it should be, nothing amiss.' He gave a sudden gasp and pressed both hands to his eyes. Tears oozed past his fingers and he wiped them away with his sleeve, mumbling, 'I'm sorry, I'm sorry.'

Di Maggio said quickly: 'A tragedy of such dimensions. It shakes us all.'

'No, you don't understand.' Vespucci rocked in his chair. 'It should not have happened. *Paloma* was well protected. There was enough halon gas aboard her to suppress any fire of such short duration. I told Alonso, we did not cause that accident.'

Di Maggio made an effort to steer the conversation back to the original complaint. 'Tell me about your son,' he began, but he was ignored. Vespucci beat his fist on the table.

'We did not cause the accident. We did not kill those people.'

250

'Good, then. Good.' Di Maggio decided to play it the old man's way. 'The gas-cylinders were delivered to Omega on Sunday, you say? Where? At the airport?'

'Yes. To the hangar where *Paloma* was.'

'Is the man who made the delivery available, *signor*? I will need to speak to him.'

'No, no, no. It was not a regular driver, the order was placed on Saturday night, he was not on duty. It was my son Alonso who took the order, he selected the cylinders and had them placed in the van. Next morning, Sunday, he made the delivery.'

'Surely that was unusual?'

'Not so unusual. We are not ashamed to work with our hands. The job must be properly done. We have a reputation to uphold.'

'Who placed the order? Someone from Omega?'

'No, it was Mr Spinner. Dove's manager. He insisted on installing fresh cylinders.'

'Why was that?'

Vespucci shrugged. 'Who knows? He was always nervous. On the aircraft that Dove leased, everything must be just so.'

'He didn't give a specific reason?'

'Alonso didn't say. Since the accident, there have been stories of terrorist threats. One can't tell if there's any truth in them.'

251

So Spinner didn't mention the Moshal scare, di Maggio thought, or if he did, Alonso didn't quote him.

Aloud, he said: 'Where were the cylinders kept, overnight?'

'Locked in the van, in our secure garage bay.'

Di Maggio glanced at Huber, who gave a faint nod. All of this would have to be verified.

'At what time did your son drive the van to the airport?'

'Nine o'clock Sunday morning, after mass.'

'Who took delivery of the cylinders?'

'Mr Kincraig, the maintenance chief. You see his signature there, on the forms. Mr Fermoy and Mr Spinner were also there. The cylinders were loaded directly on to the aircraft.'

Di Maggio knew this to be the fact, having covered the ground exhaustively with Kincraig, Fermoy and Spinner. He leaned closer to the old man.

'*Signor*, I have to ask you if by any chance the materials you supplied to Omega — the cylinders or the gases they contained — could have been defective?'

'They could not.' Vespucci's voice was vehement. 'It is not possible, unless the defect occurred outside our sphere of control.'

'How can you be sure?'

'Because we keep the law, Captain. The rules are strict, we are bound to make checks, the inspectors see that we do so. Those cylinders left here in perfect condition. We are not a manufacturing firm, you understand, we don't make the gas, we don't pack it, we are agents and sellers of the finished product.'

'Where is the gas . . . er . . . put into the cylinders?'

'France.' The old man rubbed his hands slowly down the front of his track suit. 'Marseilles, at the factory of Lecomte, Conrad et Cie. Very efficient, totally reliable. We have never had a complaint. Before he signed the contract with them, Alonso went in person to inspect their plant. Since the accident, they have run tests. They found no defective materials. I told Alonso, we have no cause to reproach ourselves, what happened to *Paloma* was not our fault. He wouldn't listen to me. He was like a madman, pacing up and down, he wouldn't talk to me or his mother, he sat watching the television, listening to the radio. He made phone calls. He was crying. It was terrible to see him so.'

The old man rocked to and fro, his head strained back. Di Maggio laid hold of his wrist and Vespucci shuddered and sat still.

'I wanted to call a doctor,' he muttered.

'Alonso wouldn't allow it. About six o'clock last evening, he made more calls.'

'To whom?'

'I don't know. He went to his own room. He screamed to us to leave him alone. After two hours, he ran from the house. He took his car, drove away. We waited for him to return. To telephone. Nothing. His mother thought he might have come here, so I drove across. She stayed home, with our daughters.'

'When did you call the police?'

'At midnight. I told them I was afraid for my son, that in his state of mind he might suffer an accident. Injure himself. The people at headquarters said it was too early to declare him missing, he could be with friends, or at the airport.'

Or drowning his sorrows in a bar, di Maggio thought. He said: 'Did you check the airport?'

'Yes. They put out calls for him but he didn't respond. At half past twelve I called Mr Huber, he came over. He called you.'

'I see. Signor Vespucci . . . has your son ever experienced depression?'

'No. He is sensitive, he is caring. This terrible disaster — he feels he should have prevented it. He kept saying, 'I'm the guilty one. I'm responsible'.'

At that moment, di Maggio's pager

sounded. He put it to his ear, moving away from the table.

'Di Maggio.'

A brisk voice rattled off a name and police rank. 'We found Alonso Vespucci, sir. He's dead. Shot through the head.'

'Where was he found?'

'In his car at the Castello parkade. It's down near the Garibaldi Bridge. I reported to Central. They said to inform you, and Huber — '

'Huber's here with me. We'll meet you at the parkade in . . . ' di Maggio glanced at his watch, 'fifteen minutes.'

He turned back to the table. Emilio Vespucci was watching him, crouched in his chair, his arms hugging his chest. Di Maggio leaned to grip a shoulder as thin as a child's.

'I'm sorry, Signor Vespucci. I'm afraid it's bad news. They have found your son. He has been shot. He's dead. Let me arrange for someone to take you home.'

Emilio clamped a hand over his mouth. He looked not shocked but resigned, infinitely tired. He said:

'No. I will come with you.'

'Better not, sir. There's nothing you can do. Better go home to your wife and family, they need you.'

'First I must see my son.' Vespucci

struggled to his feet. He thrust aside the hand that Huber held out to him.

'I will go to my son,' he said.

He walked with them to the police car. Di Maggio sat with him in the back. Huber climbed into his own battered Citroën. Siren wailing, they raced across the dark city to the riverside parking garage.

London

A copy of di Maggio's report on the death of Alonso Vespucci reached Thorneycroft on Friday morning. An hour later he took it to Geoffrey Waldron, who read it, frowning.

'Have you been able to discuss this with di Maggio?' he asked.

'Yes, I wanted to get his own views. He seems to be concentrating on the Vitagas angle.'

'Which is?'

'Vitagas supplies halon- and oxygen-cylinders to the Omega aircraft based in Rome. Technically the firm is owned by Emilio Vespucci, but the old man is semi-retired. Day-to-day management rested with his son by his second marriage, Alonso. There are three daughters by his first wife, who's now deceased.

256

'At one o'clock on Wednesday morning, di Maggio was called to the Vitagas warehouse by Huber. Emilio had reported his son as missing, in circumstances that suggested he might intend to commit suicide.

'As you know, Spinner of Dove ordered fresh supplies of halon and oxygen for *Paloma*, on Saturday night. Apparently the order was handled by Alonso himself. He delivered the goods to the Omega hangar at the airport on Sunday morning.'

'Unusual for the manager to act as delivery man?'

'Well, the order came in late. Spinner's an old woman, by all accounts. He was set on ensuring maximum security on the flight.'

'With reason, it seems. Who took delivery of the stuff?'

'Kincraig, with Spinner, Fermoy and Alonso as witnesses. On Monday evening, when the news of the crash came through, Alonso became extremely disturbed. He rushed to the airport and tried to talk to Capriati and other people at Air Traffic Control, but they were naturally too busy to attend to him. He spent that night trying to contact various key people, Spinner included, without success.

'He tried to reach both Fermoy and Kincraig. Fermoy told him to get lost.

Kincraig said the same, though more politely.'

'And Spinner?'

'He was up to his eyes, trying to deal with enquiries from relatives of the victims, the press, the authorities.'

Thorneycroft paused, looking at the report. 'It's a pity the young man didn't get more co-operation. He spent Tuesday at home, watching the reports about *Paloma*, making phone calls, growing steadily more upset. Demented, his father said. He blamed himself for the accident.'

'Could he have caused it?'

'Di Maggio doesn't think so. The gas-cylinders are handled under very strict rules. Checks by arson experts find no evidence that the goods supplied to *Paloma* were tampered with, or defective. Emilio Vespucci tried to convince his son that no blame attached to him or anyone else at Vitagas. Alonso couldn't be convinced, and at six o'clock yesterday evening he made further phone calls. Two hours later he left the house in a hurry. Didn't return, didn't phone to say where he was.

'His parents were so worried about him that at midnight they called police headquarters. When that had no result, they called Huber, who brought in di Maggio. Di Maggio and Huber interviewed old man Vespucci at his warehouse. While they were there, a call came in to di Maggio, to say Alonso had been found dead in a parking garage near the Garibaldi Bridge.

'Emilio insisted on going to the scene with di Maggio and Huber. He identified Alonso's body. Di Maggio has established that other witnesses beside the Vespucci family thought Alonso was in a very depressed frame of mind. Apparently, when he left home he drove straight to the Garibaldi Bar, down on the river bank, and stayed there drinking. The barman described him as depressed and nervous. When the bar closed, he went and sat on a bench outside. The owner of the bar, who lives upstairs, saw him sitting there at one-thirty. When he looked again, later, Vespucci was gone.'

Waldron picked up the report.

'Di Maggio says here Alonso must have walked two blocks along the river to the parkade where he left his car. He was found in the driver's seat, shot through the right temple at point-blank range. The gun, a Biretta, was found on the floor of the car. His prints were on it. Who found him?'

'The nightwatchman at the parkade heard the shot. He called the alarm company and went up to the third floor, found the body in the car. The police arrived fast, and paged di

Maggio at Vitagas. Emilio insisted on viewing the body. He identified his son, and the car.'

'How about the gun?'

'Didn't know anything about it. Rome are trying to trace it.'

Waldron sighed. 'It looks like suicide, doesn't it?'

'The pathologist who made the initial examination thought that was the likely answer, given Alonso's depressed state of mind. We'll get the detailed autopsy results in due course.'

'Why, if the gas-cylinders were not defective, would the man feel guilty enough to kill himself?'

'He took the order, loaded it, delivered it.'

'That's not enough to drive a man to suicide.'

Thorneycroft tilted his head. 'Not a man in his right mind, but reliable witnesses, including his father, say he wasn't acting normally. He was hysterical, frantic . . . '

'Suicidal?'

As Thorneycroft remained silent, Waldron said uneasily: 'You think it might have been murder?'

'I don't know. Di Maggio didn't suggest foul play.' Thorneycroft rubbed a hand over his jaw. 'We lack evidence,' he said, 'and we don't have time to find it. We need a miracle.'

Waldron frowned into space. 'Vitagas,' he murmured. 'Halon cylinders. Fire-depressant. No smoke without fire. Fire is the key.' He pulled a telephone towards him and hit buttons.

'Miracles I can't do,' he said, 'but I can find you evidence, plenty of it. Tape-recordings, computer printouts, forensic reports on the bodies and the debris, cargo manifests. Collecting the material will take a few days. Then we'll be ready to get together with Barry Coburn.'

'For what, precisely?'

'To recreate what happened to *Paloma*,' Waldron answered.

19

On Friday morning, James called his office and asked to speak to Reg Purviss.

'I had a letter this morning,' he said, 'from the Directorate of Civil Aviation. It said the official search for survivors had been called off.'

'Yes.' Reg sought for words. 'That doesn't mean . . . one can't yet presume . . . '

'That Dave is legally dead? I know.'

'They'll hold an inquest. I'm afraid we have to go through the process before we can begin to . . . to settle the estate . . . '

'That's unimportant. What I wanted to tell you . . . there's a service in our church, on Sunday. Charles Wallis says it will be for Dave.'

'We'll be there. If there's anything we can do . . . ?'

'No. Thanks. I'll see you on Sunday.'

James spent the rest of the day in David's flat in Slough. He went through the desk and cupboards, checking that everything was tidy, accounts paid, no business left unfinished. He found everything in order.

No reference to Boru.

By six o'clock he was back at Badger's Sett. He poured himself a drink and settled down to study the third of Dave's photograph albums.

It covered his last year with Sirius Freight. There were a lot of pictures of aircraft, scenery in a jungle area, a peasant village. Some of the inhabitants carried enormous backpacks, others were armed. There were pictures of Sirius crews, taken in crummy bars, or at work on a small airfield. There were also some fine landscape shots. Dave was a skilled cameraman.

In the middle of the album, James found a set of snapshots that differed both in quality and location. Six people figured in them. They had evidently been on holiday together, in a country where there were rolling hills, long beaches and luxurious buildings. The three men and three women of the party appeared on a patio, beside a swimming-pool, and on a private beach. They obviously knew one another well, they laughed a lot, and clowned about. They took turns acting as photographer.

James fetched a magnifying glass and examined the fuzziest of the pictures. Five members of the party stood together on the patio. Arms linked, they grinned at the camera — all except Dave, whose gaze was fixed on the woman standing next to him.

James knew her face.

Beneath the photo was a line of printed names, and a brief caption.

'Last happy day,' it read.

★   ★   ★

The service at Bansford on Sunday was packed with people, many of whom had known Dave since childhood. Charles Wallis said in his address:

'We are here to salute someone we dearly loved.'

When the service was over, Reg Purviss lingered to talk.

'I did tell the Woodleys,' he said. 'I'm sorry they weren't here.'

'I didn't expect them to be,' James said.

'Bloody people.'

'They spared us the hypocritical crap.'

Reg considered his friend's set face. 'The paper said there's a memorial service this afternoon, up in London. If you'd like company, I'd be happy to drive you.'

'No. I'm better off alone. It'll be a lot of pompous breast-beating. The only reason I'm going is because there'll be people I need to talk to.'

Reg eyed him uneasily. He found James's

state of mind very worrying. Certainly, in the space of a few weeks he'd lost his wife and his brother, both in ghastly circumstances. Grief would be understandable, rage, even, but James seemed to be in the grip of a sort of cold purpose. On some secret warpath. That could be dangerous. There'd be a lot of press at the service this afternoon, including reporters from the yellow press. If James chose to tangle with them, it would be all over the papers tomorrow.

'You should go easy, James,' he warned. 'Leave people to do the jobs they're paid for. Don't take the law into your own hands.'

James smiled. 'All I want to do is set up a meeting,' he said.

★   ★   ★

The memorial service for the *Paloma* victims was held in the New Holland Technikon Hall. James arrived well before time. A policeman waved him through the fringe carpark to an inner area reserved for relatives and dignitaries.

The foyer of the building was already crowded. James edged through to a gallery stairway, climbed a couple of steps, and scanned the area. The person he sought had not arrived. He stepped down and reached

265

for the official invitation in his pocket. As he started towards the door of the hall, he felt a tug at his sleeve, and turned to see the face of the man who'd spoken to him at the airport, the day of the accident. Someone's father, the flight engineer's father, Oakley, was it?

'Oakley,' the man said. 'Len's dad. You're Mr Brock.'

James shook the outstretched hand. 'I remember. Is your wife here with you?'

'No. She wouldn't come. Couldn't face it. We went to our own church, Friday night. People there, they know us. Knew Len.'

'Yes.'

'Tell you something.' Mr Oakley's mouth trembled. 'I'm sorry I came here. All they want to do is tidy things up. Get rid of us. There was a copper came to see us, Thursday. Said they'd found Len, would I go to the mortuary to identify him. But when I got there, it wasn't his body. It was just, like, the top of him. They said they'd been able to identify him by his teeth. Omega, they had the records, y'see, and they matched. They said it would be all right to bury him soon as the coroner gave permission. Permission. What's the coroner know about us? What we're going through?' Mr Oakley drew a long breath, staring at James. 'And your brother? Did they find him yet?'

'No.' Darkness, surged in James's mind, black as the deeps of the sea.

'I suppose they had to ask me,' Mr Oakley said. 'I suppose they're doing their best. So many dead.' He put a hand on James's wrist. 'I read what they said about you in the *Clarion*. Nasty, I call it, wicked what they'll print these days. If I was you I'd take them to court, I'd go to the law.'

'The law came to me,' James said.

'What? The police? Never! I hope you put a flea in their ear!'

'Actually I was glad of a chance to give them the facts.'

'You're right. That's what's needed. A bit of plain talk. The truth. We have to know what happened to my boy and your brother and the rest. Rose and me, we've made up our minds, we won't let things slide. We don't like this offer of early settlement. They won't be rid of us that way. We want a full inquiry, and once it starts, we'll be there, the both of us — as you will, I'll be bound.' Mr Oakley gestured towards a group of people standing near the entrance. 'That man in the grey suit, he's in charge of the investigations. Geoffrey Waldron. He's the Assistant Director of Civil Aviation. His picture was in the paper. Well all I say is, he's going to have to answer some questions himself before he's very much older. You and I will see to that, eh, Mr Brock?'

The old man nodded and shook James's hand, and moved away. James surveyed the crowd again, and this time saw the face he wanted. He raised his voice.

'Captain Gascoigne.'

The man turned towards him; tall, lean, with a long face and high-standing wings of wiry hair. He stared, then moved towards James. His expression was uncompromising.

'I'm James Brock,' James said. 'David's brother. You phoned me. You said if there was anything you could do . . . '

'I did, yes.' Gascoigne's eyes were still watchful. 'How did you know me?'

James drew a photograph from his pocket. 'You're in this picture. Can you identify it?'

Gascoigne glanced at it. 'Sure. It was taken when we were on holiday in the Bahamas.'

'So you know all these people?'

'Yes.'

'This one.' James indicated the woman standing next to David. 'Can you tell me how to reach her? I need to talk to her. It's very urgent.'

Gascoigne considered. He said: 'She's here, somewhere. If I find her, I'll introduce you.'

'Not in this crowd,' James said. 'There's a pub not far from here, the Happy Hour . . . '

'I know it. I'll bring her there, after the service.'

'I'd like to talk to you as well. You know there've been stories in the press that the crash was due to pilot error?'

'I know. It's rubbish. Dave was a great pilot.'

'Someone's looking for a scapegoat,' James said. 'Do you have any idea who that might be?'

Gascoigne's mouth twisted. 'Just look around and take your pick,' he said.

★　★　★

The encounter was observed by a fat woman in a purple caftan, and her thin silvery companion. The woman was smoking a Turkish cigarette, and the man fanned the smoke away with distaste.

'That's James Brock over by the stairs,' he said. His voice was resentful. 'He's talking to that Gascoigne fellow.'

'Edward Gascoigne of the Pilots' Association.'

'What's he want with Brock?'

'Probably he wants to express a proper sympathy on the death of a colleague.'

'That I don't believe. They're cooking up something. You should keep an eye on them,

Rylda, particularly Brock. He's the sort of busybody who thinks he can do our job for us. If you let him get to key witnesses like Gascoigne, he'll muddy the water. Cloud the issue.'

'Mix the metaphors.' She flicked her still-burning cigarette into the sand-tub at her side. She wished she could dispose of Clive Radnor as easily.

'Brock is serving a useful purpose,' she said.

'As what, I'd like to know?'

Rylda Warne smiled. 'As bait to draw the newshounds,' she said.

Detective Inspector Gamage and Sergeant Fay Cowper, though off duty, had chosen to attend the service. They waited in an inconspicuous corner of the foyer, a few yards away from James Brock.

'We're wasting our time,' Gamage said.

Fay Cowper shook her head. 'She'll come.'

'Why? She hates Brock's guts.'

'That's why she'll come.'

'To do what?'

'Watch him. Think what she can do to spite him.'

Gamage gave her an impatient look. Fay would never accept that a police inquiry was concerned with facts. She had this thing about putting yourself in another person's shoes, guessing how they felt, why they acted the way they did.

'You're saying she's a nutter,' he said.

'Yeah. Like her sister. Brock's wife.'

Gamage blew out his cheeks. If Candida Woodley and Clare Brock were nutters, they'd probably lied about a lot of things — like that David Brock had tried to get into Clare's bed, and James wanted David dead. And if they'd lied, if James had no reason to hate his brother, no reason to send him a boxful of incendiaries, then . . .

Fay's elbow jabbed him sharply in the ribs, and he jumped.

'What?'

'Over there,' she said softly.

He followed the direction of her gaze. Candida Woodley was moving slowly through the throng of people. Her face was pale and set, her lips pressed together. She was watching James Brock and the man he was talking to. For a moment it seemed she meant to break in on their conversation, but she halted some way from them and sat down on a wooden bench.

She sat quietly, her hands folded on her pigskin handbag, her feet neatly together. Her body swayed gently to some inner rhythm, like a snake lured by a charmer's flute.

John Thorneycroft was already in the hall. He'd been given a seat in the centre block, seven rows back, a little behind the row reserved for the Dove top brass. They took their places soon after he did, and he studied them quietly.

Daniel Roswall wore a dark suit and a sober tie. He sat with arms folded, his big head bent forward, the body language of a man not wanting attention. Still, people turned to stare at him. Roswall had the kind of magnetism that can't be switched off at will.

Dove was Roswall's brainchild. He'd created it, he loved it, he wouldn't deliberately destroy it; unless, of course, he loved something more. Like money? Maybe the Roswall billions weren't enough? One of those tycoons — Rothschild, or was it Rockefeller — when asked how much was enough, answered: 'Just a little bit more.'

Harry Solomon wasn't present. He was still in the London Clinic. Hard to see why he'd want to destroy his own aircraft. He'd collect the insurance, but as Gene Lafayette said, that wouldn't restore public confidence in his airline. It could go bust. Airlines did, these days.

Hugo Spinner was at Roswall's left. Sleek, well-tailored, and fidgety as a cat on an ant-hill. Twice he muttered into a mobile phone, and after each call he leaned towards his boss as if to make a report. Roswall listened without comment. He seemed to be treating Spinner with a sort of weary tolerance. Spinner had the reputation of being nervy, a fuss-pot. On the other hand, Dove's success suggested he had business acumen and the capacity for hard work.

Next to Spinner, and studiously ignoring him, was Kyle Parnell. He was casually dressed in tan slacks and a tussore shirt. His thick fair hair was caught at the nape of his neck in a fancy clasp: amber, it looked like, the sort of thing a girl might wear. There was nothing girlish about Parnell, though. He was well muscled and looked to be in peak condition. He sat with legs outstretched, crossed at the ankles, one elbow hooked over the back of his chair. Once he turned and stared directly at Thorneycroft. His eyes held an amused challenge. Thorneycroft had seen that expression before, the look of a man who liked to buck authority, who took risks for the rush that gave him.

Gerda Marcus was next to Parnell. She said something to him and he straightened up, and put an arm round her shoulders. The gesture was possessive and reassuring. Gerda leaned back and closed her eyes. Lovers, thought Thorneycroft, and they don't care who knows it. An odd couple, to the casual eye, but these unlikely liaisons had been known to outlast marriages made in heaven.

He wondered about Gerda's role in Dove. Gene said she was an ardent Zionist, so the boiling-pot of the Middle East was home to her. Dove had sent missions to Israel's enemies, in the past. Did Roswall's millions uphold Israel's cause? If not, would Gerda serve on Roswall's executive?

Gene would watch Gerda's links with Adri Romm. Romm would be aware of that fact. At the moment he seemed to have vanished off the face of the earth. If Gerda tried to reach him, that would be picked up by the surveillance team.

The other member of the Dove executive who was absent today, was Dieter Engel. He was in Zurich, minding his own business, which was the accumulation, safe-keeping and exploitation of big money. Engel and Roswall were spiders at the centre of very big webs. The filaments of those webs touched others. Tear one, the effect was felt round the world.

It all came back to money.

Lafayette was following the money, putting

pressure on Engel and others like him, without success as yet, but time would tell. Thorneycroft rolled his head to ease taut neck muscles. The Jerusalem Accord was due to be signed in six days.

Time was something he didn't have.

★ ★ ★

Lafayette and Todd sat in the gallery that overhung the rear of the hall. It was full of people who couldn't lay claim to a reserved seat. Rubbernecks, Todd said contemptuously, and Lafayette laughed.

'So what are we?'

Todd sniffed, and pulled a sheet of paper from his pocket. 'This came as I was leaving the office.'

The big man read the two-page fax and handed it back.

'Nothing new. Doesn't get us any further.'

'It shows he had a lifestyle way beyond his stated earnings.'

Lafayette flapped a dismissive hand. 'He inherited big bucks from his granddaddy.'

'Say what you like, Gene, my gut tells me someone at Dove was involved.'

'Forget your gut, man. Bring me facts, names to work on, maybe I'll oblige.'

'I intend to pursue my enquiries.'

'On your time, not mine.' Lafayette took a packet of Camels from his pocket, gazed at it longingly, and exchanged it for a stick of gum. Todd eyed him resentfully.

'Your little pal Natalie . . . what was she after, Monday?'

Lafayette looked blank, and Todd persisted. 'She asked if you'd heard from the NCIC and you said you hadn't. What was that about?'

'She wanted help in tracing a missing person. A personal matter. If you want to know more, ask her.'

'I did.' Todd's face reddened. 'I was tactful.'

'Naturally.'

'I said it was a question of national security.'

'And what was her answer?'

'She said, if she thought national security was in my hands, she'd emigrate to Antarctica. She called me a peeping Tom.'

Lafayette grinned. It was a fair description of Todd's investigative methods, but you had to admit, he sometimes got results.

★　★　★

The foyer was jam-packed. Hartley Blore, at his unctuous worst, ushered the Queen's representative to a place of honour at the front of the hall. Religious dignitaries and

276

guests from the diplomatic corps took their places.

Lesser lights waited their turn, bunched round the entrances to the hall. James joined the group of victims' relatives, at the central door. The queue was quiet, unlike those to left and right, where representatives from the airlines, the firms that built aircraft engines, the major insurance companies, exchanged greetings and guarded opinions, and the media people worked on the pictures and stories they would use tomorrow.

At twenty past two, solemn music began to flow through the complex, and ushers arrived to conduct people to their seats. As James moved forward, a hand grasped his elbow. 'Mr Brock? I'm Geoffrey Waldron, of Civil Aviation. We spoke on the phone. I want to express in person my deepest sympathy at this time.'

James murmured a response. Waldron was towing him through the crowd, along the aisle, talking as he went.

'I have a favour to ask of you,' he said. 'Our salvage ship has retrieved the Black boxes, we have the cockpit voice-recorder, and the Air Traffic Control tape from Rome. They cover the messages to and from *Paloma*, from the time of take-off to the moment of the crash. Would you consent to listen to the tapes? We need to have positive identification of Captain Brock's voice — it's obscured at times by other voices and background noise.'

They had reached the front of the auditorium, and Waldron stopped and turned to face James.

'As David's brother, you can make the identification, and also perhaps shed light on what he said, the nuances of his voice. It must seem a strange request . . . a cruel one to make of you . . . but I assure you that your help would be of great value to us in our investigations.' There was urgency as well as apology in Waldron's appeal.

James said: 'When do you want me?'

'Could you make tomorrow morning at ten-thirty? I know it's very short notice . . . '

'Ten-thirty's fine. Where do I meet you?'

Waldron fished a card from his inner pocket. 'It's near Southampton Row,' he said. 'It's easy to find.'

The crowd was pressing round them now, and Waldron stepped back, indicating a row of reserved seats. 'Any one of these,' he said. 'I'm most grateful, Mr Brock. Most grateful.' He started to move away, but James put out a hand.

'One moment. I need a favour in return.'

'Of course, if it's in my power.'

'I need an introduction to the head of Dove

278

International, Daniel Roswall. Can you arrange it?'

Waldron hesitated. Brock seemed mild enough, but appearances could be deceptive. He'd sent the carton that might have started the fire in *Paloma*'s hold. He could be an arsonist and a mass-murderer. Even if he was innocent, it might be a mistake to put him in touch with Roswall. The two of them would be key witnesses in the forthcoming inquiry. Any suspicion that they were in collusion could skew the court's findings.

On the other hand, Thorneycroft didn't seem to place either Brock or Roswall high on his list of suspects. It had been his suggestion that Brock be asked to listen to the tapes.

Waldron temporized.

'Mr Roswall's in the audience. I'll get a message to him that you're anxious to meet him. The decision's up to him.'

James in his turn produced a card. 'These are my numbers. I'm on leave at the moment. My mobile will always reach me.'

'I'll do what I can.'

'Thank you. I'll see you at ten-thirty tomorrow.'

★ ★ ★

The service was long.

James stood and sat with the rest of the audience, joined in the hymns, listened to the addresses and the prayers. Felt nothing.

All the words of comfort, all the fine tributes to the dead, were like flowers strewn on a coffin. Marks of respect that meant nothing to the dead.

The organ pealed out the introduction to the final hymn.

The King of Love my shepherd is. Not *Crimond*, the other one. Dave loved that hymn, a great psalm, he used to say, with two great tunes.

The audience rumbled to its feet.

When I was a little kid, James thought, I believed it was a song about Dave. I thought he was the shepherd.

Perverse and foolish oft I strayed
But yet in love he sought me
And on his shoulder gently laid,
And home rejoicing brought me.

Like the time at Waterloo when I was swept along by the crowd, I was terrified and crying, and Dave found me and picked me up and carried me.

A good shepherd, a good brother. A good pilot.

The best.

The best, even in death's dark vale. It wasn't pilot error, not an error of skill, but perhaps an error of judgement? Something Dave had done or not done, something he should have told, something he knew but kept to himself.

Dave always tried to shield the people he loved.

He shielded me because I was in hospital, because Clare died, he didn't want to worry me, so he kept whatever was troubling him to himself.

'He should have told me,' James said. 'He should have had the sense to tell me. I could have helped.'

'Are you all right?' The woman next to him was leaning a pink balloon face to peer at him. The music had stopped and everyone was sinking back into their seats.

James sat down. The blood was pounding in his head, but not with the uneven surge of the past few weeks. He felt calm. Powerful. He knew exactly what he had to do. He had to meet Gascoigne and the woman; listen to the tapes; talk to Roswall. Then he'd go to Rome.

He smiled at the pink-faced woman. 'I'm fine,' he said, and for the first time in weeks, he meant it.

20

The area round the Happy Hour pub had succumbed to development. Victorian houses and shops had given way to sprawling building-sites, vast holes, a massive crane. During the week, the workmen came for their beer, but on Sundays the place was deserted.

James carried his lager to a table in an alcove. Gascoigne joined him ten minutes later. He was alone, and he answered James's look of enquiry with a jerk of the head.

'She's making a phone call. I'll get our drinks.' He came back from the bar with a Guinness, a vodka-lime, and a bowl of chips, set them on the table and dropped into a chair.

'Where did you find that photo?' he demanded. His eyes, pale grey and shining under heavy brows, made James think of an icy sidewalk. Watch your step, Brock.

'It was in one of Dave's albums. He kept a lot of stuff in the attic at his flat. Lucky he never threw it out.'

'Lucky for some.' Gascoigne took a pull at his tankard. 'You could be opening a can of worms.'

'What do you mean?'

'If Dave was involved in some kind of scam.'

'He wasn't. I knew him. So did you. You said you could vouch for him.'

'As a pilot.'

'I can vouch for him as a man.'

Gascoigne expelled a long breath. 'Yuh. Well. As a friend, I'll go out on a limb for Dave. But I don't want her involved. She's been through enough.'

'She can't avoid being involved. She handles the insurance for the Omega crews.'

'You know what I mean.'

Before James could answer, rapid steps sounded on the tiled floor and Natalie Lomax appeared in the arch of the alcove. Her hair was windblown and she smoothed it back with both hands as she slid into the chair next to James.

'I'm sorry I'm late. I had to call my office.'

'Thank you for coming,' James said.

She gave him a hard stare. 'Ed said you wanted to talk to me, that it was important.'

James drew the snapshot from his pocket and laid it on the table. She glanced at it and said sharply,

'Who gave you this?'

'No one. It was in one of Dave's albums. Do you remember when it was taken?'

'Of course. We were on holiday in the Bahamas.'

'Enjoyable, I gather. Dave wrote under that picture: '*Last happy day.*' He was in love with you, wasn't he?'

'Did he tell you so?'

'No. It's there, in his face, the way he's looking at you.'

She sighed, and tension seemed to go out of her, leaving her soft and vulnerable.

'He wanted to marry me,' she said, 'but I chose Greg.' She touched a fingertip to the photo. 'Greg Lomax, that's him there. We were married two months later, in the States.' She turned to meet James's eyes. 'Why am I here, Mr Brock?'

'Dave wrote all your names under the picture. Your maiden name was Brian. He had a nickname for you, didn't he? Boru, for Brian Boru?'

Her mouth tightened. 'I don't have to answer your questions. The only claim you have on me is that I work for the firm that insured David.'

'Then surely it's your job to find out how and why he died, who killed him?'

Her face paled. 'There's no proof of any crime.'

James said harshly, 'Dave's dead, Mrs Lomax, and I mean to know the truth about his death. You can start by telling me about the fax he sent you. You owe him that much.'

Gascoigne leaned forward. 'Lay off, Brock, she doesn't have to take any of this.'

Natalie held up a hand. 'It's OK, Ed. He's right, I owe Dave and I owe him.' She reached into her handbag, took out a large envelope and handed it to James. 'That's a copy,' she said. 'The original's in the vault at my bank.'

The envelope contained two faxed pages, the first one a letter.

Boru, my dear,
For old time's sake and because you know I mean well, try and identify this ugly mug for me. I thought at first he was from my Sirius days, but I haven't been able to place him, and I don't have him in my photo collection. Maybe Greg's old pals could help, or the pilot organizations. Ask around, will you? It's urgent, so let me know as soon as you can. Thanks honeychile,
Always yours,
Dave

'When did you receive this?' James demanded.

Her lashes flickered. 'About . . . three weeks ago.'

James turned to the second page of the fax. It was the photograph of a man, a three-quarter shot taken from the left. It showed thick dark hair that curled over a high-domed forehead and concealed the ear. The skin of the bull neck was scarred and pitted, but that of the face seemed unnaturally smooth, no lines round the eye or mouth. The one visible eye was deep-set and lustreless. The lips were drawn back in a grimace, a snarl rather than a smile.

'Do you know who he is?' James asked. Natalie was staring into space, and he touched her wrist. 'Mrs Lomax?'

She jumped, and blinked.

'Have you identified the man in the photo?'

'No, I have not.'

'In his fax, Dave mentioned Greg's pals. Who were they?'

'They weren't his pals, they let him die!' Her voice was savage. She made an effort to control herself, clasping her hands in her lap. 'Greg worked for the Federal Bureau,' she said. 'He was with the section that dealt with illegal immigrants. Dangerous ones, criminals. He was kidnapped by a gang that wanted two of their people released from prison. Their demands were refused. The FBI tried to negotiate. Greg was killed. His body was found on a rubbish dump.

'When Dave sent me that fax, I was furious. I hated him for reminding me of that time. I didn't want to talk to those creeps who let Greg die. And I was scared. I didn't know what Dave was doing. That man's face . . . ' she glanced at the photograph, 'it's a bad face, it scared me. I thought, let Dave do his own dirty work, it's none of my concern.'

'But you made it your concern, didn't you?'

She nodded. 'I was in the States, on business. I showed the photo to some folks I know in the American Pilots' Association. They checked their files, but they had nothing on the man.

'That left the FBI. There was someone I knew, an old friend of my father, Eugene Lafayette. He's with the division that tracks down tax swindlers who send money to offshore banks. I called Gene's office, and found he was on a case in Europe. As soon as I was back in England, I got in touch with him, and last week, when he came to London, we met and I showed him the photo. He said maybe the NCIC could identify it, so I gave him a copy. I didn't show him the letter.'

'What is the NCIC?'

'The National Crime Information Centre. They have a computer in Clarksburg, West Virginia, which connects with police departments right through the States. Law enforcement personnel can ask for information about people who are missing, endangered, abducted. The questioner feeds in data from relatives, doctors, dentists, opticians — photos, if possible. You can even ask for help in identifying bodies, or body parts. They deal with millions of enquiries. I hoped they'd come up with something, but when I saw Gene on Monday last, he said they'd drawn a blank. They'd had the photo enhanced, but there wasn't enough supporting data, and they said the man had probably had surgery to his face.'

'Are you sure this Gene is telling you the truth?'

She shot him a glance. 'I did wonder. I had an almighty showdown with the Feds, after Greg's death, I gave interviews to the press. I guess the Bureau doesn't like me too much. But Gene's different. He's a family friend. He wouldn't lie to me.'

'OK, so you trust him. Does he trust you?'

She frowned. 'He asked me a lot of questions, like who sent me the photo, where did he live, what was his job. I said I couldn't

288

discuss that, it was confidential. Gene didn't argue. I think he trusts me.' She looked at James and he saw that her eyes were bright with tears. 'I have nightmares, now. I keep thinking, if I'd moved faster, if I'd done more, Dave might still be alive. I let him down.'

'No,' James said. 'You did the best you could, more than I did.' As she watched him uncertainly, he said: 'Dave never told me about this. I was in hospital, and I'd just lost my wife. I suppose he was trying to spare me. He always tried to protect the people he loved.'

'Yes, he did. You in particular. What will you do now?'

'Go on looking for the man in the photo.'

'The FBI failed, what chance have you?'

'They may not have failed, they may still be working on it.'

Gascoigne laughed. 'Pigs might fly.'

James turned to face him. 'What about your Pilots' Association?'

'I'm working on it,' Gascoigne answered. 'There's not much chance anyone can identify a bad photograph of a man who's had his face altered, but I'll keep trying.'

'What about the gang that kidnapped your husband?' James asked Natalie. 'You said they were illegal immigrants. Do you know where they came from? What racket were they in? Were they terrorists?'

She shook her head. 'They ran drugs. I never heard them described as terrorists.'

'Were any of them ever arrested?'

'Not to my knowledge.'

'So the case . . . your husband's kidnapping and murder . . . it's still open?'

'I suppose so.'

James picked up the two faxes. 'May I keep these?'

'Yes, of course.'

He twitched a paper napkin from the holder on the table, and wrote his address and telephone number on it.

'If you hear from Lafayette, will you let me know? I'll be moving about tomorrow, but I'll be home in the evening.'

She nodded silently.

James slid the faxes and Dave's holiday snapshot into his pocket and got to his feet.

'Thank you both for your help,' he said. 'I'll be in touch.'

Gascoigne sketched a salute. Natalie sat without moving. There were more people in the pub now, a couple of men sitting at the bar, and a group of students at a corner table.

James made his way out to the car park. To left and right stretched the excoriated land. The giant crane reared its dinosaur neck against a sunless sky.

It was like a bombsite, James thought, like the empty site of the Trade Centre. Whole cities could look like this, if they didn't get it right in Jerusalem.

He wondered if Natalie Lomax had told him the truth.

And if she'd lied, would Ed Gascoigne back her up?

They were still in the pub, no doubt talking it over, making up their minds which way to jump.

He climbed into his car and drove back to Bansford.

★   ★   ★

As he reached Badger's Sett, the telephone was ringing.

He sprinted from garage to hall and reached the phone in time.

'Mr Brock?' The voice was deep and resonant, a tiger's purr. 'This is Daniel Roswall of Dove International. Geoffrey Waldron said you wished to speak to me.'

'I'd like to meet you, Mr Roswall. I need information about your organization.'

'What sort of information?'

'It's probably confidential. That's why I want to talk to you in person.'

'A moment.' Roswall appeared to be consulting someone. When he spoke again, the purr was closer to a growl. 'Can you come here to my home? It will save time.'

'Yes, I can. When?'

'Tomorrow afternoon? Half past three?'

'Fine. Can you give me directions?'

Roswall gave them. At the end, he said: 'I must tell you, Mr Brock, that all of us at Dove held your brother in high esteem. He was a fine pilot and he was liked by everyone.'

'Not everyone,' James said. 'Someone hated him enough to kill him and all those others.'

'Isn't that a rather wild statement?' Roswall sounded shocked. 'We don't know it was sabotage.'

'My brother believed that someone close to Dove was involved in a criminal racket.'

'Indeed? Then why didn't he speak to me, or to his principals at Omega, or the Rome police?'

James said flatly: 'He didn't know who he could trust.'

'I presume he trusted you; did he tell you of this . . . concern?'

'No. I was in hospital with severe head injuries, he didn't want to involve me.'

'So how did you learn of this suspected racket?'

'We can discuss that when we meet.'

'Very well.' Roswall seemed to hover between anger and amusement. 'Is there anything else I can do for you?'

'Yes. I need information about *Paloma* — the aircraft, the crew, the cargo, and I would be grateful if you would give me the CVs of everyone employed at Dove, and the missions they've been part of. Especially to places in the Middle East.'

'May I ask what you propose to do with this mass of data?'

'I'll use it to help me find whoever killed my brother.'

'And, as you put it, 'all those others'. They were my people, you know.'

'Yes. I imagine that's why you're prepared to see me.'

Roswall was silent for a moment, then he said abruptly: 'I'll give you all the material I can. Is there anything else?'

James considered. 'Could you arrange for the other members of your executive to be there tomorrow?'

'Why should they be?'

'To help me understand the mass of data.'

'Umh. I can promise that Gerda Marcus and Kyle Parnell will be here. Our manager, Hugo Spinner, left for Rome early this evening. Dieter Engel is in Zurich, Harry Solomon is ill, in the London Clinic.'

293

'Thank you, I'll be glad to meet Mrs Marcus and Mr Parnell.'

Roswall sighed. 'To be honest, I think you should leave the inquiry to those who have the skill and experience to handle it.'

'There's no time,' James said.

To his surprise, Roswall did not contradict him, merely saying: 'We'll talk tomorrow. Half past three.'

The receiver went down with a snap.

James sat thinking for a while, then went to the study and despatched a number of e-mails. The task completed, he opened the gun-safe set in the wall and lifted out a Smith & Wesson automatic. He loaded it, slipped a spare clip of ammunition into his pocket, and went upstairs to bed.

294

21

London

James left Bansford early on Monday
morning. The air was cold, and the sun rolled
red through a heavy ground mist, so that
trees and buildings seemed to burn with
infernal fire.

He drove slowly, needing time to think. He
had no illusions about the people he would
meet today: first Waldron and Thorneycroft,
then Roswall and his cronies. Each group had
its private agenda. Neither would give a shit
for the wishes of an outsider. Waldron
claimed he wanted to identify Dave's voice,
and gauge his state of mind at the time of the
accident. What in God's name did he think
the pilot of a burning plane would feel? And
why invite Thorneycroft to the party?
Thorneycroft was a police dog appointed to
sniff out criminals.

As for Daniel Roswall, everyone knew he
was obsessed with Dove; it was his invention,
his memorial to his dead son. Roswall would
do whatever it took to protect Dove. If there
was no proof of pilot error, he'd look for

someone else to blame.

Like, for example, J. Brock.

So how did J. Brock save his hide?

One option was to take Roswall's advice, quit and run.

Unacceptable.

Another was to play possum, say nothing, let them all sweat for answers; but if he gave nothing, he'd get nothing. If he was obstructive, he'd be obstructed, and Dave's killer would go free.

There was no safety in silence. Dave took that road, and he was dead.

The third option was to act as if there were no tigers in the jungle, tell everything he knew, step on to open ground, wait for the killer to come after him.

The letters he'd posted, the e-mails he'd sent, would safeguard his knowledge, but not his person. If he was attacked, other people could take up where he'd left off and see justice done, but that was second prize.

First prize was staying alive.

The car rocked as a massive pantechnicon roared past. James glanced at his dashboard. Two miles to go before he reached the slip road for London.

He was sweating like a pig. Scared witless, that was the truth of the matter, scared of responsibility, of failure, of dying.

Especially dying.

He took long deep breaths. At the hospital they'd explained about the terrors. Post-traumatic shock syndrome was the big name for them. You had this accident, your wife died, you suffered near-fatal injuries, and the syndrome got you.

You relived the accident, you woke up screaming night after night. Then you went into denial. You told yourself none of it ever happened. You didn't speak about it to anyone, because you needed to stay in your little cocoon. After that came the anger, the big why me? And finally you faced the fact that you had to find a way to go on living.

All true, except no one mentioned there could be a second trauma more terrible than the first, which landed you in a morass of death and loss and fear. The pundits had no formula for that. You had to find the way through for yourself.

You had to decide to stay in the deal, or leave the table; take the London road, or give it a miss and carry on to Ashford, where you had a secure job and friends, and a future.

The mist on the road paled and thinned. The traffic formed two streams, the right-hand lane for Ashford, the left for London.

James bore left.

The address on the card given him by

Geoffrey Waldron was 7, Mill Yard, Cutpurse Lane, Holborn. Mill Yard proved to be a cobbled square enclosed by Victorian brick buildings, number 7 occupying the northern side. Across its bricked-up first-floor windows ran a signboard, COOLIDGE LABORATORIES.

James climbed a flight of stone steps and rang the doorbell. An android voice responded and the door swung back, admitting him to a lobby that looked like a giant sterilizer. Walls, tiles and reception desk were grey. There were no pictures or flowers. The receptionist matched the décor, silver hair and nails and an aseptic smile.

She studied James briefly, and nodded.

'Take the lift, Mr Brock. Top floor, third door on the right, Mr Waldron is ready for you.'

And I, thought James grimly, am ready for him.

Waldron met him as he stepped out of the lift. He seemed out of temper, and as they walked along the corridor, he said abruptly:

'I hope you won't mind if there are other people present today? Robert Abercrombie from the forensic science laboratory has done a transcript and analysis of the cockpit voice-recorder, a great job considering he's had so little time. Thorneycroft you know about. The others are Mrs Rylda Warne and

298

Sir Clive Radnor from the Home Office.'

'What's their interest in the tapes?' James asked.

'Politics.' Waldron sounded less than pleased. 'Time was when we ran an investigation, but the War on Terror's changed that. Now, an air disaster has a ripple effect on NATO, the United Nations, every diplomat in the world wants a finger in the pie. Our Home and Foreign Offices have to keep everyone informed, see there aren't any international incidents. That said, you have a right to privacy. If you say the word, I'll send them packing.'

James hesitated. He resented the intrusion. It would be bad enough listening to Dave's voice, sharing his last few minutes of life, without having strangers around: but if they were people of importance, they might be of use to him.

'Let them stay,' he said.

Waldron nodded, and opened a door. The room they entered was lined on three sides with machines: computer equipment, two huge television screens, video-recorders and players, and a number of devices James didn't recognize. The fourth wall was covered with enlarged photographs, diagrams and charts. The air in the room was neither hot nor cold, there were no draughts, no smoke; it was an

299

atmosphere designed for the well-being of the machines.

Three people stood in the centre of the room, watching one of the television screens. Waldron ignored them and indicated a gnomish man in a laboratory coat who was working at a laser printer.

'Robert Abercrombie,' he said. The man turned, gave James a brisk nod, and resumed his task.

The screen-watchers looked round as Waldron spoke, and he led James forward.

'Sir Clive Radnor,' he said, indicating a pink-cheeked, paunchy man with a pettish mouth. Sir Clive took James's hand between both his own.

'My dear Mr Brock, may I offer you my deepest sympathy on your loss, and my gratitude to you for allowing us to be here on what must be a most stressful occasion. It is my earnest hope — '

'Mrs Rylda Warne,' interrupted Waldron, moving to indicate an immensely fat woman in a dark-blue caftan. Her fat, thought James, looked as hard as rock. Bumping into that bosom would be like hitting a submerged reef. Her face was broad with full white cheeks, her nose was small and hooked, her eyes large and brilliant.

Meeting her luminous stare, James saw

powerful intelligence, a watchful vigilance, but no shred of compassion. This was a natural predator, a hawk with talons stretched. As if aware of his recognition, she dropped her gaze and murmured some phrase of sympathy. Her mouth twitched in what might be annoyance or a cynical amusement.

'Dr John Thorneycroft,' Waldron said.

The man holding out his hand to James was above average height, spare and tough-looking. His eyes were very dark, their expression hard to read. Someone had broken his nose for him, at some time.

James said: 'I saw you at the memorial service. You were sitting just behind me.'

'So I was.' Thorneycroft smiled, and the smile made him look more approachable. 'Inspector Gamage told me you were observant. It's a good quality in a witness.'

'Am I one?'

'Oh yes. Gamage also said you were helpful to him and Sergeant Cowper. A free and frank discussion, he said you had.'

Was anyone ever completely free and frank with the police, James wondered? He doubted Thorneycroft was the man to lay all his cards on the table.

He looked at Waldron. 'You want me to listen to the tapes,' he said.

Waldron nodded. 'Sit here, Mr Brock.' He indicated a chair opposite a row of tape-recorders, and sat down next to him. Radnor, Mrs Warne and Thorneycroft took their places.

'I must explain,' Waldron said, 'that the board of inquiry has invited Coolidge Electronics Laboratory to work on all the tapes relating to *Paloma*, so that we have the fullest possible picture of the aircraft's last half-hour. There are four tapes in all. Three of them — the digital flight data recorder, the cockpit voice recorder, and the quick access recorder, were recovered from the wreckage in the sea by our salvage vessel, *Seascanner*.

'I won't trouble you with the DFDR and QAR tapes. They're concerned with technical stuff relating to the aircraft and its handling, the experts will interpret them for us. What we want you to listen to is the tapes that record the in-flight conversations aboard *Paloma*.' Waldron looked at James. 'You'll hear your brother, and other members of the crew, and also a lot of background noise that the mikes picked up.'

'Right,' James said. 'May I stop the tape, listen to a part of it again if need be?'

'Certainly. Abercrombie will stop it any time you give the signal. What we want, above all else, is accuracy.'

James nodded. 'You mentioned four tapes. What's the fourth?'

'The Air Traffic Control tape,' Waldron answered. 'It's the recording made at Rome airport — the other half of the plane-to-land link. The main voice on it is Benno Capriati. Head of Rome ATC. I suggest we run that tape first. It sets the course of events, from take-off to the time Captain Brock reported the smoke alarm in *Paloma*'s hold, and on to the final messages exchanged. Once you have the overall picture, we'll run the CVR tape.

'I want you to listen to your brother's voice on both tapes — to identify it every time it occurs. That isn't always easy. *Paloma* was fitted with hot-microphone systems. The mikes on the flight deck picked up all sounds there, not just the pilots' voices. At times, particularly near the end of the tapes, there's a confusion of sound. It's hard to tell who's speaking — but you, knowing your brother's voice so well, can give us the most accurate answer possible.'

Waldron tapped a small box attached to the arm of James's chair. 'You see this button? I want you to press it each time you hear Captain Brock's voice. The signal is linked to the machine over there, which carries an accurate timing of everything recorded on the tape. By comparing your signal with our record, we can confirm that it was David speaking, or even pick up words and phrases we missed.

'Once we've heard the ATC and CVR tapes, we'll do a repeat run without breaks, and I'll ask you to do something more difficult, and that is, tell us what you believe was David's state of mind at each stage of the flight. Was he calm, agitated, was his voice normal or muffled, did he have breathing problems, physical pain, mental confusion? Did he panic?'

As James started to speak, Waldron said earnestly: 'Please, I know how hard this must be for you, but it's a matter of great importance, national importance.'

'I've already said, I'll do it.'

'Good then.' Waldron drew a long breath. 'We've made printouts of both these tapes. They may not be accurate in all respects. I'd like you to take copies away, and study them. You'll see that they're set out like a radio script: the time of each speech, hour, minute and second, is in the left-hand column. The name of the speaker, where known, follows, then the words spoken. There are interpolations that describe other sounds, as for example the ringing of the smoke-alarm bell.

'When you study the tapescript, see if anything strikes you, anything we missed, any anomaly, anything that could help us understand what happened to *Paloma* last Monday.'

James held out his hand for the transcripts and laid them on the low table in front of him.

'I must emphasize,' Waldron said, 'that we've made no cuts in the tape. There are periods when there's no communication between *Paloma* and Rome. Be patient, and listen. Maybe, as I say, you'll pick up something we missed.'

He picked up a remote control and started the ATC tape. David's voice, precise and cool, began to recite the pre-take-off cockpit checks.

James pressed the button on his monitor.

Paloma took off, climbed. James sat quietly, head bent to catch the phrases that reported airspeed, course, altitude. When a muffled voice announced that the aircraft had reached the height of 26,000 feet, he held up his hand.

'Again, please,' he said.

The tape was rewound a fraction and replayed.

'Not Dave,' James said.

'We believe it was the co-pilot, Rossi.' Waldron restarted the tape. The screen before them showed a time of 16.21.04. David spoke sharply: 'Roma. Roma. This is Omega one-niner-seven, do you read me?' He was acknowledged and said: 'We have a problem. A smoke-warning from the main-deck cargo-hold. We are proceeding on emergency checklist for main-deck cargo smoke. We are assessing the position in the hold. I will report to you as soon as possible. Over.'

Rome answered: 'Roger, Omega. We will await your report.'

There followed voices speaking Italian, high-pitched and indecipherable. Then, more clearly: 'Benno. PAN! PAN!'

James signalled, and the tape was stopped.

'Do you know who gave the PAN signal?' he asked.

'Capriati's second-in-command,' Waldron answered. 'He was giving notice there was an emergency, serious but short of a mayday signal.'

The tape resumed. Background voices, a spell of silence, then David's voice calling Rome. Told to go ahead by a deep authoritative voice. Capriati, evidently well known to David.

'Chief,' David said, 'our fire-fighter reports heavy smoke in the main-deck cargo-hold. The probable source is one of the portside containers at the rear of the stack. The fire-fighter and his assistant are in the hold

306

and will try to locate and extinguish the fire.'

Capriati asked if the smoke was confined to the hold, or had penetrated to the passenger cabin or flight deck. David replied that 'as of now' it was confined to the hold. There was another pause, the murmur of voices off-mike. Then David again:

'Roma. Request clearance for an immediate descent to flight level one four zero.' Capriati gave the clearance, hesitated, then asked if Omega 197 wished to declare a full emergency.

'Affirmative,' David answered.

Capriati asked for *Paloma*'s exact position and flight details, and Rossi gave them.

David asked what was his nearest suitable airport and Capriati told him, Rome. 'Marseilles has a ground-crew strike,' he said, 'also gale-force winds. Advise you return to Rome.

Then came the first long silence. Four and a half minutes, interminable. James stared at the screen. The time signal clicked steadily on. He wanted to stop the clock, turn time back. He wanted to shout some warning, anything.

16.30.23.

Dave called Rome for the third time.

'We've located the source of the smoke. It's

307

in the rear portside container, main-deck cargo-hold. Our fireman is dealing with it but there's been a small amount of smoke leakage to the passenger cabin. We're moving them forward.'

A burst of sound, voices shouting, drowned out David's voice. Capriati asked for *Paloma*'s present altitude, and David said it was one four zero. 'We are operating the checklist for smoke evacuation.'

Capriati gave the course to be followed to Rome, David acknowledged it. Then there came a confusion of sound, someone shouting. James flung up a hand and Waldron stopped the tape.

'The noise you hear is aboard *Paloma*,' he said. 'The cockpit mikes must have been left on, instead of being switched over to Rome.'

David's voice overrode the babble, yelling something about circuit breakers. Then: 'Ted? Ted do you read me? We have circuit breakers down. What is the temperature . . . '

His voice disappeared in a vast surge of sound.

Rome again, Capriati's voice, hoarse with tension.

'Omega one-niner-seven, this is Roma, please respond.'

Beside him a voice said: 'What is it, are

308

they opening the entry doors?'
Capriati kept calling, over and over again.
There was no answer.
The time was stopped on the clock.
16.32.25.

22

Rome — Police HQ

Vincent di Maggio hated Mondays and he hated paperwork. Mondays brought paper-work, like the mound of stuff on his desk right now. When the internal phone on his desk rang, he snatched up the receiver and snarled, 'What?' in a voice to deter all but the desperate.

The man on the front desk was not deterred.

'Captain,' he said, 'Signora Vespucci is here. She insists she must see you.'

'Not possible. I have too much to do. Make an appointment for tomorrow.'

'Sir, she won't leave, she says if you won't see her she'll go to the Chief. The newspapers.'

Di Maggio swore, looked at his watch and snapped: 'Bring her in. Find Lamberti and tell him to get here, fast.'

The woman who arrived minutes later with di Maggio's duty sergeant was like Mrs Noah: short, busty, her greying hair drawn to the top of her head and skewered with hairpins. She was dressed in black: suit, stockings, shoes, a massive black handbag. An old-fashioned mourning-brooch containing a twist of dark hair was pinned to her lapel. Di Maggio rose to greet her.

'Signora Vespucci, how may I help you? I fear I have very little time . . . '

She sat down in the chair facing his. Lamberti retreated to a seat by the wall, notebook in hand.

'I won't keep you long,' she said. Her voice was hoarse and her eyes bloodshot, all tears exhausted, di Maggio guessed. Her fingers rose to touch the brooch. 'I have come to tell you my son did not kill himself.'

Di Maggio opened his mouth to speak and she raised thick fingers to silence him.

'Alonso would never do such a thing. Suicide is a mortal sin. He loved his family and he loved God. He would never have killed himself.'

'*Signora* . . . when the mind is disturbed by a great disaster, the normal restraints may fall away. Religion and family feeling may go by the board.'

'I know that. I also know Alonso did not shoot himself. He was murdered. You must treat his death as murder.'

'We are naturally pursuing every avenue.' The phrase sounded trite in his own ears, and he sighed. 'According to your husband, your son was greatly distressed by the loss of the aircraft. He felt in some way responsible.'

'He did not kill himself.'

'Your husband believes he did.'

Anger burned in the woman's eyes. 'Emilio sees as the world sees,' she said. 'He thinks of what people will say, the damage to our name and to his business. A man's immortal soul is more important than money, or reputation.'

Di Maggio ran a hand through his hair. 'Others beside your husband have testified that Alonso was extremely upset — in fact, hysterical. He went to the airport, he tried repeatedly to speak to officials there, he said several times that the accident was his fault. But we have ascertained that the canisters he delivered were in good condition, there was nothing wrong with them, the Marseilles suppliers vouch for them. They were full of halon gas, and the Vitagas checkers assure us they were correctly stowed at your ware-house, the airport loaders confirm they were properly placed aboard *Paloma*. There was no negligence, no error. Your son was in no way responsible for the tragedy that occurred.'

'He had too much money.' Signora Vespucci seemed to be pursuing her own thoughts. 'He was careless about money. I knew that. I should have warned him to take care, but I saw no danger . . . until the man came.'

Di Maggio felt a prickling of the scalp.

'What man?'

She blinked. 'Excuse me?'

'The man you said came. Who was he, when did he come?'

'I don't know his name. It was about two months ago. It was the night my youngest grandson played in the soccer match. All the family went to watch him, except me and Alonso. I was in bed with a sore throat, and Alonso had work to do, at home. About nine o'clock there was a ring at the back door. Alonso went to answer it. He brought the man through to the hall. I looked down from the top of the stairs. I heard Alonso say in an angry way: 'Why have you come here, I told you not to come here.' The man said: 'It was too much to leave over. I have to deliver it tomorrow.' Then they went to the office and shut the door. I couldn't hear any more. About fifteen minutes later, the man left.'

'Did you see his face?'

'Not clearly. It was raining and he wore a hat pulled down, over his eyes. I didn't know him.'

'A business associate, was it? Perhaps your son didn't like a customer bothering him after hours?'

She stared at him with shadowed eyes.

'I asked him who the man was, I asked him why he was angry. Alonso said it was nothing for me to worry about, but I did worry. I felt something was wrong. I said: 'Is he a crook? Do you owe him money?' Alonso laughed, and said I mustn't think such nonsense, it was honest business, to help charity. So I said: 'If it's honest, why did you shout at the man?' Alonso said: 'I don't want him coming to the house, you know how papa is about charity workers coming here.' That is true, Captain. Emilio gives to charity, but the donations are made by the business, not the family. So I believed what Alonso told me, but then, the night of the crash . . . '

She broke off, and di Maggio saw tears well in her eyes.

'Yes?' he prompted. 'That night?'

Her lips moved soundlessly as she struggled for calm. She said: 'He saw he'd made a mistake.'

'About what, *signora*?'

'Someone. Something.' She pressed her hands together. 'He was like a madman. He said: 'I killed all those people.' He wouldn't listen when we told him it wasn't his fault. He tried to talk to people at the airport, he came home and made many phone calls. No one would listen. No one answered. About six o'clock on Tuesday evening, he made one last call.'

'Who to?'

She turned a blank gaze on him. 'I don't know. He used his mobile. He went into another room, I couldn't hear what he said. Perhaps he made an appointment. He left the house about eight . . . He drove off, very fast.'

'He went straight to the Garibaldi Restaurant,' di Maggio said. 'We checked the times. He stayed there drinking until late. Then he walked a couple of blocks to his car.'

She shivered. 'To meet the person who killed him.'

She began to rock her body to and fro. Di Maggio signed to Lamberti to pour her a glass of water, and she drank it and set the glass aside.

Di Maggio said: 'Have you told your husband all this?'

'Yes. He said I was imagining things. He forbade me to speak of it to anyone. He said: 'Alonso is dead and we can't bring him back. For the sake of our daughters we must let things rest. There must be no more scandal'.' She turned to gaze at the window where rain had begun to streak the summer dust. 'Emilio left the Church many years ago. He does not believe in the immortal soul.'

Di Maggio remembered a time, how old

was he, fourteen? — when his mother propelled him up the steps of the village church, her voice hissing in his ear: 'Sinners like you will burn in hell, Vincenzo.' He couldn't recall the sin, only the terror in his mind. He spoke aloud now, his father's comforting words.

'God is merciful.'

Signora Vespucci gazed at him hollow-eyed, uncomforted. She rose to her feet.

'I've told you all I can,' she said. 'Alonso made a mistake. It proved to be a very bad mistake and he felt terrible remorse. He tried to put things right, but before he could do so, someone shot him dead.' She laid a hand on her breast. 'These things I know to be true.'

'True, perhaps, *signora*, but not proved. Without proof that a crime has been committed, I can do nothing.'

She stared at him for a long moment, and then said quietly:

'You will do what is in your nature, Captain, as I will.'

Gathering up her handbag, she left the room. Di Maggio watched her stocky figure plod along the corridor, a black-clad Mrs Noah who saw no rainbow in her rain-filled world.

Lamberti came forward.

'What's she mean, she'll do what's in her nature? What's she after?'

'High Mass for her son's soul.' Di Maggio was rummaging through the stack of files on his desk. He found a computer printout and spread it open on his blotter. He began to whistle through his teeth.

Lamberti, knowing the signs, stirred uneasily.

'Sir?'

'Yuh?'

'You don't believe her?'

Di Maggio leaned back in his chair. 'I told her we were pursuing every avenue. I was wrong. She's opened up a new one.' He turned the printout so that Lamberti could see it. It was the list, provided by Nokia, of the numbers called by Alonso Vespucci on his mobile phone, the night of the crash.

Lamberti frowned. 'We checked them all. They were all no replies.'

'Exactly, and we allowed that to persuade us that Vespucci committed suicide. He felt responsible for the crash, he felt terrible remorse, he tried to reach people in authority to talk about it, they were all too busy to speak to him. In despair he sat drinking alone for several hours and then blew out his brains. Nice neat theory, *hein*? Solves our case for us.'

'His own parents say he was acting like a lunatic.'

'All right, we accept he was in distress, weighed down by guilt, but why, Lamberti? What was he guilty of?'

'Vitagas supplied the fire-depressant cylinders to *Paloma*.'

'And every check, by our own arson experts, by the Marseilles factory, by Vitagas itself, shows that those cylinders were in prime condition, correctly filled, sealed and stamped, transported under secure circumstances, properly installed on the aircraft. The installation was supervised by Vespucci, Omega Airlines' chief engineer Iain Kincraig, warehouse manager Andrew Fermoy, and Dove manager Hugo Spinner. All experienced men.'

'Even experienced men make mistakes.'

Di Maggio slammed a fist on the printout.

'If Alonso Vespucci had thought there'd been a cock-up with the gas-cylinders, he'd have been calling the Marseilles manufacturers, the shippers, his own warehousemen. The numbers he called last Monday and Tuesday don't have anything to do with those people. He called top brass at Da Vinci Airport, at Omega Airlines, at Dove International. He left messages on their answering machines, asking them to call him back. They didn't

318

— couldn't — because they were focused on *Paloma*, organizing the rescue operations, informing relatives, they had their hands full.'

'I don't see how what the old lady said changes anything.'

'Her story suggests a new angle, doesn't it? A man came to the Vespucci's home a couple of months ago, someone known to Alonso but not to his mother, a man who talked about a large amount of money . . . '

'We don't know it was money.'

'Well, a large amount of something valuable, which had to be moved urgently. 'Too much to leave till tomorrow' the man said.'

'Vespucci told his mother not to worry. He said it was charity work, nothing dishonest.'

'Maybe he believed that, at the time; but after *Paloma* crashed, he saw he'd made a mistake, one that contributed to the crash. He went to the airport to tell them about it, drew blank, came home, made phone calls. There are two telephones in that house, but he used his mobile, probably wanted to speak without his family hearing. He left the same message everywhere. 'Call me back'. At eight, he went to the Garibaldi, sat drinking, waiting for someone to call him. No one did. Finally he decided to go home. Walked to his car two blocks away. Someone met him there, sat in the car with him, talked, realized that Alonso was about to spill his guts, and shot him dead. Put Alonso's prints on the gun and dropped it beside the body. Slam-locked the passenger door and walked away, leaving us to form our suicide theory.'

Lamberti rubbed his nose. 'Why did he go to the Garibaldi? It's way off his home beat.'

'The place he usually met the mystery man? The place he expected him to come that night?'

Lamberti declined to theorize. 'So what do we do now?'

Di Maggio's mouth twisted. 'What's in our nature, son. We make enquiries, check the *signora*'s story, try to find the man who called at the Vespucci's house. Recheck all the calls on that list, and speak to the recipients, again.' He began to press buttons on the intercom. 'Forensic must go over Alonso's car with a fine-tooth comb, see if they can find traces of recent passengers. And tell Gina to get in here, I have to send a report to England.'

★ ★ ★

James leaned his elbows on his knees and closed his eyes. Sweat trickled down his temples and his hands were ice-cold. He fumbled for a handkerchief and wiped his face.

Someone far off said: 'Too much for him . . . wait a little . . . '

He sat up straight. They were all looking at him with concern, except for the woman; she stared at him as if he was a specimen in a bottle. She had a spider's eyes and mouth. Revulsion surged through him, and it helped. He picked up the transcript of the tape and flicked over the pages.

'This doesn't fit,' he said.

Waldron leaned towards him and James pointed to the passage he meant.

'Dave said there was no smoke in the cabin, then a few minutes later he said he was operating the checklist for smoke evacuation.'

Waldron nodded. 'We think there may have been a sudden inrush from the hold — or possibly Captain Brock was preparing for a worst-case scenario.'

'He brought *Paloma* down to fourteen thousand feet.'

'Right. The altitude at which one can breathe without an oxygen-mask, the level that would allow the crew to open the doors of the aircraft, to let smoke escape.'

'Safely,' James said.

'What?'

'If they opened the doors at level one four

zero, fresh oxygen would flow in.'

'Eventually, yes.'

'Oxygen feeds a fire. So Dave must have thought the fire was a minor one, or he wouldn't have considered opening the doors. I don't think at that stage he was considering a worst-case scenario. He was in control. He thought they'd make it back to Rome, or wherever.' James laid the transcript aside. 'I'd like to hear the other tape,' he said.

Waldron hesitated. 'Are you sure you're up to it? I'm afraid you'll find it more distressing than the first one.'

'I'm all right,' James said.

Waldron pressed the remote-control button.

The time on the screen was 16.17.00.

A voice James recognized as that of co-pilot Rossi grumbled about the coffee. Someone else talked about buying a smallholding near Luton.

A bell rang sharply and a third voice spoke loudly, drowning out the others.

'Skip, we have a smoke alarm. Detector number four in the main-deck cargo-hold.'

Dave answered: 'Yes, we have it here too.' The bell was abruptly silenced. 'Is the passenger cabin clear?'

'Clear, yes. No smoke. Yet.'

Rossi was arguing that it couldn't be a

fire, that everything was flame-proof. Dave said it could be a fault in the detector or the electricals. He spoke to someone called Len — that would be Oakley, the flight engineer — and told him to fetch up the checklist for main-deck cargo fire/smoke. Then he spoke to Ted.

'Ted, you and Wally get kitted up fast, and make a hold inspection.'

Clicking noises sounded. Switches being operated? The bell rang a second time and voices muttered in the background. Len Oakley was reading aloud from the checklist, technical stuff that James didn't understand. Dave and Rossi were checking *Paloma*'s systems, looking for defects and finding none.

Dave spoke to Ted. 'You and Wally ready to go in?'

The response was muffled. 'Going in now.'

'Check the hold,' Dave said. 'Make sure the smoke barrier is secured once you're through it, report conditions ASAP.'

'Roger.'

James looked at the screen. Just over two minutes had passed since the first alarm bell sounded. Dave and the crew were working fast, they were in control, no panic. Oakley asked when Dave would talk to the passengers, and Dave said: 'Soon as I know what we have back there.' He told Rossi to go

323

and check the situation in the cabin, sent Oakley to brief the crew and to tell someone called Liz to be ready to move the passengers forward and help them on to oxygen, if necessary.

Then Dave called Rome, the message they'd already heard on the ATC tape, announcing they'd had a smoke warning, talking about the checklist for smoke in the hold. Not smoke evacuation, yet. They were assessing the position in the hold.

As the transmission ended, the Rome controller called to Capriati, yelled 'PAN! PAN!' Then the ATC link was cut and the CVR took up Ted's voice.

'Skip, we have heavy smoke in the hold, visibility's fuck-all. Looks like there's a fire in one of the rear portside containers. We'll try to locate and extinguish.'

As David acknowledged the call, Rossi's voice spoke, close to the mike.

'There's no smoke in the cabin, but they know something's wrong, you better talk to them.'

'OK. Are the cabin signs operative?'

'Yes.'

Dave spoke, telling the passengers there was trouble in the cargo hold, it was being dealt with, there was no cause for alarm but the flight plan might be altered. They must remain calm and do as the crew told them.

Dave's voice was level and firm. No cause for alarm, he said. Had he believed that, had the passengers believed it?

The time was 16.25.00. Dave called Rome again and Capriati answered. Dave reported that there was heavy smoke in the hold, probably from a rear portside container. The fire-fighters would try to find the source and extinguish the fire. Capriati asked if there was smoke in the passenger cabin or on the flight deck, and was told there was not.

Then Dave requested clearance for an immediate descent to flight level one four zero. Capriati gave the clearance. He sounded perturbed at the request and he asked if Dave wished to declare a full emergency.

'Affirmative.' Dave said.

Full emergency. Worst case scenario? Dave and Capriati were the experts. They knew the danger and they were doing what they could to avert it; fixing *Paloma*'s exact position and flight details, agreeing that *Paloma* must return to Rome.

Dave knew they were in a crisis, but he was holding steady, he was in full control.

The light on the screen was stationary. They had reached the long pause in transmission. James imagined Capriati, busy

325

preparing the airport for emergency procedures, fire engines and ambulances, other aircraft diverted to leave the airlanes clear for *Paloma*. And Dave, turning the great aircraft back towards Rome, watching the signals on his instrument panels, perhaps sensing through his own body the response or failure of *Paloma*'s systems.

The silence was broken by a burst of sound that swelled and was cut off by the slamming of a door.

'What happened?' Dave said, and Oakley answered, hoarse and out of breath.

'Wally freaked, bolted to the cabin, brought some smoke through with him. Rossi's talking to the passengers, going to move them forward.'

'Are they under control?'

'Pretty good.'

'How much smoke is there? Are you sure it came through with Wally, and not through the ventilators?'

'I'm sure. It's not heavy. We can clear it by opening vents.'

A brief pause, then Dave said, 'Get me the checklist for smoke evacuation.'

'I don't think that's necessary, sir. We can clear it . . . '

'Get the list!'

Dave was shouting and another voice

crackled across his.

'Skip? Skip, this is Ted, I've located the source of the smoke, it's coming from the aft portside container. Dove's stuff.'

'How bad is it?'

'There's a lot of smoke, visibility's still poor, but I can fix it.'

'Do you need back-up?'

'Nah! On'y get in my way. This shouldn't take long.'

'Report as soon as you've got it under.'

'Roger.'

16.30.23.

Dave called Rome, told Capriati that they'd located the source of the fire and were dealing with it, there'd been some leakage of smoke to the passenger cabin and the passengers were being moved forward. At that point, Dave's voice was obscured by sounds of hammering, voices shouting. The interference stopped and Capriati intervened.

'Omega, what is your present altitude?'

'Altitude is one-four-zero. We are setting up the checklist for smoke evacuation.'

'Roger, Omega.' Capriati gave the course for Rome and David acknowledged the instructions.

Dave called Ted Doubleday.

'Ted. What's the situation?'

'Smoke's still coming. I'm going to use the

extinguisher attached to the container. Going in now.'

A woman's voice interrupted, speaking a little off-mike.

'We've moved them forward as far as we can. They're very stressed. Is there anything we can tell them?'

'Yes. Ask Sandy to talk to them, explain that we have things under control, we're heading back to Rome.'

A door opened, letting in a babble of sound. Closed again.

Dave said: 'Set it up.'

There came faint clicking sounds. David swore. 'Circuit breakers.' Then loudly, 'Ted, do you read me? We have circuit breakers down. What is the temperature . . . '

His words were drowned by a huge burst of noise, rushing, sucking, and across it Capriati shouted,

'Omega one-niner-seven, do you read me?'

The roar grew louder, then ceased altogether.

Capriati kept calling, but there was no answer.

Nothing but silence.

23

'My dear fellow, a dreadful ordeal for you, we fully appreciate how you must feel.'

Clive Radnor had risen from his chair and was advancing on James, teeth bared in a travesty of sympathy. Waldron rose to bar his way.

'Do you need us to run the tapes again, Mr Brock?'

'No!' James's voice sounded loud in his own ears, and he said more quietly: 'There's no need. I can tell you now what I think was the state of Dave's mind.'

Waldron resumed his seat at once. Radnor moved slowly, shaking his head.

'I strongly advise a rerun. It's so easy to miss something: a nuance, a phrase imperfectly heard. But if you're sure . . . '

'I am sure,' James said.

They were all watching him, Waldron concerned, Radnor disapproving, Mrs Warne impassive. Thorneycroft sat chin on hand, attentive. James spoke to him.

'Dave and I were close. We understood each other. When he was seven and I was five, our parents went to China as missionaries.

They died there soon after. We were left with my father's parents, who didn't want to be lumbered with young children. We were shuffled about between aunts and uncles and boarding-schools. It was Dave who raised me, more than any adult. I was totally reliant on him. He was my security, my guide. I loved him and he loved me.

'Because we couldn't rely on the people who were supposed to care for us, we learned to keep our thoughts and feelings to ourselves. We learned to communicate with each other, without speech. It's not an ability you lose. Listening to the tapes, I didn't just hear Dave's voice, I felt what he felt. I was with him.'

Thorneycroft smiled and nodded, but Mrs Warne flapped a hand, as if dispelling smoke. 'You say you loved your brother, Mr Brock, relied on him, trusted him. Your sister-in-law Candida Woodley presents rather a different picture. She claims your brother was having an affair with your wife, and that out of revenge you sent him a box containing inflammatories.'

'Have you checked her story?'

'It has been checked. You did send a carton. It was loaded on to *Paloma* in the Dove container, which is where the fire seems to have started.'

'There was nothing inflammatory in the box. It was examined at Heathrow, and again at Rome airport.' James turned to Waldron. 'Do you want to hear what I think about the tape?'

'Please.'

James picked up the transcript of the cockpit voice-recorder.

'At the start of the flight,' he said, 'Dave was completely calm. The crew was relaxed, chatting to one another. Then the smoke-alarm sounded. As you'd expect, Dave was tense, but he didn't panic. He was in control of himself and the situation. I think he was confident that the fire, whatever it was, was small and could be extinguished without difficulty. He knew that *Paloma*'s anti-fire measures were excellent.'

Thorneycroft lifted his chin. 'How do you know that? Did he discuss it with you?'

'Yes, when Omega bought the new-style containers. He told me they were state of the art, flame-resistant, and each one fitted with its own extinguisher. The fire-fighter just had to lift the hose from its clamps, shove the nozzle through an easy-access vent, press the release, and extinguishant gas would squirt over the contents and put out the flames.'

Waldron said: 'I've seen them work well at

ground trials, but an in-flight emergency is another matter.'

'Dave had faith in them — and in his fire-fighters.'

'Misplaced, it seems,' said Rylda Warne.

Waldron shot her a look of dislike. 'The chief fire-fighter Ted Doubleday was competent and brave,' he pointed out. 'He said the smoke leakage to the cabin wasn't great, he said he could control the fire.'

'Events proved him wrong.' Mrs Warne fixed her gaze on James. 'Your brother never put out a Mayday call. How do you explain that?'

'I think he believed he could bring *Paloma* to a safe landing at Rome. He believed they could extinguish the fire. He brought *Paloma* down to 14,000 feet, he was preparing to evacuate the smoke. He'd have opened the doors to let the smoke out. He wouldn't have taken those steps if he'd thought the fire was going to run out of control.'

'How can you be sure?'

'Because ultimately, when the pressure in the plane equalized with the pressure outside, oxygen would have flowed into *Paloma*. That would have fuelled the fire. Dave didn't make a Mayday call because he didn't think it was necessary.'

'And did Captain Brock maintain this

admirable sangfroid to the end? Did he have no inkling that the aircraft was going to crash?'

'Not until the final minutes.'

The woman's gaze sharpened. 'Pray explain what you mean.'

'The circuit breakers started to drop,' James said. 'Their purpose is to confine damage in the electric wiring of an aircraft. A big modern aircraft isn't flown by men pulling levers, but by systems, mechanical and electronic systems, activated by hundreds of miles of wiring. If a major part of these systems is damaged or destroyed, the aircraft is in danger . . . ' James turned to Waldron. 'Do the DFDR and QAR tapes indicate any serious malfunctions during the flight?'

'None that we've found so far. We're making in-depth examinations.'

Clive Radnor cleared his throat. 'It appears, Mr Brock, that you know a good deal about aircraft.'

'Only the basics,' James said. 'I'm qualified to fly small planes. Dave taught me to fly.'

Thorneycroft intervened. 'Returning to the question of your brother's state of mind . . . you say he appeared to be confident of bringing *Paloma* safely back to Rome, until the final minutes?'

'Yes.'

'You think his attitude changed, at the end?'

'Yes. It's here, in the transcript. Dave asked Ted Doubleday what the situation was, in the hold. Doubleday said the smoke was still coming, he was going to use the extinguisher attached to the container. Then there was a short pause. Dave spoke to an air hostess, he told her the co-pilot must talk to the passengers and tell them things were under control. He told someone to 'set it up'. I take it he wanted Oakley to start smoke evacuation.

'Then there were clicking sounds. Dave swore, and said 'circuit breakers'. He called Doubleday again, told him there were circuit breakers down, asked 'what is the temperature'. Then there was this huge sound — a rush of air, or gas. The tape cut out. I think there was a flash fire.'

'A what?' said Mrs Warne. Waldron answered her.

'Something combustible starts to burn — in the cargo, or perhaps in a passenger's luggage. It may smoulder for a long time, or flame up quickly. The fire releases gases that rise to the ceiling of the cargo hold. If those gases ignite, you can get a fire where flames flash from end to end of the enclosed space. All oxygen is consumed. The temperature at ceiling level may reach two thousand degrees. Such fires can last from thirty seconds to a few minutes, but during that time you have a total inferno.'

'That's what we heard on the tape,' James said. 'That roaring noise, like a petrol explosion.'

Thorneycroft looked at Waldron. 'Geoff? Do you agree?'

Waldron said slowly: 'We haven't found evidence of an actual explosion, either on the wreckage or in the human remains, but yes, there could have been a flash fire. It's a possibility we're considering. In time, we may be able to establish exactly what happened.'

'You don't have time,' James said, and Mrs Warne's head snapped round.

'What do you mean by that?'

'The Jerusalem Accord,' James said. 'According to the newspapers, the authorities — that's all of you — are scared political extremists may create an incident to abort the Accord. Do you think *Paloma* was destroyed to create an incident?'

No one spoke for a moment, then Thorneycroft hunched his shoulders.

'I'm just a doctor. Ask the politicians.'

James looked at Rylda Warne.

'Well?'

335

She gave him a venomous glance.

'It's possible, I suppose. What did your brother know of the Accord?'

'Very little, I imagine. Dave wasn't into politics.'

'A pity. His lack of concern may have cost him his life. If he discovered something . . . disquieting . . . he should have reported it.'

'I didn't say he wasn't concerned. Politics wasn't his field, but if he'd suspected a political plot, he'd have reported it.'

'He suspected some sort of plot, Mr Brock. He sent a fax to the mysterious Boru, but said nothing about it to his colleagues at Omega or Dove. Mr Spinner questioned him about the fax in the carton, and Captain Brock was evasive. Why was that?'

James shrugged. 'Perhaps he wasn't sure of his facts. Perhaps he didn't know who to trust.'

'Did he trust you, Mr Brock? Did he appeal to you for help?'

'No. I was in hospital with a cracked skull. I was no use to anyone at that time.' James looked at Thorneycroft. 'You've seen the fax my brother received from Boru?'

'I have.'

'But not the fax he sent?'

'Not that, no.'

James held out copies of the photostats given him by Natalie Lomax. Thorneycroft studied them carefully, laid them aside.

'Where did you get these, sir?'

'I was given them by a friend.'

'And the friend's name?'

James remained silent and Radnor exclaimed in exasperation: 'For God's sake, Brock, as a lawyer, you know the penalties for withholding information.'

James kept his eyes on Thorneycroft. 'You can keep those copies,' he said. 'There are others in safe keeping.'

Thorneycroft leaned back in his chair. 'Just what do you expect me to do with the documents?'

'Use it to trace the man,' James said. 'You have resources I lack, and you can work discreetly. I want the people who killed my brother; publicity would send them scuttling for cover.'

'You've not gone to the press, then?'

'Not yet. If you won't help me, I may have no other course.'

Thorneycroft's mouth twitched. 'Threats will get you nowhere,' he said. He bent to study the photo again. 'Has he a criminal record?'

'I've no idea. All I can tell you is that he may have had plastic surgery.'

'Yes.' Thorneycroft trailed a finger. 'Probably here, to the jawline.' He sighed. 'It's a needle in a haystack.' He slipped the two photostats into his briefcase.

'If you trace him,' James said, 'let me know. I'll do the same for you.'

'Right.' There was no irony in Thorneycroft's voice. 'Where will I reach you?'

'This afternoon I'll be at Mallowfield. I'm meeting Daniel Roswall and some of his people. Tonight I'll be home, in Bansford.'

'You're not back at work yet?'

'I'm taking leave. I may go to Italy.'

'Beware of newshounds.'

James looked at Waldron. 'Is there anything else?'

'Copies of the tapes.' Waldron handed over a couple of cassettes. 'I'd be grateful if you'll listen to them again, let me know if anything strikes you.'

'Sure.'

James took his leave. Waldron walked with him to the lift, shook his hand and thanked him for coming.

Outside the sky was clouding over, the air was oppressive and sour. James drove slowly, impatient of the London traffic. He felt tired, but he was pleased with what he'd learned, not only from the tapes but from the people he'd met. Waldron was practical and

338

sympathetic. Radnor and the Warne woman were cagey, following some agenda of their own. The technician Abercrombie was interested only in his computer. And Thorneycroft? Thorneycroft was an enigma. He missed nothing, said little, gave nothing away. He was the sort of man who could be useful or dangerous, perhaps both.

James wondered who had appointed Dr Thorneycroft to the *Paloma* inquiry, and why.

★ ★ ★

In the projection room, Waldron stood beside Abercrombie.

'Did you get it all?' he said. Abercrombie nodded and pressed a button. James Brock's voice blared out and he turned down the volume.

'Make copies,' Waldron said. Abercrombie nodded again and turned back to his machines.

Clive Radnor, who had been pacing about the room, confronted Waldron.

'What possessed you to invite Brock here? He's a menace! Talking as if he invented God, trying to tell us our business! You should never have given him copies of the tapes. He could use them to wreck the inquiry, you've made him privy to vital evidence. I'm surprised Thorneycroft didn't put a stop to it.'

Thorneycroft, hearing the diatribe, said calmly: 'I asked Geoff to invite Brock.'

'What? You must have been out of your mind! Brock's a prime suspect. It's probable he caused that fire.'

'No.'

'What d'ye mean, 'no'? Brock quarrelled with his brother, wouldn't allow him to visit him in hospital and with good reason. The sister-in-law is prepared to swear that David Brock seduced Clare Brock, result was the poor woman committed suicide. James responded by sending the carton that destroyed *Paloma*, those are the plain facts.'

'Clare Brock was a manic depressive,' Thorneycroft said. 'According to her doctor, she was neurotic and extremely manipulative. She'd made two earlier attempts at suicide. I don't believe for a moment that David Brock seduced her, or that the fire on *Paloma* started in that carton.'

Radnor's lips puffed in and out. 'If you choose to ignore the facts, Thorneycroft — '

'Sit down, Clive.' Rylda Warne's voice was soft, but it stopped Radnor in his tracks. 'Sit down,' she repeated. He groped for a chair and subsided into it.

She folded her hands in her lap. 'Dr

Thorneycroft was appointed to this investigation because of his special skill as a profiler. His job is to study all aspects of the *Paloma* disaster, and the people who are involved with it, however remotely. He has to study facts, theories, even rumours, and bring them into focus for those of us who have more specific and partisan aims. He has to take us where hard evidence and laboratory tests and expert opinions cannot take us. He must attempt to enlighten us about the motive for this crime, if crime there was. He must describe for us the sort of criminal who could have planned and executed the crime.'

'Poppycock,' Radnor muttered. 'Fanciful speculation.'

'Visualization,' Thorneycroft corrected. 'A short cut to the solution we desperately need.'

Radnor scowled. 'Why do you defend James Brock?' he demanded.

Thorneycroft was silent for a space. 'Let's assume that there was a crime, that *Paloma* was sabotaged. People who commit mass murder share one salient characteristic. They lack empathy. They do not — cannot — put themselves in the shoes of their victims. The coldness often stems from deprivation: lack of parental love, of food, money, opportunity, understanding, any or all of these things can produce a psychopathic loner, a monster

341

who'll set fire to a crowded church, plant a bomb on the school bus, poison a reservoir. It's not an invariable rule, of course. A psychopath can be the product of his genes rather than his environment.'

Mrs Warne's eyes glinted. 'James and David Brock were deprived. Deserted by their parents at a tender age. Not wanted, pushed from pillar to post.'

'Yes, but it didn't cripple them. Somehow they both learned to form normal attachments. They loved each other, found friends, got on well with others, served their communities well.'

'David Brock never married.'

Thorneycroft laughed. 'Many women, no wife. If that defines a psychopath, the world's in serious trouble.'

She sniffed. 'What about James Brock?'

Thorneycroft considered. 'On a brief acquaintance, he struck me as being honest, and loyal to his brother. He showed courage in coming here today. He has a blunt manner. I don't think he has much respect for authority, a quality you may admire or dislike.'

She tossed her head. 'Is he intelligent?'

'Very, I'd say. Listening to those tapes upset him badly, but that didn't deter him from picking up the salient points, like for instance that Captain Brock brought *Paloma* down to level one four zero before there was much smoke in the passenger cabin. He also saw that something crucial happened right at the end of the tape. He suggested it might have been a flash fire — a diagnosis supported by our own experts.'

'So tell me,' interposed Radnor, 'why did this model citizen refuse to tell us who gave him that photograph? Why did he refuse to identify this Boru?'

'He was protecting his source.'

Radnor threw up his hands in disgust. 'Heaven save us, man! The Middle East's a tinderbox, we could be plunged into World War Three by a wrong move, and *Mister* Brock chooses to indulge in petty heroics!'

Rylda Warne ignored Radnor, keeping her bright gaze on Thorneycroft.

'Why do you think he's going to Italy?'

'Probably to talk to his brother's mistress, and to others who knew David well.'

'Rome police have already questioned Pia d'Ascani. I gather she told them nothing.'

'Perhaps they asked the wrong questions.' Thorneycroft rubbed his jawline. 'Just before I left to come here, I had a call from Captain di Maggio. Alonso Vespucci's mother had been to see him with a story that two months ago, a strange man called at their home, to discuss some kind of trade. Alonso didn't like the visit, and sent the man packing.'

'What has that to do with *Paloma*?'

'Perhaps nothing. But Signora Vespucci insists that her boy didn't shoot himself, he was murdered.'

'Why?'

'Because he knew something about the *Paloma* crash. He felt responsible for it. He tried to get in touch with key people. Di Maggio thinks he could have been about to spill his guts, but someone stopped him.'

'What's di Maggio doing about it?'

'He's rechecking the forensic reports, getting traces from Alonso's car, his home and office. He'll requestion all the witnesses, everyone Alonso tried to reach, particularly on the last night of his life. Vespucci made the calls on his mobile phone. Di Maggio has the list. Incidentally, one of the names on it is Pia d'Ascani's.'

'The assumption being that one of the people he called read the danger signals and shot him?'

'Yes.'

'Tenuous, to say the least. What about the man who called at the house?'

'They'll try to trace him, but it's a faint hope.'

'Does di Maggio have a copy of the fax that

was in the carton?'

'It was sent to all investigating formations, but he doesn't have this.' Thorneycroft held up the photostats James had given him.

'Send it to him. If anyone can identify it as Alonso's visitor, we may get somewhere.' Mrs Warne heaved herself to her feet. 'Clive, we must go, we have a lot to do.'

'Wait,' Thorneycroft said. 'What about James Brock?'

'What about him?'

'If he goes to Italy, and tries to question the people close to David Brock, he could run into serious danger.'

She rolled her heavy shoulders. 'Not my worry. There's nothing I can do for him, on foreign soil.'

'There's plenty you can do! He's a British citizen, he's co-operating with us, it's your duty to look after him.'

'My duty,' she said with swift venom, 'is to look after the interests of this country. My duty is to ensure that meddlesome Mister Brock doesn't cause an international incident.'

'How the fuck can he do that?'

'Very easily, my friend. He's admitted he's out to find his brother's killer. He's already attracted the attentions of the yellow press. Everything he says or does in Italy will receive wide publicity. If he makes accusations about an individual or a state, there could be repercussions. There are plenty of factions, and one or two states, that would like an excuse to end the truce and withdraw from the Accord. I will not allow Brock's theories about *Paloma* to prejudice our work. The situation must be handled by professionals, not bumbling amateurs.'

Thorneycroft stood up to face her.

'Brock is our best chance, perhaps our only chance, of nailing the people responsible for the *Paloma* crash.'

'That is where we differ. You see, John, you deal in profiles — guesses, I'd call them. I deal in facts, accurate information obtained from reliable sources. What has Brock to offer but a load of sentimental claptrap? A blurred photograph that the FBI with all its resources cannot identify. Brock is a nothing, a red herring.'

'So you'll leave him to the sharks, is that what you're saying? Are you hoping that some paid assassin will do your dirty work for you? With Brock out of the way you'd be free to draw a neat veil of silence over this awkard atrocity. But what if you're wrong, Rylda? What if it turns out that *Paloma* is significant, that we should know why she crashed? What if you're the bungler, not Brock?'

'I don't have time for these childish arguments.' She tried to push past him but he caught hold of her plump wrist.

'I'm not letting you get away with this. I will see that Brock gets protection.'

She thrust her face towards him. 'Then watch your step. I've said, Brock must take his chances, and if you try to cross me up, you'll have to take yours.'

She pulled free of his grasp and headed for the door. As she passed Radnor she lifted a hand and snapped her fingers. He snatched up his briefcase and trotted after her.

Waldron, who had moved to answer a telephone at the end of the room, returned in time to see the departure.

'Where are they going in such a hurry?' he asked.

'Hell, I hope.'

'What's Hell done to deserve them?'

Thorneycroft shook his head angrily. 'I shouldn't let her get to me. She has a job to do.'

Waldron collected the original cassettes from the machine and slipped them into the pockets of his lab coat.

'Are you free this afternoon?'

'Yes, if it's important.'

'I thought we might go down to the debris centre. Coburn's assembled a lot of data, and we can add what Brock supplied. He was helpful, wasn't he? He'll make a good witness.'

'Very,' Thorneycroft said, 'provided we can keep him alive that long.'

24

Waldron and Thorneycroft reached the debris centre at two o'clock on Monday afternoon. They were met at the main door by Barry Coburn, who led them across the vast floor with its piles of detritus, to a long room at the back of the hangar.

Maps and charts relating to *Paloma* papered its walls. There was a rank of telephones, another of computer terminals, a television and video area. Along the outer wall, trestle-tables were spread with piles of reports and photographs. At the far end of the room, machines clicked and clattered, spilling out slow coils of paper.

Coburn gestured to a row of chairs facing a bare table. 'Park yer butts,' he said. 'What can I do for you?'

Waldron said slowly: 'Give us your picture of what happened.'

Coburn pulled down his mouth. 'Too early for that, mate. All I have is preliminary findings. We'll hafta run a helluva lot more tests before we can swear on any bibles. The engines are being checked by the makers. The metallurgy tests'll take a while, so will the DNA and path. analyses. Mind, if you want educated guesses . . . '

'We need all the help you can give us,' Waldron said.

'Yeah, well, I'll give you a run-down, shall I? You got any questions, stop me.'

He moved along the trestle-tables, selecting documents and photographs which he spread before them.

'First question,' he said, as he sat down facing them, 'is: what made *Paloma* crash? Broad answer is: fire in her gut. I can tell you what didn't bring her down, and that's lack of maintenance.

'*Paloma* was in good nick. Her systems worked, so did her navigational aids. We've run the DFDR and QAR tapes and so far as we can tell there was no engine or structural defect. *Paloma* had a refit couple of years ago and her fire precautions were upgraded. She had fire-resistant linings in the holds, her smoke-detectors were effective, she had all the halon gas she needed.

'Because of the scare about Joel Moshal, special steps were taken before the flight: meticulous service, new supplies of oxygen and halon. Cargo was double-checked.

'She had a clean record, no previous accidents — '

Waldron interrupted: 'Yet last Monday,

350

there was a failure in her electrical circuits.'

'Yeah, right,' Coburn answered. 'That's my point. At her last maintenance check-up, her electricals worked fine, but fifteen minutes after leaving Rome last week, the circuit breakers went crazy. The electricals were knocked to hell. That has to be because something wrecked the wiring. It takes a lot of heat to do that, so my guess is, there was huge heat generated very fast, in the main-deck cargo-hold. Lemme show you.'

He held up a bunch of photos. 'Here's what the heat did to a graphite racket, to the metal-mesh safety barrier, to the wiring of the Black boxes. Ate 'em up like toffee bars. Those boxes are bloody near fireproof, but they're damaged, the wiring's eaten away; in other words, they were disconnected by the fire. So the tapes stopped recording.'

'Do you know at what time they stopped?' Thorneycroft was leaning forward, studying the photographs closely.

'16.32.25,' Coburn answered. 'The first smoke-alarm sounded at 16.18.03. In around fifteen minutes, enough heat was built up to do the damage you see in those pics.'

Waldron said: 'Flash fire, or explosion.'

'We'll come back to that,' Coburn said. 'Let's first deal with what we know. Let's think about human competence. *Paloma* had

351

good pilots, crew, maintenance workers, freight-handlers. No health problems. Ted Doubleday, the chief fire-fighter, was well trained and steady. His assistant Wally Prout was a weak link. The CVR shows he panicked and ran out of the hold into the passenger cabin. Took some smoke with him, which caused trouble, but the rest of the crew got things under control.'

Coburn paused, then pushed another photo along the table. They stared at a lump of blackened flesh, bone and gristle.

'Ted Doubleday,' Coburn said. 'They identified it by the dental records. He must have been exposed to enormous heat — remember he was wearing a protective suit and helmet. The post mortem didn't find any metal fragments in him. In an explosion, molten metal flies out and lodges in anything soft. It didn't happen aboard *Paloma*.'

Waldron buried his face in his hands.

Thorneycroft said: 'Were any of the victims wearing life-jackets?'

Coburn shook his head. 'It must have been quick at the end, they didn't expect to die, poor swine.'

'But *Paloma* didn't explode?'

'Don't think so. We've found soot and fire damage on the wreckage, but no signs of explosive force.'

'What about the fire-depressants?'

Coburn handed over a typed document.

'*Seascanner*'s picked up a couple of unused halon cylinders. The gas in them is halon and the cylinders functioned, even after that impact with the sea . . . '

'Illegal cargo?'

'There could've been, though this flight was very carefully supervised. Mr Spinner was so fazed by the Moshal scare, he ran extra checks. They found no unauthorized cargo.'

Coburn paused. 'There's something bugs me. The fire started in the rear portside container, back of the stack, right next to the Black boxes.'

'The Dove container,' Waldron said.

'Yeah. So, why would anyone planning to bring down the Dove aircraft plant a fire-starter in the Dove container? The container most likely to be searched by both the Dove and the airport security, the container fitted with fireproof framework and a patent fire-extinguisher?'

Thorneycroft said: 'You're saying there was a fire-starter in that container?'

'Must've been. Doubleday said that's where the smoke was coming from.'

'Could there have been some sort of spontaneous combustion?'

Coburn met Thorneycroft's eyes. 'You think there was?'

Thorneycroft shook his head, frowning.

Waldron said: 'The initial autopsy reports state that soot has been found in the respiratory tracts of the victims, and blood samples show a high carbon monoxide content. The samples were taken from closed chest cavities, so the gas didn't come from outside the aircraft, it was inhaled by the victims aboard the aircraft. Yet the CVR tape suggests that there wasn't a lot of smoke in the passenger area.'

'The tape stopped at 16.32.25,' Coburn said. '*Paloma* hit the sea at 16.42.00. I reckon that during that ten minutes, there was a massive increase in the force and scope of the fire. Smoke entered the passenger area, perhaps through the ventilation systems. The victims inhaled smoke and gases.'

'Weren't they wearing oxygen masks?'

Coburn shrugged. 'Seems not. The plane was at level one four zero, remember; maybe they were breathing easy until those last minutes, then the fire hit and there was panic. We can't know for sure. With the tape cut off, there's no sounds of coughing or choking, no screams, to tell us what was happening in the passenger cabin.'

Waldron said heavily: 'We had James Brock

listen to the tapes this morning. He said Captain Brock was calm right through to the last moments of the tape. Then the circuit breakers began to drop, he tried to contact Doubleday, there was this colossal thump and roar, like gas igniting.'

'I think that's what it was,' Coburn said. 'Gas igniting in a flash fire.'

'Can a flash fire develop that fast?' Thorneycroft asked. '*Paloma* took off from Rome a few minutes after four p.m. By a quarter to five, she'd burned and crashed.'

'A flash fire can develop within three to five minutes of the point of ignition,' Coburn answered, 'but way I look at it, this one was helped along. A smoke- or fire-device was planted in the Dove container, to produce fumes and maybe flammable gas. The smoke activated the detectors in the hold.' He paused. 'The device was placed in the Dove container because it had a patent extinguisher. Whoever sabotaged *Paloma* knew that the fire-fighters would locate the source of the smoke, and use that extinguisher to douse the fire. But if the extinguisher didn't contain halon, if it was loaded with some highly flammable substance, it'd act like a flame-thrower. The gases in the hold would ignite with huge force. That's your sound on the tape. Whoosh. A fireball that killed

Doubleday outright, wrecked the wiring in the rear structures, spread the fire and smoke forward through the aircraft.'

'Can you prove that?' Thorneycroft asked.

Coburn shook his head. 'It's a theory that matches what we know from the tapes. I can't say if it would work in practice.'

'Can you run tests on the ground, see if you can produce what you just described?'

'Sure.' Coburn's dark eyes switched to Waldron. 'If I'm given the go-ahead.'

Waldron nodded, and Thorneycroft said: 'How fast can you get results?'

'Fast,' Coburn answered. He got to his feet and left the room. They heard his voice shouting in the depths of the hangar.

Waldron said: 'If Barry's right, and the fire was deliberately set in the Dove container, that means the saboteur was someone with access to the warehouse.'

'Not necessarily,' Thorneycroft said. 'We've been working to the wrong time-scale. We've assumed that what triggered the sabotage was connected to Joel Moshal. We've concentrated on the week leading up to the disaster. But if Barry's right, the thing could have been planned weeks ago. The cylinder on the Dove container could have been switched weeks ago, maybe when *Paloma* was in the Far East.'

356

'What about the smoke-starter? A device like that would have a timer, wouldn't it, you'd have to set it . . . '

'Not necessarily. A device could be triggered by pressure. The aircraft reaches a certain height, the device is switched on. Or they might have used chemicals to cause smoke and fire. The point is, scores of people outside of Omega and Dove had access to the aircraft during those weeks. A good many had access to the Dove office and the warehouse.' Thorneycroft looked at his watch. 'I have to get back to London. You ready?'

As they crossed the hangar, they saw Coburn conferring with a group of technicians. He lifted a hand with thumb and forefinger joined.

Waldron was looking at the piles of wreckage, the skeletal shape of *Paloma*. 'Why?' he muttered. 'Why would anyone kill all those people? If Moshal wasn't the target, who was?'

Thorneycroft didn't answer. Ideas whirled in his head. He had to fit them together, convey their meaning to a number of people who would waste time arguing and putting obstacles in his path.

Five days to the Accord.

He used his mobile phone to call the local

traffic police, and broke the speed limit all the way back to central London.

★   ★   ★

Driving south to Mallowfield, James thought about the people he'd met at the laboratory. Waldron was honest and efficient, but too busy to take up side issues. Radnor was a puppet. The woman pulled the strings. She had clout, but she wouldn't use it on Dave's behalf. Thorneycroft was as clever as the woman, he seemed to be taking his own line. He'd try to trace the photograph, and probably Boru as well. So good luck to him.

James glanced in his rear-view mirror. The estate wagon that had been behind him since London pulled away and turned off the motorway. Was he being followed? Would he be able to spot a trail, and if he did what could he do about it? Company might even offer him some protection.

He stopped at a roadside café to buy a Coke and a ham roll, and ate as he drove. The miles rolled smoothly away. Ideas that had hung free in his mind began to cohere and take shape.

Dave had not panicked. He'd been in control right to the end. It was only after the electricals went mad that he'd sounded scared.

He'd never thought *Paloma* would crash. There was smoke, but not a lot, and he thought they could deal with it.

No smoke without fire.

How much, how it was caused, was something for the experts to decide. Let them analyse the technical tapes, DFDR and QAR, let them run their tests and make their reports.

He could go where they couldn't, into Dave's mind. He could talk to Dave's friends, and get answers they wouldn't give to the police.

It was a week since Dave died.

It felt like a year; not real time, nightmare time.

It was no use thinking about that. He had to focus on what he could do, here and now.

Focus on Dove, on Daniel Roswall and company.

★ ★ ★

Mallowfield was a fortress, complete with electrified fence and automatic gates, guard-house and dog-patrols. There was a helipad to the left of the property. A chopper stood on the tarmac.

A billionaire needed maximum security. What was Roswall protecting? Paintings, jewels, a drug racket, his own person?

The guards waved James through the gates. The driveway led through formal gardens and through a second set of gates to a yard with garages and stables. As James parked his car, a big man dressed in jeans and a checked shirt strolled towards him.

'Mr Brock?' The voice was deep and husky, the smile perfunctory. 'I apologize for the security checks. We've had gatecrashers in the past.'

James shook hands. Roswall's fingers were surprisingly slender for so burly a man. His face was sallow, shadows under the eyes suggested sleepless nights. The eyes were small, a pale, cold brown, alert and watchful.

'I'm deeply sorry,' Roswall said, 'about the death of your brother. I knew David for four years, and I liked and admired him. He was a fine pilot and very much his own man.' As he spoke he was drawing James across the yard and into the house.

They walked along a broad passage with a staircase to their left. On the lowest landing a young girl sat, cradling in her arms an enormous tomcat, white with a black spot over one eye.

'My granddaughter Lucy,' Roswall said.

'She's staying with me for a bit.' There was warmth in the iced-tea eyes. James smiled at the girl and reached up to tickle the cat's ear.

'Watch out,' Roswall warned. 'That's a killer cat. He chases guard dogs for fun.'

But the cat leaned to the banister and offered its chin to be scratched. The girl said: 'He knows you like him.'

'They always know,' James said. 'What's his name?'

'Bojangles.'

'Fine figure of a cat.'

Roswall led the way along a side corridor to a sitting-room large enough to host a convention. At one end shutters had been opened to reveal a fully stocked bar. The opposite end was taken up by a television centre. James guessed there would be a computer terminal somewhere near at hand. In the middle of the room chairs and sofas had been arranged round a coffee-table. As Roswall and James approached, a young man with yellow hair, and a stocky woman in a track suit rose to greet them.

'I'm Gerda Marcus,' the woman said. 'Dove's PRO. This is Kyle Parnell, our computernik. Would you like a drink, or coffee?'

'Nothing, thanks.' Despite their cordial manners, these people were not at ease, James thought. Their distrust surrounded him like invisible laser beams. One false step, and the alarm bells would ring.

Roswall waved him to a chair, took the one next to him, and indicated a bulky folder on the table.

'The CVs you asked for,' he said. 'They are of course confidential. Before I hand them over, I must know how you plan to use them.'

'They may help me find my brother's killer,' James said.

Roswall's shoulders hunched. It was like watching the hair rise on a mastiff's neck.

'You think *Paloma* was sabotaged?'

'Yes I do.'

'No terrorist organization has claimed responsibility. The authorities haven't declared it sabotage.'

'Not yet.'

Roswall tilted his head. 'And what can that possibly have to do with my people?'

James answered at a tangent.

'I've just come from a meeting with DCA Geoffrey Waldron, and Dr John Thorneycroft. You've met them?'

'Waldron, yes. My senior colleagues and I have been questioned by assorted policemen, but Thorneycroft wasn't among them.'

'He's a forensic psychologist, a consultant

to the police, one of the new profilers. He and Waldron are under pressure from the politicians to soft-pedal on the *Paloma* inquiry.'

Roswall's mouth curled. 'They tell you so?'

'No.'

'Why would such pressure be exerted, Mr Brock?'

'I think there's a perception that the crash is linked to the Middle East crisis.'

Roswall grunted. 'It's not only the politicians who believe that. The business world, the oil cartels, the tourist companies, all share the same view. There are extremists — Arabs, Jews, Christians and the like — who will commit atrocities for political gain.'

'And there are dealers who supply the extremists with the means to commit atrocities — arms, explosives, other banned materials.'

'Certainly there are rogue governments, and renegades ready to deal with them — '

'I'm not talking about governments, I'm talking about dealers much lower on the scale. Middlemen, if you like.'

'Make your point, Mr Brock.'

'Certainly. It's this. My brother hated the drug trade. Before he joined Omega, he was with Sirius Freight in the Caribbean. He left them because some of their crews took to drug-running, and the drugs financed the Colombian warlords. He told me once that soon the dealers would diversify to chemical and biological trade. He was right, wasn't he? The Iraqis used poison gas against the Kurds, and in the build-up to the Gulf War they set up factories to produce germ cultures.'

'What has that to do with me, or Dove?'

'You employ chemists and biologists, Mr Roswall. No doubt most of them are — were — model citizens, but it's possible some may have been ready to sell their expertise to the highest bidder. Hand over formulas, give advice on the production of germ cultures and antidotes, arrange the purchase of innocent commodities that can be misused, to make weapons of mass destruction.'

'You listen to me!' Roswall leaned an elbow on the arm of his chair, finger levelled at James. 'The people I employ are selected with the utmost care. They conform to the strictest standards. They work for peace, they don't kill and destroy — '

'They visit the trouble spots of the world. If one or two of them are looking for illegal sales, they'll find buyers — not fanatics or extremists, necessarily, just mercenaries happy to strike a bargain.'

For a moment Roswall neither spoke nor moved. Then he said gently: 'Have you any evidence to support this wild theory?'

'No. All I have is my knowledge of my brother — and a fax that was sent to him by someone called Boru.'

Roswall waved an impatient hand. 'I know about that. It was found in the carton you sent to your brother. It was examined by my manager Hugo Spinner, and Dove's warehouse controller Andrew Fermoy, both of them trusted employees. Mr Spinner taxed Captain Brock about the message when he handed over the message to him. Captain Brock explained he'd sent the query to a friend, because Omega was looking for new staff. I fail to see how you connect murder and arson to such an innocuous request.'

'Not innocuous; crucial,' James said. 'I believe Dave suspected that someone in Dove was involved in illegal trading, using an agent in Rome. I think he obtained a photograph of the agent but couldn't identify him. He sent the photograph to a friend, asking for help.'

Kyle Parnell spoke for the first time.

'Do you have the photo?' Parnell was moving forward, hand outstretched. His eyes shone, he looked like a hunting-dog on a scent.

'I have it,' James said, and looked at Roswall. 'Do I get the CVs?'

Roswall hesitated, then nodded. Parnell

365

picked up the folder and handed it to James, James took a copy of the photograph from his briefcase and gave it to Roswall. Parnell and Gerda Marcus moved to Roswall's side to study the picture. None of their faces showed any sign of recognition.

'Not one of ours,' Gerda said.

Roswall laid the picture aside. 'Kyle has contacts. He might be able to trace the man.'

'We can't use computers,' James said. 'Put his face on the web, and he'll run for cover.'

Parnell had picked up the photo and was tilting it to the light. 'It's a poor shot,' he said. 'Not an official mugshot. It shows him three-quarter-face, not profile. There's no skull-form with all that hair. The skin of the cheek looks too smooth. He may have had a skin graft.' He glanced at James. 'Who's Boru?'

James shook his head. Parnell looked ready to argue, but Roswall waved him away.

'Leave it, Kyle. Sit down. Mr Brock, do I have this right, you think that someone in Dove has been dealing in illegal materials?'

'I think it's a possibility.'

'And this person became the target of someone anxious to . . . protect his investment?'

'Yes.'

366

'You're saying that to silence one guilty individual, a hundred and fifty-four innocent people were slaughtered? Frankly, I find that beyond credibility.'

James said nothing. Roswall leaned back in his chair. 'What do you want me to do?'

'Help me identify the man in the photo.'

'Surely that is a job for experts? The police?'

'The British police and the American FBI have so far failed.'

'God help us!' Roswall rubbed a hand over his eyes. He looked old and tired. He said: 'Gerda, we must talk. Kyle, see Mr Brock to his car. Give him my unlisted telephone number. You are to assist him in any way you can — funds, contacts, whatever he needs he gets. Do not at any time disregard his wishes.' He gave a nod that was clearly dismissal. 'Thank you for coming, Mr Brock, and for your frankness. I owe you. We'll stay in touch. Good day.'

⋆   ⋆   ⋆

The girl Lucy and her cat had vanished from the stairway. James had the uneasy feeling that they represented Roswall's one link with normality, and that without them this house would become a stronghold ruled by a despot.

Kyle Parnell was silent as they crossed the

367

yard, but when they reached the car he said abruptly,

'That guy you spoke about — that dealer — he had to be a nutcase.'

James shrugged. 'Not in the legal sense. He knows what he's doing and he knows it's wrong. He's just abnormally greedy. He's probably already very rich, but he's not satisfied. He wants more and he'll commit mass murder to get it. Sane or insane, he's a monster.'

'A monster who'll do whatever it takes to protect his investment.' Parnell gave a sudden crack of laughter. 'And you're providing him with a whole new set of targets. Us.'

He looked more exhilarated than scared at the prospect. A bungee-jumper, James thought, hungry for the adrenalin rush.

'Kyle,' he said, 'I don't want that photo released to anyone.'

'Sure. I understand.'

James climbed into his car and lowered the window. 'I need more information,' he said. 'When I have it, and if I want your skills, I'll let you know.'

Parnell grinned. 'Right.' He leaned to the window. 'Computers are just machines,' he said, 'only as good as their handlers, but they're fast. If fast is what you want, any time, let me know.'

25

In his study at Mallowfield, Roswall lifted a red telephone from a drawer and set it on his desk. It was an expensive instrument fitted with a scrambling device, useful for major dealing in sensitive markets.

He dialled Hugo Spinner's Rome number and was answered at once.

'Did he come?'

'Yes. He gave me a copy of the fax sent to Boru by David Brock.'

'Was there a photo?'

'Yes. No one we know.'

'Kyle must work on it.'

'When the time is right, not until.'

'You gave Brock the CVs?'

'Yes.'

There was a silence, then Hugo said fretfully:

'I find all this unacceptable. Brock has no right to harass us. I've a good mind to report it to the police.'

'Listen to me.' Roswall's voice was soft and cold. 'This is no time to whine about minor issues. Your job is to warn Fermoy, Kincraig, all our key people, that if James Brock shows up they are to treat him politely and with honesty, but they are not to volunteer information. Is that understood?'

'Yes. Of course. All I want — '

'We have to be on our guard. We have to avoid wild statements. If Brock or anyone else accuses Dove of making illegal transactions, the response will be made by me, no one else. Is that clear?'

'Quite clear.'

'Just keep your head down, and hold your tongue, Hugo; we'll do all right. Good-night.'

Roswall replaced the receiver and contemplated Gerda Marcus, who was perched on the edge of a chair, watching him.

'Well, my dear,' he said, 'why the frown?'

'James Brock levelled with us,' she said. 'He told us all he knew.'

'I doubt it. No one tells all they know.'

'He gave us the photo.'

'That was his game plan.'

'For God's sake, Dan, this isn't a game! Brock wants to find his brother's killer.'

Roswall's eyebrows rose. 'Don't we?'

Gerda levelled a finger at him. 'You gave him nothing. A bunch of lousy CVs, nothing of value. You were closer than a Scottish clam!'

'But what's to tell? We know little more than he does.'

'Rubbish!' Gerda held up a hand, counting off fingers. 'We know that Joel Moshal cancelled his flight on *Paloma* at Mossad's insistence. We know Moshal reported money was being sent from a Middle East source, through Italy, to a Swiss numbered account. Adri Romm hinted that Dove provided the courier, and that the money goes to buy war materials on the black market.

'We know that Dieter Engel warned us there are US federal agents in Europe, ostensibly to track down tax-dodgers, but in fact to learn who's cutting deals with hostile regimes and who's laundering money. We know that the Jerusalem Accord is on a knife edge, and if it fails we could all slide into a full-scale nuclear war. I didn't hear you discuss any of that with Brock.'

'Because he can't do a damn thing about any of it. If I show my hand, it will be to someone with authority, with power, not to some small-time lawyer in last year's suit.'

Gerda stood up and started for the door, but he called her back.

'You know very well,' he said, 'in today's world it's each man for himself. At least admit that I take care of my own.'

'Do you? Did you take care of the people on *Paloma*?'

Roswall paled. 'That's unfair!'

'Unfair? For pity's sake, look around you! Who's to say what's fair or unfair? The world's a mess; overcrowded, overexploited, national boundaries mean nothing, trade barriers are drowning in a global economy, there's no morality, no common humanity, no respect for God or the Devil, just each man for himself. Anarchy, Dan. People don't know who they are, where they're going, where to put their trust . . . '

'Where will you put yours, Gerda?'

She stared at him in silence for a moment. Then she smiled.

'In a small-time lawyer in last year's suit,' she said.

⋆ ⋆ ⋆

When Gerda had left the room, Roswall sat thinking for some time, then dialled an unlisted number in Zurich. Dieter Engel took the call himself, sounding annoyed.

'I'm in conference,' he said. 'I'll call you back.'

'No. Get rid of whoever's with you. This can't wait.'

Voices rumbled in the background, a door closed. Engel came back on the line.

'Well, what is it?'

'We've had a visit from James Brock, the

372

brother of *Paloma*'s pilot. He's trying to identify the photograph of a man he believes controls a syndicate that sells banned goods to the Middle East. Brock thinks they used one of Dove's employees as a courier. He thinks that to prevent exposure of the operation, *Paloma* was sabotaged.'

Engel made a sound of disbelief. 'Has he any proof?'

'No.'

'Then why are you wasting my time?'

'Let me refresh your mind, Dieter. You recall that the Thursday before *Paloma* crashed, the Dove executive met here at Mallowfield.'

'Naturally I remember.'

'You told us then that US federal agents were investigating certain people who were thought to have secret accounts in Switzerland. We asked you to find out if that could concern any member of Dove.'

'Yes. Well?'

'The following Wednesday, after the disaster occurred, we met again. You said you'd made enquiries but had learned nothing. At that same meeting, Gerda told us that Adri Romm had warned her that a cartel in Rome was laundering money from the Middle East and sending it to Zurich. It would be used to buy materials prohibited by international law.

373

Romm hinted that the agent transferring the money might be employed by Dove. You agreed to make discreet enquiries about that possibility. Have you done so?'

'I have. It is a wild-goose chase. Every Middle Eastern state conducts arms deals, legal or illegal. Much of the finance is handled here. The details are not discussed, even among friends.'

'To your knowledge, has any member of Dove been party to such deals?'

Engel made no reply. Roswall persisted. 'I must have an answer, Dieter. If I can't count on your full support, I can't work with you. I will have to put an end to all our current undertakings.'

'You threaten me?' Engel's voice was shrill with rage. 'Thirty years I've backed you, you were nothing but a barrow-boy. I've helped you build an empire!'

'We've helped each other. Now we have to decide, do we go on together, or part company? All I want from you is a name.'

'I can't give you names! I have a duty to my clients. To my profession.'

'And I have a duty to Dove, and to my people who died.'

'They're dead. You can't bring them back. Forget them. Think of the living who still need your help, don't destroy what you've built up, all these years.'

'Give me the name.'

'I don't know it. I don't want to know it, you hear? *Lieber Gott*, don't you know how dangerous this is? Don't meddle, Dan. Forget it. Forget *Paloma*.'

'Dieter, listen to me. All I'm asking . . . '

As Roswall spoke, a clock far off in Zurich began to strike the half-hour. Before the last stroke sounded, the telephone line was dead.

★   ★   ★

Roswall called the London Clinic. The nurse on duty told him that Mr Solomon was asleep and not to be disturbed. Dan left a goodwill message.

As he replaced the receiver, Gerda Marcus appeared in the doorway. She was carrying an air-travel bag. Dan beckoned her in.

She came to stand in front of him.

'I'm sorry,' she said. 'I shouldn't have yelled at you. I know you'll do what's best for Dove.'

'Dieter wouldn't agree with you.'

Her eyes narrowed. 'What's he been saying?'

'It's what he won't say that troubles me.'

'Ach, he'll come round. He'll never risk losing your custom.'

'He's already dumped me. Seems I don't yet glitter as brightly as the oil cartels. Besides, I think he's shit-scared.'

'Of what?'

'Of having his throat cut, I imagine.'

She stared at him. 'Did you speak to Harry about it?'

'No. He's too ill.' Dan gestured at her travel-bag. 'You can unpack that. I want you here.'

'But . . . what about Hugo? You know what he's like; when he hears about Dieter, he'll go into orbit.'

'He won't hear,' Roswall said, 'not till I'm ready. I shall bring him back here. If there's to be a showdown, we'll face it together.'

★ ★ ★

Gerda had hardly left the room when the red telephone buzzed. Roswall lifted the receiver and a voice crackled across bursts of static.

'Sod this bluidy phone!'

'Hamish?' Roswall said. Under stress, Trotter lapsed from impeccable English into broad Scots.

'Aye, it's me.' The static ceased and the voice boomed. 'It's blowing a gale this side. Can ye hear me?'

'Loud and clear. What's your problem?'

'The ROV's fetched up a piece of baggage. A briefcase, evidently the property of one o' the passengers. It's a fine case, strongly made, but there's not much intult. Mebbe broke open on impact, not locked ye see? Nae doot the man was busy with it when the fire started, and wasna able to — '

'What man, whose case was it?'

'The name's Kesh, Jerome Kesh. There were papers in a sealed pocket.'

'What papers?'

'Well, I'll tell ye, if ye'll stop interruptin'. It would seem Mr Kesh was buying a substantial property in the Siena district. He had the final contract, but he'd not yet signed it. The option lapses ten days from now, and Porteous is of the opinion Kesh may have kin will need to give thought to what's to be done. We'll be sending the case over to the debris centre right away, so's you can see to things.'

'Thanks, Hamish. Was there nothing else in the case?'

'Aye, there was a two-three bits paper, tucked in with the contract. A memo, it could be, referring to the purchase o' goods.'

'What sort of goods?'

Trotter chuckled. 'Over a hundred drums of castor-oil beans, and bulk orders of beef-extract. There's dates given. I'd say Kesh was keeping note of orders made on Dove's behalf. He was a doctor, was he not?'

'Of biology, not medicine. Was there anything else on the memo? A supplier's name, an official stamp, an order number?'

'No.'

Roswall grunted. 'Fax me copies of all the papers, will you, the contract and the memo? Send the originals with the case to the debris centre. Mark them *For urgent attention of Mr Geoffrey Waldron and Mr Barry Coburn.* I'll sort it out with them. How's the salvage going?'

'Fine. We lifted some of the heavy stuff today . . . now . . . weather. Sea's running . . . ' Static drowned out Trotter's bellow.

Roswall said: 'You're breaking up, Hamish, I'll call you tomorrow.'

The connection cut, he pressed a button on his intercom.

'Kyle? Come over here, will you?'

He went to stand beside the fax machine. It signalled delivery and the sheets rolled through. He collected them and returned to his desk. As he finished examining them, Kyle came into the room. Roswall handed him the papers.

'Trotter's salvaged Kesh's briefcase,' he said. 'Most of the contents were missing, but these were in a sealed compartment. What d'you make of them?'

Kyle leafed throught the contract and laid it aside. He glanced at the memo and shook his head.

'Beats me.'

'What would Kesh want with all that castor-oil and beef-extract?'

'Research, perhaps? His field was animal diseases, maybe he needed the stuff for that? Ask Hugo, he handles all the bulk orders.'

Roswall rubbed his chin. 'Castor-oil and beef-extract. It rings a bell, something I saw on television, some documentary.'

'When?'

'A while ago. I think it was about the time of Desert Storm.'

'If Kesh did place an order with Hugo, it'll be on record.' Kyle moved to the computer terminal, switched on and set to work. Roswall watched.

'Nothing like that for Dove this year,' Kyle said. 'Let's take a look at Kesh's own file.' He watched the screen, muttering.

'*Nada. Nada.*' He glanced at Roswall. 'You said Desert Storm?'

'Umh.' Roswall picked up the property contract.

A villa near Siena, with a good piece of land. Gardens, pool, outhouses. The price was steep, justifiably so in a prime area. Roswall leaned back and closed his eyes. Steve had always loved Siena, a comb full of honey, he called it. Small, street-level shops that sold quality goods and delicious food, the market on high ground where massive caravans gathered on fair-days, huge churches with great murals. Saints. Vistas. The Pallio.

Roswall dozed, chin on chest, and woke calling Steve's name; but it was Kyle standing at his side, sombre-eyed.

'I found the programme,' Kyle said. 'I remembered the rumours, that Saddam Hussein spent ten billion dollars to build a nuclear bomb, and set up factories in the desert to make anthrax and botulism and gangrene cultures. Horror stories, I thought they were, but after the war, when the inspectors went in, they found factories and also evidence of missiles that could have dumped germs on whole cities.'

Roswall rubbed a hand across his eyes. 'I remember, but how does it tie up with Kesh?'

'He was a biologist.'

'So? I'm a chemist, but that doesn't mean I'm into making chemical weapons. Kesh taught a lot of people how to deal with animal diseases. He did a lot of research, he was working on a vaccine against airborne anthrax — '

'Which he could have sold to a buyer who was fixing to wage biological war, and wanted immunity for his own troops. That documentary mentioned castor-oil beans and beef-extract.' Kyle waved a handful of printouts. 'It's all here. Listen.

''One of the signs that a country is contemplating germ warfare is an unusual or excessive demand for the media in which bacteria can be grown: beef-extract, for example.' And later, it says, 'the castor-oil beans are crushed to produce castor-oil. The residue, after the oil is extracted, contains ricin, a deadly poison.'

Kyle laid the printouts on the desk. 'A while ago there was a guy murdered in London. Someone jabbed an umbrella-spike into him. The spike was loaded with ricin, the guy was dead pretty darn fast.'

'Wait now. The fact that Kesh jotted down a few items doesn't make him a criminal. He could have been doing research, planning a paper, anything . . . '

'He could have been a crook. He could have been the courier Moshal spotted. He was a big spender, Dan, we both know that. He spent a lot more than Dove paid him.'

'Perhaps he had private means.'

'And perhaps he dealt in drugs, castor-oil beans, beef-extract. Just where did he get enough money to buy a millionaire's pad in Tuscany?'

Roswall stared into space. 'Dieter might have arranged a loan.'

Kyle snorted. 'Dieter wouldn't advance a brass cent to anyone at Kesh's level. Dieter's only interested in the heavy money. I'll lay odds Kesh had a source. It got him killed. It could get us killed.' Kyle leaned a hand on the printouts. 'You have to tell someone about this.'

'Tell them what? That I suspect Kesh of criminal traffic, on the evidence of a few scrawled notes? If I involve Kesh, I involve Dove. It could destroy what we've taken years to create.' Roswall spread his hands, almost pleading. 'Kesh is dead, after all.'

'The people he may have worked for are still alive.'

Roswall drew a long breath. 'Yes. You're right. We have to take action. But who do we talk to? The Police, Civil Aviation, the Home Office?'

'James Brock seems to be putting his money on Dr Thorneycroft. He gave him the photograph.'

Roswall was silent for a spell, then he picked up the printouts. 'Do you have his number?'

Kyle handed over a slip of paper. 'He'll

want Kesh's details, and a mugshot.'

'See to that, will you?' Roswall pulled the telephone towards him but paused when he saw Kyle still lingering.

'Well?'

'I'm thinking of Gerda,' Kyle said. 'She's Jewish, she's Israeli. She won't want to keep quiet about this.'

'If we hand over to the authorities,' Roswall said, 'we'll have to do what we're told.'

'Gerda won't see it that way.'

'Make her. I count on you to keep her in line.'

Kyle gave a half-smile. 'That's a man-size job.'

'Then grow up,' Roswall said.

26

As Thorneycroft entered his office, his secretary handed him the receiver of a phone.

'Mr Daniel Roswall,' she said.

Roswall was succinct. He described how Jerome Kesh's briefcase had been recovered from the seabed, gave its contents and said he was faxing copies to Thorneycroft at once. He offered no opinions, merely saying that he could be reached at Mallowfield or on his mobile phone, any time of the day or night.

The fax arrived and Thorneycroft studied its several pages for some time, assessing its implications.

Crunch-point, he thought.

What he did now could be crucial, for Dove, for the *Paloma* inquiry, for the people out there who were trying to bring off a miracle peace accord.

For the past week he'd been coasting, doing what was required of him but no more, no risk involved.

The last few hours had changed that. The safe course wasn't safe any more.

If he played safe and did nothing, the effects could be disastrous. If he took action, that could be catastrophic and the blame would be at his door.

Roswall had made his choice. He could have protected Dove for a time, by keeping his mouth shut. He hadn't.

If good men kept silent, evil succeeded, et cetera.

So what sort of action should he take?

He could shift the burden on to Rylda, he could give her these papers; she'd sit on them until the Jerusalem Accord was signed or not signed, and most people would approve.

The people who wouldn't approve were small fry, they had no money and no high office and therefore no power.

He could leak the documents, to di Maggio and others. There would be results, probably the wrong ones. Heads would roll, starting with his own.

Silence or speech, action or inaction?

As he sat debating, his secretary appeared in the doorway.

'Rome wants you,' she said, 'a Captain di Maggio.'

'Speak of the devil,' Thorneycroft muttered, and signed to her to put the call through to him.

Vincenzo di Maggio greeted him in halting English. Thorneycroft answered in Italian and was complimented.

385

'My mother was from Firenze,' Thorney-croft said. 'We spoke Italian at home.'

'You received my report this morning, *Dottore*?'

'Yes, thank you. Tell me, are you now treating the Vespucci matter as a case of murder?'

Di Maggio hedged. 'It is a possibility, a strong possibility.'

Thorneycroft decided to play devil's advocate.

'In your original report you took the view that Alonso Vespucci felt responsible for the *Paloma* crash. Vitagas supplied the fire-depressants carried in the aircraft. If there was an error — if it wasn't halon in the cylinders but some flammable gas that triggered a flash fire — that would weigh heavily on the conscience of the young man. Enough perhaps to drive him to suicide?'

Di Maggio's response was categoric. 'If the wrong gas was in the cylinders, it was there by intent, not error, and Vespucci was not to blame. He felt guilt, yes, he made some fatal error of judgement perhaps, but he was not a saboteur and he did not kill himself. I believe he was executed because he was about to expose some kind of criminal operation, perhaps of international signifi-cance.'

'What was this 'fatal error of judgement', Captain?'

'He let himself be conned into working with criminals. He helped them to launder money. His mother told me 'he had too much money, he was careless about money'. He thought he was helping a charity. When *Paloma* crashed, he realized he'd been helping killers.'

'His mother says he was murdered. His father says he committed suicide.'

'Emilio Vespucci is not religious. He's a man who places the approval of society above the blessing of the Church. It's easier for him to accept that his son committed suicide, than that he had links with the Mafiosi.'

'Which parent is right?'

'Today I spoke to the priest at Alonso's church. In his view, Alonso would not have killed himself. He was strong Catholic, he was generous and did much for children's charities, he was honest in all things — but the priest says, he was naïve. Not smart about life.'

'After *Paloma* crashed, did he visit his priest? Make confession?'

'No. Perhaps he did not have time. He was concentrating on speaking to other people: Capriati, the staffs of Omega and Dove; he tried to talk to Contessa Pia d'Ascani, David

Brock's mistress. Nobody responded to his calls. I have spoken to everyone he tried to reach, they all admit they didn't talk to Alonso. They say: 'I was too busy, too upset'. Tragic, *hein*? Vespucci knew something, he wanted to disclose it, he wasn't given the chance.'

'Yet he didn't approach you, Captain? He didn't come to the police? Doesn't that suggest he was involved in unlawful activity?'

'It does, yes, but a man may become involved because he is foolish, or naïve. He's not guilty, but he's scared of the law, of publicity, of going to gaol.'

'True.'

'Another point of interest, *Dottore*. After the crash, Alonso called many people, but he made no calls to any charity. That suggests he knew the people he had worked with were not a charitable organization.'

Or, thought Thorneycroft, he felt they had nothing to do with *Paloma*. He said,

'Tell me about the night Vespucci died.'

'At six o'clock,' said di Maggio, 'he made a call to the Dove office at the airport, but it was closed. At about eight he left the house in a hurry and drove to the parkade near the Garibaldi Restaurant. The ticket in his pocket showed he checked into the parkade at eight-twenty. He reached the restaurant about twenty to nine. He'd been there before — we're trying to establish if he met other people regularly. On this night, he was alone. He dined, drank a lot of *vino*. The waiters say he watched the door as if he was expecting someone, but no one joined him.

'The restaurant closed at one o'clock. Vespucci left and sat on a bench outside. The owner of the restaurant saw him there at one-thirty. Around two, he must have walked back to the parkade. Someone followed him, or was waiting for him at the car. We think they both got into the car. The assailant shot Vespucci, pressed the gun into his hand and cleared off. The nightwatchman on the ground floor heard the shot, called the security company, and went up to the third floor. Found Vespucci dead in the car. The gunman must have left by the fire-stairs.

'The shot was fired at a quarter past two. The gun was lying on the floor of the car. Vespucci's prints were on it. We're looking for trace materials in the car. The shooter must have left something, but I don't think that will help us much. It looks like Vespucci tangled with professionals. The mob don't make that kind of mistake. Likely they hired a man to take out Vespucci. If he left traces, they won't tie him to anyone local.'

'What about the charities?' Thorneycroft asked.

'We're checking them, in particular those based in Rome, those that handle goods in transit, or have import-export permits. It has to be a set-up big enough to launder money. We're looking at the banks and loan-houses; you know how long it takes to get information out of them. It's a nightmare; you run, you don't move.'

Di Maggio's voice held bitter frustration, and under it a note of fear. Thorneycroft said bluntly:

'Have you been threatened?'

'No more than usual, but there are difficulties. Obstacles are placed in my way. The inquest on Vespucci has been postponed for a week, the forensic reports will not be ready until Monday next, I complain and they say what's your hurry, *Paloma* is not a priority. God's name, all those people dead and it's not a priority? What are the fools thinking about, what's important to them?'

Thorneycroft said slowly: 'The Jerusalem Accord. All the states in the Middle East have agreed to the truce, but some of them are looking for an excuse to pull out. If our investigations show that someone at Dove or Omega has been selling banned substances to dealers in an Arab state, that could cause strong reactions. This or that state could break the truce. The Accord could collapse.'

'Banned substances?' Di Maggio pounced on the words. 'You have evidence of such dealing?'

'I'm afraid not. Not yet. We're working on it.'

'I see.' The eagerness died in di Maggio's voice. 'Like me, you have nothing but guesses. So what do we do, *Dottore*? Pimp for the politicians?'

That's it in a nutshell, Thorneycroft thought. Let the bosses decide what is the greatest good, toe the line, *Paloma* is not the priority. A phrase floated into his head. He said:

'Your guess is as good as mine.'

'*Scusi?*'

'The gas-cylinders aboard *Paloma*,' Thorneycroft said. 'They were replaced the Sunday before the crash, right?'

'Right.'

'What about the patent cylinder attached to the Dove container? Was that replaced at the same time?'

'No, because it was new. Dove purchased the container about three months ago. The halon cylinder and hose were attached to its side.'

'So that cylinder could have been switched

391

at any time during the past three months?'

'Yes ... but ... that implies a different time-scale. It implies the sabotage was planned maybe weeks ago. Nothing to do with the Moshal scare?'

'That's my guess.'

'So what was in the cylinder?'

'An accelerant, perhaps. Flammable stuff. Barry Coburn's running tests. If you can examine the firms making or handling gas-cylinders ...'

Di Maggio laughed. 'In my spare time? Sure, I'll see to it. What else?'

'I'm going to fax you a photograph, a man we're very anxious to identify. He's not on our records, and the NCIC in the States doesn't have him. He may have had plastic surgery. He may have links with the Caribbean. It'll be a bloody miracle if we get a line on him, but I suggest you show the picture to Signor and Signora Vespucci, and the staff at the Garibaldi.'

'At once. May I know how you came by this photograph?'

'David Brock sent the original to a friend, several weeks ago, asking for help in identifying the subject.'

'A chase for wild geese!' Di Maggio seemed to relish the prospect. 'I will let you know as soon as I have news.'

'Thank you. Good hunting.'

'You also.' Di Maggio hung up.

The die cast, Thorneycroft felt a lightening of the spirit. He dispatched the photograph to Rome, then returned to the phone. A woman answered his call, then after a brief pause a man said:

'Rollo.'

'We need to talk,' Thorneycroft said. 'It's urgent.'

*   *   *

James returned to Bansford at dusk. The streets were almost deserted. There wasn't a breath of wind. Clouds rimmed with fire stood motionless over the southern hills, and the warm and languorous air absorbed all sound.

Dave used to say that the day peaked at six o'clock: in summer, the evening rise on the river; in winter fires lit, drinks poured and friends coming in.

Six was kids' time, Dave said. He liked kids. He should have married and had a family. Once when he was home on leave, he'd said there was someone he hoped to marry, but she couldn't handle the idea of being a pilot's wife. That was when he was working for Sirius.

The woman had to be Natalie Lomax, who'd married Greg Lomax in the mistaken belief that he had a nice safe job with the FBI.

Turning into the lane, James saw there was a car parked at the gate of Badger's Sett. The driver was sitting on the steps of the house, and he saw without surprise that it was Natalie. He parked the car in the garage and walked back along the path towards her. She was already apologizing.

'I'm sorry to arrive like this, I did try to call you, but there was no reply.'

'I'm glad you're here, I've been thinking about you.' He unlocked the front door and waved her through. She was still apologizing.

'I couldn't sleep last night. I felt so guilty. I should have told you yesterday . . . '

'Told me what?' He watched her gravely. The fading light in the hallway struck green glints from the nimbus of her hair. She seemed to float, like a swimmer treading water.

'The truth,' she said.

He led her into the living-room, switched on lamps and opened windows.

'Would you like a drink?'

She shook her head and sank down on the edge of a chair, her hands clasping her knees.

'You must think I'm crazy, turning up like

this. I needed to talk, you see? When someone you love dies, you need to be with other people who feel the same way. You . . . kind of hope they'll tell you things you don't know about the person. A kind of bonus.'

'You loved Dave, I know.'

'Oh yes, at first sight.' She smiled at some memory. 'I was eighteen. He was my first lover. I was too green to appreciate just how great he was — not just in bed, I mean, but as a companion, an adviser, a protector.' She stopped short. 'Did he mention me to you?'

'Not by name,' James said. He saw disappointment in her eyes and added, 'I know you're the one he wanted to marry, but you turned him down, didn't you?'

She nodded, disconsolate. 'I never meant him to leave for good. I just wanted to set terms. I was so scared.'

'Because of his job?'

'Yes. He was ferrying political refugees in South America. There were a lot of risks. Planes were shot down, and any survivors were killed on the ground, I couldn't face living with that kind of fear. My father died in Vietnam when I was five, my mother started doing drugs, and I was put into care. I grew up anxious, I guess. Craving security.

'I told Dave how I felt, and he understood. He said as soon as his contract ended — that would have been in another year — he'd leave Sirius and join a regular airline. I wanted him to quit right away. I wasn't reasonable, I made scenes, and when he wouldn't break his contract, I told him to get out. I thought he'd come back to me, but he didn't. I married Greg.

'It was a terrible mistake. There wasn't a day I didn't long for Dave. I made Greg's life a misery and ruined any chance we had of being happy. And three years after we married, he was kidnapped and murdered.'

'Did you keep in touch with Dave after your marriage?'

'No. We could none of us have borne that. Greg and I moved to New York, and Dave left Sirius the following year. I hoped I might hear from him after Greg died, but I didn't. I heard nothing until he sent me that fax.' She spread her hands in a helpless gesture. 'That's what I want to talk about. It didn't happen the way I told you yesterday.'

She paused as if she was trying to order her thoughts, then said: 'The fax reached me seven weeks ago.'

James looked up, startled. 'Seven? You said three weeks.'

'That was a lie. The truth is, Dave sent me the fax early in May and I did nothing about it. I was travelling, I was very busy, but more than that I was hurt and angry that Dave only got in touch with me when he needed a favour.

'I told myself I didn't owe him anything and I shouldn't get involved, but . . . well . . . I felt lousy. In the end I showed the fax to Ed Gascoigne and Gene Lafayette, like I told you.'

'Why did you lie about it yesterday?'

'I was ashamed to admit I took so long to do as Dave asked. I thought, seven weeks, three weeks, what's the difference? Last night, though, I couldn't sleep. I saw I was cheating Dave and the other people who died, because maybe the fax was connected somehow to *Paloma*. Was it, James? Is it important?'

'It could be. You say Dave sent you the fax early in May?'

'Yes. It reached me in the second week of May.'

'He came to England on leave about then. He stayed here. He had to leave earlier than he planned, he went back to Rome and then made a tour of duty to the Far East. While he was in Hong Kong, my wife committed suicide. She drove the car over the edge of the quarry, out there. I tried to stop her and I was injured. That was just under four weeks before *Paloma* crashed. I was in hospital for two weeks and then in a convalescent home for ten days.

'When I came home I found some of Dave's things were still here, things he might need. I packed them up and sent them to Rome.'

'I know,' Natalie said. 'I read about it in the papers. They tried to suggest something in the carton started the fire.'

'Yes, but if Dave sent you the fax in May, the whole emphasis shifts, doesn't it? It shows he started trying to identify the man in the photo weeks before the crash. All the investigations into the disaster, by the police and by the press, have focused on the last couple of weeks.'

Natalie said miserably, 'So what do we do now?'

James studied her in silence. She said 'we' as if she was already committed to whatever action he might take. But was she to be trusted? She worked for an insurance company that would be paying out huge sums to the dependants of the Omega crew. Did she have some private agenda?

He had no way of telling. He had to accept her at face value, or not at all.

Dave had trusted her.

So.

He said: 'Dave had a mistress in Italy, did you know?'

She smiled slightly. 'The Countess Pia d'Ascani. My company insures all the Omega employees, I visit their offices here and abroad, I hear the gossip. Do you think she can tell you anything?'

'Perhaps. I want to talk to her. I'm booked on the early flight on Wednesday.'

'I'd like to go with you.'

'No.' As hurt showed in her face, James said flatly: 'It could be dangerous, Natalie.'

'I don't care! Please let me come.'

James still hesitated and she leaned towards him. 'Greg and Dave both loved me, and I failed them both. I need to make amends. Please.'

It was a need he understood.

'Very well.'

'Thank you. What's the number of your flight?'

He told her and she wrote it in her diary.

'I'll phone you to confirm I'm booked,' she said.

⋆   ⋆   ⋆

After Natalie left, James studied the CVs in the folder Roswall had given him.

None of the photos matched the man in Dave's fax.

He set aside those relating to women, and tried to sort the men into categories. Some of them were obviously too young or too old to qualify as the subject. That still left a sizeable pile of mugshots.

He considered nationality. It didn't help much.

Most of the people who worked for Dove were from first world states, but some were nationals of one and resident in another. A couple held dual passports.

Religion?

There were Christians, Jews, Christian -Jews, Muslims who were Arab and Muslims who were black-African. There was one Norwegian Buddhist, three Hindus, and nineteen agnostics.

Dove was about as polyglot as you could get.

At eleven o'clock, James gave up. He locked the folder in the safe, raided the fridge and made coffee.

He thought of phoning Pia d'Ascani, to tell her that Natalie Lomax would be accompanying him to Rome, but decided against it. The contessa was probably asleep, and if she wasn't, she might not welcome the idea that Dave's ex-girlfriend was about to step on to her turf.

Instead, he called Thorneycroft's office number, left a message on his answering machine, and went to bed.

27

It was dusk when the car turned into the carpark behind Thorneycroft's office. The dark glass of its windows obscured the face of its driver, but as Thorneycroft stepped forward, the front passenger door swung open. He slid through it, and the car headed out of the yard.

'Fifteen minutes, John,' the driver said. 'I'm due at a reception.'

'Thank you.' Thorneycroft was genuinely grateful. To gain this interview he'd broken his rule never to exploit a friend, particularly one from his commando days. The man beside him, grey-haired, grey-eyed, grey-suited, still looked more like a soldier than a civil servant. His posture was relaxed, his expression alert and dispassionate. Only his voice betrayed his fatigue.

'What's on your mind?' he said.

Thorneycroft told him as crisply as he could. When he finished, the grey man frowned.

'First, the man in the photograph. Long odds, isn't it, that Brock will identify him?'

'Best odds we'll get, sir.'

The man dismissed the 'sir' with an impatient flick of the hand.

'Rylda disagrees with you. She says Brock is an attention-seeker who'll cause us nothing but embarrassment.'

'Rylda's wrong about Brock, and about the *Paloma* crash. By her theory — '

'I know her theory. I'd like to hear yours.'

'Right. I believe David Brock stumbled on a racket operated by a syndicate in Rome. Involved were the man in the photo, and a Dove scientist named Jerome Kesh. Kesh acted as courier, saw that money was laundered and conveyed to a secret account in Zurich. The banker may have been Dieter Engel. Kesh also advised the syndicate on chemical and biological weaponry, and at times supplied the raw materials prohibited by UN resolution.

'The front for the syndicate is probably a Rome charity that has links with the Middle East. The controller of the operation may be the man in the photo. Vincent di Maggio is working on that.'

'When did David Brock become suspicious of the man?'

'I think about two months ago. He associated him with past illegal activity, but couldn't put a name to him. The man is believed to have had surgery to alter his appearance, but Brock could have recognized his voice, a gesture . . . '

'Yes, yes, go on.'

'Brock obtained a photograph of the man and faxed it to an old flame, Natalie Lomax. She has contacts in the FBI and in the English and American pilots' associations.'

'Was the suspect a pilot?'

'Possibly, but it's more likely he was some scumbag Brock ran across during his spell with Sirius. Whatever the case, Mrs Lomax didn't get a positive ID on him. After David died in the *Paloma* crash, she showed the photo to his brother James, who's since given copies to me, and to Daniel Roswall who's the chairman of Dove. Rylda, Radnor and Geoff Waldron have seen it, and I've sent copies to you and to di Maggio.'

'Hmm. Not what you'd call a close secret.'

'James Brock doesn't think secrecy serves his purpose.'

'The question, John, is whether it serves ours! Rylda thinks it does. You don't agree. Rylda's convinced that *Paloma* was sabotaged for political reasons. You're convinced it was sabotaged to silence David Brock, Jerome Kesh, and possibly others on board. In other words, you think it was mass murder designed to protect a criminal operation.'

'Yes.'

'And what is your opinion of James Brock?'

'On short acquaintance, I'd say he's highly intelligent, brave, bloody obstinate, and obsessed by a need to find his brother's murderer. They were close. Orphaned young, had to depend on each other through their formative years, and remained close in adult life. James claims they thought alike, shared the same principles and objectives. So when he interprets the actions of David over the past few weeks, I tend to believe him.'

The grey man eased the car round Hyde Park Corner and turned down Constitution Hill.

'What's James plan to do next?'

'He's booked on the early flight to Rome, on Wednesday.' Thorneycroft cast a sidelong glance at his companion. 'I'm sure Rylda's told you all about that.'

The grey man answered at a tangent. 'I take it he intends to talk to Pia d'Ascani. Rome police got nothing out of her. Why should Brock do better?'

'She loved David Brock. She'll sense James's affinity with David. She'll trust him and talk to him.'

'You've seen this in your crystal ball?'

'That's my job.'

'Of course. To return to my first question, what's on your mind?'

'Pia d'Ascani may have the evidence we need to nail the bastards who wrecked *Paloma*, but to get it, we have to keep James Brock alive.'

'You think he's at risk?'

'You know damn well he is! They've massacred a hundred and fifty-five people in the aircraft, they've killed Alonso Vespucci . . . '

'Was Vespucci party to the sabotage?'

'Di Maggio says not, says he was conned into being an accessory.'

'What facts do you have to support your theory?'

'Bloody few. The stuff from Kesh's briefcase may provide some leads. I'll send his mugshot to di Maggio. Maybe Signora Vespucci will recognize him as the man who visited their home.'

'Maybe. You expect me to act on 'maybe' and 'perhaps'?'

'Rollo, all we have is supposition. If we had six months, we could pile up the evidence, but we don't have that luxury. The Accord is this weekend. James Brock may be our only chance of finding facts before the balloon goes up.'

The grey man was silent as they circled Queen Anne's Gardens and eased into Birdcage Walk.

'Very well then. Let us suppose that a syndicate in Rome is supplying a Middle Eastern buyer with the raw materials for chemical and biological warfare, and is also helping the buyer to establish a war fund in a Swiss bank. Which state do you suppose is the buyer?'

'I don't know. One can probably exclude Israel, Egypt. Jordan . . . '

'It doesn't matter a stuff which power you include or exclude! If Brock links the man in that photo with any Middle Eastern state, if he turns up proof of the sort of deals you've described, the shit will hit the fan. There will be huge publicity, international outrage. End of truce, end of Accord.'

'And if Brock is not given the chance to identify the man, we lose our best chance of exposing people who are conspiring to wage biological war.'

'Catch twenty-two. Rylda's way or yours, we lose.'

'No! No, we have to consider the motive. Rylda believes that *Paloma* was sabotaged with the sole intention of wrecking the Accord. It was political murder, she says, arranged by dissidents opposed to the Accord. So our job is to muzzle Brock and keep our mouths shut until the Accord is signed and sealed.

'I don't agree, I don't believe that any of the participating states wants the Accord to fail. The stakes are too high. Even if such a renegade state existed, it wouldn't need to create this kind of mayhem. It need only withdraw formally from the truce, to break the Accord.

'That leaves the option of some group of political fanatics, but I don't think the fire on *Paloma* looks like the work of professional terrorists. It's too clumsy, too chancy, and elaborate. I think the fire was set by an amateur, and the motive was nothing more than old-fashioned, pathological greed.'

The grey man said drily: 'So we're looking for an avaricious amateur. The list, my friend, is a very, very long one.'

'We can shorten it to the ten people Alonso Vespucci tried to reach before he died. He called them, left a message: 'We have to talk, I'll be at the usual place, call me back'. Someone went to the parkade where Vespucci always left his car, waited till he showed up, shot him . . . or arranged for someone else to do the job.'

'You've had your fifteen minutes.' As Thorneycroft made no answer, the grey man grunted. 'All right, which ten people?'

'Daniel Roswall,' Thorneycroft said. 'Wealth and power are the focus of his life.

He may have used Dove as a front for illicit deals. He has easy access to chemicals and to banking systems. If detected, he may have decided to cut loose and destroy the evidence. He could have hired an assassin.

'Dieter Engel has the same motive and means as Roswall. So does Hugo Spinner. He's based in Rome, and has had business dealings with Vespucci.

'Kyle Parnell is an eccentric. He's quit his multimillion family firm, and gets his kicks from risking his neck. Illegal dealing might be his latest thrill. It's also possible he's shielding Gerda Marcus. The two are lovers.

'Gerda Marcus is a fervent Zionist. If she discovered that Dove was supplying enemies of Israel with the means to create weapons of mass destruction, she might have connived at the sabotage of *Paloma*, or at least have refused to expose the saboteurs.

'Iain Kincraig is an unlikely suspect, but he had the opportunity to switch the cylinder on the Dove container. His wife claims he was at home with her at the time Vespucci was shot, but she could be lying.

'Andrew Fermoy, like Kincraig, had opportunity to switch the cylinder. He's a street-fighter, ex-army quartermaster, could have been mixed up in a criminal racket. He has no alibi for the Vespucci killing.

'Benno Capriati is not, in my view, a suspect. His record is above reproach, and he had neither the motive nor the opportunity to plan and carry out the murders.

'Harry Solomon can also be dismissed. The results of the *Paloma* crash are cataclysmic for Omega, and Solomon is too ill to have instigated the shooting of Vespucci.

'Pia d'Ascani was probably on Vespucci's list because he hoped she could give him information about David Brock's actions before the crash. She had no motive for the murders. If Brock threatened to leave her, she might shoot him, but not the others.'

'If you leave out Solomon, Capriati and the contessa,' Rollo said, 'that cuts your list to seven.'

'We can't leave them out. Vespucci tried to reach them, and we need to know why. Guilty or innocent, those ten people may be able to tell us things we must know. They should be kept under surveillance, and Brock must have full protection.'

Rollo grimaced. 'Surveillance isn't easy. You're talking skilled operators, police or special army, and we're already thin on the ground. As for protecting Brock, we'd have to set up an operation on foreign soil. You have no conception what that entails. I'd have to claw my way through a forest of red tape.'

'You've done it before.'

'There's also the fact that Rylda's a senior member of my staff. She's set her strategy, and if I override that, and events prove her right, it could mean my job — and yours.'

'There's more at stake than our jobs.'

'Thank you so much for reminding me! Sod it, John, I could cause exactly the sort of political meltdown that Rylda's trying to avoid.'

'We could avoid the meltdown. We treat this as a commercial, not a political crime. Gene Lafayette's in town and Jerome Kesh is an American citizen. Let Gene check Kesh's tax history, see if he's been stashing funds in Zurich. Put di Maggio in full charge of the Italian enquiries, he checks out Kesh's connections and he watches Brock's back for us. Rylda can't beef about that.' As Rollo sat tight-lipped, Thorneycroft said tentatively: 'I have some ideas about how we can set things up . . .'

'The last time I listened to your ideas, I spent six weeks in hospital!'

'They gave you a nice shiny medal.'

Rollo snorted. 'All right, I'll hear you out, but I make no promises.'

He lifted a mobile phone from the dashboard, and activated it.

'Chris,' he said, 'I'm coming back, I'm

bringing John Thorneycroft with me. Cancel my evening engagement, tell my wife I'm sorry, I'll be late home. Get Kevin and his team in, and fix some food and booze for us. It could be a long night.'

★ ★ ★

Thorneycroft returned to his own office at three in the morning. He dumped a sheaf of notes on his desk, sat down, and called Rylda Warne's home number. She answered through gusts of coughing. He heard a match being struck, smoke blown.

'It's dangerous to smoke in bed,' he said.

'What the hell do you want?'

'Di Maggio called me, last evening. I thought you should hear what he said.' He gave her a précis of the conversation.

'Poppycock,' she said when he finished. 'All sucked out of his thumb. He's an organ-grinder's monkey, you can tell him I said so.'

'I will, when I see him tomorrow.'

'What d'you mean?'

'I'm going to Italy. A joint operation.'

'What sort of operation?'

'Just my job. Making enquiries, talking to people.'

'Do you mean James Brock?'

'Among others, yes.'

412

'That is unacceptable. I will not permit you to endanger my plans.' She broke into coughing again and Thorneycroft took the gap.

'Rylda, if you leave Brock unprotected, you could get him killed. You could lose us the chance of finding who set the *Paloma* fire.'

'Damn you!' She was fighting to regain her breath. 'You have no authority in this.'

'But I do. The *Paloma* inquiry is my territory.'

'I'll have you stopped.'

'I doubt it. The boss gave me the go-ahead.'

'What boss?'

'Yours. Rollo.'

She sucked in air, raucously. 'You're lying. I shall sort this out with him, at once.'

'I'm afraid he's out of town. He asked me to tell you.'

'Where is he?'

'I don't know.'

'I'll go over his head, I'll go to the top.'

'We already have, we have his blessing.'

'You . . . you . . . ' she was spluttering with rage, 'you are nothing but a bloody loose cannon.'

Thorneycroft laughed. He thought of Rollo, breaking the bonds of protocol, finding the people and the money to do the impossible, just like the old days. He thought of James Brock and di Maggio, Coburn and Waldron and Lafayette.

'Loose cannons of the world, unite!' he said, and hung up.

His next call was to Badger's Sett.

'Mr Brock? John Thorneycroft. I'm sorry to wake you. It's a matter of urgency. I had your message about Natalie Lomax. Does she understand that going to Rome with you involves a certain degree of risk?'

'Yes. I told her. She's set on going.'

'I see. I'd like very much to talk to you both, before you leave. I have certain suggestions that may be helpful. Can you find time for us to meet?'

'Sure. When and where?'

'Later this morning, at your home?'

'Would eleven suit you?'

'Eleven's fine.'

'Good. I'll confirm with Natalie, and let you know.'

'Thank you. All being well, I'll see you at eleven.'

Thorneycroft settled to work through his notes. He made phone calls, left instructions on the dictaphone for his secretary to deal with in the morning.

At dawn he moved to stand at the window. The red was fading from the stone of the buildings opposite, a violet haze lay over the trees in the park beyond. Down by the river, a siren wailed and faded.

He was tired. He could do with a cup of coffee, Irish coffee. He could do with a drink.

Dutch courage, Louise used to say, giving him that flat-mouthed look. Funny how often he thought of his ex-wife when things got rough. Kind of a counter irritant?

There was a tap on the door, and he turned to see Eugene Lafayette, dressed in a track suit and trainers, levelling an accusing finger.

'This better be good, my man.'

They settled on opposite sides of the desk. Lafayette said:

'Why the dawn call?'

Thorneycroft pushed a bundle of papers towards him.

'*Seascanner's* ROV dredged up a briefcase, yesterday. It belonged to Jerome Kesh of Dove. He died in the crash. Trotter faxed the contents of the case to Daniel Roswall, who sent copies to me. I'd like to hear what you think.'

I think you are about to slip your collar, was what Lafayette thought. He'd seen it happen before. A man followed the rules for years, then something happened that stuck in his gullet, and he freaked. Thorneycroft was as twitchy as a rabbit's nose and his eyes had that certain glitter.

Lafayette paged through the papers, a property contract and a couple of extra sheets, some kind of memo.

'Kesh musta had plenty of bread,' he said, 'to buy in that area.'

'More than he earned at Dove, Roswall said.'

'You spoke to Roswall?'

'Yes, last night. Was Kesh one of the tax-dodgers you're chasing?'

'No, never heard of him. Was he an American citizen?'

'By naturalization. He was born in Prague, became a citizen of the States after his parents emigrated to Hawaii. For the past ten years he's resided in Italy.'

Lafayette scanned the loose sheets of paper and his eyes narrowed.

'Castor-oil beans and beef-extract? Yeah, yeah, a man can get rich, selling stuff like that in the wrong market. Was Kesh a biologist?'

'Yes. Seems he'd been working on vaccines against animal diseases. Anthrax, camel-pox.'

'Weapons of mass destruction,' said Lafayette softly. 'The mere threat of disease can change a lot of minds, these days.' He met Thorneycroft's eyes. 'There'd have to be factories. You know where?'

Thorneycroft shook his head. 'Kesh could have been working with dealers in Italy and the Middle East. At the time of his death he was probably a courier. Money came to him through contacts in Rome, he'd see it laundered and convey it to Zurich. He was tailor-made for the job. He worked for Dove, a well-respected charity that ran regular missions to the Middle East. He had easy access to a Swiss bank through Dieter Engel, who's on the Dove executive.'

'No wonder Engel won't talk to me!'

'He won't talk to anyone. He wouldn't name Kesh to Roswall, even at the threat of losing Roswall's billion-dollar account. Engel's probably scared witless. He knows that Alonso Vespucci tried to blow the whistle on the syndicate and it got him a bullet in the brain.'

'Syndicate? Kesh wasn't a loner?'

'I don't think so. I think Joel Moshal picked up his trail and told Mossad. Mossad cancelled Moshal's trip to the UK, but didn't arrest Kesh because they want the whole ring.'

'Who's handling the case in Rome?'

'Di Maggio. He's following up on Kesh and looking for the charity the syndicate used as a front. I've asked him to check on firms that deal in gas-cylinders.'

Lafayette's brows rose. 'Apropos of what?'

'The fire on *Paloma*. I spent yesterday

afternoon with Coburn and Waldron, at the debris centre. Coburn thinks a fire-starter was planted in the Dove container. It released smoke, the smoke-alarm sounded, fire-fighters went into the hold and one of them used the patent fire-extinguisher attached to the container. It should have released halon. Instead, it released some highly flammable substance. The result was a flash fire that wiped out *Paloma's* tail structure and electricals, causing her to crash. Di Maggio's trying to track down the suppliers of the phoney cylinder.'

'Not Vitagas?'

'No, Vitagas seems to be in the clear. Vespucci may have guessed what had happened. He tried to inform the authorities, but no one had time to listen.'

Lafayette tilted his head back. 'All very interesting, but you still haven't told me why you fetched me out of a warm bed at the crack of dawn.'

'I'm going to Rome tomorrow,' Thorneycroft said. 'Before I go, I want the answers to some questions.'

'Such as?'

'Last Thursday night, when we dined together, we spoke about the fax David Brock sent to someone called Boru. I think you knew, then, that that person was Natalie

Lomax. I think she showed you Brock's original request. You never told me. Why?'

Lafayette screwed up his face. 'You're right, Natalie showed me the fax, before the crash. She wanted me to get the NCIC to identify the man in the photo. They couldn't. Natalie asked me not to talk about it to anyone. I owe her, John. Her husband worked for me, got himself killed, we didn't handle things too well.' Lafayette met Thorneycroft's derisive stare and raised both hands. 'OK. I didn't tell you because we had our own fish to fry, and no way was I handing over to an asshole like Radnor, or that Warne wolverine.'

'You could have talked to me.'

'I didn't know where you stood with those others.'

Thorneycroft grinned suddenly. 'Nowhere, I'm happy to say. Tell me, do you trust Natalie Lomax?'

'Sure I do. Known her since she was so high. Why do you ask?'

'She's going to Rome tomorrow, with James Brock.'

'Really? What's Brock aim to do?'

'He wants to talk to Pia d'Ascani.'

'I heard Rome police tried that, and got nowhere.'

'Brock may do better.'

Lafayette nodded slowly. 'It'll make him a

target, y'know. Natalie too. You watching their backs?'

'I'll be talking to di Maggio about that. Meanwhile, we need someone to cover the Kesh angle. Check out his links with Zurich. Follow the money trail. Would you be interested?'

Lafayette rubbed his chin. 'Am I interested in a rich US citizen who's dodging tax, and dealing in germ weaponry? Yeah, pal. I'm interested.'

28

London Airport was opaque under drizzle. Crowds in raincoats and wetproof jumpsuits moved with slow purpose towards the lifts and escalators, and clogged the stalls.

Natalie muttered: 'They've forgotten already. I feel like I'm in a bad dream, outside of the real world.'

James took her arm. She was trembling and her face was very pale.

'You don't have to come, no one would blame you.'

'I'm going to Rome!' she said fiercely. 'It's knowing so little that gets me. If only Dave had explained.'

'He told us as much as he could. We'll have protection. We just have to keep in touch, and do as they say.'

She glanced about her. 'Do you think we're being watched, now?'

'I hope so.' James smiled at her and she managed to smile back.

'I'm sorry to be so jittery. I didn't sleep well. Around three o'clock I looked out of the window of my apartment, and there was this van parked in the street. Most likely it belonged to someone in the block, but I felt kind of comforted, thinking it was there for me, know what I mean?'

'I know.' He thought, I've had the bad-dream syndrome since Clare died. Natalie's been through it before, when her husband was killed.

'It'll pass,' he said, and she sighed.

'It's easier, being with you.'

The flight was smooth, rainswept skies giving way to sparkling sunshine. Natalie dozed, and James reflected on Thorneycroft's instructions.

'Take only your carry-on bags,' he'd said, 'no other luggage. You'll be met at the airport by Father Stefano, Pia d'Ascani's village priest. He'll take you straight to the Villa d'Ascani. If there are developments you don't expect, keep your cool and don't improvise. Stick to the agreed plan. Go with the flow. We'll keep up with you, don't worry.'

I hope to hell you know what you're doing, James thought. He touched his shirtfront, feeling the box taped to his chest.

'Don't switch on until you're with the contessa,' Thorneycroft had warned. 'We need her to identify the photo and tell us when and where it was taken. Anything she can remember, any small detail, could be vital. The man's brand of cigarette, his posture, way of speaking, gestures, could help us to nail him. If the contessa can describe who he was with, we might trace other associates. We might be able to find it he has a criminal record.'

'Do you think he has?'

Thorneycroft hesitated. At last he said quietly: 'Your brother seemed to think so, and tried to prove it. That may have led to his death.'

★   ★   ★

They landed at Leonardo da Vinci on time, cleared customs and headed for the main concourse. There, the unexpected developed.

Father Stefano was waiting, holding up a placard bearing their names, but as they reached him they were engulfed in a rush of bodies, men and women wearing jeans, smelling of sweat, garlic and *vino*, all of them wielding cameras. Flashbulbs exploded and Natalie cried out, lifting her hands to shield her face. James threw an arm around her and tried to reach Father Stefano, who was being swept along on the crest of the human wave. Two airport policemen galloped alongside, shouting and gesticulating.

A black man with dreadlocks was propelling Natalie forward. James punched him in the ribs and he grinned.

'Go with the flow, my brother. Safety in numbers.'

They surged through the exit and on to the parking ground, fetching up at a parked Lamborghini sedan. Father Stefano was arguing fiercely with a woman who answered in earthy Italian. Cameras were levelled again. Father Stefano pressed a remote-button and the locks of the car clicked.

'In you go, love.' Dreadlocks held the door for Natalie, who slid into the front seat. James settled in the back. The camera mob stood back. At the wheel of the car, Father Stefano was almost in tears.

'Many, many apologies,' he said. 'These paparazzi have no shame. You are brother to Captain Brock, they want your picture, the papers will pay well for it because of the contessa. All week they have been at the villa, taking pictures, pictures. No respect for grief, no pity, it is horrible.' He started the car and moved into the traffic heading north.

'How is the contessa?' James asked. The old man shook his head.

'She is very low, very low. Perhaps it will help her to talk with you and the Signora Lomax. David was everything in her life. Now she has nothing.'

They circled the rim of the city and

reached open country. 'We will be in Ascani in one hour,' Father Stefano promised, 'and then we will be free of those barbarians.'

James doubted it. A carload driven by Dreadlocks followed in their wake, and behind that was a truck loaded with burly farm labourers. At the turn-off for Temi the truck was replaced by a closed van bearing the insignia of a plumbing firm. The carload of paparazzi left them at the main gate of the villa, but James saw it making purposefully for a side entrance further down the road. The plumber's van followed the Lamborghini all the way to the front door.

James climbed out and looked about him. The villa had been built close to the road. Its front courtyard was paved, with a fountain and large pots of flowering pelargonium, gerbera and lavender.

To the left, beyond a clipped yew hedge, was a swimming-pool fringed with poplars. Beyond that, lawns stretched to a stand of majestic cedars. White garden furniture with striped cushions was set out in the shade, a good place to sit in the cool of the evening. Dave had loved this property, the nearest he'd come to a home of his own.

The house was of stone, with a tiled roof, The shutters at the lower windows were closed. Those at the upper levels stood open, and on one of the deep sills a ginger cat drowsed in the sun.

Beside him, Natalie said, 'What a lovely place. How old is it?'

James pointed to the worn carving above the entrance, a coat of arms and a date. 'Fifteen twenty-six,' he said. As he spoke, the front doors swung back. A man in shirtsleeves scurried towards the van and with vehement gestures directed the driver to go round to the back yard. The driver refused. A stately figure in black emerged, silenced the first man, bowed to James and spoke rapidly to Father Stefano. The priest said:

'This is Mario, the contessa's major domo. He regrets, he has no English. The contessa makes you welcome, and asks you to join her as soon as you are ready.'

They followed Mario into the villa. The hall was large and lofty, its floor a magnificent mozaic of flowers, birds and geometric patterns. Father Stefano left them here, moving to address two young men in the robes of novice monks. James and Natalie were conducted through cool dark passages to a small salon that gave on to an inner courtyard.

As they entered the room, Pia d'Ascani rose to greet them. She wore a blue linen dress, sleeveless and unbelted. The tan of her face, throat and fleshy arms had faded to a yellowish-brown. Her features were puffy, and her pale-gold hair, streaked with grey, was drawn to the back of her head in an untidy knot. She wore neither make-up nor jewellery. Her eyes were large, red-rimmed and infinitely weary. The hand she held out to James was limp and cold.

She said: 'I am sorry I did not come outside to meet you. The paparazzi, you understand?' She gestured them to sit at a small table where there was a tray set with coffee, cream and sugar. As she poured for them, James tried to thank her for allowing them to visit her home. She looked at him in surprise.

'You are David's brother,' she said. Her gaze brushed Natalie, 'And his dear friend of long ago. When you are in Italy, this is your home as it was his.'

James said: 'You're very kind, Contessa. Unfortunately, we have only a few hours, then we must return to England, to help with the enquiries.'

She gave a faint shrug, 'Of course. We must get through all this. I am sorry you had trouble with the newspapers, these days they are a plague of monkeys, they climb trees to take their pictures.' She spoke with indifference, as if it was a matter beneath her notice.

James saw that she had built a barrier between herself and the world. He wondered how he might reach her, and decided that honesty was his best chance.

'Some of the people you call paparazzi are there for your protection, I think. Put there by Captain di Maggio.'

Colour flamed in her face. 'You believe that? That little cockroach was here yesterday, telling me I must have his spies in my house. For my protection, he said. I know what their protection is, it's to spy on me, ask me questions, trick me so they can blame David for that terrible thing. I won't allow it. I won't allow them to put dirt on his name. Never, never, never!'

She beat her fists on the arms of her chair. 'I told them, 'get out'. They came back with letters, from the Minister, the Chief of Police, the Pope for all I know, I didn't read their garbage. They dress up as monks, that's sacrilege. Today a man comes with a plumber's van, I have no need of plumbers, no need of anyone, let them get back to their monkey-house, so I can get on with my life!'

'Contessa,' James said, 'believe me, they don't blame David. They are trying to find the criminals who killed him.'

She was not listening. She stumbled to her feet, swinging her arms wildly, making for the door. Natalie rose and barred her way, spoke to her quietly in Italian, embraced the threshing arms. Pia fought her, then suddenly leaned against her and collapsed into her chair. Natalie sat beside her, holding her hand, and presently she grew calmer.

'What do you want me to do?' she said.

'Look at a picture,' Natalie answered, and held a hand out towards James. He took the photograph from his briefcase and gave it to Pia. She studied it briefly, then stared at James.

'How did you get this?'

He told her about the fax that had arrived at Badger's Sett, the carton he'd sent to Rome, his conversations at the memorial service and his meeting with Natalie. At that point, she waved him to silence.

'Very well. You are telling the truth. I'm sorry I shouted at you. These last days I have been very tired, you know? Not clear in my head. I thought, if I say nothing, they can't tell lies about David. He's gone, but there is his good name, I must save his good name.'

'That's what we all want, Contessa.'

She nodded, bent her head over the photo again. 'It's not a good picture,' she said.

'When did Dave take it?' James asked.

She shook her head. 'He didn't take it. I did.'

Rome airport

Hugo Spinner was in the Dove office at the airport. Andrew Fermoy and Iain Kincraig were with him. Fermoy lounged at his ease, pale eyes bored. Kincraig sat stiffly, arms folded.

'It was a bloody circus,' Hugo said. 'Brock and this bird arrived, and the paparazzi swarmed. The police couldn't stop them.'

Fermoy scowled. 'What's Brock here for?'

'Probably come to see his brother's lay, Pia d'Ascani. They were met by her tame priest.' Hugo lit a cigarette and blew out smoke with a hissing sound. 'Brock pisses me off. I've a good mind to tell him to keep his stupid trap shut.'

Fermoy wagged a finger. 'Dan wouldn't like that, boyo.'

'The hell with what Dan likes! He sits at Mallowfield and gives us orders, he doesn't know what we have to cope with here.'

Kincraig stirred restlessly. 'Mr Roswall is concerned for Dove. If the news about Kesh leaks out, it'll be goodbye to all his good work.'

'His good work? My work, mine! I built Dove. I built the infrastructure, found the offices, trained the staff. I made it a going concern. If Dove goes under, Dan will still be a billionaire, bum in the butter. He can build a new memorial for his darling boy. Nothing will change for him. It's us that's going to suffer. Our jobs.' He jabbed the cigarette at Kincraig. 'I'm telling you now, no one's going to blow me away! So if those press vultures come to you for stories, you better send them packing. They don't set foot on our property, they don't chat up our employees, if they try for photographs, we smash their cameras for them.'

Kincraig stood up. 'I've told you before, and I'll tell you again, Hugo, I work for Omega, not for Dove. I take ma orders from Mr Solomon, not from you. As for trespassers, you can set your silly mind at rest. There's police everywhere, guarding the hangars, ma workshop, and I've no doubt your warehouse too. Now, if ye'll excuse me, I've work to do.'

He headed out of the office and Hugo swung round to face Fermoy. 'Is that true? Are they watching the warehouse?'

'True enough. I'd to show my pass three times, this morning. If you ask me, it's us they're watching.'

'Why? What for?'

Fermoy hunched his shoulders, and Hugo leaned towards him.

'Did they question you?'

'Not yet.' Fermoy smirked. 'Don't worry, Hugo, I won't give away any family secrets.'

Hugo watched him, head lowered. After a moment he relaxed.

'Good. Right. Don't mind me, Andy, I'm feeling the pressure, that's all.' He glanced at his watch. 'I'm going to grab a sandwich. Gerda and I are flying back to the UK tonight. Dan's orders, he wants us back at Mallowfield, God knows why.'

As he started to rise, Fermoy reached out and caught hold of his wrist.

'Hugo, when you talk to Dan, stay cool. He pays your salary, remember?'

Hugo laughed, touching a finger to his nose.

'I'll remember,' he said.

29

In his office at police headquarters, Vincent di Maggio stood at the shoulder of an engineer who was fiddling with a radio receiver. At times it emitted muffled squawks, at times it fell obstinately silent.

Behind them, Thorneycroft and Lamberti watched a computer screen that displayed successive portions of a map of Rome. Stars marked charitable institutions, flags the sites of manufacturers and dealers in the gas trade.

Lamberti pointed. 'You see there's nothing close to the Garibaldi area.'

Thorneycroft sighed. 'Perhaps Brock will come up with something.'

Di Maggio punched the engineer between the shoulder blades.

'For the love of heaven, what's the problem?'

The engineer shifted his chair. 'From the villa to the van, no problem. From the van to us, heavy interference.' He began an acrimonious argument with someone called Umberto, evidently the controller in the radio van. Suddenly a voice blared out so loudly

433

that di Maggio swore. The engineer turned down the volume.

'Perfect,' he said.

Di Maggio walked back to his desk. Thorneycroft and Lamberti found chairs near the computer.

The voice of James Brock filled the room.

'Contessa, tell us about the photograph. Tell us when you took it.'

'It was five, six weeks ago, perhaps more . . . ' The woman's tone was listless, a little slurred, and di Maggio said: 'That's Pia d'Ascani. She is on medication, since the accident.'

'More than six weeks?' James prompted.

'Yes. The second week of May. And the middle of the week. We went to a meeting in Rome, it was to raise money for charity.'

'What was the name of the charity, Contessa?'

'I don't recall. It was something for children.' Pia's words trailed, as if her thoughts were wandering.

'Can you remember where the meeting was held?'

'It was in Rome. Some church hall. The Church of Santa Cecilia. I don't know the street. It was very boring, you know. We had only to smile, and make a big cheque. The hall was hot, there were no fans, we sat at the back, near the door. When we came outside, David said: 'We need a drink. There's a bar next door.' It was a little raining, but we didn't take the car, it was better to leave it in the church grounds. We ran quickly to the bar.'

'What was the name of the bar?'

'I don't know. It was a nice place, clean, but very noisy, a lot of people and the music very loud. We sat at a table in the corner. David ordered wine for me, and for himself whisky. We talked of the meeting and other things. The music was from *Titanic. Time to Say Goodbye.* That was the last time we were in Rome together.'

Pia stopped, on the edge of tears. Di Maggio shook both fists in the air.

'They played music from *Titanic,*' James said. 'And then?'

'Then two men came in. I was facing the door. I said: 'That's the man who spoke at the meeting.' David looked quickly, and then he bent down his head and said: 'Yes, that's Kesh, don't catch his eye, I don't want him yakking at me.' David was not for big camaraderie, you know, he liked to drink and go home.'

James said, 'I remember. So . . . Jerome Kesh was the guest speaker at the meeting. Can you tell us who called it?'

'Called?' The Contessa sounded distrait again, and Natalie Lomax spoke for the first time.

'Who arranged the meeting, Contessa? Who was the money for?'

Pia said slowly. 'I forget the name. It was for children. Dr Kesh spoke about children with cholera and tuberculosis and AIDS. Families starving, in Iraq I think. I didn't very well listen, I was tired. I'm sorry.'

'Never mind,' James said. 'Tell us about the photograph, the one you took. Did Dave ask you to take it?'

'No. It wasn't the man I wanted. It was the cat.'

'Cat?'

'Yes, yes. A blue Persian, very beautiful. I think it belongs to the bartender.'

'I see. Can you describe the man in the photo?'

'Well . . . it was dark and I didn't look much at him, he was not *simpatico*. A lot of hair, curly and dark, but no beard or moustache. The skin was smooth and quite dark, but the cheek was paler. Like a scar, you know, but pale? He was not tall. Fat. Fat in the stomach and the backsides. He sat at the bar and turned himself a little to face Dr Kesh. They were talking. Arguing perhaps.'

'Did they speak Italian?'

'Yes, but I couldn't hear what they said, there was too much noise. We finished our drinks, and David said we should leave. It was raining hard, and he said he would fetch the car. He went out. That is when the cat jumped up on the bar. It was so beautiful, I wished to take a photograph for my album.

'David was not very much for cats, but I love them, I have many pictures. I took my camera from my bag. The cat was on the right end of the counter and it walked along so nicely, stepping between the glasses. The man didn't see it, he had his back to it.

'I was ready to take my picture. I lifted up my camera, and just then the cat jumped past the man, into the space between him and Dr Kesh.

'The man went mad. I never before saw such a thing, he screamed out very loud, and he threw his glass at the poor cat, the drink went all over, the cat crouched down and then it ran along the bar. The bartender caught it and shouted at the man, the man was still screaming and banging his hands on the counter, he picked up a bottle to hit the bartender. Everyone was shouting, and Dr Kesh and a girl who was serving grabbed hold of the man and took him out to the street. He was holding his throat and his face was dark red as if he couldn't breathe, you know? I think with some people, they hate cats, and the cats go straight to them.'

'Yes,' James said. 'It's a well-known phobia. Contessa, when the man started to shout, did he speak Italian?'

'No. Not Italian, not English. I think perhaps Slav, or Greek.'

'What happened next?'

'I went outside. I was upset. David came with the car.'

'Did you tell him what had happened?'

'No. It was raining, there was much traffic, he didn't want to talk. I think perhaps he was thinking about the man in the bar. When my photographs came back from the shop, I showed them to him, and he was interested. He asked me to lend him the negative, to make another copy.'

'Was Dr Kesh in the picture?'

'No. Not Kesh, and not the cat. I suppose I moved the camera.'

'Did David say why he was interested, did he name the man?'

'No, he said nothing. Only put the negative in his pocket and spoke of other things.'

'He returned the negative to you?'

'Yes.'

'And after the accident, Contessa, when the police came to talk to you, did you tell them about the evening at the bar? Did you show them the photograph?'

'No. They came with their questions when I was in grief. They made suggestions, they said maybe the accident was David's fault, they asked did he ever get drunk, did he have a problem with the heart? The newspapers made stories about pilot error, just to sell their papers. I don't speak to such people. I told them nothing.'

'I understand. Contessa, I'm sorry to trouble you, I know this is hard for you, but it's very important. I think the man is a criminal. I think he is responsible for what happened to *Paloma*. The picture may help us to get the evidence we need, so we can arrest him and punish him. Would you lend it to me for a little while?'

There was a pause. Pia d'Ascani broke it by saying suddenly:

'The Little Flowers.'

'What?'

'The Little Flowers of St Francis. The meeting was to raise money for the society. David said we must go because his boss at Omega, Mr Solomon, is a patron, and he said someone from Omega Roma must go to hand over his cheque.'

'Thank you. Thank you, that's very helpful. Will you lend me the photo, Contessa?'

'I have it in the safe,' Pia said. 'If you come with me I will give it to you.'

★ ★ ★

Thorneycroft and Lamberti peered at the computer screen. At his desk di Maggio paged through a list of names.

'Got it,' he said triumphantly. 'Society of the Little Flowers of St Francis, St Cecilia Square. That's section D on the map.'

Lamberti moved the picture on the screen, stopped, enlarged the detail. The map displayed the square, the church property, and round the corner, Angelo's bar and wine shop. Lamberti pointed to a starred area. 'The Society's office,' he said, 'and up here at the top, that's the industrial complex. The dots show firms that deal in gas — industrial and household. Three of them also have contracts with the armed forces.'

Behind him, the engineer raised a hand.

'*Dottore?* Umberto is on the line, he says Mr Brock wants to know your instructions.'

Thorneycroft said: 'Tell him he must see that the contessa signs the photograph, ask her to write a note giving the date and time it was taken. The place was Angelo's bar in St Cecilia Square, tell her. Mr Brock and Signora Lomax must bring everything back

440

here, at once. They can travel in the van. The escort car must stay with them all the way.'

He joined di Maggio at the desk. 'What have you got on the Little Flowers?'

'A fleabite,' di Maggio said. 'The Society is well established, good patrons, some big names.'

'Including Harry Solomon of Omega Airlines.'

'Yes. Also churches, society leaders, business houses. The money goes to aid children.'

'Who's in charge?'

'The manager is . . . ' di Maggio consulted his list, 'Signor Guillermo Lippi, good churchman, lives in a nice suburb but nothing flashy. No criminal record in Italy.'

'Have you met him?'

Di Maggio grimaced. 'No, I regret. There are hundreds of charities in Rome, without a name to guide us it was not possible to approach all of them. Also, the Society is closed at the moment, the staff is on summer vacation. I made a phone call yesterday and there is only a caretaker on duty. He said Signor Lippi left last night for Greece. He has a holiday home on the coast, near Thessaloniki.'

Thorneycroft grunted. 'Tuesday afternoon we had the news about Jerome Kesh, and his interest in castor-oil beans and beef-extract.

441

Tuesday night Mr Lippi leaves the country. Maybe he was tipped off?'

'Maybe.' Di Maggio sounded grim. 'When you sent me the photo, I wanted to make copies and show them to the charities and gas firms, see if I could get a name. I was . . . overruled. It was said, we don't have enough evidence, we are not in a position to disturb respectable citizens, let alone search premises or lay charges. There are political pressures. You understand?'

'All too well.' Thorneycroft frowned, thinking aloud. 'We are at least beginning to forge a chain of likelihood. We know that the Little Flowers meeting took place in mid-May, and that after the meeting David Brock and Pia d'Ascani saw Kesh and another man in Angelo's bar. Brock half-recognized the man, but couldn't put a name to him, Pia took a photograph in the bar, and when Brock saw the print, he borrowed the negative and sent a copy of the photo to Natalie Lomax, asking her to get it identified. In his fax he mentioned her association with the FBI and the pilots' organizations. That much is fact.

'Let's assume, from the reference to the FBI and the pilots' organizations, that the man was linked, in Brock's mind, with some criminal operation, and that it dated from the

time he flew with Sirius in the Caribbean
. . . the time when he first knew Natalie.

'Natalie failed to get an identification from
the pilot bodies, and the NCIC, when
approached by Gene Lafayette, said they had
no record of the man. However, the general
opinion was that he must have had facial
surgery. In describing him, Pia d'Ascani said
the skin on his face was pale, 'like a scar'.

'She said he's of medium height, sallow,
clean-shaven, dark curly hair, and overweight,
with a big paunch and buttocks. We've
established that he's presently known as
Guillermo Lippi, he lives in Rome, has been
here long enough to acquire property and
status, and to be entrusted with the running
of a respected charity. Pia's report of Kesh's
speech to the Little Flowers Society shows
that it sends aid to children in the Middle
East.

'Kesh and Lippi weren't just drinking
together at Angelo's, they were arguing,
which suggests a more than formal acquaintance. Lippi is linked to Dove International
not only through Kesh, but also through
Harry Solomon. Solomon is one of the
Society's major patrons, owns Omega Airlines, and is a member of Dove's executive.

'Lippi owns property in Greece, which
shares a boundary with Turkey, and might

provide a staging-post for shipments of banned materials to the Middle East.

'Finally, we now know that Lippi has one unusual attribute: his phobia for cats. Cats not only give him the screaming heebies, they also bring on some sort of allergic reaction that affects his breathing.

'So what we're looking for, Vincenzo, is a slimebag with all the above characteristics and the most useful of them could be his cat phobia.'

'We need the big computers,' di Maggio said. 'Wiesbaden, London, FBI and NCIC. We must confirm the man's identity. If the records show he's wanted, anywhere in the world, that will put a hook in his mouth and we can reel him in.'

'I'll get on to London right away,' Thorneycroft said. 'There are a couple of other calls I need to make. Can you give me a secure line?'

★ ★ ★

James and Natalie said goodbye to Pia d'Ascani in the hallway of the villa. She kissed James on both cheeks and clung to him for a moment.

'I am so glad you came,' she said. She stood back, smiling. 'You are like him, you

444

know. The eyes, the voice. The kindness.'

'Next time I come, we'll talk more about him.'

Her eyes filled with tears. 'Oh yes, I would like that.' She turned to embrace Natalie, and murmured something in Italian. Natalie smiled and nodded.

Father Stefano was standing beside the van in the courtyard. James took his hand and thanked him for his help. The old man shook his head.

'I did nothing. The help was from God, and from St Francis. Did you know he is our patron saint, here in Ascani? That is why the contessa gave money to the Little Flowers Society.'

James and Natalie climbed into the back of the radio van, finding a place to sit among a welter of wires and machines. As Umberto closed the rear doors, Father Stefano raised his hand in salute or blessing.

The van headed out of the courtyard. The car with its crew of pseudo-paparazzi fell in behind it.

★   ★   ★

In di Maggio's communications room, Thorneycroft made his report to Rollo.

At its conclusion, Rollo said: 'I'll get things

moving at once. Wiesbaden and the NCIC are our best bets. I'll get back to you as soon as possible.'

'Before you go, di Maggio's keen to call at Lippi's residence and get his address in Thessaloniki. What do you think?'

There was a pause, then Rollo said: 'As long as he doesn't scare the bird. He'll know how to handle it.' Another pause. 'Thessaloniki's interesting, close to the Bosphorus and Istanbul, easy access to the Middle East by car or air. What's happening on the Vespucci case, any developments?'

'Rome forensics are taking their time, looking for traces. Di Maggio thinks the shooter was probably hired for the job, in which case it'll be hard to pin it on Lippi — or anyone else.'

'You're thinking of your shortlist?'

'Yes.'

'Well, you can cross off Solomon. He's lapsed into a coma. He never heard about Kesh's briefcase, and couldn't have tipped off Lippi.'

30

Thorneycroft spoke to Gene Lafayette in Zurich, and told him about the interview with Pia d'Ascani. Lafayette said he'd had difficulty in trying to reach Dieter Engel.

'The bugger's playing possum,' he said. 'He's holed up in his private residence, won't let anyone on the property, not even the delivery boys. I spoke to him on the phone, told him about Kesh. Engel won't admit he had any links with Kesh, won't admit Kesh was a client, denies all knowledge of money coming from an illicit trade.

'I reminded him that there's an international alliance to fight terrorism, and that people who aid or abet terrorists risk having their funds cut and could face other severe penalties.'

'What did he say to that.'

'Nothing. Just breathed heavily. He's scared, for his skin and for his bank. If you can get the dirt on Lippi, link him to the sale of banned substances and to Kesh, I can put a lot of pressure on friend Dieter. Reckon he'll crack. He's not the heroic type.'

'I'll get back to you,' Thorneycroft promised.

He spent a little time checking the whereabouts of the remaining names on his shortlist. Daniel Roswall was at Mallowfield with Lucy and Kyle Parnell. Andrew Fermoy and Iain Kincraig were pursuing their lawful occupations on the airfield and at the Dove warehouse. Gerda Marcus and Hugo Spinner were at the Dove office.

Thorneycroft took time out to make notes about the day's events, and then returned to di Maggio's office.

* * *

Luigi Lamberti's strong point was that he didn't look like a policeman. In uniform he was nondescript, out of it he almost disappeared. It was a trait that a number of malefactors had cause to regret.

Now, trudging up the drive of the Lippi residence, jacket off and shirt clinging to a sweaty torso, he seemed to present no threat to man or beast. He stopped to talk to a gardener at work on a flowering border.

'Signor Lippi, is he home?'

'No.'

Lamberti brandished an envelope. 'I have

something for him from the Church of the Holy Family.'

The gardener shrugged. 'Put it in the postbox.'

'I can't.' Lamberti's tone became agitated. 'It's a donation for the Little Flowers. I was told to give it only to Signor Lippi.'

'Have to grow wings, then.' The man showed tobacco-stained teeth. 'He's in Greece.'

'Greece? Do you know the address?'

'No. Ask at the house.' The man went back to his task. Lamberti tramped on and rang the front-doorbell.

The woman who answered was taciturn. Lamberti waved his envelope but kept it out of her reach. At last she went away, to return with a slip of paper bearing an address.

Lamberti was careful to walk slowly as he made his way back down the drive, but once out of sight of the gate, he jumped into his car and drove with all possible speed back to headquarters.

★　★　★

Di Maggio glanced up as Thorneycroft entered his office. 'Lamberti got Lippi's address,' he said. 'Not that it's much use to us. By now he could be out of Thessaloniki.

449

Even if he's still there, we can't touch him, we can't go near him without raising a diplomatic hornet's nest.' He ran a hand over the back of his neck. 'Did you speak to London?'

'And Zurich. Lafayette's twisting Engel's arm. He says if we can link Kesh to illicit trading, Engel will very likely crack.'

'We're working on it. I have men checking out the gas manufacturers. We're on to the Little Flowers, of course, but you know how long it takes, going through the books, talking to the staff . . . '

As he spoke, the fax machine at his side signalled delivery, and both men moved quickly to watch the message come through.

It was from Rollo. Thorneycroft drew out the first page and read aloud:

Wiesbaden came across. I quote:

Helmut Shandel, aka Helga Sorenson, convicted nineteen eighty-nine of dealing in narcotics, rape and murder, is at present in maximum security prison in Berlin serving a life sentence.

Albert Hyams, convicted in Hong Kong nineteen ninety-nine of robbery with extreme violence, now serving five years in that city.

Wayne Carolus, died in Toronto in

February of this year, in a gang-fight.

Paul Ionescu, wanted for illegal arms deals in Cuba and Colombia, and for drug-running in Haiti. His present whereabouts are unknown.

The details of all four suspects follow.

NOTE: Our records show three hundred and seventy-four men who fit your general description, but only the four above-mentioned are known to suffer from allergic reaction to felines. Ionescu bears the closest resemblance to the photo you sent us. The likeness is not conclusive, but as you say, the facial structure may have been altered by trauma or surgery. A preliminary study of the dimensions of the skull shows a significantly close match with an early photograph of Ionescu in our possession (copy is attached) The photo was taken in late 1984.

There is strong evidence that Paul Ionescu and Guillermo Lippi are one and the same person, and we consider that full investigation of Ionescu's present circumstances and activities is desirable.

Pages were still churning out of the fax machine, and Thorneycroft picked out the one giving Ionescu's history.

'Ionescu, Paul, born nineteen forty-six in Bucharest, Romania. Parents Loyola and Elisabet comfortably circumstanced, father a doctor of chemistry, who sympathized with the Nazi regime and with the purging of ethnic minorities such as Jews and Turks. Paul began training as a chemical engineer, but did not obtain a degree. At age 20 he was arrested for dealing in stolen goods, but was never prosecuted, possibly because his father intervened.

'Paul moved to Greece, joined a Communist cell, and in nineteen seventy-four visited Cuba. He remained in the Caribbean, ostensibly as a chemist. In nineteen eighty-six he became involved with a syndicate conducting illegal arms deals with Cuba and Colombia, and drug deals with an Haitian cartel. Also suspected of smuggling cocaine into the USA. Warrants for Ionescu's arrest issued, but he was never arrested.

'In nineteen ninety-three, off San Juan, Puerto Rico, his private launch was challenged by the coastal customs boat. Ionescu and crew tried to shoot their way out. Two customs officers were killed, Ionescu was shot in the head and presumed dead, but the launch was not captured.

'Ionescu's death has never been confirmed.

It is possible that he survived his wounds and underwent plastic surgery to repair his face. He was not seen again in the Caribbean.

'It is believed he stashed large sums of money in Zurich and the Cayman Islands. He was known to be obsessed by a desire for wealth. He is known also to be ruthless, cunning, and violent. If located, he should be approached with extreme caution.'

Lists of names were now emerging from the machine, but di Maggio ignored them. He laid the Wiesbaden photograph alongside Pia d'Ascani's snapshot and David Brock's enlargement.

'It's him. We can finish this piece of dirt.' He shuffled the pictures together and held out his hand for the first pages of the report. Thorneycroft shook his head.

'I need copies, Vincenzo.'

'Sure, but first I must tell the Chief, we have enough now, he can act.'

'When?' Thorneycroft said.

Di Maggio eyed him uncertainly, and Thorneycroft said quietly: 'You think the pressure's off? Can we hope for action before the Accord? How long will Ionescu wait?'

'I have to report this, John.'

'I know.' Thorneycroft smiled slightly. 'No harm in giving me copies for my file, is there?'

453

Di Maggio stared, then muttered, 'I don't know, I don't ask, I don't want to know.' He made copies of the photos and the report and handed them to Thorneycroft.

'Stay out of gaol,' he said.

★ ★ ★

Thorneycroft left the building and walked to the far end of the parking lot. He took out his mobile phone and tapped in a number. A male voice answered, and he said:

'My name is John Thorneycroft. I'm helping with the inquiry into the *Paloma* disaster. I need to speak to Mr Adri Romm, on a matter of great urgency.'

The voice said: 'I am sorry, Mr Romm is not at present available. May I take a message?'

'Yes, tell him it concerns Paul Ionescu, the son of Dr Loyola Ionescu of Bucharest.'

'I will give Mr Romm the message. What is your number?'

Thorneycroft gave it. The voice thanked him and the connection was cut.

He glanced at his watch. Seven minutes past three. Give it ten minutes, he thought. He leaned against the bonnet of a Uno and waited. Five minutes, six, the mobile buzzed and Romm's voice said:

'Dr Thorneycroft? Adri Romm. How can I help you?'

'You know the history of Loyola Ionescu?'

'I should do. As a young man he helped the Nazis give lethal injections to my grandparents.'

'His son Paul appears to be a chip off the old block. I think we should discuss it.'

'Where are you?'

Thorneycroft told him, and Romm said, 'I will be there in ten minutes.'

He arrived in under that time, riding a scrambler motorbike. He remained astride the bike and interrupted Thorneycroft's attempt to introduce himself.

'We know who we are, Doctor. Why are we here?'

'Common interest,' Thorneycroft said. As Romm remained silent, he added, 'In Dove International. My interest began when I was appointed to the inquiry into the *Paloma* disaster. Yours, I believe, is of much longer standing. Israel's vital concern is to protect herself against weapons of mass destruction — the atom bomb, chemical and biological warfare. You suspect that people inside Dove have used the organization as a front for dealing in WMDs.'

Romm's face was expressionless. He

reached up and loosened the strap of his helmet.

'What has this to do with Paul Ionescu?' he said.

Thorneycroft told him about the Boru fax, Barry Coburn's theory of the cause of the fire in *Paloma*'s hold, the finding of Kesh's briefcase and the tracing of Paul Ionescu to the Little Flowers Society. At the end, Romm demanded:

'Where is Ionescu now?'

'In Thessaloniki.'

'If there are warrants in the USA for his arrest, why don't they extradite him?'

'It would take too long — documents, legal mumblings. Ionescu won't wait, we have to move fast, and there's a certain . . . hesitancy in the diplomatic world, right now.'

'I am aware.'

'Then you must also be aware that if some fanatic has been stockpiling germ cultures, Jerusalem could be the target of attack. Jerusalem could be blanketed with inhalation anthrax.'

'Maybe, maybe not. Doctor, even an Israeli requires some proof of guilt against an opponent. You have nothing but circumstantial evidence against Ionescu.'

'You won't find proof by sitting on that bloody bike: God damn it, you've been looking for these bastards for months, years! I'm telling you, Ionescu has been selling germ cultures. He knows who's buying, he knows the next link in the chain. I can't reach him. You can.'

'And if I do? I have no right to question him. I have no authority in Thessaloniki.'

'You had none in Entebbe.'

Romm stared at him in silence. He raised both hands in a gesture of acquiescence.

'What's his address?'

Thorneycroft handed him a slip of paper. He tucked it into his breast pocket. The motorbike accelerated between the lanes of parked cars, and roared out into the traffic beyond the gate.

★ ★ ★

At six o'clock, his business with di Maggio and Romm completed, Thorneycroft drove to the airport with James and Natalie. They were joined on the concourse by Gerda Marcus and Hugo Spinner, and from that point on received VIP treatment. They were ushered into a private lounge, and later driven in a stretch limousine to the small-craft departure zone.

This luxury did nothing to ease tensions. Thorneycroft answered their questions in

457

monosyllables, his face was pale and his eyes hooded with exhaustion. When they reached the plane, he boarded last, and went at once to the flight deck, to talk to the pilot.

Gerda and Hugo found seats at the front, Natalie and James at the back. Natalie refused to take a window seat.

'I don't want to look out. I don't want to see where it happened.'

'We won't see anything,' James told her. 'There's too much low cloud.'

She was not mollified. She scowled at Thorneycroft's back, framed in the doorway of the cockpit.

'We should have taken a regular flight,' she said. 'Why do we have to go in this horrid little thing, why do we have to do what he wants?'

'He thinks we'll be safer out of the public eye,' James said.

'Well, I hate it. It's scary. We gave him the photo. Now I want to go home. Why does he want us to go to Mallowfield?'

James hesitated. 'Mallowfield's very secure, you know. No one can break in.'

'And we can't break out! I feel like a prisoner.' She was close to tears. She fumbled for the straps of her seat belt and slammed home the buckle with shaking hands.

Gerda and Hugo appeared to be quarrelling. Their voices carried in the almost-empty plane.

'More of Dan's crap,' Hugo said viciously, 'getting us all into his lockup. I have work to do. As for dropping Dieter, that was lunacy.'

'Dieter's a rat,' Gerda retorted. 'I'm damn sure he knew Kesh was into some racket. He should have warned us. He's only interested in money.'

'That happens to be his job! He's done Dove proud — '

'He's done Dove in, you mean. He's tied Dove to monsters who promote germ warfare. Dove is finished, thanks to him.'

Hugo slammed both fists on the arms of his seat, but before he could speak, Thorneycroft walked past them and took his place behind them. The plane began to taxi, halted, turned and took off. They caught a glimpse of fields and sea, before long swathes of cloud engulfed them.

Hugo kept up a mumbled incantation against all and sundry. Gerda closed her eyes and ignored him.

The roar of ascent settled to a steady drone. James sat quiet, thinking about David, friends they'd shared, holidays, tunes they'd liked, so many small memories.

'James?' Natalie leaned towards him. 'I'm

sorry I snapped at you. I was scared, I hate flying. I guess I'm not very brave.'

'Dave thought you were brave. He sent you the fax, he relied on you, and you did your best to help him.'

She smiled. She had a great smile. He was amazed at the pleasure it gave him. He held out his hand and she took it, lacing her fingers through his.

'Home soon,' he said.

31

Greece

On his property outside Thessaloniki, Guillermo Lippi was making a final inspection of his empty poultry houses. He was proud of what had been achieved there. His turkeys, hens and ducks had been in demand with the local hoteliers, and the money from table birds and eggs had gone directly to the Little Flowers office in the city. It made good publicity, and concealed the fact that a proportion of the birds were used in the production of anthrax and other cultures.

Lippi regretted having to destroy such a lucrative little sideline, but he had ordered its destruction the moment he had news of the *Paloma* crash. He knew that the inevitable enquiries would involve Dove, and possibly expose Jerome Kesh's interest in biological and chemical weapons. The jump from Kesh to himself was too short for safety.

Caution and planning were the foundation blocks of Lippi's immense fortune. He had always known when to cut his losses and disappear. The Italian operation was over. His retreat from it had been swift, but orderly. The offices of the Society, in Rome and elsewhere, would be found to be innocent of any wrongdoing, their records in apple-pie order. Here in Greece, the factories that transferred accelerants and other banned materials to buyers abroad, were equally immaculate, displaying nothing but cylinders of oxygen and household gas.

In due course, all these premises would be sold to reputable buyers, and the proceeds would go to the Little Flowers Society. There would be many who would lament the demise of Mr Lippi in a tragic accident. Perhaps there might even be memorial plaques from grateful citizens.

There was no paper-trail for the financial sniffer dogs to follow. His money was safe and sound, some of it already in Zurich or the Cayman Islands, and substantial amounts transferred to his new field of operations in the Far East.

There would be no foolish haste, and no mistakes. He would leave Thessaloniki on a routine mission for the Society. He had filed a flight plan, citing Tel Aviv as his destination, but the plane would never arrive there. His route to his new stamping ground would of necessity be roundabout, involving numerous changes of transport and appearance. His untimely death would be presumed, just as it had been in the Caribbean days, and after an interval he would surface in his new identity and take up the reins of a new life.

From now on he would abandon the do-good persona, and be truly himself. He would travel, enjoy leisure, food, wine, and the plump little boys he preferred. He had worked hard all his life, he had achieved success, now he would enjoy the fruits of his labour.

Leaving the poultry yard, he strolled to the end of the property, where a large shed housed the Society's jet plane. Its presence justified the electrified fencing and security systems on the estate. The plane bore the insignia of the Little Flowers Society, and had completed many charitable missions. His pilot Heine and his bodyguard Powell were ready for the journey, and Lippi chatted to them for a few minutes. Later it might be necessary to dispose of them, but not until they had served his purpose.

'We leave at nine,' he said. 'Bring the plane up the runway as usual.'

Nine was a good time to leave, the dusk sinking into a dark that would make an organized search for the plane impossible.

He returned to the house, which already had the look of desertion. The servants who had doubled as guards were already on their way to their own homes, to enjoy their holiday money. There was nothing of value in the house. No animals. He hated animals, they were dirty and demanding and they brought on his asthma.

Tomorrow, Philippou would come to see that everything was in order. Philippou was the Society's lawyer in Thessaloniki, an honest man, conscientious, with a good grasp of the law; qualities that inspired public confidence in the Society. He had an unshakeable faith in God and humankind. That made him an idiot, albeit a useful one.

Checking his watch, Lippi saw that it was already half past seven. In less than two hours, he would be on his way to a new life. He carried his light suitcase to the wide front veranda, fetched a glass and a bottle of retsina, and settled in a lounger to relax.

He felt vigorous and calm. Everything was going to plan. He sipped his wine and scanned the view. The sea was milky blue and irridescent. There were plenty of ships and small craft in these waters, serving industry and the pleasure tours. On the motorway behind the house, traffic was still heavy.

He watched a skein of pelicans fly along the coast, heading for some roosting-place in a quiet bay. A hawk hovered over his empty chicken houses for a moment, then swung south to the ring of trees that marked his neighbour's boundary. He admired the way it hung in the air, wingtips curving upwards, body suspended on the ascending warm currents. A flight of pigeons, wheeling above the farmer's house, scattered in alarm and plunged down towards shelter. Shots sounded, and Lippi grinned. The old man missed, as usual and the hawk soared out of range and disappeared.

Lippi half-dozed. Time passed, the sun sank towards a sea that flamed then darkened, smooth as a Nubian's skin.

Five minutes to time. Lippi sat upright. The plane should be coming, and there it was, trundling out from the hangar, executing a half-turn on to the lighted airstrip and rolling towards the house. It stopped thirty yards from where he sat. He stood up, lifted his case, and walked across the stretch of coarse turf to the open door of the plane.

A hand reached out to take his case, then without warning gripped his arm and yanked him through the door. As he stumbled forward, something struck him on the back of the head. He crumpled, his assailant caught him under the armpits and dragged him to a seat in the tail of the plane.

★ ★ ★

'Paul. Paul Ionescu. Wake up, fat man, you're not dead yet.'

The voice was speaking Italian. Ionescu moaned. His head was bursting and hot bile rose in his throat. He opened his eyes, and through the window on his left saw the backswept wing of the plane, and beyond that a black sky heavy with cloud. He realized that he was strapped to his seat at wrists, ankles and throat. A hand reached out and wrenched his chin sideways. He stared up at a stranger with dusty-fair hair and eyes as bleak as the winter steppes.

'Who are you?' Ionescu croaked.

'My name is Romm.' The man had switched to Romanian, and it terrified Ionescu. His eyes rolled wildly.

'Where are Heine and Powell, what have you done with them?'

'They are not dead, but sleeping. We put them in the cargo hold.'

Ionescu licked dry lips. 'If it's money you want . . .'

'We're not open to bribes, Ionescu.'

Ionescu's rat-genes rallied. He said hoarsely: 'You are mistaken. My name is Guillermo Lippi, I am a charity worker, I demand an explanation — '

466

'You are Paul Ionescu,' the fair man said, 'the second son of Loyola Ionescu of Bucharest. There are many who remember your father's part in the pogroms.' He put out a finger and touched Ionescu's jaw. 'The surgeons rebuilt your face once. Lie to me and there'll be nothing for them to work on. Do you understand?'

'What do you want? Why am I here?'

'We want you, Paul — alive if you do as you're told, dead if you don't.'

'You are hijackers, criminals . . . '

'Not at all. We are taking you to Tel Aviv, the destination you filed in your flight plan. Of course, it could be you had no intention of sticking to that. You have a fine collection of passports in your suitcase. Excellent work, they must have cost you plenty.'

'Who are you? Where are you from?'

Romm ignored the questions. He beckoned, and a man in camouflage uniform came quickly down the aisle towards them. He said something to Romm and they both laughed. Ionescu realized they were speaking Hebrew, and cold panic assailed him. The band round his neck was choking him. He couldn't breathe. He looked desperately at Romm.

'Asthma pills. In my pocket. Please!'

Romm smiled at him. 'Funny, Seth was just

467

saying we should give you a dose of your own medicine.' He held out his palm and the uniformed man placed something on it. Romm held it up for Ionescu to see. It was a small plastic phial, containing a little colourless liquid.

'We found it in your sample case, in the hold. It's not labelled.'

'Vaccine,' Ionescu gasped.

'Really? Against what? Anthrax, perhaps? Or is it ricin? Whatever it is, I'm sure it will do you a power of good.' Romm leaned forward and took hold of Ionescu's wrist.

Ionescu screamed, 'No! You can't!'

Romm tightened his grip. He said softly: 'You ask me what we want, I'll tell you. We want your syndicate, your associates, your couriers and agents. We want your buyers, your whole murderous scorpions' nest. We'll start with Rome. If you live long enough, we'll spread the net wider. We know Jerome Kesh worked with you. Who else is on your payroll?'

Ionescu laboured to breathe. He folded blue lips, and shook his head. Romm unscrewed the stopper of the phial and let two drops fall from it on to Ionescu's forearm.

'Give me the names,' he said. Ionescu swore at him, and he settled back on the arm of the seat across the aisle.

'It takes a couple of minutes to act, I'm told,' he said. Ionescu fought against his bonds, staring at his arm. The skin around the liquid was already reddening, becoming turgid. He whimpered, sucking in gulp after gulp of air. His over-inflated lungs laboured. His eyes bulged.

Romm watched him dispassionately. The man called Seth came to stand next to him, a glass in his hand. Romm nodded, and Seth bent to hold the glass to Ionescu's lips.

'Drink,' he said. Ionescu swallowed, dribbling some of the liquid on to his shirt. The pressure in his chest slowly eased. Romm's voice reached him through the roar of his own blood.

'The drug is cumulative, I believe. It will build in your system with each dose.' Romm's voice swelled in his ears.

'Give me the names.'

Weeping, Ionescu shook his head. Romm reached for the left arm this time, poured on the liquid. Ionescu choked. The walls of the plane were contracting, squeezing him in a stifling cocoon. He slid into a void streaked with scarlet, and woke to find himself sodden with sweat and urine.

The plane was in a dive. The stars whirled and scattered like sparks from a fire. He knew he was going to die. The scream of the engines, mingled with his own screams and he felt blood trickle from his nose. The plane levelled and climbed. The stars grew still. Romm appeared, phial in hand.

'The next dose could kill you,' he said. He poked at Ionescu's cheek, denting the puffy flesh. 'Be sensible, Paul. Give me the names. You have nothing to lose except your life.'

At eleven-thirty, Ionescu began to babble between chattering teeth. Seth approached with a tape recorder. Romm's voice questioned, threatened, cajoled. Finally Ionescu broke into anguished sobbing.

'I don't know, I can't remember. Please. Please.' He stared into Romm's eyes and saw no hope there. He said dully: 'Kill me, then. Kill me.'

Romm studied him. 'It would be a pleasure to dump your carcass in the sea,' he said. 'You're a perverted murderer. You peddle weapons of mass destruction. The world would be cleaner without you. On the other hand, you can serve some purpose. It would be a pity to waste you. Let's consider your options.

'The future you planned for yourself is not an option. In a few hours, your description will be released to the police forces of the world. The countries of your choice will not harbour you. You will be branded a terrorist and your funds will be blocked. So what choices remain?

'We could sell you. We could arrange a sale that would be advantageous to Israel. You're in demand, you see. Haiti wants you for your part in heroin-running. The USA wants you for selling arms to Cuba and certain South American rebels. Italy and Greece want you for drug-deals, fraud, money-laundering. Britain wants you for the sabotage of Omega Airlines aircraft *Paloma*.'

'No!' Ionescu tried to shake his head, and choked. 'I had nothing to do with *Paloma*. Nothing.'

'You supplied the device that started the fire, and the cylinder of accelerant that turned it into a flash fire which destroyed the electrical systems and tail structure, causing the plane to crash.' As Ionescu started to protest, Romm caught hold of his hair and jerked his head back.

'Don't lie to me. Lying is not an option. Hold your tongue and listen.' Romm took a packet of cigarettes from his pocket, lit one, and blew smoke. 'As I've said, there are governments who'll compete for the job of dealing with Paul Ionescu. To be honest, I don't think it's the legitimate authorities you should fear most. It's your own kind, the

471

fanatics and terrorists, the greedy scum you made your trading partners. They're killers, and when they find you've sold them out, they'll come and get you.

'Maybe they'll buy you. They can pay money some people might find irresistible. Or maybe they'll exchange you for hostages. Maybe they'll just use force of arms, but get to you they will, and when they do, you'll be a long time dying.

'Don't kid yourself that you have the option of silence. It's too late for that. You've given us names and we've passed them on. Your people will be rounded up. They will supply more names, addresses, dates. You've put a thread in our hands that will unravel your whole lousy fabric.

'There's a third option. We could simply release you, having first spread the word that you turned informer. You would be the target of a feeding frenzy, first come first served.

'So, all things considered, your best option is to co-operate with us. Keep talking, and we'll see that you stay alive. I have to tell you that your friend Dieter Engel is being most helpful. He's supplied details about your financial transactions in Rome, how money was laundered there by you, and conveyed to numbered accounts in Zurich. He's named Kesh as your courier. He's also named the

472

state from which your buyers operate. You can gain nothing by withholding information.

'Think it over, Ionescu. Don't take too long about it, we'll be landing in fifteen minutes.'

Romm strolled away to the front row of seats, where Seth was sitting. He said in Hebrew: 'Did you check the other prisoners?'

'Yes. They're still out cold. What are you going to do with them, Adri? They're going to scream kidnap.'

'Heine and Powell won't give us any trouble. They're old pros, they'll cut a deal. We'll send them home and let their own fuzz sort them out.'

'And Ionescu? There'll be hell to pay in Tel Aviv . . . '

'We won't land at Tel Aviv. We'll put down at a nice quiet military airstrip on the edge of the Negev. It will emerge that Ionescu filed a flight plan for Tel Aviv, but that the aircraft developed engine trouble and had to make a forced landing. Our patrols will board the aircraft and find two pilots and one passenger. They will also find cases in the hold that contain chemicals which, when examined by our forensic experts, will prove to be the raw materials used in making weapons of mass destruction. We've made a major breakthrough, Seth. We've uncovered a syndicate involved in chemical and biological warfare. The doves may complain about our methods. The hawks will look after us.'

'You really found banned chemicals in the hold?'

'Oh yes.' Romm's smile was bland.

A thought struck Seth. He said in alarm. 'What about germ cultures? That stuff you gave Ionescu, we handled it without gloves. If he dies . . . '

'He won't.' Romm glanced at the phial he still held. 'This isn't from his stock, it's not lethal, except to slugs. It's a pesticide developed from vegetables. Aaron sprayed this cabin with it, before we left Thessaloniki. It's dicey stuff. It was tested in our laboratories a while ago, but discarded because of its side effects on hyperallergic humans. Ionescu, for instance, is hyperallergic to cats. In him, the spray caused violent asthma spasms, a skin rash, and acute anxiety symptoms.'

Romm looked out of the window. They were crossing the coast, and the lights of Jaffa twinkled some miles to port. He yawned.

'Ionescu,' he said, 'could be described as something the cat brought in.'

32

Thorneycroft and his party arrived at Heathrow on time, but there they met with delays. Their luggage was searched by customs officials with what seemed unnecessary thoroughness, and when at last they were released, they were informed that the helicopter which was to take them to Mallowfield had not yet touched down. A hostess conducted them to a small lounge that boasted neither a bar nor a television set, and Thorneycroft was apologetic.

'I know how irritating this is for you. I believe you are safer here than you might be in your own homes. There have been developments that give us concern for your safety.'

'What developments?' demanded Gerda.

Thorneycroft regarded her thoughtfully. 'Dieter Engel is being questioned by the Swiss authorities,' he said. 'He admits to having assisted certain individuals to avoid tax in their own countries by opening secret accounts for them in Zurich. One of his clients was Jerome Kesh, who we suspect dealt in the sale of substances used in the manufacture of chemical and biological weapons.'

'How does that concern us?' Hugo said. 'We don't have secret accounts.'

'Engel has asked to be taken into protective custody.' Thorneycroft answered. 'He's afraid for his life. He says Kesh had dangerous associates.'

As Gerda and Hugo started to speak together, Thorneycroft backed towards the door.

'I'm sorry. I have things to attend to before we leave. Just stay here, don't make any phone calls, and you'll be quite safe. There's a guard on the door. I'll be back as soon as I can.'

He was gone. Hugo retired muttering to a chair in the corner, and opened a newspaper. Gerda settled as far from him as she could. James and Natalie sat together, talking quietly.

The shadow of Jerome Kesh lay across the room, filling them all with foreboding.

★ ★ ★

Thorneycroft found a pay-phone that worked, and made two calls. The first was to Rollo, who had little to say.

'Nothing yet. ETA Tel Aviv is plus-minus

476

twelve-thirty. I've spoken to the Minister. Soon as we get anything definite, he'll move.'

'We're leaving for Mallowfield in twenty minutes,' Thorneycroft said. 'I'll call you from there.'

He reached Lafayette at his hotel in Zurich. The big man sounded upbeat.

'I left Todd to stand the graveyard watch,' he said. 'Engel's still buzzin' with the fuzz. Slow and solid, that's them. How's things your side?'

Thorneycroft told him, and ended by saying: 'I've been thinking about that property in Siena. The price tag was high. Maybe the purchaser needed extra funds, maybe he put pressure on his associates, to get what he needed.'

'You thinking about what Gerda Marcus said — we should look closer to home?'

'Yes.'

'Two down and one to go?'

'Yes. The purchaser may have taken out insurance. If you can persuade Zurich to search the purchaser's security-box in Engel's bank, they might find something of interest.'

'Yeah. I'll work on that, right away. Where'll I find you, if the need arises?'

'Mallowfield. We'll be leaving in fifteen minutes.'

'Don't step in anything nasty,' Lafayette said.

★   ★   ★

It was after midnight when the helicopter landed at Mallowfield. The air struck cold after the warmth of Italy, and the lights round the helipad cast a greenish glow on a sluggish ground mist.

Two men in police uniform approached Thorneycroft as he ducked from under the slowing rotor-blades. He stayed talking to them while his companions moved towards the big house.

Natalie shivered. 'Those policemen have guns,' she said.

James nodded. Security had been beefed up. Arc lights swung their beams across the sky, and probed the fence on the edge of the estate, and there were more dog patrols than he'd seen on his first visit.

The main door of the house stood open. As they entered the hall, Daniel Roswall came to meet them. He moved stiffly, his shoulders stooped. He shook hands with James and Natalie, nodded to Gerda and Hugo.

'Thank you for coming,' he said. 'I'm sure it's the last thing you want, at this time, but Thorneycroft insists it's important for us all to be here.'

'Why?' Gerda demanded. 'What's he after?'

'I have no idea. He asked me to stand host to you tonight. I complied. My impression is, he intends to talk to us.'

'What about?'

Roswall gave a faint shake of the head. 'We must wait and see.' He turned to James. 'I gather the Contessa helped to identify our unknown?'

James nodded, but didn't respond to the unspoken question.

Roswall sighed. 'Well then. Would you like to be shown your rooms now, or later?' No one answered, and it seemed to James that the group moved closer together, like animals scenting a predator.

'Thorneycroft has matters to attend to,' Roswall said. 'In the meantime, I suggest we have a drink, and something to eat.'

He led them to the living-room. It looked, James thought, like the lounge of a five-star hotel, luxurious but impersonal. The curtains had been drawn across its long windows. Near the bar area were tables loaded with cold and hot food. Kyle Parnell stood behind the bar, and Lucy Roswall was curled on a sofa nearby, the cat Bojangles on her lap. James went over to her.

'Hullo, Lucy. How are you?'

She lifted thin shoulders. 'Spooked,' she said. 'All these cops. I have to keep Boje indoors because of the dogs. He hates that.'

James scratched the cat's bristly neck and was rewarded by a reluctant purr. Kyle Parnell called to James.

'Brock? What'll you have?'

James joined his flight companions at the bar and accepted a scotch and water from Kyle.

'I hear the Contessa pulled the rabbit out of the hat,' Kyle said.

'Who told you that?' James asked, and Kyle blinked.

'Gerda did. So what's the guy's name?'

Again James hesitated, but Gerda said, defiantly:

'Ionescu. Paul Ionescu, known in Rome as Guillermo Lippi.'

Hugo said sharply, 'How do you know all this?'

'I asked Thorneycroft.'

'And he told you, just like that! Naturally you kept it to yourself, you never thought to inform the rest of us!'

Gerda turned her shoulder to him and bent her head over her hands. Hugo insisted: 'Does Dan know? Did you think to tell him?'

Gerda didn't answer. She pushed her

480

empty glass across to Kyle, who recharged it. He watched Gerda uncertainly. It was plain she hadn't taken him into her confidence.

Footsteps sounded out in the corridor, and Thorneycroft passed the open door, accompanied by a group of policemen.

'What the hell's going on?' Hugo said. He stared at Gerda. 'Why did Thorneycroft choose you?'

'I told you, I asked him, he answered, I don't know his reasons!'

Roswall, who had been standing some way away, approached them.

'What's the problem?' he asked.

There was a silence, then Kyle said: 'They've put a name to the man in the photograph. It's not one of ours.'

Gerda turned to face Roswall. 'It's a man named Paul Ionescu. His father was a war criminal. He died before we could hang him.'

'I see. As Kyle says, not one of ours. Something to be thankful for.' Roswall sounded very tired. 'No doubt it will all be explained to us in due course. Please help yourselves to food, and wine. It will help to pass the time.'

They moved to the buffet, filled plates and found places to sit. Gerda and Natalie moved off together. Hugo settled on the sofa next to

Lucy and reached out to ruffle her tangle of hair.

'So, Luce, how goes it? Decided to stay in England, have you?'

'I want to, but Grandpa says it all depends.'

'On what?'

'On the inquiry into the crash. He says if it goes badly, there'll be a lot of scandal and Dove will have to close down. And the court may not give him custody of me.'

'I doubt if it'll come to a court case. Your mama knows which side her bread's buttered. She'll settle if the price is right.' Hugo dangled a sliver of smoked salmon in front of Bojangles, who clawed it down and devoured it with noisy pleasure.

'Salmon's his favourite thing,' Lucy said.

'Fat cat,' Hugo said.

James saw that Roswall was sitting alone and went to join him. The big man pushed food round his plate, and drank steadily, tossing back his wine like a man seeking oblivion. James asked him when he thought the board of inquiry would start its work, and Roswall grimaced.

'Not yet awhile. They'll have to complete the salvage work, and let the boffins run their tests.' He turned his empty glass in his fingers. 'Inquiries take a long time, and resolve little. You listen to witnesses polishing their apples, you hear evidence from God knows how many experts, all it does is keep the pain alive. It leads to legal battles and financial wrangles and bitter accusations, and at the end of it all the verdict may tell you nothing at all.'

'I suppose we each have to reach our own verdict,' James said.

Roswall's eyes narrowed. 'What do you mean?'

'Those of us who've suffered loss — human or material — will have to decide how to deal with whatever comes out of the inquiry, decide what's true and what's false, what to keep and what to discard. We'll have to arrive at our own settlement.'

Roswall's gaze shifted to Lucy. 'Yes. If we can.' He seemed ready to say more, but at that moment Thorneycroft entered the room and Roswall rose to his feet.

'I'm sorry to have kept you waiting,' Thorneycroft said. 'I'd like to talk to all of you now.'

'Right.' Roswall moved to stand near the bar, raised his voice.

'People, will you please gather round? Dr Thorneycroft wants to tell us why we're here.'

They took their seats at the bar-counter, Thorneycroft standing in the barman's place. He rested his hands on the polished wood, gathering his thoughts.

'When I asked you to come to Mallow-field,' he said, 'I told you it was for your own protection, and that's true. This place is secure — '

'Against what?' Kyle Parnell said. He was sitting with his arm round Gerda's shoulders, and the amber light above his head made him shine like a heraldic lion, rampant, regardant.

'Against physical attack,' Thorneycroft answered. 'Each of you is linked in some measure to the *Paloma* disaster. You've lost a family member, friends, colleagues, and wittingly or unwittingly you know things that put you at risk from the people who sabotaged *Paloma*. You have a right to know the facts, so that you can guard yourselves against them.

'Since the tragedy, a great deal of work has been done by a great many people. When the board of inquiry opens, you'll hear the details of those investigations. I want to concentrate on facts that are of immediate concern to you.

'Some weeks ago, Captain David Brock and his friend Countess Pia d'Ascani attended a charity fund-raiser in Rome. It was convened by the Society of the Little Flowers of St Francis. The guest speaker was Jerome Kesh.

484

'After the meeting closed, Brock and the countess went to a neighbouring tavern for a nightcap. So did Kesh and the manager of the Society, Guillermo Lippi. Later, Captain Brock went to fetch his car from the carpark, and while he was away, the countess took a photograph. By chance, the photo included the man called Lippi. When Captain Brock saw the developed print, he thought he recognized Lippi as someone he'd met years before, during his employment with Sirius Freight. He associated the man with criminal activity, but couldn't put a name to him.

'Captain Brock sent you a copy of the photo, Mrs Lomax, because you knew people in the FBI and pilots' associations who might be able to identify the man.'

Natalie nodded. 'Yes, but I didn't succeed.'

Thorneycroft turned to James. 'Mrs Lomax sent a fax to your brother, at your home in Bansford, Kent. She signed it BORU. That meant nothing to you, you put it in a carton with other things belonging to Captain Brock, and sent it to Rome. It arrived there two days before *Paloma*'s last flight, and was passed from Omega's office to the Dove warehouse next door to Rome airport. Mr Spinner and the warehouse foreman, Andrew Fermoy, examined the contents of the carton.'

485

As Hugo started to interrupt, Thorneycroft motioned him to silence.

'The existence of the fax was known to Mrs Lomax and to Mr Brock. That knowledge could pose a threat to the people who destroyed *Paloma*. It places them in danger. Mr Spinner, you also read the fax.'

'Yes. It made no sense to me. I handed it to Captain Brock next day. Sunday.'

'Did you ask him about the signatory? BORU?'

'I did. Captain Brock more or less told me to mind my own business. I was on edge at that time, because Joel Moshal had cancelled his flight to our conference, I was afraid of a possible terrorist threat. Captain Brock told me the fax related to a recruiting drive by Omega. The fax didn't concern Dove, or me. I took no further action in the matter.'

'But like Mrs Lomax and Mr Brock, you knew about the fax. You shared what might be dangerous knowledge.'

'I suppose so.'

Thorneycroft continued:

'After the memorial service for the *Paloma* victims, Mrs Lomax gave Mr Brock the original fax sent to her by Captain Brock. It included the photograph of an unidentified man. Yesterday the Contessa Pia d'Ascani handed over the original negative of the

486

photograph. She confirmed it was of a man known as Guillermo Lippi, manager of a Rome charity. Acting on information supplied by the contessa and others, we have identified the subject as Paul Ionescu, a criminal wanted in various countries for dealing in drugs and illicit arms, as well as for fraud, smuggling of banned substances, money-laundering, and murder.

'Ionescu made Rome his headquarters for several years. Ostensibly he was head of a charity that sent aid to children in the Middle East, supplying food and clothing to famine victims, and medicines and equipment to hospitals. Under cover of this, he exported substances to create chemical and biological weapons, cultures of such things as anthrax, botulism and cholera, and also chemical poisons and accelerants.

'Ionescu owned a factory near Thessaloniki in Greece. We have reason to believe that it produced the fire-raisers and accelerant gas that caused a flash fire in *Paloma*'s hold, causing the crash that killed everyone on board.'

Hugo slid off his bar stool and pointed a shaking finger at Gerda.

'You knew about this! You knew and you told us nothing!' He swung to face Thorney-croft. 'Why did you tell her? You should have come to Roswall, or to me.'

'I spoke to Mrs Marcus because I knew she was in touch with Adri Romm,' Thorneycroft answered. 'I told her we had identified Ionescu. I guessed she would pass the news on to Romm.'

Hugo drew back his fist as if he would hit Gerda, but Roswall caught his wrist.

'Is this true, Gerda? Have you been communicating with Romm?'

She looked at him defiantly.

'Yes, since they found Kesh's briefcase. He dealt in weapons of mass destruction. Israel would be the first victim in such a war.'

Kyle Parnell took Gerda's hand. He met Thorneycroft's eyes.

'Gerda's right. I think you used her. You wanted Romm to know.'

Thorneycroft was silent, and Kyle said:

'Kesh worked with Ionescu, right?'

'So it seems. Kesh had money he didn't earn from Dove, but he was greedy. He wanted more, to buy luxury items like a mansion in Siena.'

'So he blackmailed Ionescu, to get it?'

Before Thorneycroft could answer, Roswall spoke.

'This monster, this Ionescu ... you've arrested him?'

'He's in custody,' Thorneycroft said. 'He

attempted to steal an aircraft owned by the Society of the Little Flowers of St Francis, but it was forced to make an unscheduled landing in Israel. The military patrol that boarded the plane found samples of banned substances in the hold. Ionescu and his two crew members were detained and are being questioned by the Israeli authorities. He has named his buyers, and has admitted to working with Kesh.'

Thorneycroft paused, looking from face to face. Nobody moved or spoke. He said:

'I've told you all this because it impinges not only on your safety, but on my job. I'm part of the team appointed to uncover the truth about *Paloma*. The task is by no means completed, but I can tell you that it very soon will be.

'From the beginning of the investigation, two questions have demanded answers. The first is, why did *Paloma* crash? The second is, how was that crash caused? It was not an accident, it was sabotage. If we know why, and how, we will know who. We will know the name of the saboteur.

'The 'why' begins with what I'll call the Ionescu syndicate, which peddled death to a bunch of fanatics in the Middle East. David Brock came close to exposing the Rome ringleader. Jerome Kesh, in search of a large

489

sum of money, tried to blackmail one or more of his associates into providing it. Both David Brock and Kesh threatened the existence of the syndicate. They had to be removed, and *Paloma* was made the vehicle of their death.

'How was the crash achieved? According to our technical investigator Barry Coburn, a fire-starter was planted in the Dove container, which was strategically placed in the tail of the aircraft. Attached to the container was a patent extinguisher, filled usually with halon gas. On that final flight, however, the cylinder contained an inflammatory gas. When it was used by the fire-fighter, it ignited a flash fire, which destroyed the tail structures. *Paloma* went out of control and crashed.

'Which brings us to the 'who'. Who had access to such lethal cylinders? Who had the opportunity to switch the normal cylinder for the lethal one? Who stood to profit by the deaths of Captain Brock and Jerome Kesh?'

'Ionescu,' said Roswall harshly.

'Ionescu provided the materials for sabotage, but he couldn't have installed them. He had no access to the warehouse.'

'He paid someone.' Roswall's face was streaked with sweat, and he brushed it away with his sleeve.

'There's another point to be considered,'

Thorneycroft said. 'The shooting of Alonso Vespucci, whose firm supplied Omega with its routine cylinders of oxygen and halon. The Rome police have established that directly after the crash, Vespucci tried to get in touch with all the people most closely connected with Dove and Omega. When he couldn't reach them in person, he phoned them. We have a list of their names. Ionescu — Lippi, as he was known in Rome — doesn't figure on that list.

'I believe that Vespucci, being in the trade, as it were, realized how the fire could have been engineered, and wanted to discuss it with someone in authority. In making the attempt, he alerted the killer. He was enticed to a parking garage, and shot.

'One hundred and fifty-six people died to preserve not only a vicious criminal organization, but the front that concealed it. They died to preserve Dove.'

'No!' Roswall's cry was agonized. 'Dove is for peace, for healing . . . '

Thorneycroft looked at him with pity.

'The Dove you created has been destroyed. It's been used to recruit experts with deadly skills, to launder money, and to supply terrorists with the raw materials of biological and chemical warfare. When I arrived here tonight, I received calls from London and

Zurich. Ionescu has given the Israeli authorities the name of the head of the syndicate, and the Swiss police have confirmed it. Kesh left documents in his deedbox in Engel's bank. They include details of many deals conducted by the syndicate, and give the name of the person he attempted to blackmail.'

'Not Dove.' Roswall lurched to his feet, swaying, and behind them Lucy cried out. Hugo went quickly to her side, drew her from her seat, the cat still clutched in her arms.

'Come, Luce, come away now. It'll be all right, I promise.'

Thorneycroft advanced on them. 'Let her go, Spinner. Now, at once!'

Hugo's grip tightened. His free hand gripped the tangle of Lucy's hair, pulling her head sideways across his forearm.

'Stop where you are or I'll break her bloody neck.'

'It's over, Spinner. Let her go.'

Two policemen were moving towards them from the main door of the room. Hugo cast a wild glance at the windows, and started to drag Lucy backwards. She was still holding Bojangles, and he slapped at the animal, screaming to Lucy to let it go. His flailing hand struck the cat's nose, and it hissed and sank its teeth into his fingers. Its claws lashed out, raking Hugo's jaw and throat.

Hugo released Lucy and tried to run. The policemen seized him and he fought them, shrieking, his eyes asquint with rage and fear. As he was dragged to the door, he cursed Thorneycroft, Roswall, the world, in a dark litany of hate and greed.

'Mine!' he kept repeating. 'My work, my money! Mine!'

His screams faded along the corridor, and Thorneycroft approached Roswall.

'Sir, will you come with me, please? Spinner must be placed under arrest and removed to London at once. We'll need your say-so at the helipad.'

'Of course.' Roswall straightened, shaking off the lassitude of shock. He reached out a hand to Lucy. She set the cat down on the sofa and ran to his side. He bent and kissed her forehead.

'Stay with Gerda,' he said. 'I'll be back soon.'

He followed Thorneycroft from the room.

★ ★ ★

Before leaving for London, Thorneycroft spoke to Rollo. 'We've charged Spinner with assault and resisting arrest. We'll take it from there, when we reach town. What about Ionescu?'

'He's under lock and key. Israel's delighted, Jordan's jubilant, they've collared all Ionescu's pals.'

'How's Rylda taking it?'

'Basking in the glow of your success. Says she always knew Spinner was suspect. I told her, that's more than I did. Just when did you fix your beady eye on him?'

'Once Coburn gave us his theory of how the fire started, Spinner had to be the prime suspect. Jealous, greedy, unable to form good relationships, and the facts built up against him. He saw the Boru fax, he must have known Brock was suspicious and would keep digging. Brock and Kesh were both threats to the syndicate, and Spinner planned to be rid of both at once. I think he obtained the cylinder and fire-starter from Ionescu well before the crash, but when Moshal cancelled his flight, Spinner seized on it as the perfect cover story. He made a song and dance about terrorist threats, and insisted on taking extreme precautions, creating a belief in the public mind that *Paloma* was a target for terrorists. It suggested a political motive for the tragedy, though in fact neither Spinner nor Ionescu cared a stuff for politics. Their sole concern was money.

'Spinner was the only member of the Dove executive who had easy access to the Dove warehouse. He owned a key to the staff entrance, and regularly came and went that way. He could load what he chose in the Dove container, saying it was needed at the conference. He had the motive, the means and the opportunity to commit mass murder.'

'Can you prove that in court?'

'We'll have a bloody good try. Is the Accord on track?'

'So far,' Rollo said, and added under his breath: 'Watch and pray.'

Spinner had been taken to the helipad under police guard. Thorneycroft was still making phone calls, and the rest of the party waited in the hall to bid him goodbye. Lucy leaned against Roswall, her face tear-streaked.

'I liked Hugo,' she said piteously. 'He always talked to me. Why did he do such horrible things; is he mad or something?'

Roswall stroked her hair. 'He lost his parents when he was very young. He was poor, and lonely.'

'So were you, but you didn't do anything horrible. You tried to help Hugo. You gave him everything.'

Roswall said sadly: 'The things he really needed . . . self-knowledge and the ability to love . . . aren't in my gift.'

'Is it true what Dr Thorneycroft said? Is Dove finished?'

'In its present form, yes.' As Lucy's tears began to flow again, Roswall hugged her closer. 'But we're not finished, darling. When all this is over, we'll start again.' He glanced uncertainly at Gerda and Kyle. 'Although we've lost so many good people.'

'We'll replace them,' Gerda said. 'Kyle thinks we should relocate. Africa maybe. We'll talk tomorrow, Dan. What we all need now is sleep.'

She said goodnight and set off up the stairs, followed by Lucy and Kyle.

Thorneycroft appeared, and Roswall, James and Natalie walked with him to the helipad. Spinner was already aboard the chopper, seated between two policemen.

Thorneycroft attempted to thank Roswall for his hospitality, and was silenced by a wave of the hand.

'When the boat starts to sink,' Roswall said, 'everybody bales.' He glanced at Spinner's stony profile. 'I suppose we'll have to face a lot of publicity, about him and Kesh?'

Thorneycroft tilted his head. 'I hope not. We have a lot of work to do still, but these days it's hard to suppress bad news.'

The blades of the helicopter began to spin, their whine increasing steadily. Thorneycroft shook hands with Roswall and turned towards James. James shouted: 'I have to thank you, on Dave's behalf.'

Thorneycroft smiled, and leaning down, yelled a reply. He ducked under the whirling rotors and boarded the chopper. The watchers stepped back, clear of the down-draught. Roswall swung round and strode towards the house, but James and Natalie waited as the chopper lifted off, climbed, hovered for a moment, then veered north.

'What did Thorneycroft say?' Natalie asked. 'I couldn't hear him.'

'Nor could I. He said: 'Don't thank me', and then he said something about 'all you loose cannons'.'

Natalie was shivering, and James took off his jacket and put it round her shoulders.

'I'm not cold,' she said. 'I guess it's just reaction. I can't believe all this. That we live in a world where people do such things I couldn't have borne it alone. You've helped me so much.'

They started back across the terrace. A rising wind was blowing away the last shreds of ground mist. The arc-lights at the boundary of the estate had been extinguished, and most of the dog-patrols had vanished. Over by the computer block, the cat Bojangles paced slowly, marking his territory.

'I've been thinking,' James said. 'I should go back to Italy, quite soon. I'd like to tell Pia about Spinner and Kesh and the rest. She shouldn't have to read it in the papers. I thought perhaps you might like to go with me?'

She looked up at him, and he said hastily: 'You don't have to decide right away. Let the idea stand awhile. It may improve with age.'

'No, I'd like to go. I'd like to very much.'

Roswall was waiting in the doorway of the house, and they quickened their pace to join him.

THE END

We do hope that you have enjoyed reading this large print book.

Did you know that all of our titles are available for purchase?

We publish a wide range of high quality large print books including:
Romances, Mysteries, Classics
General Fiction
Non Fiction and Westerns

Special interest titles available in large print are:
The Little Oxford Dictionary
Music Book
Song Book
Hymn Book
Service Book

Also available from us courtesy of Oxford University Press:
Young Readers' Dictionary
(large print edition)
Young Readers' Thesaurus
(large print edition)

For further information or a free brochure, please contact us at:
Ulverscroft Large Print Books Ltd.,
The Green, Bradgate Road, Anstey,
Leicester, LE7 7FU, England.
Tel: (00 44) 0116 236 4325
Fax: (00 44) 0116 234 0205

Other titles published by
The House of Ulverscroft:

THE IMPOSTOR

June Drummond

Handsome Lord Hector Finch Wycombe's life is one long round of pleasure. His disapproving brother, Hubert, lays a wager that Hector is incapable of a useful week's work ... As plain Mr Finch, Hector applies for the post of tutor to young Jason Carey, the troublesome son of Admiral Sir William Carey. It is not long before Hector faces trouble of a different sort, for the Admiral's spirited and beautiful niece, Serena, suspects that Mr Finch is not quite what he appears to be.

THE GENERAL'S ENVOY

Anthony Conway

Seconded to China by a vengeful Indian Army high command, Captain John Caspasian finds Shanghai a cesspit of despair and corruption. He is glad to escape on a solo mission to contact a general whom the British see as a bulwark against the revolutionary leader Chiang Kai-shek. Once he has left the International Settlement for a gunboat on the Yangtze, though, Caspasian smells danger. The supposedly friendly General Mok turns out to be a bloodthirsty sadist. And Caspasian has made two implacable enemies. One is a Chinese criminal. The other is a former British officer . . .

THE SIRIUS CROSSING

John Creed

Jack Valentine has been in the intelligence game too long and it is starting to show, but he accepts one more mission — he always does. It seems like a simple task but it throws up deadly questions and he doesn't know the answers. What were American Special Forces doing in Ireland twenty-five years ago and why does it matter now? What is the thread which leads from a deserted mountainside to the offices of the White House? Suddenly Valentine has information that everybody wants and he finds himself the quarry in a pitiless chase . . .

THE ANGRY ISLAND

James Pattinson

When Guy Radford goes to visit an old college friend on the West Indian island of St Marien, he is blissfully unaware of the trouble he is flying into. Divisions of race and wealth have created such tensions between desperate workers and powerful plantation owners that a violent showdown is inevitable. When Radford unwittingly becomes caught in the crossfire, he finds his own life in danger. And, as the conflict intensifies, the fact that he has fallen in love adds merely one more complication to an already tricky situation . . .

COGAN'S FALCONS

Colin D. Peel

In one of the world's largest swamps, it is easy to follow trails that are not what they seem to be. For air accident analyst Jim Cogan the trails lead him into an unmanageable and obsessive relationship with a young woman for whom the swamp has become a refuge. Determined to unravel the mystery of her past, Cogan takes her to a desolate region of Iraq. There, the development of a frightening new weapon system is threatening to destabilize the whole of the Middle East. Against a backdrop of terror and betrayal, Cogan and the woman find themselves fighting simply to survive . . .